WOLFEBLADE

A Medieval Romance

By Kathryn Le Veque

De Wolfe Pack Generations

KATHRYN LE VEQUE
NOVELS

Author's Note

Welcome to Andreas' story!

And… oh, boy!… what a story!

Now, something you may not have realized – Andreas is the second oldest de Wolfe/de Norville grandchild as Troy's son. William "Will" de Wolfe, Scott's eldest, is less than one year older. The boys were born close together and we're going to find out why – at least in Andreas' case. They were also born, in some cases, twenty years before their cousins. They were the EARLY grandchildren.

I was so excited to realize that Andreas' story was going to be set back when William and Paris were still alive because he's much older than the other de Wolfe Cubs who have had their stories told – Markus, Tor, and Cassius. Even though Andreas' story is the fourth one of the series that I wrote, chronologically, he's really the first because he's so much older than the others.

I'll take any chance I can get to write about William and Paris and Kieran again, so the prologue to this novel is going to be back in the midst of the original de Wolfe Pack. Such bliss! But I digress… the prologue is only the kick-off to a novel that's really going to take you for a wild and unusual ride, so be prepared to be sucked into this one. The Helm of Shame makes an appearance. Or, as my husband calls it, the Ass Hat. Appropriate!

Now, back to Andreas. He's essentially the strong, silent type. He's got de Wolfe on one side and de Norville on the other, but he's managed to inherit his grandmother Caladora's quiet personality. He was named Andreas because de Norville males (and his maternal grandfather is Paris de Norville, William de Wolfe's best friend) always have a Greek name – i.e. – Paris, Hector, Adonis, etc.), and his father, Troy, was named for Paris, so Troy and Helene simply carried on that tradition.

Andreas is actually a fairly common name in antiquity and even up through Georgian times. He has a nickname, as most de Wolfe Cubs seem to have – Dray. We've met Tor (Thomas) and Cass (Cassius) in the de Wolfe Cub series, so now we have Dray. When you realize how his name is pronounced, shortening it to "Dray" makes sense – an affectionate term within the family. Drè is actually the Flemish nickname for Andreas – I'm just spelling it phonetically.

I just want to make a mention here of Troy, Andreas' father, and his mother, Helene. You, as the reader, are going to get some insight into how the two of them met, and they were "together" at a very young age, which kind of makes Troy's story (DarkWolfe) all the more tragic. I specifically didn't introduce Helene into this story because I didn't want to create a greater sense of tragedy. If you got to "know" her, and bonded with her, then that would make her eventual ending more difficult to bear.

Something to note in the "Holdings and Titles of the House of de Wolfe" at the back of this book – you'll note that this book takes place anywhere from ten to thirteen years before the first three books in the series, so the "holdings" list reflects the holdings as they were at that time. For example, WolfeSword hasn't "happened" yet, so Cassius de Wolfe isn't the Duke of Doncaster – yet.

This is a book with a LOT happening in it – lots of little details you'll want to eat up. Frankly, the Scots borders are getting really crowded now because of so many de Wolfe Pack novels and, of course, everyone has to have his/her own castle.

One of the castles that plays a prominent role in this story is a castle called The Hermitage, which is quite a famous place. There were legends (for real) that the family who owned the place was involved in witchcraft, among other things. I've (conveniently) used those legends for this story, and the family name and castle. The name, The Hermitage, derives from the old French *l'armitage,* which means guardhouse. In this book, the castle is referred to as Hell's Guardhouse.

Good stuff!

What else can I say about this story? Huge highs and lows. There are some very low moments and some very laughable ones. This one is grittier and more brutal than any book I've written in the past couple of years, so it's great to get back to my "battle roots".

Now, the usual pronunciation guide:

Andreas – On-DRAY-us

Gavriella – Gah-vree-ELLE-uh. Basically, Gavriella with a "v" instead of a "b"

Theodis – THAY-uh-dis

I could go on and on, but I'll stop here. You've got a big book to read – enjoy it!

Hugs,

De Wolfe Pack Generations

The grandsons of William de Wolfe are referred to as "The de Wolfe Cubs". There are more than forty of them, both biological and adopted, and each young man is sworn to his powerful and rich legacy. When each grandson comes of age and is knighted, he tattoos the de Wolfe standard onto some part of his body. It is a rite of passage and it is that mark that links these young men together more than blood.

More than brotherhood.

It is the de Wolfe birthright.

The de Wolfe Pack standard is meant to be worn with honor, with pride, and with resilience, for there is no more recognizable standard in Medieval England. To shame the Pack is to have the tattoo removed, never to be regained.

This is their world.

Welcome to the Cub Generation.

De Wolfe Motto: *Fortis in arduis*

Strength in times of trouble

PROLOGUE

Castle Questing
1255 A.D.

H E SAW HIM **coming.**
William de Wolfe, the greatest English knight on the Scottish border, was all-seeing and all-knowing when it came to matters of northern England. He had the pulse of the politics and the players but, unfortunately, he had missed something occurring within his very own family. He was still kicking himself because of it.

The truth was that his sons were becoming young men.

Young men with the natural needs of young men.

His twins, Scott and Troy, had just turned twenty-one years of age and their brother, Patrick, was fourteen months younger and a full-fledged knight. All of them were back with their father at his seat of Castle Questing after having spent years training at Kenilworth Castle, Norham Castle, and then Bamburgh Castle when the lord of Bamburgh lost several men to an illness. It was only temporary, but it had been good experience. Now, they were some of the most highly trained knights in all of England, a tribute to their magnificent father.

The rest of his sons – James, Edward, and Thomas were in

various stages of training. All of them growing up, all of them turning an eye to young women.

And one son in particular, he had just found out, had done more than simply turn an eye.

Now, there was trouble.

"Papa!" Patrick de Wolfe was in the doorway of his solar. The tallest man in the family at several inches over six feet, he'd reached that height at an early age and was still growing. "Uncle Paris is here!"

William was calm, watching his oldest and dearest friend, Paris de Norville, ride in through the massive Castle Questing interior gatehouse astride a fat, gray war horse. A few of Paris' soldiers followed, but they remained back by the gatehouse in an uncertain bunch. They didn't follow their liege towards the keep.

There was a reason for that.

"I know," William said steadily.

Scott, the first-born twin, was suddenly in the doorway next to Patrick. "Papa?" he said, sounding anxious. "Did Atty tell you?"

Atty was what the family called Patrick, a childhood nick-name for the little boy who couldn't pronounce his name correctly.

William nodded.

"He did," he said. "I can see him from here."

Patrick and Scott looked at each other, trying not to appear too panic-stricken.

"Papa," Scott hissed. "He's *here*. You know why!"

William turned to his sons. "You will keep your apprehension under control," he commanded quietly. "Seasoned men do not let their emotions show. You know this."

Scott was trying not to, but he was an emotional man to begin with. "I do not think you understand the seriousness of the situation," he said. "We have tried to explain it to you. Troy has explained it to you. You know why Uncle Paris is here and yet, you stand there calmly? I do not understand."

"What would you have me do?" William asked, looking between them. "Run out there and beg for mercy? Better still, draw my sword against him? He has every right to come here and you both know it. I understand the seriousness of the situation fully. But we will discuss this calmly, like men. There will be no bloodshed this day and most especially not between Paris and Troy."

He meant what he said even if Scott and Patrick didn't look convinced. He returned his attention to the bailey, completely calm until he caught movement. His son, Troy, was making his way out into the bailey, dressed for battle. The man was armed to the teeth, everything dark and deadly reflecting the light as he walked.

So much for composure.

William bolted.

He pushed in between Patrick and Scott, charging towards the entry of Castle Questing's massive keep. He'd nearly reached the door when his second in command, and another old and dear friend, came off the stairwell.

"Paris is here," Kieran Hage said grimly. "He just came through the gatehouse."

William threw open the door. "I *know*," he said. "Worse still, Troy knows. Come, Kieran. I will need your help."

Kieran didn't hesitate. A massive man with dark blond hair and dark brown eyes, he was William's right hand at Castle Questing. Kieran and William and Paris had known each other since they had been squires and they'd bonded over adventures, misadventures, and everything in between. There were no bonds stronger in England, so much so that William, Kieran, and Paris had married three women who were cousins. Now, they were family and those family bonds were unbreakable.

But those bonds were about to be tested.

William knew that. God help him, he did. Kieran knew it, too. Unfortunately, they'd been so focused on Paris and Troy that they didn't notice they'd lost Scott and Patrick. The brothers had run off to collect their own armor and weapons, determined to protect Troy against what would surely be a battle to the death.

For certain, Paris was mad enough to kill.

No one really blamed him.

Troy was standing at the base of the steps leading from Castle Questing's keep. It was a temperate day in late May, still moderate and lovely, before the warmer days of summer would come. There wasn't a cloud in the sky overhead, the deep blue expanse alluding to the fact that it could have been a glorious day.

Could have been.

But at the moment, it was a very uncertain one.

William barked at his son.

"Troy," he snapped quietly. "Back away. Go and stand by the entry door."

Troy turned to his father. Dark and handsome, he wasn't as tall as William was, but he was powerfully built. Even at his young age, he showed skill well beyond his years. He'd also inherited an innate Scots rage from his mother's side of the family, a woman born and bred in Scotland, because he was faster to temper than almost anyone William knew. He wasn't afraid to act on that rage.

And that was William's fear.

"I will not," Troy said. "This is my battle, Papa. Kindly stay out of it."

William shook his head. "I cannot and you know it," he said quietly. "Let me speak with your Uncle Paris first before this gets out of hand."

"It is already out of hand."

"Please, Troy," William begged softly. "Stay here with Kieran. Just… humor me. *Please*."

Troy wasn't pleased. "Papa, you are not involved in this," he said. "I did what I did and I shall face it. Alone."

William cocked an eyebrow at his stubborn son. "You involved me when you came home and confessed everything to me," he said. "You pulled me into this, so do not tell me I am not involved. You are my son. I will always be involved in anything that affects your well-being."

Troy stiffened, preparing for a fight with his father now, but Kieran put himself between William and Troy in an attempt to defuse the situation. Big, gentle Kieran was dearly loved by all of the de Wolfe and Hage and de Norville children, a man who was supremely patient and supremely wise. William could hear Kieran's soft, deep voice speaking steadily to Troy as he headed off in Paris' direction.

Paris, too, had come dressed for battle. He was wearing all of his mail and plate protection, with weapons strapped all over his body. Paris was a big man, muscular and agile, and he had been at William's side in many a battle. William trusted him with his life and he had, too many times to count. William knew very well what the man was capable of. As Paris dismounted his war horse, William went to meet him.

"Paris," he greeted. "I will not pretend to be ignorant as to why you are here, but I want to hear it from you."

Paris met William's gaze a moment before looking around him, seeing Troy with Kieran.

"Get out of my way, William," he said. "This is between me and your son."

William wouldn't budge. "Tell me why you have come or I will not move."

"You said you already know why."

"I also said I want to hear it from you," William said. "Do you think so little of me that you would not give me that courtesy?"

Paris looked at him. "This is not about you," he said. "This is about your son. He thinks he is a man, so let him handle this like a man."

"I am waiting."

Paris took a step back, his jaw working angrily. "Very well," he said. "If that is what you wish, then I shall tell you why I am here. You have raised a scoundrel for a son, William."

"Why?"

Paris snorted, his cheeks beneath his three-point helm turning pink. "Did he tell you that Helene is pregnant?"

"He did."

William said it so emotionlessly that Paris ripped off his helm, throwing it down in a rage. "My daughter is fifteen years old, William," he snarled. "Fifteen years old and seduced by… by that feral cat you call a son. He seduced her!"

"He loves her."

Paris' jaw was ticking so furiously that he was close to snapping teeth. "I told him that he could court her," he said. "I did not tell him that he could fuck her. That's what he did, like a dog after a bitch in heat."

William was struggling to keep his cool. He didn't like to hear Paris calling his son names. "It is my understanding that she was a willing participant," he said, trying to slow down Paris' building fury. "She loves him, too, Paris. You know this."

"I also told him that she was too young to marry!"

"My mother married at thirteen."

Paris began to stomp around, kicking at anything that came near his foot. "I told you that this is not about you," he said. "Your son has defiled my daughter and I shall have my satisfaction!"

William just stood there and shook his head. "What satisfaction?" he said. "Killing my son? And just how do you think I will respond to that? Did you ever think about that?"

Paris came to a halt, facing William with wide eyes. "I have every right to seek satisfaction."

"If you do, then I have every right to seek revenge."

That brought Paris great pause. He stood there, staring at the man he loved best in the world, a man who was closer to him than any brother. But at the moment, he was flabbergasted that William didn't see his point.

Paris, as usual, only saw what he wished to see, in this case, the man who had impregnated his fifteen-year-old daughter. It didn't matter to him that they were in love. It didn't matter to him that Troy wanted to marry Helene. All that mattered was that his daughter was pregnant out of wedlock.

He simply wasn't being rational.

"You would do that?" Paris hissed. "You would punish me for something that is my right?"

William was starting to harden. He was no longer the understanding friend, but the father put in a position of defending his son.

The situation was turning dark.

"It is not your right to kill my son," he said, lowering his voice. "Stop being so ridiculous and understand the situation for what it is – there is no slander against your daughter. She loves Troy and he loves her. They demonstrated that love. May I remind you that you demonstrated your love to your children's mother, many times, that resulted in your eldest child's conception before you were married, only Caladora didn't have an enraged father to defend her honor."

Cracks were appearing in Paris' stance. "That is completely different."

"It is not."

"Caladora was not fifteen years old!"

"Even so, you were the feral cat that you accuse my son of being, as you've been a feral cat your entire life," William snapped back. "They say that it takes one to know one, and having known you since you were a child, I have seen your collection of deflowered women, so your anger against Troy is not only ridiculous, it is offensive. You were exactly what you accuse him of being, Paris."

Paris stiffened. "That may be," he said. "But those days are gone. I have daughters to protect – three of them. Your son violated my trust when he bedded my daughter."

William could see that Paris wasn't going to relent so easily. The man was angry, and incensed, and his argument kept moving from one reason to the next. William just looked at his friend, realizing that no matter what he said, Paris was going to find an excuse to punish Troy. He felt the de Norville family honor was at stake somehow.

Perhaps that was really what this was all about.

William finally looked away.

"You want to punish my son?" he said. "Then punish him. Do what you will. But whoever draws the first blood is the winner and when you leave, in whatever condition you happen to leave in, you will never return here. Ever."

Paris' brow furrowed. "What do you mean?"

William looked at him, angrily. "You are forcing me to take sides," he said. "Very well; I shall take a side. I shall take Troy's side and anyone who tries to harm my son is my enemy. Even you, Paris. So, if this foolish surge of manly honor is worth the risk, then go ahead and fight my son. But if you do, it will be the last time I ever speak to you."

With that, he turned away, heading back to where Troy and Kieran were standing. But as William drew near, he saw two more heavily armed knights emerging from the keep. It took him a moment to realize he was looking at Scott and Patrick, armed to the teeth as they prepared to defend their brother.

William was so angry at Paris that he was going to let them.

"First blood drawn is the winner," he told Troy and Kieran as he walked past them. "Troy, if Paris de Norville lifts his sword to you, you have my permission to defend yourself. But if he insists on fighting you, then he is dead to me. I think you should know that."

As William continued towards the keep, Troy and Kieran passed concerned glances. Troy looked positively shocked. Kieran finally held up a hand to Troy, silently asking him to remain where he was as he went to speak to Paris.

Paris was in the process of picking his helm off the ground, grunting unhappily when he realized he had scratched it up by throwing it into the dirt. When the man saw Kieran coming, he looked away quickly, trying to ignore him as he put on the helm.

"Save your breath," he told Kieran. "I have nothing more to say."

Kieran came to a halt. "Maybe you do not, but I do," he said. "I was told about the situation with Troy and Helene. I take it you have come to avenge your daughter?"

"I would be a poor father if I did not."

Kieran watched Paris, his jerky movements, and knew this situation was close to exploding. But he wondered if Paris really did.

"William says you are dead to him if you lift a sword to his son," he said. "Knowing that Troy loves your daughter and wants to marry her, and knowing your daughter loves Troy and wants to marry him, are you still prepared to go through this ridiculous farce?"

Paris' head snapped up, his blue eyes narrowing. "And just

what would you do if one of your daughters became pregnant without the benefit of a marriage bed?"

Kieran shrugged. "I would not try to kill the son of my best friend," he said. "Paris, you are angry for the wrong reasons. And given your past, I would think you would have some understanding when it comes to unrestrained young men."

More cracks were appearing in Paris' determination. "I know this cannot go unanswered, Kieran," he said. "Troy bedded my fragile flower, my Helene. What in the hell would you suggest I do about it?"

"No daughter of Caladora Scott is a fragile flower," Kieran said. "Did she come to you crying and carrying on that her virtue had been stolen?"

Paris frowned. "Of course not."

"Did she beg you to avenge her?"

"She begged me not to."

Kieran's eyebrows lifted. "And still, you are here?" he said, incredulous. "Do you know what I think? I think you are doing what you think you should do. I think you are doing what all of those angry fathers did when you compromised their daughters. You know nothing else, so that is how you are behaving. Because it happened to you. The difference is that you ran from these fathers – do not deny it for I know it to be true. William and I helped you fight your way out of at least two instances that I can recall. And still, you want to kill Troy? Of course you don't. I do not truly believe that. If you try, it is going to ruin your relationship with William."

"Then he should have raised his son better."

"What if the situation were reversed and it was William at Northwood, wanting to run Hector through?" Kiera fired back softly. "What would you say to William for wanting to kill your son for this same offense?"

The cracks in Paris' determination were starting to join up, weakening everything about him. "I would understand, of course."

"Would you let him kill your son?"

Paris didn't answer for several long moments. "I would not," he finally said. "But I would be…"

Kieran cut him off. "Is your pride worth the high price this is going to cost you, Paris?"

Kieran was hammering it home as only Kieran could. Paris was starting to calm a little, realizing that he was on the precipice of something he didn't want to topple from.

Was his pride worth William's friendship?

Pride, with him, had always been his problem. But in this case, he was going to have to swallow it or risk everything.

But he wasn't sure he could. He'd never had to. Paris had never believed himself to be wrong, under any circumstances, but much of what Kiernan said was true. He was here to fight Troy because he believed it was expected of him. There was a sense of family honor at stake. He was mad enough to kill, but truly mad enough to kill Troy? Nay, he wasn't. The reality was that he wasn't.

Damn Kieran for forcing him to face that very truth.

Bless Kieran for forcing him to face that very truth.

"It is not worth losing William," he finally said. "But Troy must be punished. Mayhap it is foolish to think that family honor is at stake here, but it is, Kieran. I cannot let this go unanswered."

Kieran was saying a silent prayer that the man was seeing reason. In fact, he was more relieved than he cared to admit. "I know," he said. "And he should be punished. But this is not worth his life, Paris. He is a good man and he loves your daughter. Would you really try to kill him over this?"

Paris sighed heavily. Kieran had a way of defusing a situation and making one see reason. "Nay," he said reluctantly. "I…

I would not kill him, in any case. But I am furious enough to beat the humors out of him and then some."

Kieran held up a finger as if an idea occurred to him. "He's young and strong," he said. "And he would fight back, so you would risk injury if you tried. Therefore, your punishment must be creative."

"What do you mean?"

A glimmer of deviousness flickered in Kieran's dark eyes. "Sometimes, humiliation is far worse than death. It is just as permanent but doesn't leave a mark. At least, not physically."

Paris was listening, but he didn't understand what Kieran was suggesting. "What do you mean?"

"Remember the Helm of Shame?"

Paris' eyes widened. "Of course I do."

"Would you say that is something a man would consider adequate punishment?"

"God's Bones, it is. More than adequate."

"Something he would be unwilling to tell his friends or brothers and suffer silently?"

Paris nodded firmly. "Indeed," he said. "What do you have in mind?"

Kieran held up both hands. "Stay here," he said. "Please… just stay here. Do not move, do not advance on Troy. I shall return."

Paris watched the man run off towards the keep. He wondered what Kieran, a man with a truly devious mind when it came to dirty tricks, was up to.

He would soon find out.

The Helm of Shame was one of those brilliant, nasty tricks used for punishment on lazy knights. They all knew of it, every last one of them, because it was legendary. It had all started a few years ago at a battle near Whiteadder Water when someone cut the garter off the mail of Kieran's left leg during the heat of battle. The mail slid down and took his breeches with it, and suddenly, Kieran was fighting with his bare arse exposed.

Once the fighting stopped, Kieran was so angry at the rebelling Scots that he refused to pull up his breeches. He left his backside hanging out and made it all the way back to the encampment that way. But it didn't end there; he went to the Scots prisoners and made them all look at his bare buttocks to punish them for their insurrection.

And so, came the Helm of Shame.

As Kieran was walking around, holding up his breeches in the front so his manhood was covered, he came across a knight from Northwood Castle. The young knight was named Corin de Fortlage and he had pulled out of the battle early, pleading exhaustion. Kieran was so angry at Corin that he pushed the man to the ground and sat on his head with his bare buttocks. He called it the Helm of Shame and told Corin if he ever left the field of battle early again, he would punish him with the Helm of Shame. It had been particularly ghastly for Corin because of the way he'd fallen on the ground – when Kieran squatted on him, from the angle of his head, the man's testicles were right by Corin's nose.

Corin was always the last man to leave the field of battle after that.

The Helm of Shame was legendary amongst the de Wolfe armies and it was something that Kieran had done more than once. If a young knight displeased him, they were threatened with the Helm of Shame. No one else could do it better than Kieran and the older knights began using it as a threat to the younger knights or misbehaving squires. William, Paris, and Kieran had even used it on their own sons to keep them from being naughty.

Paris didn't know why he hadn't thought of it before.

It was the perfect way to punish Troy.

And he was going to use it.

Unfortunately, Kieran had a time pulling William out into the bailey again. William had remained stubbornly in his solar until Kieran managed to coax him out with the inference that Paris wanted to apologize. Still frustrated and hurt, William came back out into the bailey, walking past Troy and Scott and Patrick, who were still in full armor. Young knights, still ready to fight for their cause.

But William didn't look at them, nor did he acknowledge them. He was focused on Paris, still standing where he had left him. Marching up on him, he came to a halt and folded his arms across his chest expectantly.

"Well?" he said.

Kieran spoke before Paris could reply. Things were so fragile that he didn't want them to get off on the wrong foot.

"I have an idea, William," he said. "First of all, I lied to get you out here. Paris has not offered to apologize to you, but I believe we have hit upon a compromise to satisfy everyone."

William scowled. "What?"

"The Helm of Shame."

William had been gearing up to blast both Kieran and Paris, but when he heard Kieran's words, he cocked his head at the man in confusion.

"The Helm of Shame?" he repeated. "What are you talking about?"

Kieran focused on him. "Would you be willing to admit your son should face some measure of punishment for his actions?"

William sighed sharply. "What he did was not ideal, but…"

"And if Hector impregnated Evelyn, would you say the man needed to be punished?"

"I'd bloody well kill him."

He said it so fast that he didn't really have time to think on what he said and, in that moment, Paris looked at him in shock. Realizing he'd been caught with the same attitude that Paris now had, William rolled his eye and looked away.

"So now you have it," he said. "I would kill the man, but not literally. But I'd certainly make sure he felt my rage."

Kieran was fighting off a grin. "Exactly," he said. "And Paris wants Troy to feel his rage, as well. As a father, that is his right. Would you not agree?"

William bobbed his head impatiently. "Fine, Kieran," he said irritably. "What do you have planned? Clearly, you have something on your mind."

"As I said, the Helm of Shame would be ideal."

William couldn't help it; he started to smile, but he bit his lip. "Troy would rather face Paris in mortal combat than assume the Helm of Shame."

Kieran was trying hard not to smile. "Not if he does not know it is coming."

"What do you mean?"

"Are you willing to help?"

William eyed him dubiously. "Me? Help?"

"He's your son. If anyone should deal out punishment, it should be you. He damaged the de Wolfe name by impregnating a young girl."

"The impetuousness of youth."

"And if some impetuous youth did that to *your* daughter?"

He was bringing that reasoning to bear again and William threw up his hands in surrender. "Very well," he said quickly. "I get your point. But what in the hell do you want me to do?"

"Like Paris, you are going to stand by while I deliver the punishment."

"You? Why you?"

"Because I have no stake in this," Kieran said. "I am simply the vessel by which to deliver the fair and just punishment. You and Paris are going to present a united and agreeable front to such judgment. Troy will take it like a man or risk completely shaming the de Wolfe name."

"And he wouldn't dare."

"Nay, he would not."

William sighed heavily again before looking at Paris. "And you agree with this?"

Paris nodded, once. "I do."

"And you will be satisfied?"

"I will."

"And Troy will marry Helene and this will be the end of it?"

"Indeed."

Because Paris agreed, William agreed. "Very well," he said. "But how do you intend to do this? Troy will not make an easy target."

Kieran shrugged. "That will be up to you," he said. "Take him to the stable and have Troy remove his armor and weapons. Paris brought several soldiers with him. I saw them outside of the gatehouse. Those soldiers will pin Troy down while I deliver the punishment."

William wasn't so sure. "Someone might get hurt. Troy will fight viciously."

"Not if he doesn't see them coming."

William still wasn't sure about this, but it was better than Paris trying to kill his son. Maybe there was a small part of him that didn't want to see Troy humiliated like this but, on the other hand, Troy did do wrong. He did deserve to be punished.

Maybe this was the lesser of the evils.

"Go on," Kieran said. "Let's get this over with."

As he turned towards the stable, William turned for the keep but Paris stopped him.

"William," he said quietly, firmly. "Wait a moment."

William stopped, turning to the man he knew best in the

entire world. "What is it?"

Paris cleared his throat softly. "I really wouldn't have killed your son," he said quietly. "I just wanted to get in a few good licks, something he would remember from his future wife's angry father. I… I am sorry if I sounded unreasonable."

William simply shook his head. "You *are* unreasonable," he said. "You're a big, unreasonable dolt and sometimes I want to shake you until your head falls off and your bones turn to dust. But I also love you, you idiot. Just do me a favor."

"What?"

"If any of our children marry in the future, and my sons become too amorous, don't do this again. We can always reason through any situation if you'd only stop being so stubborn."

Paris gave him a smirk, like he wasn't entirely sure there would be a time when he wasn't utterly stubborn, and William smirked in return.

All was right in the world again.

But the worst was yet to come.

William managed to convince the de Wolfe brothers to stand down. He told Patrick and Scott that Paris had decided not to violently seek his revenge and instructed the pair to go into the keep and stay there. They did, but it was begrudgingly, as William took Troy out to the stables.

The stable was mostly void of servants, as it was after the animals had been fed, so they were out in the yard while William and Kieran and Troy were quite alone. But the moment the three of them entered the stables, William and Kieran began to strip Troy of his weapons and armor.

Troy protested at first, but gradually just stood there, exasperated, as his father and uncle stripped him down to a tunic and breeches. He was puzzled at what they were doing, but he suspected that he was in for a tongue lashing from Paris and they didn't want him armed. He was willing to accept that in lieu of a physical fight.

But he had no idea what was coming.

He soon would.

His first clue that something was out of the ordinary was when he was hit from behind. He'd been standing with his back to the stable door, but that had been intentional. Bodies with many arms and legs slammed into him and he went down, face-first, into the dirt of the stable. He tried to fight, but he'd fallen on his arms and because he'd instinctively put his hands out to brace himself for the fall, he was fairly certain he'd broken a wrist.

There were a lot of men piled on top of him.

Troy could hardly move, but he was giving it his best. He could move his head because he was only pinned from the shoulders down. He caught a glimpse of his father's boots a few feet away.

"Papa!" he demanded. "What is happening?"

William crouched down next to his son's head, dipping low so he could look the man in the eye.

"Punishment," he said simply. "Troy, Paris must have his satisfaction for what you have done. I know that you love Helene, and that she loves you, but she is now unwed and pregnant. If that happened to one of your sisters, I cannot say my attitude would not be the same as Paris'. The offender must be punished."

Troy had no idea what his father meant as far as punishment. Not that he exactly disagreed with the fact that he had punishment coming his way, because he understood that what he did was frowned upon. He understood that, in a sense, he had violated Paris' trust and had essentially shamed both families. All of that, he understood. But what he didn't understand was what was happening at this very moment.

Something told him this wasn't going to be good.

"What is Uncle Paris planning?" he asked, grunting because he was still straining against those who held him down. "And who are these men, Papa? Will you not help your son?"

William sighed heavily. "You took liberties," he said. "Now you must pay the price. Paris' price."

"What in the hell does that mean?"

A shadow fell over him and, abruptly, there was a naked arse on his head. Troy knew immediately what was happening.

"God!" he groaned, trying to turn his head so butt cheeks wouldn't be on his face. "Not this! Papa, *nay!*"

William stepped away as Kieran planted his big, taut arse right on Troy's head. He could hear his son howl and it was an effort not to laugh. He felt so badly for him but, on the other hand, it was probably less than he deserved. Looking at the soldiers pinning Troy down, and there were eight of them, they were all grinning. They thought it was hilarious. And it was.

For everyone but Troy.

As Kieran began to wriggle his buttocks, grinding them into Troy's head, William noticed that Paris had disappeared. As he was wondering where in the hell the man went, he suddenly reappeared, carrying something with him. He had an object in each hand. As William watched with curiosity, Paris went to the fresh water barrel and dunked the object in his left hand.

"Kieran," Paris said. "Get off. I have something I must do."

Kieran stood up, pulling up his breeches, as Paris knelt down beside Troy's head. He bent over so he could look the young man in the eyes.

He was much calmer than he had been when he'd first entered the bailey. He looked into the face of the man he'd known since the day he was born, a man who was named for him, in fact. Troy was the strong but sensitive child who had grown into a strong but sensitive man.

Sensitive and reckless.

He smacked Troy on the head.

"That is for doing something to my daughter you should not have done," he said as Troy winced. "And the rest… well, this is so you will never forget my wrath. Let your punishment be a testament to any more de Wolfe or even Hage lads who get it into their heads that they want to treat my daughters with any less respect. The next time your brother, Scott, eyes my Athena in an amorous way, you will remind him of what happened to you when you showed no restraint with her sister."

With that, he pulled out the object he had dunked in the water. It turned out to be a lumpy bar of soap and he rubbed it into Troy's hair on the right side of his head. Troy turned away, trying to avoid it, so Paris ended up lathering one side and the back of the man's head.

Then, he pulled out the object that had been in his right hand. It was a razor. As Troy yowled angrily, Paris proceeded to shave the back of the man's curly, rather long hair. Because Troy was moving around so much, he ended up shaving about half of the right side of his head, too, and then part of the left. Troy ended up with a big patch of uneven, unshaved scalp on the top of his head. When Paris was finished, it was all William could do not to burst out laughing at his son's humiliation.

It was absolutely hysterical.

"May I?" Kieran asked Paris, indicating their victim.

Paris nodded. "By my guest."

As Troy begged for mercy, Kieran resumed the Helm of Shame, now on Troy's freshly shaved scalp. He went so far as to fart on the back of Troy's head and William lost his composure completely. He laughed until he wept, turning away from Troy so the man wouldn't see him. Paris, too, could no longer hold back the laughter, especially when Kieran farted a second time and Troy started gagging. It was horrible and humiliating and hilarious. The soldiers on Troy's back weren't as discreet as the knights were; their laughter was long and loud.

After about an hour of sitting on Troy's head and eking out a series of farts, Kieran finally stood up and pulled up his breeches. Paris called off the soldiers, who left the stable as Troy, humiliated to the bone, was finally allowed to sit up. As the man ran his hand over his newly shaved scalp to see just how much damage there was, Paris went to stand in front of him.

"Do you have something to say to me?" he asked.

Troy was furious and ashamed. "Like what?"

"An apology, mayhap?"

Troy lurched to his feet, standing in front of Paris in an angry stance. William and Kieran were watching closely, hoping Troy didn't ruin all of this by trying to punch Paris in the face. But admirably, he kept his fists at his sides.

"An apology for what?" he finally said. "For loving Helene? I have loved her for as long as I can recall and I will never apologize for that. She is the embodiment of all that is pure and beautiful in this world, and with every breath she takes, I am reminded anew of what a fortunate man I am that she loves me in return. I am not nearly good enough for her and I know that, but I will swear to you that I will love her until the end of my life and beyond. And you want me to apologize for that? I won't. You can take out your sword and cut me if you wish, and punish me for demonstrating that Helene is my all for living, but I will not apologize for loving her. Not ever."

By the time he was finished, Paris was looking at him with a great deal of emotion. His speech had been beautiful and succinct, if not a bit angry.

"Oh… lad," he said softly. "That was magnificently put. You make me sorry that I… well, not entirely sorry. You deserved it. But I hope you weren't injured in all of this."

Troy was still furious, but Paris' show of concern had him

unsteady. "Nay," he said, rubbing his wrist, which was sore but not broken. "I am uninjured. But my hair is in ruins and I do not know if I shall ever recover from Uncle Kieran farting on my head."

Paris couldn't help but laugh. "Your hair will grow back," he said. "And you have endured the Helm of Shame with honor. You took your punishment like a man."

"Like a de Wolfe."

"Indeed. And the sooner you marry my daughter, the better."

Troy lost his anger at that moment. "Do you mean it?"

"I do," he said. "She is at Northwood. If you wish to retrieve her and bring her back here, we can have the wedding here at Castle Questing."

"Now?"

Paris nodded, looking at William. "Are you agreeable?"

William was smiling. "I am," he said. "Troy, ride to Northwood. Retrieve your bride, but bring all of Northwood with you. Leave no one behind. I will go tell your mother that we are to have a wedding when you return."

A smile flickered across Troy's lips as he bolted towards his war horse, in a stall at the end of the stable. Paris came to stand next to William and Kieran as Troy quickly prepared his mount.

"That was a most appropriate punishment," William said, looking to Paris and Kieran. "I thought shaving his head was a clever touch."

Paris was trying hard not to smile. "He's going to get married like that now," he said. "I had an uncle who looked like that. He was bald in spots, so he grew his hair long to try and cover up the bald and it ended up looking like a jester's cap."

William chuckled, looking to Kieran. "And Troy will never look at you the same way again."

"That is good," Kieran said. "If he thinks we're going to catch him again so I can sit on his head, he should behave himself from now on."

William continued chuckling, finally shaking his head. "God's Bones," he muttered. "What friends I have."

"The best," Paris muttered.

As Kieran nodded fervently, Troy suddenly charged past them, riding his horse over to the next stable where the tack was kept. As he blew by, William pointed a finger at Paris.

"The best, indeed," he said. "But the Helm of Shame is only the latest tool in an arsenal of tools we have collected over the years. Back when we were forcing Kieran to wrestle other squires and place bets on the winner, we had a tool for collecting bets from those who would not pay. Do you remember what it was?"

Paris burst out laughing. Given how this day had started, it was so good to laugh with William and Kieran again. Being at odds with them simply wasn't natural.

"Of course I do," Kieran said because Paris was still chortling. "We would find them, tie them up, strip off their clothing, and twist their nipples until they screamed."

William started laughing. Just the sound of Kieran saying that as if they'd had every right to do it made him laugh. Self-righteous torture was always hilarious.

"God," he muttered. "We bruised many a young squire that way. I seem to remember putting hay in between their toes and lighting it on fire, too."

"We were cruel," Paris said. "Cruel, vicious, and conniving. No wonder they separated us. How old were we when they did that? About fourteen years of age?"

"Something like that," William said. "It was great fun coming of age with you two. I do not know what I would have done without you."

The feeling was mutual. They spent several minutes reflecting on their time at Kenilworth, when William ran a large gambling ring that had made them all very rich until the master knights found out. After that, it was big trouble for the brilliant squires, young men who couldn't seem to keep out of trouble.

William had managed to tame his naughty streak over the years and, nowadays, he kept it well buried, but he wasn't beyond indulging in a game of chance now and then. No one would play with him, however, because he always won. As evidenced by the events of the evening, Kieran really hadn't tamed his naughty streak, either, nor had Paris, although they only gave in to the urge under appropriate circumstances.

As the three of them reminisced about a particular gambling circumstance when Kenilworth had competed in a tournament in Gloucester, their revelry was cut off when two small, beautiful women entered the stables.

Jordan, William's wife and Troy's mother, charged into the stable, her expression nothing short of murder. Right behind her came Jemma, Kieran's wife. Instantly, all smiles were gone as Lady de Wolfe and Lady Hage glared at the men.

"Who did that tae Troy?" Jordan demanded. "In the name of Christ and his saints, if ye dunna tell me, I'll take a stick tae every last one of ye. Who did that tae my lad?"

Her Scottish burr got heavier when she became angry, making her sound quite intimidating, but William was trying desperately not to laugh. His wife was enraged and all he could picture was Troy with his head half-shaved, looking like an idiot. He tried to push that image out of his mind so he wouldn't start giggling.

He didn't think his wife would take too kindly to it.

"Troy was punished for actions you are well aware of," he said steadily. "You will not interfere, Jordan. If Troy wants to be a man, then he must take his punishment like a man."

Jordan's gaze moved to Paris. "Ye did this," she said, her voice low. "Ye came here tae punish my lad and ye made a fool out of him."

Paris lifted an eyebrow at a woman he genuinely liked. "He made a fool out of me when he betrayed my trust, bedded my daughter, and beget her with child," he said. "I took my pound of flesh, Lady de Wolfe. I had every right. Be grateful I did not do more than that."

Jordan was furious, but she was also sensible. She knew she didn't have a leg to stand on. Her son had gotten himself into a predicament, impregnating Paris' daughter, and she knew the man had every right to exact justice.

Still, the sight of her son's head shaved except for a rough patch on the top of his head was something she'd never forget. After a moment, she simply shook her head.

"Did ye take yer lesson from one of the many fathers whose daughters ye undoubtedly compromised?" she wanted to know. "Did someone do that tae ye, Paris? Do ye remember the humiliation? That is what Troy is going through right now. Why would ye do tae him what was done tae ye?"

"He's a devil, that one," Jemma growled. She and Paris had shared a contentious relationship since the day they'd met. "Wicked and stupid. He shamed yer lad and is laughing about it."

Kieran caught his wife's eye, shaking his head faintly at her, but it did nothing to shut her up. She simply glared at him.

"And ye?" she said. "Did ye cheer him on or did ye try tae stop him?"

Big, calm, and wise, Kieran had married a spitfire of a woman. He'd had eight children with her and he loved her to his very bones, but she was a handful even in the best of times. He decided to take the bull by the horns because he wasn't going to spend all night arguing with her.

"I did not cheer him on," he said, heading out of the stable. "I was too busy sitting on Troy's head. He had earned the Helm of Shame and he's fortunate that his punishment was so mild."

Both Jordan and Jemma looked at him in horror. "Ye did that disgusting thing tae him?" Jordan cried. "How could ye do it?"

William and Paris were following Kieran's lead. If they stayed in the stable, they'd be arguing with women all day long.

"Troy took his punishment like a man," William said as he walked past his wife. "And I will no longer discuss this with you. This is Paris' business and you will kindly stay out of it."

Jordan and Jemma stood there, mouths open, as William, Kieran, and Paris headed out of the stable, out into the day that was deepening. Looking at each other in both surprise and outrage, the women followed them out of the stable but they were cut short when Troy, astride his war horse, came rushing towards them.

"Mother!" he said excitedly. "Did Papa tell you?"

Jordan could hardly stand to look at her handsome son with only one patch of long hair on his head, hanging in his eyes.

"Tell me what?" she said. "Troy… do ye want me tae shave the rest of yer skull? It'll grow back, sweetheart."

Troy was beaming, unusual for a man who didn't smile very often or very easily. "That?" he said, flipping back the hair in his face. "No time. Uncle Paris told me to ride for Northwood. I am to collect Helene, and everyone else, and bring them back for the wedding. I shall marry Helene tomorrow!"

With that, he dashed back into the stable where his armor and weapons were, left there when William and Kieran stripped him. Jordan and Jemma stood there in the wake of his excitement before looking at each other in resignation.

"Mayhap we are those in the wrong here," Jordan said, lifting her shoulders. "My son has half his head shaved, and suffered the Helm of Shame no less, and he's as happy as a lark."

Jemma shook her head in disapproval. "'Tis those men we married," she said. "Sassenach beasts. 'Tis their twisted sense of justice, shaving a man's head only part way and then sitting on it with bare buttocks. God's Bones!"

Jordan could see Troy in the stable, quickly gathering his things. The more she looked at that crazy patch of hair on his head, the more comical the situation became. Suddenly, she burst into laughter.

"Saints preserve us," she said, turning for the keep. "The man looks like an idiot. And he's happy about it!"

In spite of herself, Jemma fought off a grin. "My husband has a big arse," she said. "I'm surprised he dinna suffocate Troy."

Realizing there was no use in them fretting over something that could have been much worse, they giggled as they headed back to the keep of Castle Questing. Of course, they wouldn't know until years later just how close Paris and Troy had come to mortal combat. For all they knew, Troy had received his humiliating punishment, but he hardly cared because, in the end, he got what he wanted. He married the fair Helene. Six months later, a fat baby boy was born in Andreas de Wolfe.

Paris was the first one to hold the grandchild who nearly tore apart the Houses of de Wolfe and de Norville.

He prayed the lad had been worth the trouble.

CHAPTER ONE

Year of Our Lord 1291
Hell's Guardhouse Castle
The borders of Scotland

"YOU ARE A prophet, man. I have given you the best food and the finest wine, and now I demand you look into the future and tell us how we are to achieve the wealth and power we desire. Speak, True Thomas!"

The older man, whose name was barked so savagely, winced. He didn't like shouting even though he was desperately hard of hearing.

Standing in the great hall of a dark and stormy castle on the Scottish border called Hell's Guardhouse, all he could feel were the cold, steely fingers of fear gripping at him as he faced off against a father and son. Men he had found camaraderie and companionship with lately, men who listened to his prophesies even when the church would not. They called him a sorcerer, a blasphemer.

But not John de Soulis and his son, Nicholas.

They wanted something from him.

The great hall was only a hall in the literal sense but, mostly, it was a dark and cavernous hole. The wooden floor was wet and slick and moss grew on the walls because the roof leaked and the water trickled down the walls, making them green and shiny. In fact, the entire north wall was green with moss and the wooden floor was weak in places because of the rot.

The entire hall smelled of rot.

It smelled like the name – a gateway to hell.

"It is not as simple as you believe," True Thomas said after a moment, seated at the feasting table that was filthy and splintered. "But I told you that I would do this for you, my friends, so I have come prepared. Tonight is the night. Are you prepared to know your fate?"

Lightning flashed and the storm pounding heavily outside seemed to increase. Standing next to the table, John sighed heavily.

"We have been waiting for almost a month," he said. "You told us that it must be a full spring moon, with a hint of dew in the air, and the birds will have come to roost in the pine trees to the east. All of this has finally happened and I will wait no more. You have demanded food and shelter for weeks until the conditions are right and, finally, they are right. Do what you said you were going to do. Tell us what we wish to know."

True Thomas knew he'd been living off of the rich lord for the past month. He didn't feel bad about living like a king while they paid for everything because the pair were an evil lot. Everyone in the western Lowlands knew it.

Stay away from Hell's Guardhouse, they'd whispered.

But True Thomas hadn't listened. A prophet, a soothsayer, or whatever the church wished to call him, he was all of those things and more. He was an outcast, so it was rare to find comfort and companionship.

But he'd found it now.

And he was prepared.

"Is my iron bowl hot?" he asked.

He was pointing to the enormous hearth, which was spitting out more smoke than it was evacuating from the chimney. Nicholas, the son, went to the hearth and bent over a thick, iron bowl that True Thomas had placed on the coals. He touched it, drawing back quickly.

"It is," he said.

"Fetch it to me."

Nicholas used the corner of his heavy tunic to pick up the bowl and bring it over to the table, where he sat it in front of the old man.

"And the hen's egg?" True Thomas asked.

John produced the egg, handing it over. True Thomas held the egg up over the bowl, but before he cracked it, he looked at Nicholas.

"Cut your finger," he instructed.

The dirty young man frowned. "Do *what*?"

"I said cut your finger. I need your blood."

Nicholas sighed sharply, looking at his father, who simply nodded. They'd come this far and John wanted his future divined from the man that all of the border region knew as a prophet. He'd spent a month with the smelly, drunken old man and he refused to wait any longer, so Nicholas cut his finger.

True Thomas cracked the egg, right into the bowl.

It sizzled.

Grabbing the finger dripping with blood, True Thomas let a few drops plop into the egg that was cooking from the hot bowl. Once he had what he needed, he spat upon them. Using a dirty, long nail from his little finger, he stirred it up a bit, watching the patterns emerge.

Nicholas and John crowded closer.

"I see… a horizon," he muttered after a moment, watching the egg and blood and spit mingle. "I see great change, but not without sacrifice."

John and Nicholas were trying to see what he was seeing. "What sacrifice?" John demanded.

True Thomas used his nail again, swishing through the mixture. As it settled, he watched the omens emerge.

"There is a great power on the border," he finally said. "I see a wolf's head. The House of de Wolfe rules the border. But I see a new power arising from the gates of Hell. A new power from the west."

Nicholas couldn't hold back his excitement. "Us?" he asked. "Is it us?"

True Thomas turned the bowl, watching the contents congeal. "It will not be without great cost," he said. "Blood must be spilled for this to happen. A sacrifice."

John looked at the old man. "What kind of sacrifice?"

True Thomas didn't answer right away. He kept turning the bowl, watching the patterns emerge, scraping it with his dirty nail until everything was a jumbled mess at the bottom. Then, he closed his eyes and lowered his head as if praying over the bowl.

John and Nicholas watched curiously. It seemed to them that the old prophet wasn't even breathing at that point. He simply kept his head down, his eyes closed, and meditated. When they thought they could stand no longer, he lifted his head and opened eyes that were the color of clouds. Normally, the man had brown eyes but, at this moment, they were cloudy and gray. It was enough to cause John and Nicholas to step back, their curiosity now mingled with fear.

"A child must be sacrificed," True Thomas said hoarsely. "An infant of de Soulis blood, as that is the blood that must be spilled at the ring of the nine stones. Take the child to the stones at summer solstice and spill the blood upon the stones. Bury the body to feed the stones, to nourish the dominion of demons, and the House of de Soulis shall rise against the wolf.

The brimstone of Ba'al Zebub shall be your strength. Do this and everything you seek shall be yours."

With that, his head slumped and he pitched forward, collapsing on the table. John and Nicholas simply stood there, watching him with a good deal of surprise at his prophesy but without much concern for True Thomas himself. In fact, they made no move to help him. They simply looked at one another in awe.

"An infant," John repeated. "We need a child of de Soulis blood. But we have *no* child."

Nicholas looked at him. "Not now," he said. "But that will not be difficult. I can create one."

John eyed his brutal, lawless son, a man so vile that at forty years and one, he had never married. No decent family would give a daughter to him. But hearing his son's words, he knew what the man meant.

Creating a child wasn't difficult for a determined man.

If no one would give him a daughter, then he'd find one.

"How?" he said. "Do you intend to find some hapless woman to impregnate?"

Nicholas nodded, clearly cooking up at idea. "Grandfather did it."

John conceded the point. "He did, but he had other reasons."

"And I have mine," Nicholas said. "It is the perfect solution, really. True Thomas says we need a child of de Soulis blood, so I simply find a woman to bear my child. When it is born, it shall belong to me. It is really very simple."

John scratched his head. "Possibly," he said. "Mayhap a woman we do not know or does not know our family name. Obviously, we cannot tell her what the child is for. Will you marry her?"

Nicholas snorted. "I do not have to marry a woman in order

to beget her with child."

That was true, but John wasn't clear on what his son meant. "Then mayhap it should be something simple, like a servant or a farmer's daughter," he said. "Pay her well enough and she will agree to bear the child. Will you bring her here to have the child, then?"

Nicholas shook his head. "Nay," he said. "She may have it wherever she wishes, but I will return to claim it. Call it a business transaction and nothing more. She shall be my breeding stock. When we pay for a finely bred horse, the horse does not have born under our roof, does it?"

John shook his head. "It does not."

Nicholas turned away from the table, heading towards the fire as it continued to spit smoke and sparks into the hall. As he stared into the flames pensively, True Thomas let out a groan and lifted his head. John and Nicholas looked to him, somewhat anxiously, wondering if there was more to come.

"This child," John said. "This sacrifice – must it come from anyone special? May we select the woman or will we be given a sign as to who it may be?"

True Thomas' eyes were still cloudy as he stared at the distant wall, unblinking. "Where the dead and the water meet," he said. "The dead and the water is her belonging."

His eyes closed and his head tilted to one side. When he began breathing heavily, John and Nicholas looked at each other.

"What does that mean?" Nicholas said, frustrated. "The dead and the water?"

John looked at him, puzzled. "The dead and the water," he muttered slowly. "A church? A cemetery? There is one near us, near a brook."

Nicholas shook his head. "A woman would not be at a church," he said. "Unless he means we should find her there as she worships?"

John snorted. "All we would find at that church are women who know who you are and would never enter into an agreement with you."

"I do not need their agreement. I simply need a woman of breeding age."

The comment didn't bother John. Coming from Nicholas, it was normal. It was also truthful. They were literally prepared to make a deal with the devil for what they felt was their due, their right, and a reluctant female wasn't going to stand in their way. They'd waited quite some time for the prophesy from True Thomas and now that they had it, they were going to make sure they did everything in their power to ensure that it became truth.

A blood sacrifice meant nothing to them.

Not even of their own blood.

Therefore, an agreeable female or a resistant one was all the same to them.

John suddenly held up a finger.

"Wait," he said as if a thought had just occurred to him. "The dead and the water. Do you not understand? *Deadwater.* He must mean the village of Deadwater."

Nicholas' eyes widened. "Of course," he hissed. "It is not far from here. But it not on our lands."

John shook his head. "Merek de Leia of Falstone Castle," he said. "He is the lord of Deadwater's village. God's Bones… I've not thought of him in some time."

"That is because he is worthless to us," Nicholas sniffed. "He should be closer to us than he is, but he refuses any alliance at all. Instead, he is allied with de Wolfe from Rule Water Castle."

John's eyes narrowed. "The Lair," he muttered, using the term for the massive de Wolfe garrison known as Wolfe's Lair.

"In my quest to assert myself over de Wolfe's dominance, I've overlooked their smaller allies like de Leia, mostly because they mean nothing to me. I can easily quash them. But de Leia… Deadwater is his domain. And he has a daughter, his only child."

Something in Nicholas' eyes flickered, like a flame of evil igniting. "A child from a de Wolfe ally would surely fulfill the prophesy better than any other woman," he said. "Think of it, Father – we have often spoken of this moment, the moment when we obtain the necessary alliance to rise against de Wolfe and push back. We have watched them encroach upon the border, drawing closer to us, swallowing up our eastern lands and daring us to challenge them. This is *our* moment, Father. Do you disagree with me?"

John shook his head. "That is why I kept True Thomas here," he said. "That is why I sought him out to begin with. The House of de Soulis has been on these borders longer than the House of de Wolfe, yet de Wolfe and his connections have gradually swallowed up everything. Soon, they will swallow us if we do not resist. Nay, more than resist – defeat. And this child will give us the power to do that because we shall have the greatest ally in all the world. God would not help us, so let Lucifer have his due. I will gladly give him a sacrifice of de Soulis blood if it will rid us of de Wolfe."

Now, it was spoken plainly, the very reason they had summoned True Thomas and kept the man close until the conditions were right for his prophesy.

Now, they knew what had to be done.

A child of de Soulis blood and a de Wolfe ally.

"I will go to Deadwater and I will continue to return until I can discover information on de Leia's daughter," Nicholas said, feeling some excitement now that a plan was set. "Deadwater is on her father's land, so surely she is not a stranger to the village."

"Assuredly not," John said. "But you must be cautious. If her father hears you are looking for her, he will keep her safely tucked inside the walls of Falstone."

Nicholas shook his head. "I will be careful," he said. "I have not been to Deadwater in years, so I will not be recognized. But make no mistake, Father – this is a hunt. And I shall be very careful in my hunt."

"As you lie in wait."

"Exactly."

That was exactly what John wanted to hear. The prophesy had been delivered. Soon, so would a child.

A child that would cause the fall of the House of de Wolfe.

PART ONE
LONDON

CHAPTER TWO

Year of our Lord 1292
London
The Pox Tavern

"D RAY! *DOWN!*"

A very big man in the midst of throwing a punch suddenly fell to the floor as another man, who had rushed up behind him with a chair held aloft and intending to smash it on his head, went sailing over his head and crashed into a wall.

It was time to get out.

Andreas de Wolfe, his two cousins, Thomas "Tor" de Wolfe and William "Will" de Wolfe, and his close friend Theodis de Velt, had come to the legendary London tavern known as The Pox. It was a rather large establishment, situated in a seedy part of London, and nestled down by the riverbank where the cogs would come to shore and anchor. The Pox had been around for over one hundred years and, in those years, had established a reputation as a lively place with a deadly underbelly.

But The Pox was unique.

So unique, in fact, that it drew a massive crowd from the lowest of the low to princes and kings. Everyone wanted to spend time in a place that wasn't fashionable, or beautiful, but had reputation built on two distinct things – excellent food and drink, and a gambling reputation that was second to none.

At The Pox, anyone could bet on anything – literally.

That's exactly what Andreas and his cousins had been doing. They had come into the tavern to sample the good food and drink that they had heard so much about, but they ended up in a drinking game that had become quite revolting.

It had all started because Theodis had purchased several different medicaments from a local apothecary, stuff that was difficult to find in the north. He'd purchased ingredients that were guaranteed to ease a fever, some to cure a cut or a puncture, some to fortify the blood, and yet another that guaranteed to evacuate the stomach at an alarming rate. It was called a "purge" and it was used when men ingested poison or rotten meat, or something that needed to come out of the body quickly.

And that had given the knights an idea.

The premise was simple – one of them added a tiny bit of purge to the cheaper ale they were drinking. The glasses were then shuffled and distributed, and the men bet on who would be drinking the glass with the purge.

There was an element of danger as well as an element of hilarity. Too much purge could kill, but a small amount would do terrible but recoverable things to a human body. Whoever got the drink with the purge in it would know very quickly, because within a minute of drinking it, everything would come right back up again.

At first, it was just the four of them indulging in the game, but then others began to see what they were doing and they wanted to join in. Very quickly, there were ten to twelve men indulging in the vomiting game that was becoming the focus of the entire tavern.

Andreas was a man who would be considered the strong

and silent type. He wasn't one to say much, but when he did have something to say, it was worth listening to. He'd built a reputation for giving sage advice and a fighting skill that was one of the very best in England. His particular attributes made him quite dangerous because he was adept at hiding his emotions and his expression would maintain a neutrality even if, inside, he was plotting a man's death. One could never tell what Andreas de Wolfe was thinking at any given time, and that included during the stupid drinking game.

He had gotten the purge once during the entire game. He had vomited so hard and so far that, now, they were taking bets on just how far men would and could vomit. They had cleared away several tables while they passed around the drink and waited to see who would erupt and just how far they could go with it.

It had been messy, but it had been quite funny. There was an added benefit to drinking the ale with the purge in it because it evacuated the alcohol out of the stomach, meaning the person drinking was delaying their path to drunkenness. But those who couldn't hold their liquor very well were already quite drunk, regardless of having the misfortune of the purge in one of their cups of ale, and the bets were flying fast and furious as vomit covered the floor of the tavern.

Even now, as it grew late into the night and the River Thames outside of the tavern's front door lapped softly upon the rocky shore, The Pox was filled to the rafters with questionable women and even more questionable men, at least half of them indulging in the messy and sometimes violent vomiting game.

Every time someone vomited, the roof was practically lifted off the tavern by people laughing and cheering. Andreas and his cousins had been having a marvelous time, but that quickly changed when one of the men betting suddenly decided that the game was somehow rigged. He couldn't quite explain why he thought that or how he even knew that, but he was unhappy because he felt as if he'd lost too much money trying to predict just how far someone was going to puke. He began arguing, Will delivered a well-aimed insult as only he was capable, and the entire room deteriorated into an all-out brawl.

And that was where Andreas found himself now, throwing himself onto the floor so he wouldn't be crowned by a chair. Once his attacker was sprawling several feet away, he leapt to his feet and turned to make sure his cousins were unharmed.

"It is my sense that we need to leave this place," he said to them. "Poppy warned us against coming here, but we did not listen."

"Poppy" was his grandfather, William de Wolfe, the mighty Wolfe of the Border. He was the greatest knight in northern England, and probably all of England, having served three kings. He had been to The Pox in his youth and had tried to dissuade his grandsons from venturing to it on their visit to London, but like moths to the flame, they were drawn to something legendary, dastardly, and exciting.

And now regretting it.

Mostly.

"Come on." William "Will" de Wolfe, the oldest of the de Wolfe grandchildren and named for his famous grandfather, grabbed his younger brother and was moving for the door. "This place is full of clay-brained halfwits. Dray, grab Theodis! We leave!"

Andreas whirled around, looking for his best friend in the entire world, a massive and frightening beast of man who was part of a family whose entire foundation was built on brutal conquest and death. Theodis de Velt was a true-blood of those lines because he had three of their most defining characteristics – being enormously built, having long and dark hair, and two-colored eyes.

The most well-known de Velt with that trait was Ajax de Velt, a man who had conquered half the Welsh Marches and was starting in on the Scottish Marches when he met the woman who tamed him. He had brown eyes except the left one had a big splash of bright green in it. That trait, to varying degrees, was carried by the male line of his family and, in some cases, even the women had it. Theodis had it, but his was quite pronounced – his right eye was brown, while his left eye was brown except for the pupil being encircled with a ring of bright green. It was beautiful, bold and startling, something that only enhanced the interesting nature of a very handsome, and very volatile, man.

In fact, he was being volatile right at this very moment. Andreas spied him over near the kitchens as he threw punches with a very large man who seemed to have murder on his mind. As Andreas headed in that direction, Theodis caught sight of him and decided to end his brawl once and for all.

One big fist in the face and his opponent went out as quickly as blowing out a candle.

"Come on," Andreas said, motioning the man to follow. "We're leaving."

Theodis grinned as he joined Andreas, a gesture that most men saw as rather frightening because his canines were prominent. It made him look like a fanged beast.

"Why?" he asked, keeping his fists balled in case someone decided to charge him. "Look around you, Dray – it's a party."

Andreas had to chuckle. "A party, is it?" he said. "This is one party I no longer wish to attend."

"Why not?"

"Because this place smells like vomit, you wretch. I need fresh air."

Theodis laughed, pushing him through a still-writhing

crowd to the front door where William and Tor were waiting. Together, the four of them rushed the front door, ending up on the muddy road outside with the River Thames before them.

Andreas drew in a long, deep breath.

"God," he muttered. "I can finally breathe. Well, it was fun while it lasted."

William, a serious and somewhat shy man, scratched his dark head. "It was some of the better entertainment we've had," he agreed. "What now? Do we retire to Lothbury House?"

Theodis shook his head. "We are *not* retiring," he said. "I haven't been to London in a few years and I am not going to miss a second of it. Are you lads up for a new adventure?"

The three of them looked at him. "*What* adventure?" Tor demanded. Big, handsome, strawberry blond Tor attracted women like horses attracted flies. "What do you have in mind?"

Theodis tapped is head as if he had a grand idea. "I realize you de Wolfe lads don't get to London too often, you poor little country mice," he said, taunting them. "I think your family likes to keep you all bottled up, afraid of what will happen if you get a taste of the decadence London has to offer."

Tor sneered at him. "And you're so worldly," he said sarcastically. "Well? Tell us what you have in mind so we can get this over with."

Theodis was grinning as he looked around, getting his bearings. "This way."

Curious, and slightly irritated, the de Wolfe men followed.

"Where are we going?" Andreas asked.

They were heading in the direction of the Tower of London on a moonlit night. The moon was reflecting on the waters of the Thames and the smell from the river was strong, like rotten fish and sewage. Theodis pointed towards the Tower.

"The last time I was here, I came with men I had served with long ago," he said. "We were in town for a funeral of a lord we had once served. We'd heard through some other knights that there was a miraculous place here for the taking, a place so scandalous, so filled with debauchery, that only the rich, handsome, beautiful, or utterly outrageous were permitted entry."

Andreas frowned. "What kind of place *is* this?" he said. "I've not heard of it."

Theodis grinned, his fangs reflecting the moonlight. "It's called Gomorrah," he said. "It's beneath the old St. Dunstan's Church, an old Saxon church that burns down every time the church rebuilds it. The church was built atop the ruins of an ancient Roman temple and no church built upon those ruins has ever survived. It is said that the property itself is cursed."

In spite of the suspicion, he had their attention. "So what is the place you're taking us to?" Tor asked.

"I told you," Theodis said. "It's an exclusive guild where every fantasy can come true. It was started a long time ago by a Hessian lord who married an English noblewoman, Lady Camberwell. The Hessian used the Camberwell money to buy the property from the church and start his guild, which costs a small fortune to access, but the family pays the church part of those proceeds so they look the other way with what goes on there. There is feasting, drinking, entertainment, fornication – whatever you want is provided. Anything and everything."

Now, they were more intrigued. "*Anything?*" Tor said.

"Anything."

"But you said it costs a small fortune to access," William said. "How much?"

"A pound."

That brought outrage. "A *pound?*" William spat. "I could buy a week in London and live well for that much."

Theodis shook his head. "But you'll not live like this," he said. "You must experience this once in your life, Will.

Consider it an enrichment of your education as a man and as a knight. Tell them you're a de Wolfe and that will be your key to entry. They only take the elite and the rich and the beautiful. I tell them I'm a de Velt and, terrified of my family name, they admit me. Truly… you must experience this place."

He said it passionately enough that they were intrigued to the point of being agreeable. William looked at Tor, who lifted his big shoulders and nodded. Then they both looked to Andreas, who was usually the level-headed one in the group, and he simply shrugged.

"We may as well," he said. "We've experienced Sodom back at The Pox – let us experience Gomorrah beneath this dead church."

Theodis put a big arm around Andreas' neck and began pulling him down the street. "You are going to live to regret this," he told him. "But you are going to have the time of your life doing it."

Andreas wasn't sure if that made him feel better or worse. Having no idea what they were in for, he tried to keep an open mind. He was a man who could judge things evenly, from all sides, and deliver what he considered a fair and just decision. Within the family, he was known for that ability and Andreas' judgment was unchallenged in any case.

But he wondered if this was going to be one of those rare bad decisions.

The look on Theodis' face told him that it very well might be.

The quest for this mysterious and scandalous guild took Andreas, Tor, William, and Theodis more than half a mile down the road that paralleled the River Thames, heading in the direction of the Tower of London. The area, in particular, was known for high crime with plenty of murders and robberies and other unsavory deeds. It seemed strange that the area next to the Tower of London, such an icon for a just and right civilization, should be considered the seedy side of London.

Therefore, the four of them were on their guard as they traveled. Not that they expected any trouble, because they were four extremely large and well-armed knights, but one never knew when fools would attack. The moved further away from the section in town that contained the taverns and hostels, a quieter area that was rather dark and without much traffic.

In fact, the very air seemed ripe with darkness and murder.

An exclusive guild in this section of town? Andreas wasn't entirely sure that Theodis was leading them in the right direction, so he started to open his mouth when Theodis abruptly took a left turn and headed up a small alley, away from the river.

A dark trek became darker – literally.

There was hardly an ambient light in the alley called Beet Street. It was only a block or two from the walls of the Tower of London, so they were generally familiar with where they were. This was the older side of town, the side where the Romans had left their mark and the Saxons had built their timber city. It had a feel all its own, like something wild and uncivilized, which simply went along with the general seedy nature of the district.

But it was more than that.

Andreas felt as if there were some kind of otherworldly and barbaric flavor to this part of town, mostly because many of the buildings that were still there were of Saxon design, something the Normans modified once they took control of the City of London. In his rare trips to London throughout his life, he'd only been on this side of town while traveling to the Tower, and that was always the sense he got from it –

Barbaric.

Traveling up Beet Street, the knights came to a fork in the road. The fork heading northeast would take them through more of what they had just passed through, and the fork to the south would lead to the Tower of London. They took the fork to the northeast, traveling up the road and passing shabby businesses and residences.

St. Dunstan's Church was on Hart Street, an offshoot of Beet Street. It was near the wall of London but in an area that was not well traveled. In fact, there was a dumping ground on this side of the city used for rubbish, so the stench kept people away for the most part.

Except for those heading to a particular burned-out church.

They could see St. Dunstan's Church as soon as they turned onto Hart Street, the bones of the church pronounced against the moonlit sky. As Andreas looked at the distant church, he recalled Theodis speaking of the location as being cursed and he could instantly see where that opinion came from. The church had been built out of timber originally when the Saxons built over the old Roman temple, but when the Normans had come, they ripped down the wood and replaced it with stone. Still, the wooden roof had been vulnerable and St. Dunstan's had burned three times before the church finally decided not to rebuild.

Therefore, it was a skeleton that existed these days, looking forlorn and macabre against the night sky. The closer the knights drew, the more Andreas wondered if this was really a good idea. Theodis certainly thought so and he was more than excited to take his friends through an adventure they would all remember.

But Andreas… not so much.

They ended up moving in the shadows of the burned-out structure until they came to an enormously heavy door with iron braces. Theodis held up a hand, bringing the group to a pause.

He knocked once.

Several seconds later, he knocked again.

That went on twice until the door lurched open and two big men, heavily armed, stood in the doorway.

"*Da verbum*," the first man rumbled.

"Gomorrah," Theodis replied.

The man looked to the three massive men behind him. "Name?"

"De Velt and de Wolfe. Northumberland has arrived."

The man looked at him, registering some surprise. Or perhaps it was approval. The names of de Wolfe and de Velt carried weight all over England, no matter what the situation. The man took Theodis' money, quite a lot of it, and retreated back into the church with his companion.

"Enter," he muttered.

Theodis turned to his friends, flashing that big-toothed smile.

"Now," he said quietly, "it begins."

Andreas was the last one in. He wondered what, exactly, "it" meant. *What* was beginning?

He was about to find out.

CHAPTER THREE

The Asher Manor
London

"Gavy! Gavy, awaken!"

She could hear a woman's voice in her ear, a voice she recognized. But she was still entrenched in a haze of sleep that had her within its grip. Her dreams had been warm, dreams of her home in the north, and she was reluctant to leave them.

But someone was hissing in her ear.

"Gavy!"

Lady Gavriella de Leia's eyes popped open. For a moment, she didn't recognize her surroundings. It took her a moment to orient herself.

Then she remembered.

I'm in London.

The familiar pangs of grief hit her. She was here because her father had sent her here. Not because she wanted to be here. She'd never wanted to come, but here she was.

Caged.

Trapped.

Rolling onto her back, she saw her cousin, Lady Camilla de

Kennet. Camilla had just come of age and beneath that pale, innocent-looking exterior beat the heart of a rebel. Gavriella had learned that the first day she'd come to London. Camilla's sister, Lady Aurelia de Kennet, was older by two years and even worse, only Aurelia had a titian-haired sensuality about her that she wasn't afraid to weaponize. If she saw a handsome man, that sensuality would be put to good use.

Camilla had learned quite a bit from her scandalous sister.

"Gavy!" Aurelia was in the chamber now, hissing at her cousin on the bed. "Get up, do you hear? We are going out."

Gavriella sat up, rubbing one eye. "Going *out*?" she repeated. "But… but it has to be the middle of the night. Where on earth are we going?"

"Shhhh," Aurelia put her finger to her lips. "Not so loud. Mother might hear you."

Camilla was dragging her out of bed. "Hurry," she said. "We must hurry!"

"Hurry for what?" Gavriella was quite confused. As Camilla tried to pull her night shift over her head, Gavriella held fast and pulled away. "Tell me where we are going or I will not budge an inch."

Aurelia was in the wardrobe. She pulled forth a beautiful red damask gown with pearls embroidered on the sleeves and the bodice.

"This should do," she said, ignoring Gavriella's question. "It's Cammie's gown and a little small for you, but it will make your breasts look full."

"They'll pop out over the top of the neckline!" Camilla giggled.

Gavriella didn't want to pop out of anything. She had no idea what her naughty cousins were up to, but she wasn't going anywhere with them in the middle of the night unless they were clear about their intensions. She folded her arms across her chest stubbornly.

"Tell me or I will not go," she said.

Aurelia tossed the gown on the bed. "Then we shall go without you."

"Go and I will tell Aunt Drucilla."

Camilla shrieked in fear as Aurelia eyed her country cousin unhappily. She'd really only met her three times in her life because Gavriella lived in Northumberland on the border with Scotland. That was quite far to the north and visits with that branch of the family had been infrequent.

In fact, this most recent visit had been quite unexpected.

Gavriella had appeared a few days ago, unannounced, with a small contingent of de Leia men and a missive to their mother. Drucilla de Kennet had read the contents of the letter and promptly brought Gavriella into their enormous manse called The Asher. It was a beautiful home to the northeast of the Tower of London and it had been in the de Kennet family, the Earls of Blackburn, for decades.

It was one of the prized jewels of London.

Aurelia wasn't sure how she felt about her cousin, to be truthful. She was beautiful – *too* beautiful and Aurelia didn't like the attention being taken off of her. She was sweet and obedient, but that's where the problem was – she was *too* obedient. There was no nerve in the woman, no bravery. She seemed to cry easily and didn't seem very happy.

Aurelia suspected that Gavriella had been sent here for a reason.

But *what* reason?

Her mother wouldn't tell her, nor would Gavriella. But it just seemed strange that the woman would show up one day like a beaten dog. Something about her seemed… crushed. Defeated. She seemed too meek and quiet for Aurelia's taste, but rather than be understanding of that trait, Aurelia had turned into a bully.

Everyone at The Asher did as she wished. Gavriella would be no different.

There would be consequences if she were.

"You will not tell my mother because if you do, I'll tell my mother than you have been stealing and lying and demand she send you home," Aurelia fired back. "You will listen to me, you little country mouse, and you will listen well. You are going to do as I say or there will be trouble. Why did you even come here, anyway? We have not seen you for ten years and, suddenly, you show up unannounced? *Why*? Why did you even come?"

Gavriella didn't back down, but she also wasn't going to answer her bossy cousin's questions. She'd never had much of an opinion of Aurelia because she'd never spent an inordinate amount of time around her, but the past week had seen that changed.

She wasn't sure she liked her cousin.

"Please, Gavy," Camilla pleaded softly. "We're going to a place that is full of fun and music. Don't you want to come?"

Fun and music.

Gavriella wasn't sure such things existed anymore. *Did they*? Ever since her life changed last year, things like joy and laughter didn't exist in her world anymore.

Was it possible that people here still laughed and enjoyed themselves?

Camilla seemed to think so.

So did Aurelia.

"Fun and music?" she repeated. "Are we going to a feast, then?"

"In a way," Aurelia said. She'd spent enough time discussing the point with her killjoy cousin. "Come with us or don't come with us; 'tis all the same to me. But if you don't come, you'll not say a word to my mother or I'll have her send you back where you came from."

It was a threat, pure and simple. Gavriella eyed her cousin as Camilla pulled the shift over her head. Whether or not the threat was real, returning home at the moment wasn't an option.

She was relegated to London until her father sent for her.

"Come on," Camilla said, pushing her to move. "Hurry and dress. We're going to have such fun!"

At that point, Gavriella didn't have much choice. She had already implied that she would comply simply by getting out of bed, and she honestly wasn't strong enough to fend Camilla off. Therefore, she stood there while Camilla dressed her in the beautiful red silk with the pearls. Gavriella didn't own anything quite so fine and, in truth, she was a little intrigued by the soft and lovely garment, and the way it emphasized her full breasts.

Breasts that so recently had been engorged with milk for a baby they no longer needed to feed.

In fact, her entire body was a curvier version of the slender woman she used to be before … before the event that changed her life forever.

It was something she would take to her grave, something so horrific that it wasn't anything she could ever repeat, and especially not to her cousins. Aurelia had asked her why she had visited unannounced, or in her words, simply showed up. Gavriella couldn't tell her the truth.

The truth was too horrible to even speak of.

She'd been sent to London because her father couldn't bear to look at her anymore. That was the truth of it. Merek de Leia knew that sending his daughter to his sister in London would get her out of his sight, but it was only a temporary measure until something more permanent could be arranged.

And that is why Gavriella was here.

She hated every minute of it.

Now, her bossy and disobedient cousin wanted them to go gallivanting around in the middle of the night. Gavriella wanted to get back into bed, but that wasn't going to happen. Therefore, she stood still as Camilla dressed her in the beautiful gown that was just a little too snug. Her full breasts popped up over the top and then some. As Gavriella tried to minimize that pop, Camilla pinned back the front of her hair and then braided it with red ribbons woven into the braids. The gown came with a matching cap, sewn with tiny seed pearls, and Camilla pinned that on the top of her head.

As Aurelia sat at a small dressing table and primped before a polished bronze mirror, Camilla took great delight in primping her country cousin. She, too, had noticed how beautiful Gavriella was with her long, blonde hair and gray eyes shaped like a cat's eyes, but unlike her sister, Camilla wasn't threatened by it. She knew that was why her sister was being so mean to their cousin.

It was pure jealousy.

Timid Gavriella had only been there a week and Camilla was fairly certain her sister's nastiness was only going to get worse, especially when the young men started taking notice of Gavriella more than Aurelia.

"There," Camilla said, satisfied. "The red color is beautiful on you, Gavy. You look very beautiful."

Aurelia, hearing her sister's praise for their cousin, glanced over her shoulder and saw the magnificent woman. But she downplayed it. "She'll do," she said. "Come on, now. We must hurry. If it becomes too crowded, they'll close the doors and will not let us in."

Camilla put a black cloak on Gavriella's shoulders as she grabbed her own blue cloak with white rabbit lining. Aurelia was already moving into the adjoining chamber, gathering her things, including her coin purse. Slinging her cloak over her shoulders to cover up a gown the color of emeralds, she faced her sister and cousin.

"Now," she said softly. "We must be very quiet. Follow me and do not speak. Is that clear?"

Both Camilla and Gavriella nodded. Satisfied that they were going to do as they were told, Aurelia slipped out.

The Asher was something of a labyrinth. It was built just like any other manor house in London, with a central courtyard in the middle of the house. There were four levels to it and a myriad of staircases, making it a large and complex structure.

Aurelia led her sister and cousin down a darkened corridor. She came to a halt at one point, putting her hand on what looked like a wooden panel, but when she pushed the panel, it swung open to reveal a narrow staircase. The women traveled down the staircase in the dark, trying not to fall in the darkness, as they made their way to the level below, which happened to be a servant's pantry.

The pantry was connected to the scullery which was connected to an inner hall with a fortified exterior door. The door led out into a side yard, which was used for tradesmen when they came to do business with the manor. Because of this, there was a postern gate lodged into the massive wall that surrounded The Asher. The postern gate was guarded by a pair of soldiers, but Aurelia was prepared. She slipped the soldiers each a coin, ensuring their silence and cooperation, and they opened the gate for her.

The women slipped out into the night.

The Asher was located on a quiet road in the northeast section of London's walled city. Aurelia moved quickly and confidently through the darkened streets, which smelled like animals and rubbish. They were heading into the warmer months and the weather had been mild, with no rain, which meant the smells of the city were starting to become more evident. This was a time when people kept their windows closed purely to block out the stench of the city.

That was something Gavriella was still trying to get used to, that sharp and acrid stench of human habitation. Smells like this in the north where she came from were only common in the larger villages and certainly not usual where she lived. Her home was on the gently rolling hills of the borders and the only smells other than the stables and the moat were of the blooming heather or other flora and fauna.

Thinking about it made her miss it terribly.

Here she was, in this unfamiliar city with people she barely knew, and it was difficult not to become overwhelmed with grief. So far, there wasn't anything about London that she liked and she longed to return home. Aurelia made it difficult to want to stay in London, as her father wished, but at least Camilla made it a little more bearable. Whereas Aurelia was bossy and scheming, Camilla was truly sweet and a little silly. Her sister had great influence over her, that was true, but Gavriella wondered if that damage could be undone.

She was sorry to see vulnerable Camilla fall subject to her sister's deviousness.

In fact, she had fallen victim to it, too. Aurelia had threatened and bullied, and she'd gone right along with it like a submissive little cow. The proof of that was right before her – she was out running around in the middle of the night on the dangerous streets of London, following her cousin as the woman led them towards some unknown destination. They were allegedly going to a feast of fun and music, but given how sly and underhanded Aurelia was, Gavriella wondered if that was the truth.

Where Aurelia was concerned, anything could happen.

Something told her they were going to a tavern they'd visited once before, a terrible place called The Pox, but knowing Aurelia, it was probably someplace worse. Still, she followed like that stupid cow, with no mind and no ability to make a decision for herself. She felt dumb and fearful, but not dumb and fearful enough to turn around and go home. Maybe there was a small part of her that wanted to make sure Camilla was protected, even if she really didn't care what happened to Aurelia.

As far as she was concerned, her cousin would get what she deserved.

They were getting closer to the river now. Gavriella could smell the fish and the rot as it radiated off the River Thames. She had noted that smell earlier in the week because her aunt had taken her to the street of the merchants, which was near the river itself. That rotted river smell seemed to permeate everything it could touch.

Thoughts of smells and stupid cows were pushed aside as she noticed a silhouette against the backdrop of the moonlit sky. She could see a bell tower and walls that clearly indicated a church, but as they drew closer, Gavriella could see that there was no roof on the church. It was derelict. The walls looked like great rib bones of a dead and desolate beast, eerily dark, and Aurelia took them onto a smaller street that ran alongside the church to the east. They stayed close to the walls of that burned-out church, making their way in the darkness until they came to a massive door built into the side of the building.

Aurelia knocked twice, two heavy knocks, several seconds apart. The response wasn't immediate and as they stood there, eyes darting nervously about the darkness, fog began to roll in from the river. They could see it snaking through the street and alleyways and cresting over the tops of the buildings like the wave of a great storm. Something about that fog rolling in over the darkened streets of London gave them a measure of apprehension.

Gavriella watched the fog edge closer and closer. Aurelia lifted her hand and knocked in the same fashion again, two heavy knocks with a long pause between. As the fog grew closer, encroaching on them, Gavriella felt Camilla lean into her fearfully. The fogs of London were known to be extraordinarily thick at times and if a truly heavy fog rolled in, it would be difficult to see their hands in front of their faces. No one wanted to get caught in a fog like that.

Evil things lurked in fog.

Especially in the darker side in London.

Just as the fog began to roll over the skeleton of the old church, the door opened. Two very large men, heavily armed, were standing in the opening. They looked at the three women huddled there without a hint of warmth or welcome in their expressions.

"Da verbum," one man growled.

Aurelia was without fear. "Gomorrah."

"Name?"

"De Kennet. Earl of Blackburn."

Like magic, the men took her coinage and backed away, permitting the women to enter. Just as the fog enveloped the burned-out ruins, the heavy door was shut behind them. But for a small torch on the wall, they were in complete darkness.

It felt like a tomb.

One of the men pushed past them and took the torch off the wall.

"Come," he said.

The man led them through a small, dark corridor and towards a stairwell that led down into the depths beneath the old church. As Gavriella's eyes adjusted to the darkness, she could see that they were in a sublevel beneath the floor of the old church.

There were tombs down here, and crypts, from long-forgotten burials. The smell of rot was heavy down here, the dampness thick. London had a high water table, which meant that not many things were built below ground, but places like churches often built vaults beneath them to accommodate burials.

This was one of those places. Beneath the old church, an entire world was opening up.

Gavriella tapped Camilla on the shoulder.

"Where *are* we?" she hissed.

Camilla glanced at her as they were heading down the stairs. "This is the old church of St. Dunstan's," she whispered. "The Lords of Camberwell own it now because the church believes this property to be cursed. Down below this level are the remains of an ancient Roman temple dedicated to the god Eros. Camberwell has turned those ruins and catacombs into a guild that is so exclusive, so secretive, that only the fortunate few know about it."

Gavriella looked at her with some apprehension. "A guild? What *kind* of guild?"

"Fantasy," Aurelia said. They had reached the bottom of the stairwell and were now in a small chamber where women dressed in filmy, gauzy garments came forward. They put a glorious mask on Aurelia's face. "This is a guild where you can live out whatever fantasy you wish and do so without fear of recognition and retribution. You can do anything, say anything, be anything, but keep your mask on at all times. If you are here, you are not meant to be known or recognized."

The same women who had put the mask on Aurelia were now putting one on Gavriella. It was a wooden mask, painted elaborately like the upper part of a cat's face – nose and eyes only. The mask had jewels set within it and feathers for whiskers. In truth, it was astonishingly beautiful and fastened onto Gavriella's head with red silken ribbons.

She was unsure about the mask, her fingers flitting over it, as she looked at Camilla, whose mask resembled a mouse. Aurelia had one that looked like a proud peacock, with great peacock feathers on it.

"I do not understand," Gavriella said. "What kind of fantasy?"

Aurelia smiled at her, but it wasn't a pleasant gesture. She reached out and took Gavriella's hand.

"Come," she said quietly. "Let me show you."

The same young women who had put masks on their faces then proceeded to open a heavy, iron reinforced door. Aurelia led Gavriella into the next room but not before Gavriella realized that the women in the thin, gauzy clothing were naked underneath. One could see right through their clothing to their young, nubile bodies beneath. They, too, were wearing masks so no one could see who they were.

As Gavriella would soon realize, it was all part of the fantasy element.

As soon as she passed through the door with Aurelia leading the way, she could hear music. There were people milling about, all of them wearing masks, and as she watched, a man came up to Aurelia, grabbed her around the waist, and proceeded to kiss her deeply.

Aurelia responded lustily.

Gavriella watched in shock as Aurelia kissed a man she probably didn't even know. There were no names, no acknowledgement, and as Aurelia had said, no one was supposed to know the true identity, so Gavriella could only assume she didn't know who the man was. But she was sure kissing him like she knew who he was. He stuck his tongue in her mouth and she let him.

Then, as quickly as he had grabbed her, he let her go and moved on.

When Aurelia saw the shock on Gavriella's face, she laughed.

"This is a place where you can live out your wildest fantasies, Gavy," she said. "If you see a handsome man you wish to kiss, then do so. He can kiss you, too. Everyone is free to do as they wish."

Gavriella was coming to suspect that she was going to sorely regret coming to this place. "This establishment is called Gomorrah?" she asked, repeating the word she'd heard Aurelia give to gain them admittance. "As in Sodom and Gomorrah?"

Aurelia giggled, which told Gavriella everything she needed to know. "You'll enjoy yourself," she said. "You must learn to relax and enjoy life. You're so serious. You must learn to smile more and be less obedient to convention."

Camilla was next to her, chiming in. "Gavy knows how to smile," she said. "I have seen her. But she will love this place, I know she will!"

Aurelia gave her an appraising look, as if she didn't quite believe that. "If she cannot be happy here, then she cannot be happy anywhere," she said flatly. "Since no one is supposed to know your real name, you must have a pretend name. A name you only use when you are here."

Gavriella was dubious of the entire strange concept. "Why would I not give my real name?"

Aurelia sighed sharply. "Because no one must know *you*," she said. "In a world of fantasy, nothing is real. Do you not understand? Here, you are anyone you want to be. You are not real. You are simply a woman in a cat mask, with no past and no future. You are a dream and a dream is you. Therefore, we shall call you... Kitten."

Gavriella resisted the urge to roll her eyes. "Kitten?"

"Perfect!" Camilla said. "I am always Angel and Aurelia is always Venus, the Goddess of Love. That is all anyone knows of us!"

Gavriella stared at them for a moment, her seemingly prim and proper cousins, who evidently had a naughty side. She had an inkling that this place was much darker than she had been led to believe.

God's Bones, what have I gotten myself in to?

But it was too late to leave as Aurelia continued to lead them deeper underground. Because the church had built their structure over the old temple, the ceilings were very low. Everything seemed tight and close. There were fires burning in copper bowls to give off light and warmth against the dankness of the sublevels, but it wasn't enough to stave off the true darkness of the place.

They went deeper.

Aurelia took them into a larger room that had one wall that was shaped like a half-moon. In this room, fatted torches burned upon the walls, creating a layer of smoke against the wooden ceiling that had been reinforced with great beams. This chamber contained food, and not just any food – any and all food imaginable. They were great tables spread with the stuff and, for the first time since entering the establishment, Gavriella showed some interest in her surroundings.

Aurelia gave her a moment to look over all the food, and most of it prepared in a Roman fashion. One entire table was fish; fish baked in pies, fish fried and fat, fish stuffed with breadcrumbs and other fish, fish swimming in wine and vinegar sauce, and fish roasted on small iron spits. It was an incredible amount of fish.

Another table was strictly beef – beef prepared twenty different ways, with different sauces and different spices. There was even a bull's head on the table, cooked, with grapes for eyes and a crown on its head. Yet another table was chicken and other birds. Crowning that table was a giant peacock that was cooked, yet the feathers had been reattached so that it looked as it did in life.

People were simply walking up to the tables, using their hands and removing chicken legs or knuckles of beef. She saw one man stand there and use his hands to scoop out big chunks of a beef pie and shove it in his mouth. Against the wall was a table dedicated to sweets and there were probably more sweets than Gavriella had ever seen in her entire life, and still another table that was full of drinks. A nearby servant made sure that the table never ran dry.

It was more food than Gavriella had ever seen in her life.

Gavriella took a skewer of candied grapes, but Aurelia didn't let her examine the food too closely before she was pulling her along to show her the rest of this mysterious establishment. As Gavriella quickly devoured her grapes, she had no real hint that the worst was yet to come.

In fact, it was in front of her.

Because the grounds had once been a Roman temple, there were small cells that were meant to house priests or even soldiers. They were sleeping rooms complete with stone beds that had been built there a thousand years before when the Romans ruled Londinium. What they were used for now, however, was not what the Romans had intended.

There was a strange smell down here, incense burning in bowls to cover up the stink of human bodies and sex. There were curtains in front of some of the cells and not in front of others. Gavriella turned away quickly when she realized that in one cell, two girls were kissing and stroking one another as a man watched. In the next cell, virtually the same thing was happening. At that point, Gavriella realized what Aurelia had meant by living out fantasies.

Unholy, sexual fantasies.

Gavriella was starting to feel sick.

Most of the cells seem to be filled with people doing things they probably should not have been doing. She tried not to look into any of them because some of them were wide open with no curtains to shield their activities. She happened to catch sight of a man lying on the stone bed while a woman put her mouth on his manhood. After that, she simply shut her eyes and let Aurelia lead her on.

She didn't want to see anything more.

The music they had heard when they first entered the labyrinth was growing louder and at the end of the corridor that was lined with cells, they spilled out into a vast, low-ceilinged chamber that was full of people dancing. There were minstrels lining the wall on one side and they played a lively tune as drunk men and drunk women danced together, loudly and happily.

Camilla had apparently reached the event she wanted to participate in and she ran out into the chamber, losing herself amongst the dancers. Aurelia still had a hold of Gavriella when a man in a dog mask grabbed Aurelia and pulled her out onto the dance floor. Gavriella nearly got yanked along, but she let go of Aurelia and let the woman plunge into the writhing crowd.

She wanted no part of it.

Now, Gavriella was all alone in this horrendously sinful place, watching men in dog or stag masks dance with women in cat or bird masks. The masks were all elaborate, and quite beautiful, and they were divided for the sexes. The dance that the group was participating in was not an unknown one, a folk dance that Gavriella had danced to herself from time to time. But it seemed so long ago. Any of her memories and experiences from home seemed like centuries ago.

It was as if she had been away forever, missing it now more than she ever had.

Gavriella backed up, pressing herself against the wall as she watched the dance go on. On more than one occasion, she watched a man wrap his arm around a woman and fondle her breasts as she danced. The women didn't seem to mind at all, but the last thing Gavriella wanted was to be fondled against her will.

That had already happened once.

She wasn't going to let it happen again.

She had to get out.

Unfortunately, she had no idea how to get out. She had followed Aurelia into this large chamber, but her eyes had been closed some of the time because she had been trying to protect herself from what was going on around her. Unfortunately, that meant that she was completely lost.

The music was loud. *Too* loud. It wasn't even enjoyable. Gavriella turned in the direction she thought they had come from but there were so many people it was difficult to tell. She saw what she thought were a couple of doorways, so she made her way towards one of them. It seemed to be dark and still inside the doorway, so she stepped into it and removed herself from the room where men and women were dancing sensually.

The corridor had torches on the walls, with the same sooty smoke billowing against the ceiling. At the end of the corridor was a light and she made her way towards it, but she quickly realized this wasn't the way she'd come in because there were no cells lining either side of the corridor. But she saw a light up ahead and assumed there must be servants around who could tell her where the exit was.

She proceeded.

Unfortunately, the corridor only took her deeper into the maze. Gavriella felt as if the ground were sloping, as if she were walking downwards, and she ended up in a chamber where both men and women were gambling. They were rolling bones and engaging in any number of other gambling games.

Gavriella wasn't very familiar with gambling games, so she could only really guess what they were playing. When a cry went up over to her left, she saw a woman stand up and reveal her breasts to the whole table of men because she had evidently lost the game. Gavriella decided this was not the place for her.

She moved on.

When she turned to go out the way she'd come in, she realized that there were two other doors next to the one that she had come through. In fact, they all looked alike, and she chose what she thought was the correct door. It looked like it, and it smelled like it, so she headed back out towards the light at the end of the tunnel.

Sadly, for her, it only took her into another room.

In this small chamber, filled with smoke and fumes from the copper brazier, scantily clad women were dancing for an audience of men. They were wearing the thin, flimsy clothing that the women who had given them their masks had been wearing, clothing that was transparent. As Gavriella watched, a man in the corner played his citole and the women gyrated.

Nipples flashed.

Gavriella was starting to become panicky.

Whirling around, she left the way she'd come. She was trying desperately not to lose her composure, but this place was a vast collection of tunnels and small chambers, all of them looking and smelling alike, and not one of them leading the way out. If she could at least make it back to the room with the food, she might be able to find her way to freedom. Perhaps Aurelia and Camilla thought this place was a good deal of sophisticated fun, but Gavriella did not.

She thought it was horrible.

The place was maze of corridors and more corridors, of smaller chambers and larger chambers, and every one of them full of people. The more Gavriella wandered, the more disoriented she became. She tried to find her way back the way she had come, but she just ended up going deeper into the labyrinth of Gomorrah. She had just entered another small chamber when a man grabbed her from behind.

"Come 'ere, girl," a man slurred. "Come 'ere and give us a kiss, you tasty morsel."

He was big and smelly. He also had a lot of hair, because when Gavriella put her hands up to stop him, all she could feel was hair.

He was too close, too sweaty, and too nasty.

His mouth clamped down over hers.

Gavriella let out a scream. Suddenly, she was back in the north, in that little village where she had been cornered by men in mail and weapons. They had sighted her like a hunter sights prey, and they had followed her until they trapped her.

And then, she had been grabbed.

As the big, hairy man tried to kiss her, Gavriella was taken back to the worst moment in her life. At the time, she had been shocked and confused. She had lived on the borders her entire life, a peaceful existence, and she had never been fearful when out of her father's home of Falstone Castle. She had taken weekly trips to town to go to the marketplace or to visit the various merchants. She had lived her entire life with relative freedom and had never feared for her safety.

Until the only incident she'd ever experienced became the biggest event in her life.

Now, the amorous man smothering her brought it all back.

Helpless…

Terror…

Her composure vanished.

Gavriella began to scream and fight for all she was worth. She hit the man in the face, dislodging the bear mask he wore. As he grunted in pain and his hand flew to his nose, which now had a trickle of blood, Gavriella took off running. It didn't even matter which direction she was running, only that she was.

Only that she had to.

She had to flee.

Dark and angled corridors confused and terrorized her, but she continued to run. She was running wildly, banging into people, smashing into things, but still she ran. She didn't even know where she was going. Somehow, she ended up in another room where men were drinking heavily; she could smell the alcohol in the air. There was a minstrel playing a harp and a woman singing softly which, given the chaos of the rest of the establishment, seemed oddly out of place.

The chamber had a small alcove off it, only Gavriella thought it was another corridor. She ran into it only to smash into the wall and hit her forehead, which knocked her back. The alcove was apparently another one of those cells where people could go off and do things that were all part of the fantasy world because there were cushions and furs on the floor.

It smelled like innocence lost.

Head spinning and ears ringing, Gavriella ended up on her behind, having fallen on one of the cushions. She could hear gasping, realizing that it was her own. There were tears on her face and she ripped off the mask, tossing it aside.

She was, literally, in hell.

There was no escape.

She could feel something in her left hand, realizing that it was a blanket of some kind. Frightened to death and unable to run any further, Gavriella pulled the blanket up over her head, huddled against the wall, and wept.

She just wanted to go home, but she couldn't find her way out.

She was going to die here.

70

to plenty of feasts that had been far more lavish and better attended, although he had to admit that there were dishes presented that even he had never seen before. He'd managed to taste quite a bit of it before Theodis had dragged him off. Then, they had passed by the cells where prostitutes were doing what prostitutes did and men were enjoying every minute of it.

After that, they'd moved into a rather large chamber that was filled with people who were dancing to very good music. But it wasn't so much dancing as it was publicly fondling one another. Sure, they were dancing in the literal sense, but he saw more than one man grab a woman's breast uninvited or another pull a woman into his embrace so he could suckle on her neck.

It was sexual debauchery without restraint.

As they watched the dancing, they had been brought drinks by a servant dressed in transparent clothing who had served them a heavily mulled wine that, Andreas thought, had something else in it that made his head swim. When he realized that the wine was spiked with something unpleasant, he went for ale that seemed to be free of any kind of stimulant. Tor and William followed his lead, as they weren't too thrilled with the wine, either.

Theodis wasn't even drinking. They'd lost him when he ran out onto the dance floor and grabbed a woman to dance with, who quite happily appreciated his company. But he didn't try to kiss her or caress body parts. He simply wanted to dance and she was more than happy to comply. He was a perfect gentleman, in truth, and the girl apparently grew bored with his good behavior and moved on with another partner who stuck his hand down her bodice.

But Theodis took it in stride. He left the throng of dancers and took his friends into yet another corridor that led to a chamber that was probably the most outrageous thing Andreas had ever seen. It was full of men, and even some women, all focused on a woman who sat on a table at one end of the chamber.

The woman was quite lovely and she was dressed like a queen. All of the men in the room seemed to be very excited about her presence and Andreas had no idea why until the woman laid back on the table and spread her legs, knees bent, as a man stood next to her with a big bunch of red grapes. As Andreas and the others watched in fascination and curiosity, the woman promptly shoved a grape into her woman's center and, as the men cheered wildly, shot the grape out and into the crowd of men.

The roar of their approval was deafening.

Andreas couldn't help it; he started laughing. Tor and William, too. They were all laughing heartily as the woman shot grape after grape from her private parts, and the men who were so enthusiastically waiting for every single grape were trying to catch them in their mouths. The woman was very good with her aim and she was able to shoot it into a mouth more often than not.

It was the wildest thing Andreas had ever seen.

A woman who could shoot grapes across the room from a body part meant to pleasure a man and birth children.

They watched the grape lady for quite some time and Andreas began to wonder how he was going to explain such a thing to his stepmother and grandmother. He wasn't looking at it from a sexual standpoint, but rather from a standpoint of skill. The grape lady had a good amount of skill to be able to shoot those grapes out from between her legs with such accuracy. He thought it was quite fascinating but realized quickly that his beloved stepmother and adoring grandmother would not be so fascinated.

They would probably box his ears for being so lewd.

When the novelty of the grape lady faded, Theodis move

them away from the performance. He also moved them because the audience was becoming quite rowdy and a fight erupted. When the fists started to fly, the four of them moved into another corridor that took them back to the chamber where everyone was still dancing. There were a few doorways off of that chamber and they picked one, ending up in an incredibly tame chamber given the riotous nature of the establishment. Men were simply sitting around, drinking ale and listening to a woman sing as a man accompanied her on his harp.

Andreas with more comfortable in this room than he had been in any of the others, so he found a place to sit along with Tor and William and Theodis, and the four of them listened to the music and sampled a few good ales that the servants provided for them. The alcohol in this chamber didn't seem to be spiked.

"So," Andreas said, smacking his lips as he tasted an ale that had hints of apples in it. "I think you really did bring us to Sodom and Gomorrah, Tay."

Theodis grinned. "Only the best for my dearest friends."

Andreas cocked an eyebrow. "If you do this for your dearest friends, I would hate to see what you would do for an enemy."

Theodis laughed, pouring more ale for them from a pitcher brought by a servant. "Truly, this is a festive place," he said. "Where else can you see things you would not normally see outside of Paris?"

William, seated on Andreas' other side, smacked his lips at the surprisingly good ale. "So this is the Roman temple, is it?" he asked. "I had no idea it would be so elaborate."

Theodis nodded his head. "Indeed, it is," he said. "It was a temple dedicated to Eros."

"The god of love," William muttered. When the others looked at him with some surprise, he tapped his head. "I remember my education. Ancient gods and goddesses always fascinated me. But I doubt Eros could have imagined what the Hessians would do to his temple."

They all started chuckling, remembering the grape lady when Theodis mockingly spread his legs. "That was… charming," William said, lifting his eyebrows. "I'm sure her father must be proud."

"Mayhap he is. Mayhap he's the one who put her up to it."

"Mayhap it's her mother's profession."

Deeply, they laughed. "Can you imagine what childbirth will be like for her?" Andreas asked. "The midwife will have to stand back from the bed and catch the infant as it shoots out into the room."

"Mayhap she'll catch it in her mouth," Theodis said.

That brought more laughter and more drinking. The woman singing the lovely songs had a haunting voice, made more haunting by the harp that accompanied her. A servant brought around some food on a tray, food from the main feasting room. There were small tarts with beef and raisins, along with sweets. They were only supposed to take a few from each tray, as there were more people in the chamber listening to the woman's lovely singing, but Andreas took the entire tray from the servant and he and William and Tor and Theodis made short work of it.

Now that they were away from the debauchery of the rest of the establishment, it really wasn't so bad. Copper bowls in the corner of the chamber burned with peat, keeping the room nice and warm as they listened to the dulcet tones of the harp. There was a variety of ale and they sampled each one, enjoying the camaraderie in a peaceful moment. Times like this were rare for fighting men such as them, moments when their entire existence didn't revolve around a life or death struggle.

But such was the way of their lives.

In fact, Andreas was in town because his grandfather had

sent him to deliver a missive to the king. William de Wolfe was the Earl of Warenton and he, his sons, and his allies essentially controlled England's border with Scotland from one end to the other. There was always something happening with the Scots and Andreas had brought a report to the king of the last several months, including some odd happenings between Clan Maxwell and Clan Johnstone. Clans that had been at each other's throats for decades were now becoming even more belligerent, which concerned William.

A clan war was something they all wanted to avoid.

In fact, each man had their own reasons for being in London. Andreas had come to deliver missives, Theodis had come to procure ingredients from the apothecary, while Tor and William had come purely on business for their father. It seemed that their father wanted to reinforce his ranks at his castle in Cumbria and having picked through the local population of men, he was hoping to find more interested parties in a bigger city.

Each man with a different directive. But each man now enjoying the adventure of a new experience.

After about an hour of steady drinking, however, Andreas was starting to feel his exhaustion. All of this on top of the time they had spent in The Pox, so they had already had quite a full evening. With his business for his grandfather concluded in London, Andreas was thinking of the journey home and how long that would take. It was July and the weather had been good, so their journey from Northumberland to London had taken them somewhere around eighteen days. They had been in London for about two weeks and they knew that it was imperative that they head home soon because once September rolled around, the rains would come and they didn't want to get caught in the autumn rainy season.

As Andreas finished off a hard apple cider with quite a kick, he thought that this should be the last drink of the night. With all of the food and drink, and his bout with the purge, he had to admit that he wasn't feeling all that great. They were staying with his uncle, Edward de Wolfe, a diplomat for King Edward, a highly positioned advisor who had a home outside of London but also a townhome, Lothbury, that was in a more tony part of the city.

Edward and his wife, Cassiopeia, were uncle and aunt to Andreas, William and Tor, but not in the usual way – Edward was their fathers' brother and Cassiopeia was their mothers' youngest sister, so they were related to them from both sides of the family. Andreas didn't think Uncle Edward would appreciate them staggering back home at dawn and was about to comment on such a thing when a frantic woman suddenly blew into the chamber.

Being that they were trained to handle startling situations in a calm and rational manner, the four of them simply looked at the woman who rushed in. The first thing they looked for was weapons; she wasn't carrying any. But she was gasping as if terrified. She seemed in a panic. The next thing they realized, she was running into what she evidently thought was a doorway, only it was a small and secluded alcove.

They all heard a loud thump.

The woman didn't emerge.

Curious, and perhaps slightly concerned, Andreas set his ale cup to the table and stood up, going to the partially concealed alcove and peering inside. It was dark except for the ambient light from the larger chamber, but he could see something trembling in the corner. Looking closer, he could see something quivering beneath a silk coverlet.

He stepped into the alcove.

"My lady?" he said. "Do you require assistance?"

It took a moment, but she pulled the coverlet off her head,

gazing up at him with a mask-free face. Andreas had understood that to be forbidden. Everyone was to cover his or her face because it kept the element of mystery and fantasy. But the woman had yanked hers off and tears were streaming down her face.

It was a very pretty face.

"I just want to leave," she whispered tightly. "I cannot seem to find a way out and a man grabbed me and tried… he tried to kiss me, and I know that sort of thing is allowed here without repercussion, but I do not want to be kissed. I only want to leave. Can you please tell me the way out?"

It didn't take a genius to figure out that she was hysterical. Andreas could have done the easy thing at that moment and simply walked away, but he couldn't seem to do it. He had sisters, after all, and a stepmother he loved. He had a grandmother he adored and a variety of aunts and female cousins. If one of them was in distress and he wasn't around to help, he would hope that someone would be kind enough to lend a hand.

"I am not entirely sure how to get out of this place," he said. "I have never been here before. Is it your first time, too?"

She nodded, fear reflecting in her eyes. "My cousins brought me here," she said. "I do not even know where they are. They disappeared and left me… alone."

"Then you have no escort?"

"I never did," she said. "My cousins demanded that I accompany them here, so we left the house after their mother went to sleep."

"Then no one knows you have come?"

"Nay," she said, guilty and confused. "My cousins said this would be a place of feasting and fun, but… I find it vile. I just want to go home."

She sounded so forlorn. Andreas could see that perhaps the

young woman had gotten more than she'd bargained for when her cousins had forced her to come to this unusual and decadent place. The woman's cousins had told her of feasting and fun, and she'd found debauchery and excess. Being a chivalrous man, he knew he had to do something to help her.

He held up a hand, to beg patience.

"Do not fret," he said. "I will return shortly. Will you stay?"

She wasn't going anywhere, curled up against the wall with a silk coverlet over her. But she didn't respond, perhaps too frightened to, and Andreas ducked out of the alcove, looking for the servant with the drinks. He caught sight of her over near one of the copper braziers and he took two cups off her tray.

He returned to the alcove.

"Here," he said. "Drink this. It will make you feel better."

He was extending one of the cups to her, but she stared at it like she had no idea what to do with it. "What… what is it?"

"Ale," Andreas said. "It has fruit in it. It's quite good. It will help calm you."

She stared at the cup a moment longer before lowering the silk coverlet and hesitantly claiming the drink. Andreas watched as she gulped it, thirstily, draining nearly half the cup.

She licked her lips.

"It *is* good," she agreed quietly. Then, her gaze moved to Andreas, perhaps looking him over a little. "You are very kind to bring this to me."

He smiled faintly. "It was no trouble," he said. "Frankly, I am grateful for the diversion. I don't think I like this place very much, either."

She licked her lips again and took another drink. "Then why are you here?"

He threw a thumb over his shoulder. "Because my friend brought us."

"Us?"

He nodded. "My cousins and me," he said. "The four of us are in London on business and my friend, who has been here before, thought it would be a great adventure for us."

He saw her take a deep, fortifying breath before taking another drink of the ale. "I would agree that it is an adventure," she said after a moment. "But not a great one. It is one I could have done without."

A smile flickered across his lips. "I am coming to think that as well," he said. "I would never begrudge a man for living out his fantasies, but a place like this… my grandmother will murder me and bury the body if I tell her I visited such a place."

She lifted her eyebrow as if in full agreement and Andreas found himself studying her face. She was blonde, with delicately arched brows and the most beautiful eyes he had ever seen. They tilted up at the ends, like the eyes of a cat. She had a pert nose and lips that seemed rather lush. Aye, she was more than pretty.

She was beautiful.

"If you truly feel as hostile towards this place as I do, then you shall leave here and forget you ever visited," she said, gulping more ale. "I intend to leave and never look back no matter what my cousins say. And I shall never let them bring me here again."

Andreas was watching her closely, seeing that she had calmed with quiet conversation and the ale. At least she was no longer panicking.

"They like this place, do they?" he asked.

"They do," she said. Then, she snorted ironically. "They woke me from a dead sleep for this. I should have stayed in bed."

She said it with great regret and he grinned. "And I wish I was in mine," he said. "This was interesting for the first few minutes, but no longer. Will you accompany me, my lady?"

She looked at him suspiciously, appraising him again with those glittering eyes. "Forgive me, my lord, but given the nature of this place, I must ask *where* I am to accompany you."

"Out," he said flatly. "I shall take you home."

"Mine or yours?"

He chuckled. "Yours, of course," he said. "My lady, I realize that in a place like this, you should probably suspect the worst from everyone you meet, but I assure you that my intentions are purely chivalrous. You seem distressed and I am offering my services to take you home safely."

He could see that she was considering it. But after a moment, she shook her head. "I am afraid that I cannot," she said. "You are a stranger. I do not know you. And I am not in the habit of entrusting my safety to strangers."

He nodded. "Fair enough," he said. "I do not blame you, of course, but I am going to leave nonetheless. If you would like to follow me out, you are welcome to do so. I will not trouble you further."

Her focus lingered on him a moment before lowering her eyes and draining the rest of her ale. The alcohol was settling in her veins, taking away the sheer terror she had been feeling so that she was able to think more clearly.

She eyed the enormous man crouched a few feet away.

"I do not mean to sound ungrateful," she said. "And I do not mean to impugn your honor, but it would be foolish of me to trust someone I do not know."

"Very true."

"And we are not supposed to know anything about one another, so I cannot even ask you who you are."

"I am a knight."

She looked at his mail, his tunic. He was wearing a green tunic with a black dog's head. She pointed at it.

"I can see that," she said. "It looks familiar but, then again, there are probably fifty such standards around England with a dog's head on it."

"Not like this one," he assured her quietly. "This one is unique. And it is not a dog."

"What is it?"

"A wolf."

"Is it your family crest? Or your liege's standard?"

"My family crest."

She pondered that for a moment. "We are not supposed to ask for names, but do you have something you are called?" She reached over and picked up the mask she'd torn off her face. "I am to tell everyone that my name is Kitten."

She put the mask back over her face, showing him that it was a cat's face. He smiled. "It suits you," he said. "I suppose you can call me Wolf."

His mask was a dog's face, elaborate and painted. "Wolf," she repeated. "I would like to thank you again for bringing me the drink. You did not have to bother with me, but you did. I feel better now."

"Would you like more?"

She shook her head. "I simply want to leave, if that is agreeable," she said. "I will follow you when you are ready to go."

"I am ready."

She sounded stronger now, in control of herself. He stood up from his crouch as she tied on her mask before tossing aside the coverlet. She stood up, stiffly and perhaps a bit unsteadily, revealing herself in a beautiful red silk that made her breasts appear quite large. Andreas would have had to have been a blind man not to notice that.

In fact, along with her beautiful face, he'd never seen a finer woman. *A woman like that finding her way home, alone?* Not bloody likely. He couldn't just help her find her way out of this place only to leave her alone on the dangerous and dark

London streets. He suspected he was going to follow her home, which wouldn't be well met if she saw him. He could just tell by looking at her.

In fact, he couldn't believe that she was without a man, period.

A woman like that was surely spoken for.

With those thoughts on his mind, he headed out of the alcove. As he stepped out, Theodis called to him.

"Where are you going?" he demanded. "Our evening is not over yet."

Andreas paused. "It is for me," he said, glancing at the woman as she emerged behind him. "I will see you at Lothbury."

Theodis was set to argue with him until he took a good look at the woman. She was stunning. That screaming mass of hair and silk that he'd seen blow by was actually something quite spectacular and he suspected that Andreas had found someone to keep company with, so he didn't argue with him. Gentle Andreas, who could have any woman he wanted with his comely looks and kind demeanor. Theodis simply waved at him, as did William and Tor. All of them waving at a man who was probably one of the most discriminating men in England when it came to women.

Andreas wasn't a hound when it came to the fairer sex.

In fact, he was a paradox.

Big and handsome, he was hell on the battlefield but sweet and gentle when it came to women. He always had been. But there was something of a problem with him – Andreas was rather old to have never been married at thirty years and seven, but it wasn't for the lack of his family trying. They'd tried too many times to count, but he had never found a woman he would consider spending his life with.

Unfortunately for him, he had a legacy to uphold.

Andreas was the oldest son of Troy de Wolfe, who would have been the eldest son of The Earl of Warenton had it not been for his twin being born a few minutes before he was. But Troy was a powerful warlord in his own right and had multiple properties and allies, including a great alliance with Clan Kerr because he had married a chief's daughter as his second wife.

As Troy's eldest son and heir, Andreas would wield a great deal of power upon the death of his father. He would have property in both England and Scotland in addition to inheriting his father's title of Lord Braemoor. Much was expected of Andreas because he was one of the oldest male de Wolfe grandchildren and that included an advantageous marriage.

But Andreas had other ideas.

His mother had died when he had been a youth, drowned in an accident that also took the lives of his younger sisters. Andreas had been away fostering at the time and the news had been devastating because he had been close to his mother, who had been quite young when she had given birth to him. When he had been a small child, she had been more like a sister and a playmate than his mother. They had spent an inordinate amount of time together and he had been an only child until he was nine years of age.

That meant that he and his mother had been very close.

Sometimes, he still talked about her. His mother had been a small woman, with blonde hair and big, blue eyes that she had passed down to her son. She had been lighthearted and witty, and sometimes Andreas said that he could still hear her silly giggle. She'd had a way of giggling that had made anyone who heard it want to giggle right along with her. Andreas could remember his father putting his hand over his mother's mouth when that giggle grew out of control, but it had never been mean-spirited. Her death, and the deaths of his two younger siblings, had left Andreas as the remaining child of a man who was grieving too deeply to function.

It had been a difficult time for them both.

Those in the family thought that it was perhaps his mother's death that prevented Andreas from marrying. The last woman he had been close to and had loved unconditionally had died, and her death had left a son who had incorporated that loss into the very fiber of his existence. Once Troy came to grips with the loss of Helene, he tried to speak with his son about it, but Andreas didn't want to discuss it. He lived with that loss as part of him and he wasn't willing to deal with it. When he grew older, it was still part of him, and Andreas felt no sense of urgency to take a wife. To be close to a woman ever again.

Some wondered if he ever would.

Which is why this moment was of particular interest to William and Tor and Theodis. Andreas had apparently found a woman to keep company with, as shocking as it was, so they were more than happy to let Andreas find his evening's entertainment elsewhere. They didn't want to get in his way.

As Andreas headed out of the chamber with a luscious blonde trailing behind him, they looked at each other and smiled. Perhaps Troy de Wolfe would finally get that wedding he'd been hoping for, with Andreas finding a bride, in all places, at a guild called Gomorrah.

Or perhaps it would be another dead end.

Knowing Andreas, the latter was more than likely.

CHAPTER FIVE

H E WAS A very big man.

Maybe not the tallest, for Gavriella had seen taller, but the sheer breadth of his body and arms was simply solid and big. And his hands, embraced by enormous leather gloves, were the size of her head when contracted into a fist.

In truth, she was a little awed by the man. He had been very kind to her and had helped her calm a great deal with his steady manner and offered drink. She still wasn't sure why he had paid any attention to her, considering she had been running around like a madwoman and, like an idiot, she had even smashed into the wall. She would have been embarrassed about that had she not been so terrified.

There would be time to be embarrassed about it later.

The knight's appearance had been unexpected. She probably should have been more suspicious of him than she had been because in a place like this, it seemed like everyone wanted something. A kiss, a dance, or something far more intimate... everyone seemed to want something.

She wondered what this knight really wanted.

From her.

But he had been very polite and he had offered to show her

the way out, and being desperate to leave, she had accepted his offer. Perhaps it wasn't the brightest thing to do, but desperate times called for risk. She was going to risk herself to get out of this hellscape, even if she had to place herself in the care of this enormous knight to do it. Suspicion was there, but so was curiosity.

He was intriguing.

Although she couldn't really see his face very well because of the mask he wore, she thought he had rather a nice face. At least, everything between his nose and his chin, which had a big dimple in it. He had smiled, although not broadly, and she had caught a glimpse of massive dimples in each cheek. He wasn't wearing a helm or anything on his head, even if the rest of him was dressed in a tunic and mail. The dog mask he wore covered a good portion of his face and all of his forehead, but she could see his hair. It was close cropped and blond from what she could tell.

He was quite something to look at, in truth.

But that didn't mean he was trustworthy.

Even as she followed him from the alcove and into a corridor, she knew she was being stupid. She was going to follow him all the way out and then hope he didn't try to abduct her or, worse, molest her on the street because she'd been dumb enough to fall into his hands. Although his manner didn't seem to convey that type of man, she didn't know him, so she really had no idea of his nature or his character. Those men who had cornered her last year in her village hadn't seemed wicked in nature until their intentions were revealed. It wasn't strange that the incident that changed her life also made her distrustful of any man, no matter how kind he was.

And that's what made this moment so very difficult.

Desperation was causing her to do something she wouldn't normally do.

Trust a man she didn't know.

As Gavriella followed along behind him, she made sure to stay out of arm's length. He never made any attempt to touch her or pull her along, and so far, he had turned around to make sure she was behind him only once. They entered a corridor, dark and angled, that took them into a room crowded with men who are watching a woman who was sitting on a table, and her escort seemed to move faster when they entered that chamber for some reason. Because he picked up the pace, she picked up the pace, and they were soon through that chamber and into another corridor.

She could hear music.

Gavriella's heart began to flood with relief, realizing they were near the chamber with the music and the dancing. That was where she'd last seen Aurelia and Camilla, and she was starting to feel as if she might actually break free from this horrid place. She knew that the music-filled chamber was near the chamber that was filled with all of that marvelous food, and beyond that were the rooms that connected to the outside world.

Closer!

She was drawing ever closer to leaving. It was strange how she seemed completely oriented now, whereas earlier, she seemed to become more and more lost with every turn she took. Her new friend, the man who called himself Wolf, seemed to have a good sense of direction because he was leading her back the way she had come. He seemed to know which way to go and which door to take, and she was starting to hope that, at least for the moment, following him had been a good idea.

But that was her last calm thought before someone grabbed her.

They had just entered the room with the music and the dancing, and the room was full of people dancing to a lively folk tune. The musicians were quite good and they were playing adeptly as a room full of dancers leapt and twirled gaily. But the moment Gavriella stepped into the warm, smoky room, someone grabbed her by the wrist and started yanking her towards the writhing throng.

Immediately, she dug her heels in and began to fight to free herself. The man who had hold of her was big and smelly, and he yanked her so hard by the wrist that she felt pains shooting up her arm. She thought she even heard something crack and, suddenly, she was in a good deal of pain as the idiot pulled her towards the dance floor. The more she dug her heels in, the more he pulled, and she finally screamed at him to let her go. He barely had time to turn around and scowl at her before there was suddenly a big body in between them.

His hold on her wrist abruptly released and he was on the ground.

The man she knew as Wolf had his big arm around her shoulders and begin pulling her quickly back to their original course.

"Come along," he said steadily, but then he noticed she was cradling her left arm. "What happened? Did he hurt you?"

Gavriella wasn't sure what to say. The man *had* hurt her, but she didn't want to tell the man called Wolf because she didn't want him to think she wanted him to tend her or, worse, punish the man who hurt her. She didn't want him to feel any sense of responsibility towards her whatsoever. He wasn't her escort – he wasn't her anything. Just a man trying to lead her to the exit.

But she had to admit his chivalrous action had been rather endearing. She'd never experienced anything like it.

"Nay," she lied. "I was simply… startled."

"Are you certain you are not injured?"

"I am not injured."

His gaze lingered on her as if he didn't believe her, but he didn't contradict her. He simply let go of her once they reached the darkened corridor and went on ahead of her as she followed along behind.

Now, they were in the feasting room. It smelled glorious and Gavriella's determination to leave was deterred by the fact that she was hungry. She'd had an entire cup of ale to calm her nerves and her head was swimming a little, so she swiped a beef tart as she walked by a table.

She began shoving it into her mouth as they reached the chamber where the women in transparent clothing were, the women who had put their masks on when they had first arrived. As they entered the dimly lit chamber, the women seemed to come out of the shadows, untying their masks and pulling them off. Gavriella had a mouth full of tart, shoving the entire thing in, as her mask came away.

His mask came off, too.

Gavriella found herself looking at a man handsome enough to make her forget how to swallow.

The tart went spraying out.

Gavriella coughed violently as the women in the transparent clothing shrieked and began calling for servants to clean up the mess. The man called Wolf reached out, taking her by the arm and pulling her away from the pile on the floor that she had created.

"Are you well?" he asked, sounding concerned. "Mayhap you need some wine."

"Nay," Gavriella said, clutching him before he could move away. She struggled to control the cough. "Truly, I am not ill. I tried to swallow and… it… it went down the wrong way. I am not ill, I assure you."

She was gazing up into his face as he nodded, but he still looked concerned. "Are you sure?" he asked. "It will take me only a moment to find you something to drink."

Gavriella shook her head. "Truly, do not trouble yourself," she said. "I have already been an immense trouble to you already. In fact, since the moment we met, I have been little else, so I wish to relieve you of my burden as soon as possible."

He looked at her, rubbed his chin, and then shrugged. Turning away from her, he continued down another dim corridor as Gavriella swallowed hard and tried to forget the fact that she had nearly choked. For certain, looking at a man as handsome as he was had startled her. She should have suspected given his dimpled smile, but once the mask came off… well, she had made a fool of herself.

Again.

He was fair, with blond brows and pale eyes from what she could see, but she noticed that he seemed to have a faint red tint to his hair even in the dim light. Just a little, but it was there. His jaw was square, like granite, and when he turned to look at her as they passed by a torch, she could see that his eyes were a glorious shade of blue.

The man was positively magnificent.

They'd finally reached the corridor that had the two armed door sentries in it, the point of entry to Gomorrah. The armed men stood back, allowing them to the door, but once they passed through the opened panel and out into the cold night, they slammed the door behind them. They could hear the bolt thrown.

Suddenly, they were out on the darkened, dangerous London street with the burned-out church behind them. The fog that had rolled in from the river now covered everything with mist, damp and slick. Gavriella came to an abrupt halt, looking down at herself.

"I came with a cloak," she said, looking regretfully to the door they'd just exited through. "I do not even know what happened to it. It belonged to my cousin and I hate to leave it behind, but I am not going back inside."

He looked at the door also. "To go back inside would be to risk being trapped again."

"I know."

His gaze turned to her. "Where is your home?"

That was a good question. Gavriella looked around the darkened street and tried to get her bearings, cradling her aching left arm. "God's Bones," she muttered. "I have already embarrassed myself irreparably tonight in front of you, so I suppose one more embarrassment will not matter. I have not been in London long enough to know much about it. I followed my cousins here from the manse. All I know is that it is in the northeast section of town, near the priory of the Holy Trinity. If you will point me in that direction, I am sure I can find it."

He scratched his head a moment, pondering what she'd said. "If you are not from London, where are you from?"

"North."

"A small village?"

"Small enough."

He sighed. "Then I will tell you that traveling in London, and especially at night, is a dangerous thing for a woman alone," he said. "If you think the maze of Gomorrah frightened you, then you should be doubly afraid of traveling these streets. There are men lurking in the shadows now, watching us, just waiting to pounce on you. I will be frank when I say that it would not be for a kiss or a dance, my lady."

Gavriella knew that. At least, she did in theory. Her cousins had stupidly come alone to Gomorrah and they'd been fortunate not to have suffered any trouble, but now she was without an escort for her return home.

Except for Wolf.

"I understand that the streets are dangerous, but I have little choice," she said. "I cannot stand here all night and wait for my cousins to emerge so that we may walk home together."

"Then I will offer my services as an escort, my lady, to see you home safely," he said. "I've seen you through this far. You should allow me to finish my task."

She looked at him doubtfully. "I told you that I am not in the habit of trusting my safety to strangers."

"Either you trust me or you will have to fight off the rabble on your own," he said. "Are you willing to risk your life?"

He had a point and, no, she wasn't. Heavily, she sighed. "Nay," she said after a moment. "Very well, Wolf. I accept. But do not try anything or I'll scream loud enough to wake the dead."

In the darkness, his lips twitched with a smile. "I believe it. Shall we go?"

He was indicating a northerly direction and she nodded. They began to walk, heading up the muddy road as fog swallowed them up with every step they took. It was soupy and cold, with an occasional torch from the night watch piercing the veil of darkness. It was terribly difficult to see.

Gavriella was looking around nervously, more relieved than she cared to admit that he was escorting her home. A man that size would surely be a deterrent to any unsavory activity. But something occurred to her as they walked and she turned to look at him, his handsome features shrouded in the mist.

"I'm curious about something, Wolf," she said. "May I ask you a question?"

"My lady?"

"Why would you do this for a woman you do not know?"

"Do what?"

She looked around. "Risk yourself like this," she said. "I do not understand why you would do it."

He was looking around, too, but in his case, it was calculated. Years and years of being a trained knight, of being trained to always be aware of one's surroundings, had him watching every shadow, every glimmer.

"Because I am a man of honor," he said simply. "Whether or not you realize it, you became my responsibility the moment I helped you from that ghastly place. I could not simply leave you to fend for yourself once we were free of the confines."

"But I am no one to you," she said, genuinely baffled. "You just met me. You do not even know my name."

"Kitty."

"Kitten."

"I like Kitty better. It suits you."

She stared at him, having no idea what he meant by such a thing. Then, she broke into soft laughter.

"Suit yourself," she said. "But you still have not answered my question."

"I answered it plainly."

"But you did not explain why you would do such a thing for a woman who means nothing to you," she pointed out. "A man could jump out at us any moment with a dagger and you would defend me?"

"Of course."

"With your life?"

"If necessary."

She had to think on that. It made no sense to her but, then again, she had never really spent an inordinate amount of time around knights. Her father was a knight in the technical sense of the word, but somewhere over the years, he seemed to have lost the very thing that made knights who they were. Call it courage, call it dedication… whatever it was, her father's seemed to have faded. He'd lost whatever was left of it when she had been attacked. She'd seen the light go out of his eyes then.

Nay… she didn't understand much about men and their

sense of duty because her father didn't seem to harbor any hint of such a thing.

He'd given up completely.

But the man next to her had that sense of chivalry, of honor. She was coming to realize that. Of course, when they'd first met in the guild, she hadn't trusted him. Her distrust was natural. But now that she'd had a few moments of conversation with him, she began to sense something settling and calm about the man.

Honorable.

True.

She didn't know why she sensed such a thing, but she did.

It made her more curious than ever.

"You must have great experience as a knight, then," she said after a moment. "In battle, I mean. You must be very skilled."

"I have fought in my share of battles."

She could tell that just by looking at him. "Is your father a knight?"

"He's a very good one."

"And your sons? Do they train also?"

"I have no sons."

She didn't say anything more after that. He didn't seem to want to converse, so she stopped talking. He was watching their shrouded surroundings like a hawk, intensely focused. They were heading towards a main road, something Gavriella thought she recognized through the mist, but she wasn't quite sure. Everything was so dark and disorienting.

They just kept walking.

The moon finally set even though they couldn't see it because the fog suddenly became dark. There was very little ambient light at this late hour and, frustrated and a little fearful, Gavriella came to a halt. He stopped next to her.

"I thought I would recognize the street at the very least, but

I do not," she said. "As I said, I've not been here very long and this is a much larger city than anything I am used to. I fear that I cannot ask you to continue to walk aimlessly with me when I do not know where I am going. I have been far too much trouble to you already."

His gaze lingered on her a moment before he started to look around again. "You have no idea where you are?"

"None at all."

"It would probably be easier in the light."

She sighed heavily. "It would, indeed. At least I might see something that I recognize."

He looked up at the sky. "It is probably two or three hours before dawn," he said. "I think we are finished wandering around for the night if you do not recognize anything."

She looked at him curiously. "But I must keep looking," she said. "I cannot stand here on the street all night."

"That was not what I had in mind," he said. "Come with me."

She didn't move. "Where?"

There was fear in her voice right away and he paused. "Someplace safe until dawn breaks and there is light for you to see," he said evenly. "My lady, I cannot leave you standing out here on the street if you do not know where you live. I would be a dishonorable man, indeed, if I did that. I told you that you were my responsibility until I see you safely home and I meant it. Therefore, please let me take you someplace safe until the dawn comes. I swear upon my honor that I will not hurt you, nor will anyone else. Do you believe me?"

Gavriella couldn't very well say no. He'd been kind and considerate since their rough acquaintance and, truthfully, she didn't have much of a choice at the moment.

She would have to trust him.

"I do," she said after a moment. "Where are we going?"

Gently, he took her arm with one of those enormous hands. "Come with me."

She did.

Like a fool, she did.

ANDREAS TOOK HER to an inn he had stayed at on his very first night in London. He and William and Tor and Theodis had been so thrilled to finally be in London that they'd bypassed Lothbury House on that first night and opted for the food and excitement of a tavern, only this particular tavern hadn't shown them much excitement.

It had been downright boring.

Someone had recommended the place called The Fox and The Wolf, and they'd taken up seats in the common room and were treated to a spectacular meal. The place had been full of people, but a much more respectable level of clientele than most inns in the city had, and there had literally been no music, no dancing, no entertainment. Just food and perhaps the softest bed Andreas had ever slept in. The visit hadn't been a total waste, but it had been unspectacular, so he thought a place like that might be just the thing for a woman who had just suffered a harrowing visit to Gomorrah.

A woman he couldn't seem to let out of his sight.

They moved out onto a main road that had stone paving on it as part of a drainage system. There were expensive homes on this street and those with wealth tended not to like shite in the streets, so Andreas knew where they were in spite of the fog and knew exactly where he was going. He continued down the avenue for a short distance until he came to a small and cramped alleyway. It was quite dark except for a single torch about halfway down the alley.

Andreas aimed for the torch.

The Fox and The Wolf was a two-storied establishment on that cramped alley and crammed in between other buildings. The first floor hung out over the alleyway by at least a couple of feet, as was common with most buildings built around this time to maximize the interior space. The upper floors were always wider than the lower floors. He knocked on the door, several times, before it was finally opened.

The innkeeper, evidently recognizing Andreas, opened the door to admit them before shutting it behind them and bolting it.

Being that it was very late, the common room was cluttered with sleeping bodies. There were people strewn across tables, on the floor, and some of them were simply sitting in chairs leaning against the wall. The fire in the hearth burned low, giving off a little light into the chamber as Andreas spoke to the tavernkeep about procuring some food and a place to eat it. The tavernkeeper didn't have a problem warming up some food for them, but somewhere to sit and consume it was another matter altogether.

He indicated the common room, which was nearly full at that point of snoozing patrons, and he suggested using one of the rooms that hadn't been rented for the night. Often, travelers would sleep at the table they had eaten at, thus avoid paying for a bed – leaving sleeping chambers empty.

Gavriella heard the tavernkeeper suggest that they rent a sleeping room where they could eat their meal and, suddenly, she wasn't so willing to trust him anymore. A chamber with a bed? With a door he could shut and prevent her from leaving?

She wondered if this had been his intention all along.

Suddenly, she was feeling frightened again.

As they discussed the cost of such a thing, Gavriella was already backing towards the door. She reached the panel and tried to unbolt it, but the bolt was old and heavy, and she had to jiggle it for it to come loose. By that time, the man she knew as Wolf was directly behind her.

"Where are you going?" he asked softly.

She couldn't get the door open quickly enough. Her fear, her rage, was blooming in her chest again. Perhaps now more than it ever had. Whirling around, she pressed herself flat against the door.

"I heard you speak to that man about renting a bedchamber," she hissed. "I am *not* going into a rented bedchamber with you. I do not know what kind of woman you think I am, but I will not be seen as… as an easy target."

He was a bit taken aback by her outrage. "An easy target? For what?"

"I did not come here with you to warm your bed!"

She raised her voice, partially rousing a few people who were nearby. They lifted their heads, yawning and groaning, and she looked around in a panic, thinking she'd just awoken everyone. They would be angry with her. Frightened and furious, she turned for the door again yanking on the bolt until it opened. When he tried to help her or stop her – she wasn't sure which – she slapped his hand as hard as she could. She finally jerked on the door, throwing it wide and rushing out into the night.

As the woman bolted outside, Andreas followed, genuinely surprised at her reaction, but given that he was speaking to the tavernkeeper about renting a chamber, he supposed he didn't blame her for being suspicious and angry. There was part of him that absolutely understood why she'd fled in terror.

"My lady," he called to her as she ran into the fog. "Please come back. It is not as it seems. There are no tables for us to eat at. Renting a chamber would allow us a space to do that – eat!"

The fog was swallowing her up. "I will not be tricked," she said. "The last time a man asked me to trust him was... oh, it does not matter. I'll not let you touch me! Never again!"

She disappeared into the mist. Andreas watched her go, wondering if he just shouldn't let her alone this time. He'd tried so hard to be kind and polite, so hard to be chivalrous because he thought it was the right thing to do, but she had fought him at every turn. She hadn't believed him from the beginning; that much was clear. She had looked at him with such suspicion that, in truth, his pride was starting to take a beating. He'd done everything he could to be trustworthy and courteous, but it wasn't enough. Kitten, or whatever her real name was, wasn't the trusting sort.

She was suspicious of everything he did.

He could have been offended, but he ended up just feeling pity for her.

As he had told her, however, he felt some sense of responsibility towards her. She was a woman, alone in a dangerous city, and he simply couldn't turn his back on her. He wondered why she was so incredibly mistrustful because it seemed to him that it really had nothing to do with him at all and everything to do with something she surely must have experienced in her lifetime. He'd never met anyone who was that suspicious who didn't have a good reason behind it.

Before she'd run from him, he could see terror in her eyes.

There was something more to her fear.

A few moments after watching her red dress fade from sight, he followed.

NO, SHE DIDN'T know where she was going.

All she knew was that she had to get away.

The fog had thickened as she headed back the way she thought they had come, but it was so misty that she couldn't really see anything but the occasional public torches. There was a night watch because she could hear them calling to one another, distant voices in the fog.

Even so, the streets of London were treacherous.

Everything in London was treacherous.

Gavriella had never felt so lost or alone in her entire life. At least when she was at Falstone Castle, she was surrounded by people she knew, servants she had grown up with and friends from the small village that was near the castle. She was content there, living a bucolic life, or at least she had been until the events of last year.

That had changed everything.

She no longer felt safe. She no longer felt anything. As she stood there shivering in the mist, she realized that this moment was symbolic of what her life had become – dark, dreary, miserable.

There was simply no hope.

She could return to The Asher and face her cousins. Maybe they would care that she'd run off, maybe they wouldn't. She was coming to hate Aurelia for dragging her out on this night and taking her to that horrific place, and here she was, wandering in the night and looking for the only home she knew in London, only it wasn't her home.

It wasn't her anything.

In fact, she had nothing.

The knight, the one who called himself Wolf, had been kind to her in the midst of her despair, but she realized it had only been a ploy to get her into his bed. And like a fool, she'd fallen for it. She had been coming to appreciate him in the slightest, and even trust him a little, but that had all been summarily dashed when she realized what he'd been up to. Now, all she could manage to feel was stupidity.

Desolation.

Gavriella de Leia had reached the bottom.

The tears began to come. She was so very weary, at the end of any semblance of patience she'd ever had for herself. Patience in her situation, in what life had brought her. She'd tried to remain pragmatic, to hope that something better was on the horizon, but she knew nothing was. She was damaged goods now, relegated to being a companion to a scandalous cousin and a victim to a man who had just wanted to seduce her.

God, why had she trusted him?

Everyone in her life had failed her.

Now, the knight who swore he was honorable had failed her, too.

Gavriella was wet and cold and hungry, and her left arm hurt where they man had yanked on her. Cradling her arm against her body, she turned around and began to walk. She didn't know where she was going, but she began to walk. Tears streaked down her cheeks and her thoughts were those of utter despair.

Still, she walked. And walked.

Mud coated the bottom of the pretty red silk and covered her slippers. The tears turned into sobs and as she walked, she wept over everything her life had become. Tears she'd held off, trying to be brave, had found an outlet. She found herself hoping an outlaw would come out of the shadows and put her out of her misery.

Surely what awaited her in the afterlife was better than the cesspool of grief her life had become.

After what had happened last year, no decent man would want her now. She could not hope for an advantageous marriage. She couldn't even hope for a simple but honorable knight, like the man who called himself Wolf, to marry. A decent man who would overlook what had happened to her. A decent man who might even care for her.

But she realized that she wasn't worth caring for.

No man had a shred of respect for her.

Gavriella had no idea how long or how far she had walked. Her life was swept up in misery that was consuming her as a blaze consumes kindling. She was freezing cold and wet from the fog, her long blonde hair saturated with mist. She wept and walked, not focusing on anything in particular, until she came to the shoreline.

She'd ended up by the river.

The river…

Gavriella looked off over the fog-bound waters of the Thames. She couldn't see much because of the mist, but she could see enough. The cold, silent river was beckoning to her. It seemed peaceful there, far from the hell she had endured this past year. Perhaps that dirty river was her salvation from her living and breathing hell.

Perhaps it was her only way out.

God forgive her.

And with that, she climbed down from the street and onto the narrow, rocky riverbank. Her first step into the water was freezing, but it didn't matter. She took another step and another. The river was smelly and icy cold. It had a nasty, slimy bottom, but still, she continued to walk into the water until she took one step too far, slipped over a ledge, and went right into a hole.

Freezing, blissful death awaited, or at least she thought so until she held her breath so long that she needed air, but all she managed to suck in was a mouthful of water. Panic filled her. Perhaps this wasn't the peace she had hoped for. Perhaps she wasn't brave enough to withstand the pain before the calm overtook her. She started to thrash, but unable to swim, she gulped in more water.

Daggers filled her lungs as everything gradually turned to black.

CHAPTER SIX

The village of Deadwater

"YOU ARE THE physic in this village. You would know if a child was born."

Two heavily armed knights, father and son, had shoved their way into his cottage this morning. As a soft mist had embraced the rolling hills of the border, men armed for war had charged into the village and had come straight to the physic's cottage. They'd slapped around the old couple, the man and his wife, before tossing the wife in a corner and shoving the old man into a chair.

Now, they stood over him, posturing threateningly.

But the old man didn't flinch.

"Not everyone summons a physic for the birth a child," he said steadily, even though there was a trickle of red coming from the corner of his mouth. "Midwives are summoned most often."

The younger of the pair, a nasty brute called Nicholas by the older man, glared at him. "But you are summoned to care for the people at Falstone Castle, are you not?" he demanded. "The child would have been born at Falstone to Merek de Leia's daughter."

The physic blinked as if surprised by the information. "I did not hear of a child born there, nor did I attend it."

"Who is the midwife around here?"

"My wife is, but she did not attend the birth, either."

The pair immediately turned their venom on the old woman, who cowered in the corner.

"Well?" Nicholas demanded. "What do you have to say about all of this?"

While the husband was quite brave, the wife was a sniveling mess. They'd struck her on her round cheeks, frightening her more than they really injured her, but she was terrified. She put up an arm as if to shield herself from them.

"I did not attend a birth at Falstone," she said, her voice quaking. "But I did hear that two children were born there this past spring. I did not attend either one."

Nicholas looked at the older man. "One of them has to be it, Father," he muttered. "She would have given birth sometime in April."

The older man eyed his son before running his fingers through his graying hair. "The merchant who passed through our lands a few months ago confirmed that he saw de Leia's daughter with child, so we know that she conceived," he muttered, keeping his voice down so the physic wouldn't hear him. "But if the midwife knows nothing about the birth, we should send her to find out. It is her duty, after all, to tend the women and infants in this area. An inquiry to Falstone would not be out of the ordinary."

Nicholas liked that idea. Ever since he'd cornered Merek de Leia's daughter in the village those months ago and molested her in a nearby livery with his hands covering her screams of pain, he knew he'd done everything a man does to beget a child. He filled the woman with his seed and told her if she spoke of his assault that he would return to kill her. But he also told her that he would come for that child when it was born, so she had to know he'd be coming. He never gave his name, and he was certain she didn't recognize him, so there was no danger of association with the House of de Soulis. That was key. The child, if it had been born alive, would be at least three months of age by now.

And he wanted it.

He returned his attention to the woman.

"You will go to Falstone and inquire about the women who have given birth," he said in a threatening tone. "You are the midwife – it is your duty to tend to the health of the women and children in Deadwater and beyond. I want you to go to Falstone and find out who gave birth there. You are to find out everything you can about the infants and do it quickly, because I shall return soon. If you do not have any information for me, there will be consequences."

As the old woman continued to cower, now with confusion added to the mix, the old physic spoke up.

"My lords," he said evenly. "I do not know what this is all about, but if you tell me, mayhap I can help. Am I to understand that you are looking for an infant born recently at Falstone?"

The older man turned his attention to the physic. "The daughter of Lord de Leia gave birth sometime in the spring," he said. "We are looking for that child."

Harman the Wise was the old physic everyone within a fifty-mile radius of Deadwater used to cure ills, diagnose ailments, or otherwise assist with the good and bad humors of the human body. He knew everyone and everything in these parts, including events like births and deaths, and even madness. He knew the comings and goings, and he knew the families.

And that was why he was trying not to show his fear.

Even though the men hadn't given their names officially, the mention of the son's name and the father-son relationship caused him to suspect who they were. Moreover, their soldiers weren't bearing any tunics, but the horses they had ridden had brands on the rump. He could see them through the open door.

He'd seen them before, in times past.

He knew the de Soulis family.

Wicked to the bone.

He had heard about the incident last year when the daughter of Merek de Leia, Lord of Falstone, had been cornered by a group of unidentified knights. The lovely young woman had been in the village with a pair of her maids, visiting the merchant who imported silk thread, when she was set upon her.

As the story went, because Harman had not witnessed it personally, Lady Gavriella de Leia was caught off guard by the men. When they'd grabbed her and spirited her away, she'd never even made a sound. Everyone knew Lady Gavriella and everyone loved her, and there had always been such peace in Deadwater in spite of the fact that it was on the Scots border, that any kind of violence was unheard of.

And that's what her attackers had been counting on that.

News of the terrible incident spread quickly. Lady Gavriella hadn't know her attackers and that she had seen the only identifiable thing they had – a brand on one of the horses. She'd drawn it for her father, which told the man all he needed to know.

THE BRAND FOR Hell's Guardhouse.

De Soulis.

It was the same brand that Harman saw now through the open door. Those from the castle known as the Hell's Guardhouse usually didn't venture over to Deadwater. They kept to themselves, spreading their filth over the villages closer to them. The father and son pair were known as unfair lords, harsh and terrible, taxing their vassals into starvation to fund their coffers, yet the castle itself was strangely in disrepair. The fear was that they could no longer squeeze blood out of their vassals and had somehow turned their sights on Deadwater and even Falstone. They'd come into Deadwater and had caught Lady Gavriella off guard.

They seemed to know who they were looking for. They'd caught her like a cat in a trap and dashed off with her before anyone really realized what had happened. But someone sent word to de Leia over at Falstone and his men went on the hunt, only to find Lady Gavriella in a livery in the far corner of the village, bruised and beaten and raped.

Therefore, the physic had lied to the pair. He'd seen Gavriella de Leia after she'd been assaulted and raped, presumably by Nicholas from what he could now gather. The young woman had been badly beaten and her innocence taken in a most hideous manner. Nicholas also knew the rape had resulted in a pregnancy, but Harman had been truthful when he said he hadn't attended the birth and neither had his wife.

But what he couldn't figure out was why John and Nicholas wanted information on that child.

Perhaps it was time to stick his neck out a little.

"Then allow me to go to Falstone and see what I can discover," he said after a moment. "They know me and they trust me. I will do this for you, but for my service, I wish to be paid."

Nicholas started to berate him, but John held out a hand and stopped him. "What do you wish?" he asked.

"How valuable is this information to you?"

John eyed the shrewd old man. "Go to Falstone and find out what you can about Lady Gavriella and her child," he said. "Return to me with the information and I shall pay you a full pound. Tell anyone what you are doing, or breathe a word of this, and I shall return and kill your wife before your very eyes. Do you understand me?"

The old physic nodded. With a deal reached, he figured the worst of the storm was over, at least for now, so he stood up and shuffled over to his wife, pulling her off the floor. As he stood with her next to the hearth, the father and son ducked out of the cottage to where their men were waiting outside in the mud, unaware that the brand on the hip of one of the horses had been recognized, as it had been before.

"What good is it going to do to simply find out the wellness of de Leia's daughter and the child?" Nicholas asked his father once they were outside. "We want the child."

John nodded. "I know," he said. "But you must have patience, lad. We discover what we can about the child and Lady Gavriella, and then if the old physic is trustworthy enough, with enough coin we can probably pay him to smuggle the child out of Falstone. But first things first – we have to determine how the child and its mother, fare. It is possible that neither have survived to this point."

Nicholas was impatient. He swung himself onto the back of his steed. "Why are we even bothering with this?" he hissed. "Why not simply go to Falstone and take what we want?"

John nodded slowly, fussing with his stirrup. "Because Falstone has big walls, a good army, and the backing of de Wolfe," he said. "Need I remind you of that? Nay, lad, we must be careful about this. Let us take the child by stealth, not with a big show of force. That would gain us nothing. Let the physic do his work."

"And when he does?"

"When he does, we shall reward him," John said. "A very *special* reward."

Nicholas knew what his father was alluding to – death and destruction. That was always what he meant. He looked over the village of Deadwater, a surprisingly prosperous village with a gloomy name.

"When we have fulfilled the prophesy and begin our advance against de Wolfe, this village will make a nice spoil of war," he said. "I have fond memories here already."

He flashed his yellow teeth rather lewdly. John simply shook his head at his crass son, though he did not dispute him. They had the beginnings of what they'd come for – information on the infant delivered by de Leia's daughter. There was nothing more they could do but return in a few days to ensure that the task had been completed.

All they could do now was wait.

As they mounted their fat horses and headed out of town, Harman the Wise stood in his open doorway, watching them go. He'd heard their conversation because they hadn't shut the door when they'd quit the cottage.

He'd heard every word.

It was quite possible that Merek de Leia was going to hear every word, too.

CHAPTER SEVEN

ANDREAS SAW HER walk into the river.

In utter disbelief, he watched her walk right into that swirling, dark water. He was standing at the end of the avenue on the river's edge, watching her red dress through the fog. There was some illumination on the river walk because of some public torches lighting up the narrow walk that had several taverns still open for business.

If not for those torches, he wouldn't have been able to see her at all.

He'd heard her walking and weeping. That was how he'd been able to follow her so easily. Her tears weren't just of a woman who couldn't find her way home, or of a woman who had spent the evening in a guild filled with debauchery. She'd wept painfully, tears of something much deeper than what had happened that evening. He'd thought her suspicion of him was driven by something else, something deeper, and now he was suspecting it was perhaps deeper than he'd thought.

This wasn't a woman who was frightened or angry.

This was a woman who was filled with despondency.

Whatever she was feeling was something beyond the obvious and he was drawn to her. It was true that she was beautiful and it was also true that he was a man of compassion and understanding. He still wasn't sure what drew him to her because he'd known his share of women. He'd been pursued by some truly beautiful and accomplished ones.

So what made this woman different?

He wasn't sure, but something did.

And now she was trying to kill herself.

He was just setting foot on the rocky shore of the river when he saw her abruptly go under water. He was in mail, with his broadsword around his waist, and he knew jumping into the river with all of that weight would sink him right to the bottom, so he began yanking off his sword and anything else that might weigh him down, including his mail. By the time he ripped the coat over his head, several long seconds had passed and he raced to the river's side and dove in.

It was like ice.

Murky, dirty water greeted him. He was a good swimmer and went right to the spot where he'd seen her head go under and dove down, grabbing around, trying to catch hold of her somehow. He was trying not to panic, but he swam in circles, flailing about, trying to find some scrap of her. She couldn't have gone too far, but maybe she'd gone just far enough that he wouldn't be able to find her in time.

The seconds ticked away.

His lungs were screaming for air.

And then, he touched something.

It was hair.

Andreas grabbed a handful and pulled, surfacing on the water and pulling the woman up with him. She was unconscious and he swam desperately until he could find his footing. Hauling her into his arms, he carried her to the bank and lay her onto the rocky shore.

She wasn't breathing so he turned her on her side, slapping

her on the back, trying to evacuate the water from her lungs. He ended up rolling her onto her stomach, pressing her back firmly, trying to get her to breathe. After several pumping tries, she suddenly vomited up brackish river water, coughing violently as water sprayed from her lungs.

Andreas thumped on her back, helping her expel it, as her body shook with cough. Once she'd managed to evacuate what water there was, she just lay there, eyes closed, breathing painfully and sounding as if she were dying.

He bent over her.

"My lady?" he said, dripping water on her. "Can you hear me?"

She grunted softly but she didn't say anything. He rubbed her back, trying to stimulate her. "My lady?" he said again. "Can you speak?"

She drew in a long, agonizing breath before coughing fitfully again. But the coughing eventually faded and he heard her grunt again.

"It's you," she muttered. Then, she burst into tears. "Why can you not leave me alone?"

He wasn't going to argue with her. He was freezing, she was freezing, and they were both going to catch their deaths if they didn't get out of the wet clothing. Without another word, he went over to collect the things he had tossed off before diving into the water. Once he had them back on, over his wet clothing, he returned to the lady who was still laying there on the shore.

Bending over, he swept her into his arms, carrying her back up to the street level and heading back the way they had come.

But she didn't put up a fight.

Maybe the fight had finally gone out of her.

THEY WERE BACK at the tavern.

This time, Gavriella was too exhausted to run from him. She was soaking wet and nearly catatonic by the time he carried her into the small bedchamber that he had rented for what remained of the night. She could hear the tavernkeeper as he rushed to awaken his wife, who helped him lug in a large copper pot used for bathing. Hearths were stoked and hot water began to fill the tub as she lay against the man called Wolf, as limp as a wet rag. Literally.

She could feel him shivering as he held her.

But she didn't care.

She'd given up.

A fire and hot water and food was brought in. She could smell it, but she was so tired that she drifted off to sleep even as the bustle went on around her. When next she realized, he was setting her on the bed and the tavernkeeper's wife was pulling the wet red silk off her. The water had made it run, so there were puddles of red water on the floor. Gavriella noted that it was just her and the tavernkeeper's wife in the chamber. The door was shut and the man called Wolf was nowhere to be found.

They were alone.

The tavernkeeper's wife managed to get the dress off of her, the shift, her hose and shoes. She'd lost the hat somewhere along the way. Once she was stripped down, the old woman plopped her into the copper pot that was big enough for two people.

The heat from the water was searing. Gavriella closed her eyes, relishing the heat. But her brief moment of peace and comfort was brutally interrupted when the old woman grabbed a horsehair brush, and a bar of lumpy white soap, and began to scrub her from head to toe.

Gavriella had to hold on to the sides of the pot as she was buffeted back and forth by the force of the old woman's scrubbing. The woman didn't have a light touch, unfortunately, and she scrubbed so hard that Gavriella was certain she had scrubbed some skin off. She even scrubbed under her toenails and her fingernails, thorough as she was. When she was finished, she poured buckets of water over Gavriella's head and when she was certain her young charge was completely waterlogged, she used that slimy white soap to lather up her hair.

Gavriella was too tired and too weak to resist at that point, so she simply let the woman have her way. Her hair was scrubbed cleaner than it had probably been in her entire life and the woman finished her washing by pouring several more buckets of water over her head to rinse out the slimy white froth.

In truth, it was a little strange to have the woman bathe her, as Gavriella had been bathing alone since she had been a girl. She had a maid who served her at her father's castle, but the woman never really helped her bathe. That was always something Gavriella did on her own. Even now, she wasn't entirely comfortable with a strange woman bathing her, but it was too late to do anything about that, so she simply went along with it. When she had been scrubbed and scraped and rinsed from the top of her blonde head to the soles of her small feet, the old woman pulled her out of the pot and wrapped her up in a big coverlet.

Gavriella took no active role in anything that the old woman was imposing upon her. If the woman wanted her dry, then Gavriella sat there while the woman dried her. When it came to combing out her wet hair, she made no effort to take the comb from the old woman and do it herself. She simply let the woman do it for her, combing the tangles out of her hair as the heat of the chamber began to dry it.

With her hair partially dry and her body completely dry underneath the coverlet, the old woman loaned her some of her own clothing because the red dress was completely ruined. The red dye had been affected by the water, leaving big patches of white where it had washed out of the fabric. Gavriella knew that Aurelia was going to be extremely upset at the ruined dress, but there wasn't anything she could do about it now.

In truth, she didn't care.

At the moment, she didn't care about anything.

The tavernkeeper's wife pulled a shift over her head, made from wool and surprisingly clean. Over that went a heavy broadcloth surcoat that was tied at the waistline. It was too long, and a little too loose, but it was clean and comfortable. As Gavriella sat on the bed, quiet and exhausted, the old woman continued to comb through her hair before finally braiding it into a long, thick braid.

But all of the grooming had taken time and the food that had been brought into the room was cooling now. Still, Gavriella could smell it and, cool or not, she was going to eat it. The lure of bread and butter was enough to get her up off the bed. As she took a seat at the small table in front of the hearth, the old woman gathered up the damp linens and opened the door, hissing at her husband. He rushed in to help her remove the copper pot that was now heavy with lukewarm water. They lugged it out together, sloshing it on to the floor. As they departed, an enormous figure took their place.

Gavriella looked up to see the knight standing there.

"Are you feeling better?" he asked quietly.

She had a big piece of bread and butter in her hand, having

just taken an enormous bite. In truth, she wasn't sure how to answer that question. Did she feel better? Maybe physically. She was warm and clean. She had food.

Mentally was a different matter altogether.

After a moment, she lowered the bread and fixed on him. "You… I simply do not understand you."

"What don't you understand?"

"Why you will not leave me alone."

His response was to shut the door, but he didn't bolt it. He shut it just enough to give them privacy with their conversation. "I told you why," he said. "You became my responsibility when I helped you find your way out of Gomorrah."

"And that includes pulling me out of the river?"

He nodded faintly. "I could not let you kill yourself," he said quietly. "At least, not in my presence. It is a sin, my lady. Surely you understand that."

She pushed the bread aside completely, her appetite waning at the subject of conversation. "Mayhap it is, but it is *my* sin," she said. "You had no right to stop me."

He regarded her a moment and as he did, something in him snapped. He was tired of being noble when it wasn't appreciated… or wanted.

"My lady, I have gone out of my way this evening to present you with a courteous man of honor and you have done your very best to insult me every step of the way," he said, a flash of temper rising. "I can tell you, plainly, that I have no motive in all of this. I saw a lady in distress tonight and I felt compelled to help her, but that will end in a couple of hours when the sun rises and I help you find your way home. After that, I will trouble you no further. Run back to the river and drown yourself if you wish because I will not be there to pull you out. If you succeed, then God have mercy on your soul. But I will wash my hands of you and your foolish behavior. I am finished showing any measure of concern for your safety because, clearly, you do not care."

It was a scolding, probably far less than she deserved, but in those stern words, she began to see something in him that she hadn't seen before. A hardness that he hadn't shown her, a darkness flashing in those pale eyes. She sat there, looking at him, feeling indignation. Anger.

Pain.

"I never asked you to save me," she said. "All I did was agree to permit you to help me find the way out of that horrible guild. That was it. You took it upon yourself to become my protector and I never asked you to do that, either."

He just looked at her, slowly shaking his head. "God, you're an ungrateful creature," he muttered. "You may look like an angel, but you have the manners of a lout. Since you feel that way, I'll pay for you to use this chamber for the rest of the night, but you can find your way home on your own in the morning. I am sorry to have wasted my time with you. You make a good act of being fearful and weak, but when someone tries to help you, you have no idea how to graciously accept such help or even be polite about it. What do you get out of this abusive game, my lady? Some kind of sick satisfaction?"

She was taken aback by his words. "What are you talking about? How I behave is not a game, my lord."

He snorted rudely. "How you behave is as poorly as I have ever seen," he said. "God help the next man who tries to give you any measure of assistance. You're not worth any of it."

She frowned. "How dare you say such things," she said. "You know nothing about me."

"And I do not want to," he snapped back. "I honestly thought I was doing something good. You see, I have sisters and a mother and many female relatives, and in my family, we treat our women with great esteem and respect. It is natural to us. I was raised to be a chivalrous man and I thought you needed someone to be kind to you, but I was wrong. So very wrong. Therefore, I will not trouble you further, my lady. Good luck to you. You are going to need it."

With that, he turned for the door and yanked it open. Stepping through, he shut it behind him, pausing a moment because he'd just yelled at a woman who had tried to kill herself. He tried not to feel like a monster. But her ingratitude had inflamed him. He didn't expect praise, but simple thanks would have been nice.

But he'd been wasting his time.

He'd been an idiot.

With a sigh of frustration, he was about to step away from the door when he heard something.

It sounded like weeping.

Keep walking, he told himself. She didn't want his help. She'd told him to go away multiple times. She didn't want anything to do with him and she'd made that abundantly clear. Ungrateful, rude, bitter wench.

… so why couldn't he seem to leave her alone?

Idiot!

Pausing unhappily, mostly with himself, he sighed again, this time with great annoyance, and opened the door. He could see her sitting there, head lowered, sobbing her eyes out. His gaze lingered on her for a few moments. He still held the opinion that he'd never seen a finer woman. That rude, beautiful, insolent, delicious-looking creature. He stepped into the chamber again and shut the door, but he made sure to stay next to it in case she did something else to inflame him so he could make a swift exit.

"Stop weeping," he commanded softly. "It's not as bad as all that. I didn't mean what I said. I was simply frustrated."

She didn't seem surprised that he was there. Even when she

told him to go away, he didn't, and so far he'd proven adept at popping up in the most unexpected of places.

She kept her head down.

"You were right to be annoyed," she sniffed. "Nothing you said is untrue."

That was a surprising answer from her. He wasn't sure how he felt about it, but it made him feel less like a monster for scolding her. He watched her lowered head and tried to figure out why he couldn't seem to leave her alone, thinking that it had something to do with his innate sense of chivalry.

As a knight, he'd been taught to help the weak, but that usually involved a battlefield. He fought for the weak, the persecuted, and those he loved – family or otherwise. He'd never had a cause to fight for, like a religious cause, and he'd never had to fight simply to live. As a de Wolfe, his family's superiority was well established. If he thought about it, he'd had a fairly easy life. He'd never had to claw his way to the top simply to survive.

But not everyone was as fortunate as he was.

He had a feeling he was looking at one of those less fortunate right now.

"Then why have you been so ill-mannered?" he asked quietly. "My lady, if I had wanted to molest you, I would have done it a long time ago. I would have done it when I found you in that alcove at Gomorrah. I would not have waited until I brought you to a tavern with two dozen people in a common room, hearing everything I did to you. I would have done it in the dark, with music and laughter and dancing to cover up my actions and your screams. Surely you realize that."

She wiped her eyes. "I… I suppose so."

She didn't say anything more, still wiping at her eyes, and he finally shook his head. "What is so terrible that you would walk into the river and try to drown yourself?"

She stopped wiping her face. He heard her sigh faintly. "Sometimes you meet people who hide a great deal, my lord. Not everything is always… pleasant. Looks can be deceiving."

It was the most human, intelligent thing he'd heard her say. "That is very true," he said. "One cannot make assumptions about someone they do not know, like beautiful women in red silk who look as if they should not have a care in the world. If I were to see you on the street, I should think you were the most revered, honored lady with the love of her family and the adoration of her husband. But that is not the case, is it?"

For the first time, she looked up at him. "Nay," she whispered.

"Then you hide a great deal."

She simply stared at him before lowering her gaze again.

But something in those eyes pulled at him. He was starting to forget his annoyance with her, his confusion. He wanted to know why such a beautiful woman behaved the way she did. He'd suspected earlier than it had nothing to do with him and everything to do with past experiences. With what she was hiding. If he knew, then maybe he could help.

Or not.

Unfortunately, Andreas wasn't one to keep himself emotionally detached. He never had been when it came to women. He was emotional, much like his father was, so he didn't have the ability to separate himself, which was why he was very selective when it came to women in general. His family wasn't too far off when they connected his lack of a wife with his mother's death those years ago.

The truth was that, deep down, he felt comfortable with women, with grandmothers he loved and, in a sense, he was always trying to reclaim that comforting relationship he'd had with his mother. It was the horrible truth, but that was his reality. When he got too close to a woman, he ran. He was afraid of the pain that such attachments could bring. But that didn't make him any less emotional or any less intuitive when it came to the opposite sex.

An example was the sad woman before him.

More and more, she intrigued him.

"I know I am not supposed to ask you your name, but we are free of Gomorrah now," he said. "Won't you tell me yours? You do not have to tell me your family name, but won't you at least tell me what your Christian name is?"

She eyed him a moment. "My name is Gavriella."

"Gavriella," he repeated, rolling it off his tongue. "That is a unique name. My name is Andreas, Lady Gavriella."

Gavriella cocked her head slightly, looking up at him once more. "Also a unique name."

He nodded. "It is a tradition in my mother's family that the males carry a name from the ancient Greeks. My father's name is Troy and my grandfather's name is Paris."

"The Iliad," she said softly. "Those are from The Iliad."

"You know of it?"

She nodded. "My father used to read it to me. He is very keen on ancient literature."

"Is he a scholar, then?"

She shook her head. "Nay," she said. "He simply prefers his books to anything else. He used to be a knight, once. I suppose he still is in the literal sense of the word. But my mother died a few years ago and that seemed to turn him to his books for escape, I suppose. He grieves for her, still."

Andreas almost brought up how her father would react to the loss of a daughter who drowned herself in the river, but he kept silent on the matter. He had her talking and she was being as congenial as he'd ever seen her, so he didn't want to disrupt it.

"I am sorry for you," he said. "And for him. I, too, lost my mother years ago in an accident, so I understand what it is to grieve."

Her focus on him was becoming more intense. "What happened?"

"She drowned along with my two younger siblings."

Her eyes widened. "Then that's why you jumped in after me at the river," she said. "Now I understand. You did it so that I would not drown like your mother."

Andreas hadn't even thought of that and her words hit him like a hammer. He was about to swiftly deny it, but the words died on his lips. Before he realized it, he was sitting on the bed next to the door, pondering what she'd said to him.

It took him a few moments to realize that she was probably right.

Maybe that's why he had been so angry at her – voluntarily doing something that his mother and baby sisters had been given no control over.

And he hadn't been there to help them.

"That is very possible," he said after a moment. "It was a carriage accident. The bridge that they were traveling on collapsed and dumped the carriage into the river."

"And no one was there to save her?"

He shook his head. "I was not there if that's what you mean," he said. "I was away, fostering at the time. She was traveling with my aunt and my young cousins when the bridge collapsed. They had an escort who tried to save them, but their efforts were futile. As a youth, I always wondered if it would have made a difference if had I been there. Every man thinks he can save the world. Or, at the very least, his mother."

Gavriella was looking at him seriously. "My mother died of a cancer," she said. "I could do nothing for her except watch her die a long and lingering death. Sometimes I wonder if it would have been better if she had gone quickly and unexpectedly, like your mother. She suffered a few minutes of terror and mayhap even pain and then it was over. But my mother lasted a little over a year while something ate away at her chest. It is an ugly way to die."

It was a surprising show of honesty from a woman who had been closed off and guarded since they had met. Little by little, barriers were breaking down, something that wasn't lost on Andreas.

Truth be told, his barriers were breaking down, too.

"There are a thousand ways for a man or woman to die," he said. "In my opinion, only one of them is peaceful."

"What's that?"

"Going to sleep and never waking up."

"That is the best we can all hope for, I suppose."

Andreas' gaze lingered on her for a moment. He couldn't help but speak what was on his mind. "You just walked into a river," he reminded her quietly. "If you would have rather died in your sleep, why did you do such a thing?"

Her expression seemed to tighten and she averted her gaze, looking at her hands. "Because…" she said, paused, and then continued. "Because it seemed like a good idea at the time. So much… anguish. Sometimes I simply want it to end."

"What anguish?" he asked. "Surely there is comfort for you with a priest or with your family?"

Quickly, she shook her head. "Nay," she said. "Not any of them because they do not… well, it does not matter. I have found that speaking to a stranger who doesn't already have preformed opinions and a sensible outlook has been an odd comfort. And to be truthful… walking into the river was a spur of the moment decision. It was not a smart or reasonable one. I don't think I was really serious, but I slipped into a hole and went in deeper. Mayhap I thought I could pull myself out; I don't really know. I am not usually so weak, but…"

He watched her struggle for a moment, unable to continue.

"But your emotions got the better of you," he finished quietly.

"They did. I admit it, they did." She lifted her head to look at him again. "And you jumped in after me. I still do not fully understand why you would risk yourself for someone you do not know, but I suppose I understand a little more now."

She meant because of the way his mother had died. Andreas simply lifted his big shoulders. "I did it because it was the right thing to do," he said softly. "But… mayhap you are right… mayhap there is a part of me that wanted to save you from drowning since my mother had suffered that fate. I had not really considered that until you brought it up."

"I hope it did not bring back awful memories."

He shook his head. "The pain of my mother's passing has long since faded, so it is nothing that cripples me these days. It is simply part of my life, as the death of a parent is part of the lives of many, including you."

They were wise and reasonable words, something that resonated with the both of them. "Then I thank you for speaking to me about it," she said after a moment. "In fact… thank you for everything, Sir Andreas. You were correct. I was very ungrateful. Trust does not come easily to me and, these days, I am afraid my entire mood is generally poor."

They were some of the first words of gratitude out of her mouth all night. In this brief conversation, he came to understand a little about that beautiful and complicated woman. He was coming to feel glad that he hadn't left her to her tears, after all. He felt better about the evening and he hoped she did, too.

"I am sorry to hear that," he said. "You were wearing a beautiful dress when we first met, indicative of a woman who enjoys pretty and lively things, so I assumed you did, too. I have seen women have a great deal of fun in London, with the exception of those at Gomorrah. I'm not entirely sure about *those* women."

He made a face and, for the first time that night, she smiled weakly. She had a big dimple in her right cheek, something Andreas found rather enchanting. After a moment, she snorted.

"And you have never been there before?" she asked.

He shook his head firmly. "God, no."

"Nor I. Someone should burn it to the ground."

"From the looks of the church built over it, someone has already tried."

She burst into soft giggles, revealing pretty, straight teeth. "They did not do a thorough enough job."

He liked seeing her smile. "Not to worry," he said. "If people in that place keep sinning like that, God himself will come down from heaven and burn it to cinder. You remember what happened to Gomorrah in the bible, don't you?"

She nodded. "God destroyed it."

"Exactly. Therefore, I want to be as far away from Gomorrah as I can get since God may have to burn it down a second time."

Gavriella continued to chuckle, a distinct difference to her mood and manner now. A bath, some good company once she let her guard down, and she was relaxing admirably. She was relaxed enough to pick up the bread she'd set aside and take another bite.

"I will stay as far away from it as I can for always," she said, mouth full. "I am not entirely sure about my cousins, however. They seem to have a naughty streak in them that I was unaware of. We are supposed to be warm and cozy in our beds right now, yet here we are – I'm in a tavern with a man only just met and they are probably back in that den of debauchery doing something that will probably make God light the kindling to burn it down just a little sooner than He had planned. I just know they will want to return, but I will refuse to go with them. Never again."

So she had a sense of humor. Andreas found himself grinning at her comment. "As well you should," he said. "I shall refuse to go with my cousins, also."

"That is who attended you this night?"

"Aye," he said. "My cousins, Will and Tor, and my best friend, Theodis. Dirty alley cats, all of them. Well, at least Theo is. He's quite naughty. There are so many other far less scandalous things to experience in London."

"Like what?"

He thought on that. "Like the entertainment across the river, for one."

Gavriella seemed to perk up. "Across the river?" she repeated. "What kind of entertainment?"

He could see that he had her interest and, in truth, he felt a bit of a bond with her. They'd shared quite an evening together and with dawn approaching, he found that he was actually a little disappointed to think me might never see her again. He wondered if she felt the same way.

There was only one way to find out.

"There are performances given on the beds of wagons," he said. "Plays with actors wearing costumes. They pretend to be Jesus or Potiphar or a filthy beggar. Have you never seen one?"

She was intrigued. "Once," she said. "One traveled through our village and performed a scene from the bible. It was terribly depressing. They aren't all biblical plays, are they?"

He lifted his enormous shoulders. "I am not certain," he said. "But I intend to find out. Would you like to come with me?"

Her eyes widened a little. He thought she might refuse. But a smile began to play on her lips. "When?"

"Today, sometime. After I've had some sleep and after you have had some sleep." He watched the tug of war on her features, interest versus refusal. "It will be much better entertainment than Gomorrah. I shall escort you across the river and we shall watch the entertainment, mayhap sample some of their food, and then I shall return you home safely."

"Well…"

He didn't let her finish. "Come with me, Lady Gavriella," he said softly. "Let's both find something better to entertain ourselves with than that pile of shite they call Gomorrah."

He was very persuasive and she started to laugh. "Very well," she said. "You have made a convincing case. I believe I should like to see entertainment that doesn't involve dark passages and women who should wear more clothing."

He smiled broadly. "Excellent," he said. "It is settled. Now, I will leave you here to sleep for an hour or two and then I shall escort you home at dawn. Is that acceptable?"

She nodded as he stood up. "But where are you going?"

He threw a thumb in the direction of the common room. "I'll find a place to sleep out there," he said. His gaze lingered on her a moment. "I am glad this evening turned out better for us both, my lady. I have to admit, I had my doubts."

An expression of regret rippled across her features. "I know," she said quietly. "For pulling me out of the river when I behaved so stupidly… you have my thanks, Sir Andreas. And, for everything else, too."

He dipped his head politely. "It was my pleasure, my lady."

She smiled timidly and he smiled, nodding his head at her again, before quitting the chamber and quietly closing the door. But even then, he stood at the door, reliving the conversation with her and glad he had not left her, after all. It would have been so easy to do, but he was glad he had remained.

He wondered if she was, too.

With a weary sigh, he headed out into the common room, confiscating a chair next to the hearth where he would sleep until dawn.

The day looked brighter already.

CHAPTER EIGHT

The Asher

"WHERE HAVE *YOU* been?" Aurelia hissed. "Mother has asked for you this morning!"

Gavriella had entered the chamber she shared with Camilla, only to be faced with both Aurelia and Camilla, apparently in mid-argument. When they saw Gavriella, Camilla slammed and bolted the door behind the woman as Aurelia grabbed her by the arm.

Gavriella yanked her arm free.

"Where have *I* been?" Gavriella hissed in return. "No thanks to you, I have been wandering the streets of London trying to find my way home."

Aurelia was incensed. "No thanks to *me*? What does that mean?"

Gavriella had quickly decided something about her cousin. She was a bully and the only way to deal with her was to bully her in return.

She wasn't going to let Aurelia push her around any longer.

Having just walked home with Andreas, she was still lingering on the good conversation they'd had, one that revolved around some of the entertainments Andreas had seen in the past and how much he liked to watch plays. It had been a glorious conversation with a man she had mistrusted until he'd hauled her out of the river.

That had been the turning point.

Now, speaking to Aurelia was like throwing cold water on the pleasant feelings she had about the conversation with Andreas.

Pleasant feelings were so rare for her these days.

"Exactly what I said," she said angrily. "You dragged me out of my warm bed in the middle of the night to take me to some clandestine guild where people fornicate for all to see, men are free to grab any body part they wish, and people engage in things better left unsaid. How dare you take me to such a place and then run off and leave me standing there alone. If I am home late, it is *your* fault!"

Aurelia's mouth popped open in outrage. "If you cannot appreciate fun, that is your misfortune," she said. "I knew it was a mistake to take you there, you little country chit."

Gavriella's eyes narrowed. "I'd rather be a little country chit than a big city whore," she said. "You heard me correctly – I said whore. I saw what you did in that place and you probably did more that I did not see."

Aurelia's face turned red. "You're such a child, Gavriella," she snarled. "You know nothing about the ways of men and women. I would keep my mouth shut if I were you."

It was a threat and Gavriella knew it. But she was prepared. "If you think to challenge or torment me in any way, know that your first transgression will send me to your mother with every wicked thing you have done," she said in a low voice. "I'll tell her everything, Aurelia. Do not test me."

Aurelia was looking at her in shock. No one ever challenged her and most certainly not another woman her age. She could push people around with the best of them, but Gavriella was evidently sprouting some courage. She very much wanted to snap back, but she knew that Gavriella's threat was a real one. She could see it in the woman's face. She looked exhausted and angry and…

"*Where* is the dress you were wearing last night?" she demanded, abruptly noticing her clothing was not the dress she had worn last night. "That was an expensive dress!"

Gavriella wasn't going to tell her the truth. "Some man from your vulgar guild ripped it off of me," she lied. "This was the only thing they could give me to wear, so your ruined dress is *your* fault. And I am never going anywhere with you again!"

Aurelia was beyond shocked now. She had moved into the realm of outrage. Cheeks flushed and mouth working, she turned and stomped out of the chamber, leaving Gavriella standing there with a stunned Camilla. Gavriella knew she'd won the battle, but not necessarily the war. This wasn't over with Aurelia in the least.

She could only imagine what the next confrontation would be about.

Once Aurelia was gone, she heard Camilla speak softly.

"Are you well?" she asked, concerned. "You are not sick or injured, are you?"

Gavriella looked at Camilla. She was sweet and young, but her sister's influence over her was great. Gavriella knew she couldn't trust Camilla because anything she said would get back to Aurelia.

"I am not sick or injured," she said, her tone kinder than it had been with Aurelia. "I am well, I promise."

She went over to the wardrobe that contained her clothing in it and opened the doors. As she began to remove the garments that the tavernkeeper's wife had loaned her, Camilla came up behind her and started helping.

"I am sorry we left you," she said sincerely. "I thought you would dance with us, but we realized you had not. I went looking for you but could not find you. We only came home about an hour ago."

Gavriella pulled the surcoat over her head. "Cammie," she said slowly. "Do… do you really like that place?"

Camilla helped her pull the shift over her head. "It is fun," she said. "It is exciting kissing men and not knowing who they are."

Gavriella took some precious oil she'd brought with her from home, oil that smelled of flowers, and rubbed it on her skin because it was dry after the scouring she'd been given at the tavern. "But you should not be kissing men you do not know," she said softly. "You are young and pretty. How do you think a fine husband will feel if he knows you have kissed so many men before him?"

Camilla pulled forth a fine, soft shift from the wardrobe. "He will appreciate that I know how to kiss him," she said. "He does not need to know how I learned."

It was clear that she didn't understand the seriousness of her actions, of the dangers of a place like Gomorrah. Gavriella was trying to be delicate with her because Camilla was, in truth, a delicate creature, but she was also naïve. Reaching out, she put a hand on Camilla's arm.

"Sweetheart, Aurelia is leading you astray," she said as kindly as she could. "What your sister does is her own business, but you… you are better than that. You should not go to a place like that. I am afraid of what will happen to you, especially if men can have their way with you without consequence."

Something in Camilla's expression suggested that she knew that, but the truth was that she was weak. Aurelia led and she followed. It had always been that way.

"Do not worry," she assured her, helping pull the new shift over Gavriella's head. "I will not fall prey to anyone. But I do like to dance. That is the only reason I go."

Gavriella knew she couldn't talk any sense into the woman, so she shut her mouth. It was unfortunate that Camilla felt so, but there wasn't anything more she could do about it.

"Just be careful," she said before changing the subject because there was no use in continuing. "Now, I am going to sleep for a few hours. Mayhap you should, too."

Camilla nodded, yawning. "I will," she said. "But I could not go to sleep when you were missing. I was very worried about you."

Gavriella smiled at her, patting her cheek. "I am well," she assured her. "But Aurelia said your mother was asking for me. Why?"

Camilla shrugged. "She did not say," she said. "I suppose when she realized you were not in bed, she wondered where you were."

Gavriella was heading towards the big bed she shared with Camilla. "I will tell her that I could not sleep and went to walk about," she said. "I have had trouble sleeping since I arrived, so that is nothing unusual."

She climbed in, with Camilla climbing in next to her. They settled down on the feather mattress, soft and warm, far away from the foggy night and the dangerous guild in the sublevels of a burned-out church.

Far away from a dirty river that Gavriella had once entertained.

"Sleep well, Gavy," Camilla said, sighing as she closed her eyes.

Gavriella rolled onto her side, facing the wall and the door. She was exhausted, that was true, but she didn't fall asleep right away. Her thoughts were back on the handsome knight who had escorted her home, the one she had once told to go away. But he hadn't listened.

She was glad he hadn't listened.

In a few hours, he was going to take her to an entertainment across the river and she had to admit that she was excited about it. Not just the idea of watching an entertainment, but the idea of continuing the conversation with a man who had done the impossible. In spite of everything, the tumult they had been through and her own struggles against him, he had knocked a few holes in that wall she kept up around herself.

She was coming to trust him.

Truth be told, she was coming to like him just a little, too.

She knew she shouldn't – God knew, she should send the man along his way – but she couldn't seem to do it. Having a friend, a male friend, was something foreign and exciting and even a little titillating. She really hadn't known any men other than her father and the men who served him, and then after what happened last year… nay, she had no desire to be friends or acquaintances with any man.

Men only brought pain.

But Andreas hadn't. He'd been quite the opposite.

Something told her that her stay in London just became a little more bearable.

Lothbury House

"WHERE HAVE *YOU* been?"

The question came from William as soon as Andreas walked into the hall of Lothbury House, his Uncle Edward's townhome. Edward de Wolfe was an advisor to the king and, as such, needed a home near the Tower of London and also one near Windsor, which he did. It was on the River Thames off to the west, and a beautiful structure, but Edward and his cousins and Theodis had been staying at Lothbury, a hell of a fortified manse that wasn't too far from the home where he'd just left Gavriella. *The Asher*, she had called it.

He couldn't stop thinking about it.

Or her.

"Out," he told his cousins, who were seated at the big table in the hall, having a morning meal. He pulled off his big leather gloves and plopped down next to Tor. "How was the rest of the evening at Gomorrah?"

He was deflecting the subject and, for the moment, they went along with it. "Boring," Theodis said. "All of the pretty women were taken, including the one you left with. Where did you go?"

Andreas gave him an exaggeratedly coy look. "Do you truly expect me to kiss and tell?"

Will leaned into him. "Give us something to gossip about, lover," he said. Then, he sniffed the man and immediately pulled away. "Jesus, Dray. You smell like the fat and greasy river rats that populate The Pox."

Andreas poured himself some warmed, watered wine. "You were close when you said the river, actually," he said. "Mayhap I'll tell you sometime just how close. Now, back to that bawdy guild. Are you telling me that with all of the women there, I was the only one to find an attractive one? Tay, that's not like you. Usually, you have a few hanging off your arms, anywhere we go. You must be losing your charm, old man."

Theodis sneered at him. "I have lost nothing except my virginity at a very young age," he said, watching William and Tor laugh. "Dray, you do not seem to understand. We do not want to speak of our evening. We want to know about yours."

Andreas spooned stewed fruit into a bowl and took a hunk of bread. "There is nothing to tell," he said. "You saw her run into the room where we were – she was hysterical because she could not find the exit. I merely helped her find her way out."

"And?"

"*And* nothing. It was foggy, she could not remember where she lived, she tried to drown herself in the river, and I took her to an inn to wait out the mist."

He said it so fast that they almost didn't catch the part about the river. "She tried to *drown* herself?" William repeated, confused. "Why? What happened?"

Andreas stuffed his face with bread. "In truth, I still do not know," he said. "She's a sweet lass once you get past her hysteria. We had a pleasant conversation and I took her home at dawn. I am going to sleep a few hours and then we are going across the river to the entertainment over there."

Will's eyebrows lifted in surprise that Andreas should actually make a date to see the woman again. He looked at Tor, who shrugged, but Theodis was far less discreet than those two were.

He wanted answers.

"You must like her," he said. "What is her name?"

"Gavriella."

"Ah," Theodis said. "Gavriella. A lovely name. Where is she from?"

"I do not know."

"What is her family name?"

"I do not know."

Theodis frowned. "What *do* you know about her?"

"Enough," Andreas said, washing the bread down with wine. "Stop pestering me or I'll tell you nothing more."

Theodis backed down, but it was only to rethink his strategy. They continued to eat, with servants moving around the small hall delivering more food to the table, but Theodis was eyeing Andreas, as they all were, only Tor and William were more discreet about it. They didn't want to hammer their cousin too much, although they were quite curious.

Andreas and a woman was a rare thing, indeed.

"When did you want to leave, Dray?" Tor finally asked, mouth full of warmed-over beef. "With our business here finished, I see no reason to remain. Have you thought about heading home soon?"

He spoke the truth. There really was no reason to remain in London because everything they'd come to accomplish had been completed. Yesterday, Andreas was ready to head home, but now…

Now, not so much.

"We need to make it home before the September rains come," he said. "That gives us about five or six weeks at most. There's plenty of time."

Will shook his head. "Not for me," he said. "I have a family to return to. I have already been gone overlong. No offense, lads, but I want to get home."

No one argued with him, not even Theodis. They all knew the situation with Will, how his wife had been ill for the last year. A tumor in her belly, the physic said, something he couldn't remove, so pretty and frail Lily had been fighting for her life ever since. Will was a devoted husband and father, strong in the face of his wife's illness because he had to be. Outwardly, he was in control, but inwardly, that was another matter altogether.

He was struggling with a world turned upside-down.

But no one brought that up. There was no need. Still, it had been good to see Will enjoy himself, at least for a short time, something that was rare for him. When all of the puking and purging and scandalous guilds had passed, the fact remained that Will had enjoyed himself, even for a short while.

"As do I," Andreas agreed after a moment. "In truth, I miss home when I am away from it overlong, but I would like to spend the afternoon with the lady I saved from Gomorrah. I did promise her entertainment, after all. If you are agreeable, then we can leave on the morrow."

Will and Tor shrugged in agreement as Theodis smiled wickedly from across the table. The man was oozing lascivious suggestions even if he wasn't speaking them. Rolling his eyes, Andreas shoved the last of the bread in his mouth and got up from the table.

At dawn, Lothbury House was already busy with preparations for the coming day. Andreas could hear his young cousins upstairs, preparing to come down to the small hall to break their fast. There were four young girls and a new baby, his uncle's first son. He could hear the girls squealing and the baby crying, and he grinned as he hurried towards the wing of the manse that housed the young men.

His chamber was at the end of the corridor, a small one that overlooked the yard of the manse, the wall, and the street beyond. As he headed towards his room, he caught the attention of a big, sweaty servant who was bringing fresh water to the rooms. Andreas not only wanted the water, he wanted a bath because he smelled like fish guts, so the servant went running for a tub and hot water.

Andreas was fairly certain that Lady Gavriella would not like him to smell like fish guts.

Opening the door to his chamber, he stepped into the cool and dark room. There was a small hearth, but it lay dark and cold, so when the servants began to bring the buckets of hot water along with the tub, he sent them for firewood as well.

Since the room was so small, Andreas stood out in the corridor while the servants prepared his bath and stoked a fire in the hearth. As he stood there wearily, he realized that he was still hungry, having only really left the table because of the way Theodis was looking at him, so he sent for more food which was promptly brought.

With the fire burning in the hearth and a big copper tub half-filled with hot water, Andreas finally chased the servants away and entered his chamber, closing the door and bolting it. His saddlebags were underneath his bed and he pulled them out, slinging them onto the bed. Digging around, he pulled out a razor, soap, and a comb. He put everything onto a table near the tub and begin to peel his smelly clothing off.

Unfortunately, he was wearing a chainmail coat, something that rusted very easily when it was damp. Already, he could see the rust starting and he unbolted the door and tossed it to the big, sweaty servant who was still out in the corridor. He asked the man to have his mail cleaned, closing the door once more and bolting it.

With his protection being tended to, he proceeded to strip off every piece of clothing on his body, including his boots, which smelled horrible at this point. There were some parts of his clothing that were still damp, so he tossed everything into a heap with the intention of having it washed as he sank his big body into the copper tub.

He hissed as he sat down because the water was so hot, but it felt glorious. Picking up the hard white Spanish soap that smelled of mint and rosemary, he proceeded to scrub himself down. Fortunately, the heavy scrubbing eventually got rid of any mildew smell that might have lingered on his body and the scent of peppermint and rosemary filled the air as he washed his hair and face thoroughly. He even shaved, using the surface of the water as a mirror. It was strange, really, wanting to smell good for a woman he had only just met.

A woman with whom he hadn't had the easiest of beginnings.

But given the conversation with her earlier, things were starting to look up.

The hot bath felt so good that Andreas ended up scrubbing himself a second time, just because he wanted to. Gone was the smell of the river and in its place, he smelled like the wonderful herbs of a garden. He wondered if Lady Gavriella would like the smell and then laughed at himself for being foolish enough to be concerned.

It had been such a long time since he had last spent quality time with a woman that he wondered if he remembered how. He just wasn't like Theodis, who charmed women from one end of England to the other. He wasn't like Tor, who also had a fairly decent following of admiring females. Truth be told, there were a few women in the north who were declared Andreas de Wolfe admirers, but he didn't take pride in that like the others did. It didn't mean anything to him. As handsome as he was, it was inevitable that he should have a following. Following – aye, but prospects – nay.

Until now.

Well, maybe the lady wasn't exactly a prospect, but at least someone to spend some time with while he was in London. As Andreas scrubbed his fingernails to get the grime out, he began hoping that their most recent pleasant conversation wasn't a fluke. He hoped that when he saw her again, they would go right back to that pleasant moment in time and pick up the conversation where they'd let off. He hadn't felt this way in a very long time, excited to spend time with someone of the opposite sex. Honestly, he couldn't remember the last time.

But he knew one thing.

He was very much looking forward to *this* time.

Andreas sat in the water until it cooled and he was forced to get out. His big body was rosy from the hot water and the scrub down, and he dried off with a piece of linen. He ran the damp linen over his hair just to get most of the moisture out before using the comb to run it through his locks. Quite honestly, his hair was so short that he didn't even know why he bothered, but he hadn't combed his hair in a very long time. It felt good to rub the tortoise shell teeth along his scalp.

It felt good to get clean, physically and perhaps even mentally.

Now that the bath was over with, he pulled on a pair of linen braies, something he usually traveled with to wear when his usual leather breeches were too heavy or too uncomfortable. Opening the door to the chamber, he called out to the servants to remove the bathtub, and as they came in to heave the cold water away, he had them take away his dirty clothing and boots, too.

Then he sat down at the small table that contained the food and devoured everything that had been brought to him. There was more bread and butter, along with the boiled beef he'd eaten earlier with his cousins and friend. There were stewed apples and little oat cakes with currants in them, and he ate every bit. With the hot bath and warm fire, and now with a full belly, Andreas passed out on his bed like a drunkard and snored the morning away.

When he dreamed, it was of flaxen-haired maidens.

When he finally awoke some time later, it was to a dog barking outside of his window. Startled, he had no idea how long he'd been asleep and sat up quickly, rubbing the sleep from his eyes as he ran to door and threw it open. He didn't see anyone right away, but by the time he took a few steps into the corridor, the sweaty servant was there, a tray of food in his hands.

"What time is it?" Andreas demanded.

The servant blinked, surprised by words that came blasting out at him. "Just past the nooning hour, my lord."

"How *far* past?"

The servant shrugged nervously. "An hour, mayhap," he

said. "I don't know, my lord. I will have to find the…"

Andreas waved him off before he could finish. "Never mind," he said. "Bring my clothes immediately."

"I'm not sure they're dried, my lord."

Andreas was struggling not to blow up at the man. "Then tell either of the de Wolfe brothers that I require their clothing," he said. "Get what you can from them and hurry or I'll find you and skin the hide from you. And shoes! I need shoes!"

The man fled in terror.

Andreas slammed the door. He'd slept so soundly and so deeply that he was groggy and struggling to shake it off. He'd told Lady Gavriella that he'd be waiting for her across the street from The Asher just after the nooning meal and he very much wanted to make that appointment. Quickly, he dug through his saddlebags to locate any spare clothing and he came across an older pair of breeches he always carried with him, made from fine leather but having faded and worn over the years.

It was of little matter because he had nothing else, so he pulled them on. Even though his door was closed, he could hear yelling and doors slamming all throughout the manse, and suddenly, there were footfalls in the corridor.

Someone pounded on his door.

"Dray!"

Andreas knew that voice. He yanked open the door, coming face to face with his Uncle Edward. He was the diplomat of the sons of William de Wolfe, the man who had followed in his famous grandfather's footsteps by choosing a diplomatic career over a military one. Not to say that Edward de Wolfe wasn't a warrior; he was, by nature, training, and blood. He was tall and broad-shouldered, regal and masculine and handsome, and from his father's side carried the darkness of the Saracens. He had the de Wolfe dark hair and golden eyes, eyes that were now looking at Andreas in concern.

"What ails you?" Edward demanded. "You have the servants running mad upstairs, looking for clothing to fit you."

Andreas sighed heavily. "I am sorry, Eddie," he said. "I did not mean to throw them into fits, but I am late for an appointment that I must keep."

"What appointment?"

Andreas cleared his throat softly, averting his gaze. "I am going across the river to see the entertainment over in Lambethmoor," he said. "I have promised a young lady that I would escort her there."

Edward went from being mildly perturbed to being most curious at the mention of a woman. "A young lady?" he repeated. "Who is this woman?"

"I met her last night," Andreas said. "We had a long and eventful evening and I have offered to escort her across the river to see the entertainment there."

Edward studied him for a moment. The man had a most calculating way of looking at people, something that served him well in the diplomatic corps. He could look at any man and, within a few moments, read him clearly. It was a gift.

He was trying to read Andreas at that moment.

"I see," he said. "Dray, I must say that I am surprised. You of all people do not spend time with young women in social situations. Where did you meet her?"

Andreas looked at him hesitantly. "I am afraid to tell you."

"Why?"

"Because you are going to tell my father and he will tell my mother and she will try and box my ears."

Edward fought off a grin. "I promise I will not tell him," he said. "Tell me."

Andreas rolled his eyes, still hesitant, before finally confessing. "It was Theodis' fault, so do not yell at me," he said. "Tay took us all there – me and Will and Tor."

"Took you *where*?"

"Gomorrah."

Edward's eyes widened. "That place?" he hissed. "You went to *that* place?"

Andreas nodded. "And it was just as awful as you think it is," he said, putting up his hands. "Believe me, I shall not be returning. In fact, the young lady was coerced into attending by cousins. She was just as miserable and horrified as I was, so I helped her find her way out of that place. That place is like a goddamn maze."

Edward nodded. "I know," he said, his eyes alight that his noble, straitlaced nephew should go to such a lascivious establishment. He started to chuckle but put a hand over his mouth to stop himself. "God's Bones, Dray. I'm proud of you for going to such a place. Mayhap there is hope for you yet."

Andreas frowned. "Leave me alone," he muttered. "I need my clothes or I'll never make my appointment. Aunt Cassie isn't angry at me for upsetting her home, is she?"

Edward shook his head. "She is not," he said. "I stopped the servants from making too much of a fuss before she caught sight of what was going on, so do not fret."

Andreas scratched his head. "Do not tell her that I went to Gomorrah."

"I will not, I swear it. That might lead to a confession that I have been there, too, and I have no desire to be angrily chased around by my wife today."

There wasn't much of an age gap between Andreas and Edward because Andreas was the eldest son of Edward's much older brother, so even growing up, the two of them had been good friends, something that still carried over to this day. That was why Andreas didn't even address the man as "Uncle". There was a scant three years between them.

"You have been there, you naughty lad?" he said, grinning

suggestively. "I'm shocked."

Edward held up a hand. "Only in the line of duty, I assure you," he said with disgust. "We had a particular Bohemian warlord, very wealthy, who had been told of it by his interpreter and he wanted very badly to attend, so the king asked me to go with him to ensure he did not run into any trouble."

"Did he?"

Edward cocked a dark eyebrow. "Did you see that woman shooting grapes out of her privates?"

Andreas couldn't help it; he started laughing. "I did," he said. "Appalling and hilarious at the same time."

Edward clapped a hand to his forehead. "Our Bohemian warlord spent an hour in that chamber, catching grapes in his mouth. I have never seen anything so ghastly in my entire life. And then I had to explain it to the king. Edward laughed until he choked. I think he went to see for himself."

Andreas was still chuckling as servants suddenly appeared, running in his direction bearing clothing and boots, all belonging to Edward. Andreas was bigger and heavier than Edward, so the tunic was a little snug and the boots a little tight, but they would do. They were clean and well-maintained. Over it, he pulled on a stylish leather robe, lined with fur around the cuffs, something that looked quite elegant and manly on him. It draped all the way to the ground.

Because of his position, everything Edward owned was of fine quality, so the clothing was much better than anything Andreas owned. Washed, combed, and shaved, he appeared quite presentable. Edward even loaned him a belt with brass links that draped over the black leather broadsword sheath that Andreas had strapped to his waist. As he secured the sheath to his left thigh, as he was left-handed and fought left-handed, Edward brushed off the shoulders of the fine robe that was so soft and light that it had a velvety feel to it. The entire back panel was made from the finest silk damask, gold and red in color. He stood back, running a practiced eye over Andreas.

"Excellent," he said. "You look quite presentable, Dray. All the women should be going mad for you dressed like that. I usually see you only in mail and armor, so this is a definite change."

As a seasoned knight, it was unheard of to go out in public without protection, and Andreas was already feeling strange about it. "I feel naked."

"You look very handsome," Edward said, enjoying his discomfort. "Now, do you have enough money to tend to the lady's every whim?"

Andreas grinned. "Yes, Papa, I have enough money," he said sarcastically, teasing Edward, who laughed softly. "In all seriousness, I do appreciate it. And I had better go or she will think I have forgotten her."

He headed out with Edward following him. "Be careful over in Southwark," he said. "There are thieves and pickpockets over there, so watch yourself."

Andreas moved through the narrow corridor and out into the reception hall. "I will," he said steadily. "You needn't worry about me. Your focus should be on Tay. He may try to return to Gomorrah and you must not let him. I wish to return him home in one piece."

They were at the entry door that led out into the yard. As Andreas opened the panel, Edward came to a halt. "I shall tell Cassie where Theodis wishes to go," he called after Andreas. "She'll make sure he does not go there, I promise you."

Andreas lifted a hand, waving it at him with a grin. Like all de Wolfe wives, Cassiopeia de Wolfe was strong beyond measure. She wasn't beyond tying Theodis to a chair if she didn't want him to leave.

But he didn't want to think about Theodis anymore.

He wanted to think on the golden-haired angel in his future.

Since The Asher wasn't very far from Lothbury, Andreas decided not to take his horse. The animal was big and snappish at times, and he didn't want to have to worry about it as they traveled over the bridge spanning the River Thames and in the close quarters of Southwark. He only wanted to worry about his companionship, so he departed Lothbury through the fortified gatehouse and spilled out into the London street beyond. The Asher was about a half-mile east of him, so he headed off in that direction, anticipating the day more than he had anticipated anything in a very long time.

Gavriella.

The smile on his face seemed to be permanent.

CHAPTER NINE

Falstone Castle

"**I** UNDERSTAND THAT you are asking about my daughter, Harman. What do you want with her?"

Harman the Wise stood in the bailey of Falstone Castle, a compact but heavily fortified castle with an enormous yew tree growing up in the center of the bailey. Everything about Falstone was circular – the wall, the keep – with the outbuildings nestled inside. Situated just over the Scotland side of the border with England, it gave the impression of a place hunkered down on itself, expecting trouble at any moment.

As the wind kicked up the dust of the bailey around him, Harman was at the base of the stairs that led up into the keep, with Merek standing at the top. Harman had arrived at Falstone several minutes earlier, asking to see the Lord of Falstone and sending a servant for the man with one simple phrase – *I am inquiring on the health of the lord's daughter.*

Now, he had his attention.

Merek de Leia was a big man with big blue eyes and as bald as a newborn babe. He wasn't very sociable, or even very likable, but he was a fair man in all things and he had a well-trained and well-supplied army, which was essential this close to the Scots border. He was known to be a good but cautious battle commander.

But Harman hadn't come about armies or Scots.

He had come to speak with Merek about his daughter.

"My lord," he said, mounting the steps. "I have come on a most urgent matter. I must speak with you."

Merek eyed him. "About what? My daughter? You have already seen her, Harman. She does not require any more of your attention. She is… well."

"I did not come to inquire about her health."

"Then why were you asking for her?"

"What I have to say about her could be a matter of life and death. Will you speak with me now?"

Merek was reluctant. That was clear. "What could you possibly know about life or death for my daughter?"

"If you will speak with me, then you will know."

Merek's gaze drifted over him for a moment before finally grunting, which Harman took to be an affirmative, and headed inside.

Harman followed.

The interior of the rounded keep was dark and dusty, smelling like dogs. In fact, there were dogs everywhere, wandering in and out of doorways as Harman followed Merek into a chamber directly off the entry.

There were dogs in there, too.

It was Merek's large and cluttered solar. Merek had to push some of the bigger dogs out of the way, who milled around him, looking for scraps, before wandering over to Harman in search of handouts. Harman ignored the dogs, even when they jumped up on him. He simply pushed them down.

"Now," Merek said as he sat heavily in a chair next to a big cluttered table. "What's this about my daughter? And know that I am only speaking to you because of my respect for you as a physic and the fact that you have tended to my men on occasion. Were you anyone else, I would have thrown you from the walls myself."

Harman wasn't intimidated. If the de Soulis bastards couldn't frighten him, Merek de Leia certainly couldn't.

"My lord, I will come to the point," he said. "I had a disturbing visit recently by John and Nicholas de Soulis. They were asking me if I had delivered a child this past spring at Falstone Castle, specifically, from your daughter. I told them that I had not. Now, let me state that I pass no judgment upon your daughter or upon your family. It is none of my affair. But Nicholas and John want that infant. And they want your daughter, too. Is she here?"

Merek stared at him a moment before his features contorted with confusion. "*Want* them?" he repeated. "Want them for what?"

Harman could see that Merek wasn't taking the situation seriously. Whether it was confusion or lack of caring, he couldn't be sure. "My lord, I must impress upon you the seriousness of what I am about to tell you. I overheard them speaking of getting their hands on the infant your daughter delivered to fulfill some sort of prophesy. I do not know what it is, but they want the child and they want your daughter. If it is de Soulis, you know it can only be for unspeakable things. You must protect your daughter and the babe from them. They plan to have me smuggle the child out of Falstone and give it over to them, but I will not do it. That means I need your protection. My wife and I must come to Falstone. Do you understand what I am telling you?"

Merek blinked slowly, clearly in disbelief. "My God," he finally muttered. "It really *was* them."

Harman was watching the man closely. "What do you mean?"

Merek glanced at him with some suspicion, but that stance quickly faded. He stood up, running his hand over his bald head, his features twisting with disbelief.

"They told her not to speak of the incident, but she did," he mumbled. "She did not listen. She even drew the brand she'd seen on one of the horses. I knew it was them all along."

Harman was becoming puzzled. "Are you speaking of the men who abducted your daughter from Deadwater?"

Pain rippled across Merek's face. "Aye."

Harman knew that, too. The entire village knew it after the brand Lady Gavriella had drawn had been circulated, mostly to warn the villagers that the House of de Soulis was on the prowl again. In years past, they'd been known to burn, loot, pillage, and rape, but those incidents had died down for a while.

It was a genuine fear that they might be resuming their harassment.

Harman prayed not.

"My lord, when it happened, why did you not summon the Constable of the North?" he asked. "Why not punish de Soulis for what they did?"

Merek looked at him in anger. Then defeat. That defeat moved on to confusion. "You would not understand."

"I understand that your daughter was attacked," he said quietly. "But I also understand that you did nothing about it. Why?"

Merek suddenly slammed a fist against the table, rattling everything upon it. "You will not judge me," he boomed. "My daughter bears the shame of that attack, not de Soulis. It is my daughter who shamed the House of de Leia and summoning the constable to punish de Soulis? It would be useless. The House of de Wolfe is caught up in the troubles on the borders right now and this would be considered a personal matter, so I would plead my case, which everyone would hear, only to be denied."

Harman didn't agree with him. "Then you do nothing to help her?"

Merek glared at him, teeth clenched. "To help her is to let this incident fade away as if it never happened," he growled. "To help her is to let this lie. It will be forgotten, eventually."

"But you have an army…"

"I have an army of eight hundred men," he shouted like a man who had wrestled with this exact question too many times to count. "I cannot take Hell's Guardhouse with only eight hundred men. It would be futile and I would lose many men in the attempt. What happened to my daughter was… unfortunate. Of course I am outraged. But I am outraged that she allowed it to happen and to punish de Soulis would mean starting a war with him that I cannot win. And he knows it."

Harman was at a loss. He simply couldn't understand the man's perspective of his daughter's participation in an attack. "My lord, I do not believe your daughter allowed anything to happen," he said. "I was told there were several men who abducted her from the village. She had no control. But is certain that de Soulis knows about the child and now he wants it. Mayhap he even did this deliberately. Even if you will not seek vengeance for what has happened to your daughter, surely you will not let them take her or the child."

Merek seemed to calm unnaturally fast, but he still looked like a man who was struggling with the weight of the world on his shoulders. "She is not here," he said, sounded exhausted. "The child is not here. I have sent them both away so there is nothing to be concerned with. They are gone and this situation shall pass. It will be forgotten. Things like this always are."

Harman though that Merek was relying quite a bit on the hope that the situation would just go away by itself. But given what he had heard from the de Soulis father and son, he wasn't so certain that was the case.

He just wasn't sure what more he could say.

"I have come here to warn you about their plans, my lord," he said. "I hope that I did not waste my breath. Your daughter and the child need your protection, not your apathy. Do you truly wish to see John de Soulis get his hands on your daughter and grandchild? You know his unsavory reputation. You know what the man is capable of."

Merek simply nodded. "It does not matter," he said. "She is gone and the child is gone. I thank you for your concern, Harman."

Harman couldn't help the disgust he was feeling as he looked at Merek. "My concern is for myself, too," he said. "I will bring my wife to Falstone and you will protect us from de Soulis. The man intends to kill me because he has involved me in the situation. I know things that I should not know."

"Then fetch your wife and return at another time. But for now, you will go."

Harman was being dismissed. Baffled at the man's reaction to the situation, he did as he was told and left Falstone Castle, wondering if fear of the strength of de Soulis was truly outweighing de Leia's sense of responsibility to his daughter.

I have sent them both away so there is nothing to be concerned with.

That was only one concern of many in this dangerous situation. Sending his daughter away could have meant anything, anywhere, but he was clear that de Leia thought that would solve the entire problem. Was the man truly living in such denial? But Harman wasn't going to try to figure him out. He'd done what he'd come to Falstone to do – the rest was up to Merek de Leia.

And God.

Harman made his way back to Deadwater on the little pony he'd had for twenty years. It had been a foal when he'd first come into possession of it, given to him by a man in payment for treatment Harman performed on the man's wife. It was a sturdy little pony and Harman treated it like one of the family. The animal had its own room attached to Harman's cottage where the little beast was kept warm and fed well.

Harman and his little pony made it home in time for supper.

Two days later, however, the door to his little cottage burst open at dawn.

Harman's wife, who had been preparing a morning meal at the hearth, shrieked when the heavily armed men entered the little cottage. Harman was with his pony, feeding it, but he heard the commotion and came inside to see John sitting at his table while Nicholas had stolen the loaf of bread Harman's wife had made for their meal. He was shoving it in his mouth when Harman entered the common room.

"My lords," he greeted, clearly displeased at the chaos they were creating. "You are always welcome in my home. Will you break your fast with us?"

He was politely inviting them to a meal. As if he had any choice. John yawned, putting a leg on the table and scattering the utensils that were there, as Nicholas continued to stuff bread in his mouth.

"I was told you went to Falstone a couple of days ago," John said casually. "Undoubtedly, you know my men are watching this village. And you. They knew you went to Falstone. Tell me what you discovered and mind you leave nothing out."

Harman came to stand by his wife, who was very nervously cooking their meal. "I asked about the children born there during the spring, as you instructed," he said. "I came away with some interesting news. It seems that Lord de Leia sent his daughter and the child away."

Nicholas frowned. "Away?" he repeated. "Away *where*?"

Harman shook his head. "I asked, but no one could tell me," he said. "I was only told that they had been sent away."

Nicholas' frown turned into a scowl as he looked at his father. "Why would he do that?" he demanded. "He was not supposed to send them away!"

John was far calmer than his son. In truth, he didn't seem all that surprised. "So de Leia rids himself of his daughter and the bastard child," he said thoughtfully. "To a nunnery, I wonder?"

"Or mayhap there is a grandmother, somewhere, to watch over them," Harman suggested.

John looked at the old man. "And you know nothing about de Leia's family or allies that might take in a daughter and her child?"

Harman shook his head. "I received the impression that Lord de Leia kept the girl… confined, shall we say," he said. "She was not free to run about, probably kept locked in a chamber until the child was born. Once it was delivered, Lord de Leia sent them both away."

John stroked his chin. "I wonder why," he said after a moment. "A dutiful father would keep his child with him, protecting her."

"Lord de Leia does not seem to have the protective instinct when it comes to his daughter," Harman said, realizing he might have given away more than he intended. He didn't want John to know he'd spoken directly to Merek. "At least, that seems to be the general opinion at Falstone."

John mulled over the information for a few long moments before removing his leg from the table. "I do not suppose it would do any good to send you back there to find out where he has sent his daughter and the child," he said. "De Leia has no reason to tell you. He would think you were trying to probe him for information and he might become suspicious."

"That is true, my lord."

John didn't say anything more after that. He simply sat there as Nicholas, still unhappy, finished up the loaf of bread. Harman wasn't sure what more he could tell the pair, but something told him this wasn't finished. John and Nicholas had their answers, but not satisfactory ones.

"Well," John finally said. "It seems to me that we must discover where they have gone and if Harman the Wise cannot discover that for us, then we must send someone to Falstone who can."

He really wasn't speaking to Harman at that point, but to his son. Nicholas swallowed the last bite in his mouth.

"Who?" Nicholas said. "I surely cannot go."

John shook his head. "Not you," he said as if his son were an idiot. "I suppose I could take an entire army there, lay siege, and demand answers, but that would take too much time and effort and money. Nay, we must be more subtle than that. A spy, in fact. Someone we can send as a traveler seeking respite or a devoted servant, a gift from one of the de Leia allies. Someone who can ask the right questions of de Leia and find out answers."

Nicholas frowned. "Directly ask him?"

"He is the one who knows."

That was true. Nicholas noticed that there was a covered dish on the table, one his father had missed kicking off when he'd put his leg upon the table, and he pulled off the cloth to reveal boiled eggs underneath. He began stuffing them in his mouth.

"Then you send someone to get close to de Leia," he said, his mouth full. "The man isn't married, so mayhap we send a mistress to him. A woman who can get into his bed and into his mind. Women can work wonders on men if they are skilled enough."

John looked at him as if a thought had just struck him. "Giddy."

Nicholas' eyebrows lifted. "You feel giddy?" he said before he realized what his father meant. "Do you mean Giddy Garwald?"

John nodded. "The same," he said. "The woman can suck the steel off a sword. She'd discover what we want to know, straight from de Leia himself."

Nicholas knew the woman his father was speaking of – a loose woman from a local village who had warmed John's bed many a time. She was a little older, a little rounder and fuller, but she was pretty. And she knew how to use her mouth and what God gave her between her legs.

Given enough money, the perfect spy.

John smiled as if quite pleased with himself.

"A few coins to Giddy and she'll do as I ask," he said as he stood up from the table. "In fact, there's an apothecary in Gretna Green who has all manner of potions. Potions for truth, among other things. If Giddy's feminine wiles do not work on de Leia, then mayhap we can find a potion that will do the job for her. We'll send her on to Falstone well-armed. She'll find out what we want to know."

Nicholas simply nodded, grabbing more boiled eggs, as John grabbed his son and pulled him from the cottage without another word to Harman. They simply left, slamming the door behind them.

But that wasn't the end of it.

John had spoken of his plans in front of Harman, which had been careless, but in hindsight, he didn't really care. The old man was no longer of any value to him, so the moment Harman delivered his information, he had outlived his worth. It didn't matter if Harman had heard them speak of the whore named Giddy because the old man wasn't going to live to see the sunset.

John paused before he mounted his horse.

"Barricade every door, every window, and light the cottage on fire," he said. "It would not do for Harman the Wise to tell Merek de Leia what he knows."

Nicholas wasn't distressed by the command in the least. They had about twenty men with them, so he sent some to light torches and still others to barricade the doors and windows of the cottage, which shared a common wall with another cottage. Anything they lit on fire would carry to other homes.

But that didn't matter to Nicholas or the de Soulis men – they did as they were told.

Harman must have sensed that something terrible was going to happen because he and his wife slipped out of the cottage through the rear, through the pony's chamber, taking the little beast with them. They had only what they could carry, moving far enough away that John and Nicholas could not have seen them.

Then, they stayed to the shadows and watched. It wasn't long before they saw men swarming their little cottage, barricading doors, tossing lit torches in through the windows. The cottage went up in flames remarkably fast as Harman grabbed hold of his wife with one hand, the pony with the other, and made their way out of the village to the southeast. They had their lives, but de Soulis thought they were dead, so it was best that they leave – *permanently.*

He thought about returning to Falstone to tell Lord de Leia what John de Soulis had planned for him. He considered it carefully. But if valuable information involving the life of his daughter didn't move the man, surely the plan to send a spy to discover her location wouldn't move him, either.

Harman didn't feel inclined to help Merek de Leia one way or the other.

He headed east.

Back at Deadwater, the de Soulis men ended up burning down nearly half the village that day.

CHAPTER TEN

London

S HE COULD SEE him across the street.

Gavriella's heart leapt into her throat when she realized Andreas was across the street, waiting for her just as he said he would.

He's here!

Truthfully, she'd been watching for at least two hours. Ever since she had woken up next to Camilla about three hours after she closed her eyes. It wasn't nearly enough sleep, but she had been too excited, too nervous, to go back to sleep, fearful she would sleep all day and miss something she very much wanted to attend…

Andreas.

It was funny how that fearful, quiet, nervous woman who had arrived at The Asher not long ago was now starting to come out of her shell. Before she met Andreas, meeting a man she'd only just become acquainted with for an unchaperoned excursion would have been unheard of. She was fearful and jumpy, and suspicious of every man she saw. But somehow over the past several hours, that had changed.

The man she saw from her window didn't threaten her at

all.

Now came the matter of breaking out of the fortress-like manse.

From the jaunt last night, Gavriella knew where the postern gate was, but she had to go through the maze-like corridors of the house to get there and she wasn't entirely sure that she could. The only other alternative was the main entry door. The Asher was surrounded by an enormous curtain wall, but the entire front part of the manse was on the street. It wasn't set back from the avenue, nor was there a wall between the front door and the main street where people were going about their business. The entry door was right on the street, an enormous iron structure built into the wattle and daub walls.

Fortunately, she was already dressed and waiting for him.

But that had been an odyssey unto itself.

When Gavriella had awakened after those rough few hours of slumber, Camilla had still been asleep, snoring softly in the feather-filled bed. Listening to the faint sounds of the street outside mingling with the snoring, Gavriella had crept out of bed and went about dressing very quietly.

Her first order of business had been to bolt the chamber door. She didn't know where Aurelia was and the last thing she wanted was for that woman to enter the chamber just as she was getting dressed for a rather scandalous meeting. She didn't want to have to explain herself to Aurelia, especially not after the fight they'd had, so Gavriella had gone about dressing very quickly in the hopes of avoiding Aurelia altogether.

She also had a special reason for wanting to avoid her – she didn't want Aurelia to see that she was wearing one of Camilla's dresses, in yet another dress to potentially ruin. Gavriella had no real need for fine clothing in the north because her father's castle was in a rural setting and it wasn't as if their lives were a gay social whirl. In fact, it was quite the contrary.

Because of this, Gavriella owned just a couple of good dresses and she had already worn those several times since she had arrived in London. Both of those dresses had been taken to the laundry and she had nothing left but the simple broadcloth dresses she had brought with her, and quite frankly, she didn't want to wear those plain and unassuming garments for Andreas.

She wanted to look pretty.

Which meant she had to borrow another dress.

Therefore, Gavriella was very quiet as she opened Camilla's wardrobe and pawed through the dresses that were hanging on the pegs. She didn't want to wear one of the really nice garments, expensive with gold and jewels, but she wanted one that was better than her simple broadcloth. She found a red garment, made of a lightweight wool and a sheer white shift that was worn underneath it. It seemed simple enough, without any adornment, so she pulled on the shift, which was very nearly transparent, and the red dress over it.

Being that Camilla's father was an earl, her bedchamber was well equipped, including a bronze mirror that was about five feet high. It was positioned on the wall next to the dressing table and Gavriella went to look at herself in her borrowed garments. With her fair skin and blonde hair, the rich red dress looked absolutely stunning on her. Because Camilla was a little smaller than she was, the dress was snug, but it made her look quite delectable.

In fact, Gavriella had never seen herself look so… beautiful.

It was a little startling. As she ran her hands over the material, she realized that although the design was simple, the material was, in fact, expensive and the dress very well made. This was no cheap piece of clothing. It had a low neckline with the shift peeking out and long sleeves with cutouts so the nearly transparent shift could be seen underneath. The bodice was snug to her hips whereupon the skirt flared quite beautifully. In truth, it was magnificent.

And she looked magnificent in it.

Feeling confident in the lovely garment for the first time in ever so long, Gavriella combed and braided her hair, draping the braid over her right shoulder and tying it off with a red silk ribbon she found on Camilla's dressing table. The thrill of looking pretty was something she hadn't felt in a very long time. She'd just spent the past year feeling ashamed and ugly, and this was the first time in many months that she actually felt attractive and young and alive.

There was something in her that desperately wanted to live a normal life again.

Emboldened by the lovely dress, Gavriella went to her satchel and found a silk purse very deep at the bottom that contained her jewelry. She pulled forth a large golden cross on a long chain that she put over her head. Fine leather slippers went on her feet and she fastened her coin purse to a golden belt that she draped over her hips. The belt also belonged to Camilla and she silently thanked her cousin for her generosity. She knew she was going to have some explaining to do when she returned home but, at the moment, she wasn't concerned about it.

She was only concerned about the excitement in her heart.

She was blind to all else.

Fully dressed in the lovely red clothing, Gavriella then stood by the windows overlooking the street outside and watched for that tall, blond man who had been part of the eventful evening the night before. As she waited, she relived the night over and over in her mind, thinking on the very moment she met him up until he brought her home at dawn.

She thought about their conversations and about his bravery as he had pulled her from the Thames. More and more, she was feeling incredibly foolish about impulsively jumping in the river. But as she explained to Andreas, she really didn't know why she did it. All she knew was that every event in her life over the past year had built up to that moment and she was desperate to escape it, however stupidly.

But she didn't feel like escaping it anymore.

She felt something she hadn't felt in a very long time – *hope*.

Just as the wait was becoming torturous, Andreas finally made an appearance and Gavriella left the window and rushed to the mirror for one final look at herself. She turned for the door when something on her cousin's dressing table caught her eye; a golden headband that had a white gossamer veil carefully stitched to it twinkled in the dim light.

It was a headpiece that a proper maiden would wear and, impulsively, she put it on. With the gold glittering in the light and the soft veil trailing just past her shoulders, she looked prettier than she had ever looked in her life. She wanted Andreas to think so, too.

God, she needed this, more than she'd ever needed anything.

Dressed and ready, Gavriella made her way to the chamber door and unbolted it, quietly cracking it open.

The corridor outside seemed to be still and quiet, so she stepped out of the chamber and silently shut the door. She was acutely aware that Aurelia's chamber was right next door and she tiptoed past it, moving as swiftly as she could without making a sound. Since the entry door of the manse was directly below, Gavriella silently made her way down the staircase to the reception hall below.

There were a few servants moving about, but they didn't pay any attention to her as she went to the front door and threw the bolt. Pulling the door open, she was immediately confronted by two armed soldiers, but they did nothing more than shut the door behind her as she walked out. No questions, no comments. Their job was to guard the door, and guard it they had. Their job was not to question a young woman who was coming out of the manse, unescorted.

But that didn't stop them from giving her a queer look.

Oblivious to the expressions of the soldiers, Gavriella was focused on Andreas across the wide avenue. He was literally all she saw. The man had been watching the front door and when she came through, he came across the street and met her right in the middle.

For a moment, they simply looked at each other. All they had really seen of each other since their acquaintance had been in dark chambers or in the fog, or in fire-lit rooms. Never out in the sunlight where they could get a good look at one another. From the dark, dank night to the bright light of day, it was literally a world of difference.

And the difference was staggering.

"Greetings, my lady," Andreas said after a moment, a smile playing on his lips. "I am pleased to see that you thought enough of me to keep our engagement."

Gavriella smiled broadly. "And I am pleased you thought the same," she said. "Truthfully, you look quite different than you did last night. I hardly recognized you without all of the bulky things you were wearing."

He laughed softly, the dimples in his cheeks carving deep. "That is my usual attire," he said, holding out his arms to show off his fine clothing. "I confess that this does not belong to me, but to my uncle, who is a diplomat for the king. He forced me to wear it. Something about women liking men in fine clothing and not men who looked like they just crawled off a battlefield. I think he is mad, but I took his advice nonetheless."

Gavriella laughed softly because he'd spoken in a jesting manner. "Did he really say that to you?"

Andreas' smile was broad. "He did not," he said. "I just

thought to say it to mayhap gain your sympathy. A fighting man does *not* dress like this, as a rule."

Her gray eyes glimmered at him. "You'll find no sympathy here," she said. "You look very fine. I like it very much."

"Thank you," he said sincerely, his gaze moving up and down her thoroughly exquisite dress. "As do you. I… I find myself speechless, my lady. When I met you last night, I had no idea that… well, all I can say is that surely the angels are jealous of your glory."

Gavriella's cheeks turned a soft shade of pink. "You are very kind," she said. "But I stole this from my cousin because I did not have anything pretty to wear, so mayhap we can move along now? I would hate for her to come running after me and demand I return everything."

He offered her an elbow. "I would hate that, as well," he said. "Hurry, let's run for it."

Gavriella giggled and took his elbow, clutching him tightly as they began to walk swiftly down the road. Andreas took a turn at the first smaller street they came to, disappearing from the view of The Asher.

But it wasn't fast enough.

Neither one of them saw the face in the window on the first floor, looking out over the street. Had they noticed, they would have seen Aurelia watching them run off together. The very sister who had insisted on attending Gomorrah, who adored men, and was threatened by her beautiful cousin now had a reason to hate her.

A reason to be vindictive.

Aurelia had always been the queen of The Asher. She had male suitors and considered herself the most sought-after woman in London. She certainly wasn't willing to relinquish that title to any country mouse. She'd heard her cousin stirring in the next chamber and it had been enough to get her out of bed. She'd even heard Gavriella slip out of the chamber and down the stairs. She'd moved to the window just in time to see her cousin run across the street to meet a man who was perhaps the most handsome man Aurelia had ever seen.

Jealousy consumed her.

She wasn't going to let Gavriella get away with it.

She went to find her mother.

"THERE," ANDREAS SAID, slowing his pace once they were out of sight from The Asher. "We are safe now. No one can see us from your cousin's house."

Gavriella grinned, still holding on to his elbow. "Thankfully," she said. "I will admit that Camilla is not the issue. I am sure she would not mind that I borrowed her things. It is her older sister that I am worried about."

"Was this the cousin who dragged you to Gomorrah last night?"

"The same."

The fact that she was still holding on to his elbow wasn't lost on Andreas. In fact, he felt like a puffed-up peacock with her on his arm. He'd never felt like that in his life, so this was something of a new experience for him. He was struggling not to feel giddy about it.

"And you are here visiting?"

Gavriella nodded. "I am," she said. "Truthfully, I do not even know my cousins very well. I live so far away that I have rarely seen them in my lifetime, so they are essentially strangers. There are Aurelia and Camilla, and it is Aurelia who seems to be quite… bold."

"Like going to Gomorrah."

"Exactly."

They walked a few more feet as Andreas contemplated what to say next to her. He really only knew her name but nothing more and, understandably, he was quite curious.

"As I said last night," he said. "London is much different from a small village in the north. I suspect where you come from is far more sedate than this."

Gavriella was looking around, noticing the people, feeling more curious about her surroundings than she had since she had arrived in London.

"Sedate enough," she said. "I must admit that I have been very curious about London. Where I come from, people speak of London as if it is located on the moon. Far away and mysterious."

"Have you not been here before, then?"

"When I was a child, but I do not remember much," she said. "My father and my cousins' mother are brother and sister, so my father and I came for some kind of family event. I do not even recall what it was."

He glanced over at her, studying the delicate contours of her face. "Here is the part where I would naturally ask you where you came from and what your family name is," he said. "May I do so?"

She looked at him, perhaps a little coyly. "I think the only moderately enjoyable thing about Gomorrah was the fact that everyone was anonymous," she said. "It's rather fun not knowing who you're talking to. That means I can imagine a background for you. For all I know, you could be a prince."

He grinned. "Or a pauper."

"Exactly," she said. "And I could be a princess of France or I could be the daughter of the most wicked man in England. But you will never know if you only know me by my first name."

He laughed softly. "So you wish to continue that way for now?"

She grinned because he was. "It is rather fun, isn't it?" she said. "Mayhap we should only ask questions of each other with an 'aye' or 'nay' answer."

He was up for the game. "Very well," he said. "You ask first."

She thought on that briefly. "Are you a prince?"

He burst out laughing. "Nay," he insisted. "Why? Do I look like one?"

She shrugged, caught up in the man's charm. "Possibly," she said. "That is my point; one can never tell."

"That is true," he said. "Now it is my turn."

"Go ahead."

"Are you the daughter of the most wicked man in England?"

She snorted. "I am not, I swear."

"That is good to know."

They were nearing the river at this point, the smell of fish and brine heavy in the breeze. Up ahead was Thames Street, which paralleled the river, and they turned right when they came to the street. It was a busier avenue, full of people going about their business at midday. But Andreas wasn't paying any attention to the hustle and bustle; his attention was on the woman at his side.

"Well?" he said. "Any more questions of me?"

Gavriella realized she'd been off daydreaming about the handsome man next to her, now slightly embarrassed that she'd let the conversation fall off.

"Well," she said thoughtfully. "I suppose general questions are acceptable. For example, what might your favorite food be?"

It was a very tame question, considering the depth of his character and life experience, but he went along with it gladly.

"I like a good roast of beef," he said. "When I was a lad, we had a good deal of mutton and I cannot stand the smell or taste of it any longer. Beef is my favorite."

"Mine, too," Gavriella said. "Mutton always tastes like an old shoe to me."

He chuckled. "That is very true," he said. "That is something else we have in common."

"Something else?"

"In addition to our distain of Gomorrah."

Gavriella laughed softly. "That is a most important one," she said. "It is certainly something I will not miss about this place when I return home."

He looked at her, then. "Are you planning on leaving soon?"

Her good humor faded a little. "I am not certain," she said. "My father sent me here to… to spend time with my aunt and cousins. To rest a little, mayhap experience different things that I would not experience in my village. He thought the change might be good for me. And you? Are you a permanent resident here?"

He shook his head. "I am not," he said. "I had come on business for my father, but we are to return soon."

"How soon?"

He looked at her, his gaze intense. "We were to depart tomorrow," he said. "But now I am not entirely sure I wish to leave yet."

A bashful smile played on her lips and she averted her gaze.

Andreas was completely enchanted.

They had reached an intersection of another major avenue, called Bridge Street, which led right to the greater London Bridge that spanned the Thames.

It was bustling with people.

"Hold tightly to me, my lady," he said. "We enter the den of pickpockets and thieves. If they see you with me, they will be less likely to try anything unsavory."

Gavriella looked at the bridge. It was lined with structures on either side of it, some of them precariously built, and it was jammed with people. So very many people. It was like looking down the throat of a mighty beast. She looked at Andreas rather nervously, but he smiled encouragingly.

Her grip tightened.

They began their foray onto the bridge, which was essentially just another neighborhood as far as neighborhoods went. There were people everywhere as they passed by men and women conducting trade right on the bridge. One man was selling baby chicks while still another was selling bundled herbs. People were coming out of their leaning homes to buy things from these street vendors as Gavriella watched most curiously.

"I will admit I've never actually come near this bridge," she said. "It's almost its own little city."

Andreas was watching everything around him – every person, every move. He didn't like the close quarters of the bridge. The knight in him was on high alert.

"It is," he said, eyeing a vagrant who was sleeping against a wall holding a big, dull knife in his hands. "All of the troubles of a city, too, I am certain."

Gavriella wasn't entirely oblivious to what he meant. She'd seen trouble enough last year in Deadwater and therefore knew the meaning of trouble.

She moved a little closer to him.

"I'm curious," she said, pulling her skirt away from a dirty man who wandered too close. "Is that what you see when you look at a city? Trouble? You said the same thing last night."

The same man Gavriella had pulled her skirt away from was still too close and Andreas reached out a massive hand, shoving the man away by the head. He was evidently drunk and toppled over quite easily.

"I am a knight, my lady," he said. "I've been taught to view the entire world from that perspective. Everything is potential trouble, everywhere. One must be vigilant."

Gavriella watched the drunken man roll around on his back for a moment before returning her attention to Andreas.

"You have seen many battles, then? As a knight, I mean."

He nodded. "Too many to count," he said, eyeing her. "Are you sure you do not want to know my family name and where I live?"

She grinned, shaking her head. "There is no fun to it if you come out and tell me," she said. "Let me continue to ask the proper questions and see if I can discover the truth for myself."

He fought off a smile. "Very well," he said. "You already know what my favorite food is. What else would you know?"

"Are you from Cumbria?"

"Nay. Are you?"

"Nay."

"Yorkshire?"

"Nay. And you?"

"Nay. Where was your first battle, as a knight?"

He cocked his head thoughtfully. "As a knight? A nasty skirmish in Wales."

She looked at him. "Were you injured?"

He shook his head. "Nay," he said. "But I have seen friends and family injured in battle, or worse."

"What was the worst battle you've ever seen?"

Andreas thought on that. There had been so many, some he still wasn't ready to speak of. The battle in Wales that he had mentioned was one of them. His uncle, James de Wolfe, had been cut down and left for dead. In fact, the entire family thought the man was dead until he reappeared years later with no knowledge of his previous life. Andreas had been there on that horrible day, watching his grandfather as he'd held his uncle's bloodied, beaten body and wept while Andreas and other de Wolfe knights fought to save themselves and him. It was at Llandeilo, something he tried hard to forget.

Therefore, he still couldn't speak on it.

"Every battle is bad," he said, glancing at her. "I cannot extrapolate the degree of one battle against another. Suffice it to say that I have seen many battles, all of them terrible, in my twenty years as a knight."

"That is a long time to see such terrible things."

He smiled faintly. "It is my vocation and the vocation of my father and grandfather," he said. "There was never any question as to what I would become as an adult. I trained in some very fine houses and I have learned a great deal. I would wager to say that I am probably the smartest man in the world."

He said it in an exaggerated way that had Gavriella giggling. "I would believe that," she said. "I, too, fostered in an excellent home, but my reading education came from my father."

"The man with the love of books?"

She nodded. "He has a great love of literature and poetry," she said. "I must confess that when I was younger, I would act them out. The tale of Orpheus and Eurydice is my favorite."

Andreas' eyes squinted as he recalled the tale. "Where Orpheus goes into the Underworld to find her?"

"Exactly," she said. Then, she sighed. "Imagine having someone who loved you so much that they would go into the Underworld for you. That would be a devoted love."

"Indeed," Andreas agreed. "But he lost her again when he disobeyed Hades."

She shook her head. "I never understood why he did that," she said. "Hades told him not to look at her as they were departing. Why would he disobey him?"

"Because his trust was not strong enough," he said. "Orpheus loved Eurydice deeply, but his trust was not strong enough. That makes him unworthy of her and of their love."

Gavriella frowned. "But he loved Eurydice so much that he risked everything to find her. Trust has nothing to do with it."

"Trust has everything to do with it."

She eyed him, perhaps appraisingly. "I can see that you have your own strong opinions about things."

"My opinions are always right."

She was trying not to smile at that. "Come, now," she scolded softly. "Are you telling me you have never been wrong about anything in your life?"

"Not that I can recall."

"You're perfect, then?"

He paused for effect. "Aye."

She started laughing. Andreas grinned as well, his free hand coming up to grasp the fingers at clutching his elbow. He squeezed them and she continued to giggle, only now it was because he was fondling her fingers and she was loving it. It was a delightful, flirty moment.

They were nearing the end of the bridge as it dumped into Southwark. This was a less populated part of the city, but the entire area was owned by the church. There was Southwark Cathedral, a massive place, and other centers and residences that were linked to the church officials, but the one place they didn't have any jurisdiction over was an area called the Liberty of Winchester, which was an area that combined a low-rent district with merchants and open areas where minstrels and actors would ply their trades.

They came off the bridge and headed for this area. They could already hear music from the gangs of minstrels and entertainers. It was crowded with people, with children running about and dogs wandering, and people eating and enjoying the entertainment that was going on.

It was magical.

Gavriella kept straining to get a look at what was going on. She'd never seen such things in her life and it was all quite exciting. As they were entering the quarter, they passed by a man with a cart that was full of bronze pieces – little statues, jewelry, and even toys. There were also pieces of brass and as Andreas and Gavriella walked past, the man suddenly jumped out in front of them.

"Your lady needs something beautiful to wear, my lord," he said. Immediately, he held up a bracelet with red stones and yellow metal. "Look! This matches her dress!"

He was mostly standing in front of Gavriella and she let go of Andreas and moved to his other side, taking his arm and pulling him away.

"Come along," she said firmly.

Andreas was actually looking at the bracelet. "In a moment," he said, plucking the bracelet out of the man's grip. He held it up into the light. "What is this?"

"Carnelian, my lord," the man said eagerly, hoping to make a sale. "I've set it in brass. It shows off the stone, don't you think?"

Gavriella frowned as Andreas looked at the other things on his cart. "Are you a metal worker?"

The man nodded. He was short, round, with dirty dark hair and several teeth missing. "I used to work for Rothschild the Goldsmith," he said. "You know the one – there is a large establishment on Thames Street."

"But you work there no longer?"

The man shook his head. "Rothschild's son took over for his father when the man fell ill," he said. "He sent many of us along our way. Now I must make my own living with the skills I have been taught."

Andreas could see that the man's work was fine. He evidently couldn't afford the more expensive metals, but he did a beautiful job with the ones he could afford. But he put the bracelet down.

"I will not pay for brass or bronze," he said. "It will turn the skin green."

The man held up his hand as if to beg patience as he rushed to the other side of his cart, digging around in the side of it. Quickly, he pulled forth a silk pouch and came back around the cart, unwrapping what was in the pouch. He held it up for Andreas to see.

"I do have some good pieces, my lord," he said. "This is gold, very precious, with a red ruby in the middle and two pearls on the end. 'Tis a very fine piece."

Andreas took it from the man, inspecting it closely. It was a brooch, about three inches long and about an inch wide. The gold work on it was exquisite filigree, with a round, red ruby in the center of it and two lush pearls on either side. Each corner of it had a rose pattern worked into the metal.

He'd never seen finer.

"How much?" he asked.

The man was working his hands nervously. "Five pounds, my lord."

Andreas immediately handed it back. "I can buy a horse for that."

He turned for Gavriella, who was standing there with an expression of angst on her face. The man ran after him.

"Three pounds!" he said. "It was made for your lady, my lord. It will make her beautiful!"

Andreas came to a halt and turned to him sharply, his eyes narrowing. "She is already beautiful," he said. "There is nothing you can sell me that will make her any more magnificent than she already is."

The man could see that he'd angered the knight, possibly

blowing the sale. "I meant… I meant her dress, my lord," he said, gesturing in Gavriella's direction. "It would look beautiful upon her dress. It matches."

He was right. Andreas considered his offer. "Two pounds."

"Three pounds and I include a pearl bracelet to match."

That gave Andreas pause. He opened his mouth to reply but Gavriella's gentle hand grasped him.

"Please do not buy it for me," she said softly. "Keep your money, my lord. I do not need such a thing."

He looked at her, seeing that angsty expression again, as if fearful he were going to do something she didn't want him to do. In this case, buy her jewelry. They didn't even know each other very well and, already, he was considering buying her a very expensive piece of jewelry.

She was uncomfortable about it.

He felt a little foolish.

"Put it away," he told the man. "Let me think on it. If I want it, I will return before the day is out."

The man was disappointed, but not entirely destroyed. With a nod of resignation, he went to put the piece away as Andreas turned to Gavriella, took her hand, and tucked it into his elbow.

They continued on.

"What makes you think I was buying those things for you?" he said as they entered an area with merchants. "I could be buying it for my mother, you know."

She looked at him, horrified that the thought hadn't occurred to her. "I… I am so very sorry, my lord," she said. "I did not…"

He put up a hand to silence her, his gaze warm. "I am jesting with you," he said. "Of course it was for you. A token of my appreciation that you took the time to spend the day with me."

She was relieved, but she was also touched. "You did not

have to do that," she said. "You do me a greater honor by escorting me here. That is gift enough."

His gaze lingered on her. "And I still cannot ask you your family name and where you live?"

She flushed, looking away from him. "I thought we agreed that a little mystery was enjoyable."

He grunted, increasingly unhappy about the little game of mystery she wanted to play. He was a man of action, of instant gratification where possible, so he wondered how long he could play this game with her and not take her in his arms and kiss the truth out of her.

"As you wish," he said, frowning. "What do I know about you so far? That your name is Gavriella and you are from a small village in the north, but it is not Cumbria or Yorkshire. Then it must be Northumberland."

"I suppose it must," she said. "You?"

"That is my home, also."

They looked at each other. "Then we are neighbors," she said, pleasure in her tone. "But Northumberland is a very large place. Do you live near Newcastle?"

"Nay. Do you?"

"Nay," she said. "I have been there, however."

He was looking off to his left where there was a stall selling food and he was distracted from that line of questions. "Are you hungry?" he asked.

She looked over to where he was pointing. "I could eat something," she admitted. "I have brought my own money for such things."

He looked at her as if she'd gone mad. "Do you think I expected you to pay your own way?"

Gavriella shook her head. "Nay," she said. "I know you would want to pay, much as you wanted to purchase something from that peddler back there. I do not expect you to pay, nor do

I want you to. It is probably better if I pay for myself."

He frowned. "Why?"

She came to a halt and looked at him. "Because it would be rude of me to expect you to pay for me," she said, pulling forth her coin purse. "In fact, you paid for a chamber for me to sleep in last night and I must pay you back."

"You'll do no such thing."

She looked up from rummaging around in her coin purse. "Why not?"

"Because you were my responsibility last night," he said. "Frankly, I'm offended that you should think to pay me in return for something that was naturally my responsibility. And I invited you to come with me to see entertainment – since you are my guest, I shall pay for the excursion. I did not invite you so that you could pay your own way."

Gavriella looked at him, closely. Since they had met in front of The Asher, he'd been an utter gentleman, kind and considerate, and she had been completely giddy to be in his company. Truth be told, she was still giddy and the feeling was only growing worse. As much as she wanted to give in to those feelings and tell him everything about her, there was a nagging little part of her that was beginning to tell her that she had no business with this glorious knight.

He was too good for her.

What was she? Damaged goods? She seemed to remember her father calling her that after the attack in Deadwater. Her father had been torn between wanting to protect and support his daughter. He had been devastated that she had been violated and was now no longer a viable marital prospect. He had called her damaged goods more than once, in times when he thought she hadn't heard him.

But she had.

Now, as she looked at Andreas, those words were ringing in

her mind…

Damaged goods.

Andreas didn't deserve damaged goods and that was why, she realized with great sadness, that she couldn't let this go any further.

That meant she would pay for her meal.

It also meant that she didn't want him to know much more about her. It was as she had explained it to him – as long as he didn't know her full name and she didn't know his, they could imagine what they wanted to about each other. He could imagine that she was a virtuous young lady and perhaps she could imagine that of herself, as well. When she looked at his eyes, she saw that he was interested in her and as much as it thrilled her, it also broke her heart.

Perhaps the guessing game they had been playing wasn't such a good idea, after all.

"I realize you did not invite me to accompany you with the expectation that I should pay my own way," she said after a long moment. "But we hardly know one another and I feel that I would be taking advantage of you by allowing you to pay for everything. If I was simply another man you had invited along, would you be so quick to pay for him? Or would you let him pay for himself?"

He lifted an eyebrow. "You are not a man," he said. "You are a beautiful young woman who, I have come to see, is quite guarded at times and then quite sweet and charming at others. I wish I knew what I did to make you trust me in some instances but not in others."

Gavriella could see that he was genuinely becoming upset about her position. That wasn't what she wanted, but she was torn.

"Please," she said softly, putting her hand on his arm. "I am not trying to upset you, I promise. I just do not want you to think me demanding or spoiled should I let you pay for me. I would be a rude woman, indeed, if I did not at least thank you for your efforts and try not to cost you more than necessary. It is really as simple as that."

He calmed, a little. He put his big mitt over hers as it rested on his arm. "If I did not want to do this, I wouldn't," he said simply. "It has been a very long time since I have been in the company of such a charming lady and allowing me to pay for your meal and entertainment is truly a pleasure. Please do not take that away from me."

When he said it so nicely, of course, she couldn't. After a moment, she sighed, resigned. "As you wish," she said. "What are we to eat?"

He flashed a smile at her as he lifted her hand, kissed it, and put it back on his elbow. "I am not sure," he said. "But it had better be beef."

So much for thinking she wasn't good enough for him, that she couldn't let this situation go any further. The kiss to her hand erased any sense of determination she'd had about that. She was putty in his hands. He was so sweet and, God only knew, she needed that sweetness. She needed for someone to be kind to her.

It had been such a long time since anyone had been.

Andreas ended up leading her over to the stall where a man and woman were serving up big bowls made of bread, hollowed out and filled with boiled beef and peas and carrots in gravy. Andreas paid for three of them – two for him, one for her, and they went over to the shade of a yew tree to eat it with crude wooden spoons that had been provided.

Gavriella realized she was famished as she plowed into the food, listening to Andreas speak on the meal he'd had in the city of Bath when he had visited there not long ago. There was a great Roman influence in Bath, still with the great hot springs that the ancient Romans had built their big temples around. He'd had eggs drizzled with honey and chicken with a sauce made of fermented fish, honey, and vinegar. It sounded awful but he assured her that it was quite tasty.

When they'd finished with their meal, including eating the bread bowl, he bought them sweets that were flat rounds of dough that had been fried in fat and basted with honey. They were delicious and as they ate them, they walked along the avenue to their very first entertainment.

It was taking place on the bed of a large wagon, a movable stage that had a painted wooden backdrop. There were two men on the wagon bed, but six or seven in a group standing next to it. The group of men were singing the plot of the play as the men on the wagon bed acted it out, and Andreas took Gavriella's hand again as they watched the biblical story of Cain and Abel play out before them.

The actors portrayed the brothers and when Abel hit Cain over the head, he really brained the man, who fell over the side of the wagon and bloodied his nose. Infuriated, he jumped up on the wagon bed, punched Abel in the face, and a full-scale brawl erupted. That was not part of the play. Gavriella started laughing as Andreas shook his head at the antics and led her away to the next, and hopefully less violent, entertainment.

The next wagon had a good-sized crowd around it. It was a play about Demeter, the Greek goddess of agriculture, among other things, but in this play she was killing everything that moved. There were three men in this play, each one assuming several characters, and they watched Demeter kill crops, kill a goat and eat it, pull flowers out of the imaginary earth and then throw them to the audience. Andreas, being quite tall, caught one of the flowers, a white rose, and handed it to Gavriella. She held her rose quite happily, watching a play that was very depressing.

But they watched the entire thing and it had been long. Demeter ended up getting swallowed up by the underworld. When the crowd broke up, looking for the next spot of entertainment, Andreas and Gavriella wandered down the avenue to a stage that had been built from the ground up. There was no wagon here and groups of children surrounded this stage as two actors, made up as a dog and a cat, chased each other around, foiled by a third actor dressed as a rat.

The cat, the dog, and the rat ran around the stage, biting each other much to the delight of the children. Gavriella thought this play was much more fun than the other two and she laughed right along with the children. The rat was conniving, the dog stupid, and the cat frantic. It was hilarious to watch. At one point, the rat offered the dog a bowl of what was presumably dog food, but the cat smacked the bottom of the bowl and the contents went flying into the audience.

The children screamed with delight as pieces of hard honey candy rained down on them. Gavriella managed to catch two pieces and she gave one to Andreas. Together, they ate the honey candy that tasted like cinnamon. It was quite delicious. But once the honey candy sprayed out over the audience, the play was apparently finished and they clapped enthusiastically.

They moved on.

There was so much to see that time passed swiftly. The day became midafternoon, and soon it was nearing dusk. Andreas and Gavriella had seen several plays, the last one being two men beating each other with padded clubs and anyone else in the audience who strayed too close. It was quite humorous, or so Gavriella thought, but Andreas wasn't entirely sure it was proper entertainment for a lady. He walked back to the street, trying to coerce her to come with him, but she was enjoying watching the men beat up on each other.

He finally gave up trying.

Andreas stood out on the street, watching her as she laughed uproariously at the men on the stage, beating and poking each other and telling terrible jokes. He thought they were terrible, but Gavriella did not. She was enjoying it immensely and he was enjoying her. She laughed so freely that he was coming to think she didn't do it often enough. It was as if it had all been pent up inside of her and she was letting loose for the first time in a long while. Given what he'd seen last night, he believed that.

Sometimes you meet people who hide a great deal, she'd said.

He had a feeling she was hiding more than her share.

She'd kept an air of mystery about her, but that didn't stop him from wanting to be with her, to hear her laugh, or to see her eyes when they twinkled at him. Something about the way she looked at him made him feel like the most handsome, vibrant man in the entire world. He'd had plenty of women look at him, but not like that. Never like that.

No one had ever looked at him like Gavriella did.

He rather liked it.

"I thought that was you, de Wolfe."

Andreas heard the voice and turned very calmly to see three dirty, rough-looking knights standing there. They were clad in well-used protection, with big swords. He knew who they were on sight and, immediately, he went into battle mode.

Protection mode.

He needed to keep them away from Gavriella.

"De Alisal," he greeted calmly, though he was moving away from the stage where the fools were. "You're a long way from home."

The three knights bearing the yellow and red colors of the House of de la Londe, a distinct enemy of the House of de Wolfe, tracked his movements.

"As are you," de Alisal said. He was an older man with bad

teeth and a massive scar down his cheek. "Are you alone?"

Andreas shook his head. "Of course not," he said. "My cousins, Tor and Will, and Theodis de Velt are around here somewhere. Shall I find them for you?"

That seemed to bring the knights pause. Suddenly, they weren't quite so confident with the mention of those three names. "De Velt is around here?" de Alisal asked with a hint of apprehension. "Where?"

Andreas kept walking, leading them away from Gavriella as she continued to watch the fools, oblivious to what was going on behind her.

"Come with me and we shall find him," Andreas said. "I am sure he would be quite happy to see you. I think the last time he saw you was at the tournament at Northwood Castle to celebrate the marriage of Lord de Longley's eldest daughter. I heard something about an illegal joust pole when you went up against Theodis in the final rounds of the joust, but I could be wrong. Mayhap we should find him and clear up that rumor."

They were still walking, moving away from the stage and back towards the avenue lined with merchants. More opportunity for Andreas to level out the fighting field should the knights choose to attack. But de Alisal came to a halt at his comment, his face contorting with rage.

"It was nothing of the kind," he said. "I did nothing illegal."

They were far enough away from the stage of fools that Andreas felt comfortable enough to face them, but he was still edgy. Too many variables, including the fact that he didn't want Gavriella to notice he was missing and come looking for him. He didn't want her anywhere near the situation.

He had to get rid of the knights.

"I am sure de Velt could help us dispel that nasty rumor," he said, positioning himself so that he could see the area where he'd left Gavriella. "And then, mayhap, we could drink and reaffirm our bonds."

The dirty knight scowled. "I'll not affirm my bonds with any de Wolfe except those of hatred," he snarled. "You and your kind think you rule the north, like kings, but you're really like vermin that must be rooted out. You infect everything you touch."

Andreas smiled dangerously. "Strange," he said evenly. "I was just thinking the same thing about you. But since we're speaking truths, allow me to speak mine – you are a cowardly piece of filth, de Alisal. You're a shame to the knighthood. Now, let me find de Velt because he'll have a few choice words for you as well."

They weren't going to let him move and the swords came out. Andreas was acutely aware that he wasn't wearing any mail or protection, but he had his broadsword and considered himself grateful for small mercies. Still, he was concerned that he was about to be engaged in something that was going to be deadly and quick, and he was unable to communicate any of it to Gavriella, who was still over by the fool's stage more than likely still having a good time. In fact, Andreas was sorry that he was about to put a mark on what was otherwise a flawless day.

But it couldn't be helped.

"I've got no words for you that my sword cannot speak, de Wolfe," de Alisal said, flashing his blade as people around them began to run for cover. "Let us have a conversation."

Andreas sighed heavily. "It is an argument you cannot win," he said. "Are you truly prepared to engage me? When de Velt and my cousins see what is happening, you will be lucky to survive."

It looked to him like de Alisal was considering that very possibility. His comrades didn't look quite as eager to engage in a battle as he did, so there was some hesitation on their part. Andreas was hoping it was enough hesitation with the threat of three more formidable knights possibly joining the fray that it would cause them to back down. He was truly hoping for that outcome.

But it was not meant to be.

The battle wasn't started by de Alisal or his comrades. It started quite by accident. They were standing next to a merchant stall as a wealthy woman and her two guards emerged, walking straight into a group of armed men. As soon as the guards saw the weapons drawn, they immediately unsheathed their own weapons, more than likely afraid that they were being robbed.

That's when all hell broke loose.

De Alisal and his comrades were charged by the two armed guards. As a nasty fight broke out, de Alisal's comrades, possibly thinking that this had something to do with Andreas, charged Andreas with their swords lifted. Fortunately, Andreas had some time to prepare, so he was ready when the men ran at him. He easily dispatched one man who ended up with a sword wound to his belly, but the second man was a knight he had seen before, an older man who was quite seasoned but who had never had a decent reputation. Andreas didn't even know his name, but that didn't matter. The man had his weapon leveled at Andreas, clearly with the intent to do him great bodily harm.

Dropping to his knees as the man charged him, Andreas was able to bring his sword up in a beautiful move that cut the man right through the middle. As the old knight fell away, more men abruptly entered the fight and Andreas had no idea where they came from. He could see the armed guards fighting de Alisal, but more men were entering still, perhaps the armed guards who protected the many merchant stalls along the avenue.

Though this area was the low rent district, controlled by the church, and there didn't seem to be many great things of value here for sale, that didn't mean some of these merchants didn't have men on their payroll to protect what they did have. It was quite possible they thought some massive robbery was taking place or about to take place. All Andreas knew was that many armed men were entering what should have been a four-man battle.

Without his protection, Andreas knew he was at a distinct disadvantage and it was probably best if he make haste away from the fighting. He was just about to turn back towards the fool's stage when de Alisal managed to break away from the armed guards he had been fighting. He saw Andreas attempting to leave and he took exception to that. Fortunately, Andreas caught the movement and realized he was about to be attacked from behind, so he swiftly turned about and met de Alisal head-on in a nasty swordfight.

There was chaos going on all around them as the entire avenue seemed to deteriorate into an enormous skirmish. What had been a happy and pleasant afternoon now turned into something deadly and frightening. At this point, Andreas was simply trying to keep his torso from being pierced by the sword that de Alisal was swinging at him.

He simply wanted to make it out of there in one piece.

If he had been wearing his protection, he wouldn't have been so cautious and the fight would have been over much sooner. Because he was without protection, however, he was being a little more careful than usual. He was using tables and doorways as shields as de Alisal came after him with a vengeance. The man might have been an unscrupulous knight, but he had skill.

Andreas had known that from the start.

That's what made all of this so very tricky.

In fact, Andreas was trying to get his opponent into a position where he could cut him down and not risk himself doing so, using a small merchant's stall as a shield. He ducked inside as de Alisal came charging after him. Just as he turned to level his sword against the man's neck, de Alisal was hit from behind with something heavy. It looked like one of the enormous fire pokers that Andreas had seen in a nearby merchant's stall, from a man who sold all manner of iron works.

As de Alisal started to go down, Gavriella suddenly appeared. It was she who had been the wielder of the iron bar. As Andreas watched in shock, Gavriella swung the iron implement at de Alisal again, hitting him twice in the head. Once he was on the ground, she swung it yet again and ended up dislodging the man's helm. Andreas quickly overcame his shock when he realized she was swinging to kill, but before he could disarm her, she swung it twice more as she screamed at de Alisal.

"No more!" she cried. "You'll not hurt anyone again, you bastard! I hope you die! I shall kill you myself!"

Shocked, Andreas listened to her scream before he finally realized that he should probably stop her from committing murder. As she brought the fire poker up again to brain de Alisal, he managed to grab hold of the iron implement and yank it from her grasp.

But that didn't stop her. In fact, Gavriella seemed not to realize he had taken her weapon away. They were at a merchant's stall where the man had imported items from France and Saxony and other points east, including carved wooden walking sticks. They were quite beautiful, topped with brass, and she grabbed one of those and begin beating de Alisal with it as the man lay there, dazed.

All the while, she continued screaming at him.

"That will teach you to attack anyone again," she yelled. "You'll never hurt anyone again, you vile fiend. I shall make it so you can never hurt anyone again and ruin their lives!"

Andreas knew he should have stopped her.

He knew he should have taken the walking stick from her hand and stopped her from beating de Alisal, but he couldn't seem to do it. He was far more interested and, truthfully, more concerned about what was coming out of her mouth.

He was coming to get a bigger picture of her.

She was screaming at de Alisal as if he had personally harmed her or attacked her, the ravings of a terrified woman who was reliving that terror. He watched her swing once or twice more at de Alisal's head before he finally stepped in and disarmed her. Even then, she still looked around for another weapon but he wasn't going to let her continue the fight, so he tossed her up over one shoulder and carried her out of the stall through the back entrance.

The entire avenue in front of the merchant's stall had deteriorated into a fight that the local sheriff and his men were only now starting to break up. No one seemed to know how it had started, and no one would, because Andreas was going to get as far away as possible. He didn't want to be caught up in anything and he didn't want Gavriella caught up in it, either.

Because of the brawl, the activity in the entire area seemed to have come to an uncertain halt. Andreas was still carrying Gavriella as he ran past stalls that were abruptly closing with the threat of an armed incident. He ran past the stages where they had seen Demeter and Cain and Abel. He ran past all of that on his way to the London Bridge.

Predictably, news of the fight had spread to the bridge and people were running into the area to get a look at what had happened. Andreas didn't even put Gavriella onto her feet. He simply raced to the bridge and crossed it against the traffic that was going in the opposite direction.

At that point, Gavriella didn't seem to be fighting him too much. She'd stopped struggling and was mostly bracing herself against his broad back as he carried her over his shoulder.

Andreas ran all the way across the bridge and to the other side before he even attempted to set her down.

Once he set her to her feet, he looked at her with great concern.

"Are you well?" he asked. "Were you injured?"

She'd been crying. He could see where she'd wiped her face with fingers dirty from clutching an iron rod.

"I am not hurt," she said, her lower lip trembling. "I… I am sorry I was so much trouble. I saw that man… he was trying to kill you and I… I tried to help. I am sorry if I have made you angry."

He sighed heavily, relieved more than he cared to admit that she was unharmed. Reaching out, he grasped her by the upper arms.

"I am not angry, sweetling," he said, his relief causing him to call her by a term of endearment. "Are you sure you are uninjured?"

"I am sure."

He was looking her in the face, seeing great upset in her features, and he went back to what she had said when she'd been beating de Alisal within an inch of his life.

I shall make it so you can never hurt anyone again and ruin lives.

Given the situation, that had seemed strangely out of place. But in her guarded world, perhaps not. Clearly, it meant something to her, but what, exactly, was anyone's guess.

Part of that guarded woman had just revealed herself.

Gently, he released her and took her hand in his. "Did you get more sweets thrown at you?"

He was trying to change the subject, trying to calm the situation. She nodded, head hung as she continued to wipe at her eyes.

"I'm sorry," she said. "I did not save any for you."

He smiled faintly. "Not to worry," he said. "Did you enjoy yourself today?"

She nodded. "I did, very much."

"I am sorry about the skirmish. It was… unexpected."

Her head came up, then, and she looked at him. "What happened?" she asked. "How did you end up fighting that man?"

It was a complicated story, one he didn't feel like telling her. Therefore, he simply shrugged. "Things like that start so quickly and no one ever remembers why," he said. "Come, let us go back into the city and find something to eat."

He began leading her away and she looked at him in mild surprise. "Again?"

He winked at her. "I have a very large appetite."

With a shrug, she gathered her skirts in one hand and let him lead her away with the other.

The entertainment, for the day, was concluded.

But not the excitement.

There was more to come.

CHAPTER ELEVEN

GAVRIELLA HAD TO admit that she'd never seen anyone eat so much in her life.

They were back at The Fox and The Wolf, the inn they'd visited not twelve hours earlier. But this time, it was to eat. Again. Andreas had his beloved beef roast, cooked in red wine and garlic and cloves, and he'd had a goodly portion of it. Along with the roast, he had stuffed eggs, spinach and cabbage, carrots cooked in sweet vinegar, and all the bread he could eat.

He was in heaven.

For as much as the man ate, Gavriella couldn't see an ounce of fat on him. He was quite large, and very strong, but it was all muscle. She'd found that out when he had carried her out of danger, running what had to be at least a mile or more with her slung over his shoulder. It took a strong man to do that.

More and more, she was coming to see just what an exceptional man he was.

In fact, the entire adventure to Southwark has been an eye-opening experience for her. In the deliciously languid moments when all they'd done was talk, with no pressure, no expectations, she had come to see a man of exceptional intelligence and exceptional humor. He was exacting, a bit of a perfectionist, and very smart. He was also a little rigid, quite arrogant, and supremely confident. She had seen that side of him and it amused her greatly, but the side of him she liked best was the compassionate and caring side.

That was the side that was drawing her to him more and more.

She kept going back to those moments when she realized that she wasn't worthy of him, knowing that she couldn't let this acquaintance go any further than it already had. Although Gavriella did not know much more about Andreas than his name, she instinctively knew that he was from a very fine family and there were several in the north where she was from. She knew he was from Northumberland, just as she was, but as she'd said to him, Northumberland was a large province. There were several great families and innumerable warlords. It was quite possible he was one of those warlords, one of the many who battled against the Scots or fought for the king's army.

All she knew was that the man had a stamp of greatness about him.

It would have been so easy to pretend there was some manner of future between them. It would have been so easy to daydream that he was her husband, her handsome and powerful husband, and she was a wife worth having. She was coming to think that her father sending her to London had been a good thing because, here in London, she had no past and people didn't know about the shames she had suffered. Essentially, she had a clean slate but, most importantly, Andreas didn't know of her past and she could pretend that there was a future with him.

And that a man like Andreas was within her reach.

For the moment, she decided that she was going to enjoy this.

"My lady?" Andreas broke into her train of thought. "Did

you hear me?"

Startled that she'd been caught daydreaming, Gavriella smiled weakly. "I am sorry," she said. "My mind was wandering. I suppose I am more exhausted than I realized."

He smiled faintly, collecting his cup of ruby-red wine. "It was quite a long night," he said. "I did not sleep much after I returned home. Did you?"

She shook her head. "My cousin snores," she said, grinning when he laughed low in his throat. "But do not tell her I said so. She would deny it and I would look like a liar."

He shook his head. "I could never see you in such a light," he said. "In fact, what I said earlier when you did not hear me was that I had an enjoyable time today in spite of the way it ended. Thank you very much for accompanying me."

"Thank you for taking me," she said, her eyes glimmering at him. "I cannot remember when I have had such a wonderful time."

"Even with the fight?"

"Even with the fight."

A smile played on his lips. "You were quite fearsome," he said. "It is a rare lady who will take up arms like that."

Her eyes dimmed a little and she averted her gaze. "I… I do not know why I did it," she said. "All I know is that you were in trouble and I sought to help. I could not stand by and do nothing."

His smile faded, the look in his eyes growing more intense. "That is quite noble," he said. "And I am flattered. You are a rare bird, Lady Gavriella."

She dared to look up at him, perhaps surprised he hadn't scolded her. "I do not think so," she said. "I am just like everyone else, but when threatened… I will fight back. I…I have learned to fight back. But let us speak no more of the incident, if you do not mind. Today's visit shall be something I will always remember and treasure, fight or no fight. Mayhap one day, we shall meet in London again and you will let *me* take you to see an entertainment. I should like to repay the kindness."

He had been drinking his wine, now looking at her as he set the cup down. "You would like to… see me again?"

She didn't catch his meaning, not at first. "Of course," she said. "I enjoyed myself a great deal today. I do not think I have laughed so much in a very long time."

He sighed, long and slow, and sat back in his chair. "I do not get to London often at all," he said. "There is no guarantee I will ever see you again once I leave this city, so can we please dispense with this guessing game you wish to play? Won't you *please* tell me your name and where you live so that I may call upon you once we leave London?"

Her good humor fled. God, it would have been so easy for her to agree with him and tell him everything, but as long as he just knew her as Gavriella… he could pretend she was anything he wanted her to be.

But if he knew the truth…

After a moment, she averted her gaze, looking at her lap. She was trying to find words he might understand because she had to stop fooling herself. Maybe she was willing to pretend she was normal and that Andreas would make a fine husband, but that had only been for the moment.

That moment was up.

"This day has been one of the most remarkable days I have ever known," she said softly. "I was free to be myself, with no hint of where I have come from. My lord, if you…"

"Andreas."

Her head came up. "What?"

His gaze was fixed steadily on her. "My name is Andreas," he said. "My friends and family call me Dray. That is what I wish for you to call me."

She took a deep breath and lowered her gaze again. "Dray," she said quietly. "You are a truly extraordinary man. I have never known anyone like you."

"Then come to know me better," he said, a hint of pleading in his tone. "Is there something about me you do not like, Gavriella? Something that prevents you from telling me where you live? If you do not want me to call upon you, you merely need to say so. I will not ask again."

"Nay, it is not that," she said quickly. "I would like nothing better. But you are a fine knight and you deserve better than someone like me. Please do not ask me more, for I cannot tell you. What I can tell you is that I am not married and I am not betrothed. I never shall be, you see, so it would do no good for you to call upon me. I am not meant for… marriage."

He stared at her a moment, frowning. "What does that mean?"

"Exactly what I said."

He continued staring at her until a ripple of realization crossed his face. "Do you mean that you are meant for the veil?"

He'd just given her a reason for her refusal. She didn't know why she hadn't thought of it before. It would discourage him but not insult him. But it was so very heartbreaking to latch on to that excuse and use it.

She had to force herself.

"Aye," she said, tearing up. "That is why… why you cannot… and I can never… as much as I would like to. Please believe me… I would like nothing better."

He was still frowning, digesting what she was telling him. "But why?"

She blinked, trying to stave off the tears. "Because… because my father wishes it," she said. "I wish it, too. At least, I did. Dray, you will make someone a wonderful husband. I am so very sorry that it cannot be me."

That was God's truth. She lowered her head again, genuinely trying not to weep. She caught movement out of the corners of her eyes, realizing he was pushing a cup of wine in her direction. She took it gratefully and drained half the cup.

"Gavriella," he said after several long moments. "Would your father reconsider? I would very much like to speak to him."

She couldn't look at him. "Please," she begged softly. "You are just making this more difficult. I… I told you that, sometimes, people hide a great deal. You have only known me such a very short time and my life is already set. You cannot change it."

He didn't say anything. She kept her head down, looking at the cup in her hands, when he abruptly stood up. She thought he was leaving the table, perhaps going to pay for their meal, when he suddenly came around the side of the table and pulled up a chair right next to hers. Sitting down, he took the cup out of her hands and clasped them both in his big, warm palms.

"I know that I have only known you for a very short time," he said quietly. "*Too* short. I met you last night and we have not exactly had an easy time of it, but you must know something about me. I am not a man who has an easy relationship with women. I am old for a man who has never been married or betrothed and I realize that, but it was because I never found a woman that I felt any manner of attraction with. At least, not enough to marry. A woman who laughed so freely at fools beating on one another or who uses an iron poker to defend me from an attacker. I am not sure how to say this, so I shall come out with it. I see a sunrise in you, a new day, and I do not want to see that sun set. Does that make any sense? It is not the shortness of the hours I have known you. Sometimes, one simply knows when someone comes into their life that they do not want to let go."

Gavriella was taken aback by his words and proximity. He was sitting so close to her that she could feel the heat from his body, but it was nothing compared to the heat from his eyes.

She wanted so badly to give in.

"But… but people hide things…"

"I do not care what you are hiding."

Her eyebrows flew up. "You cannot say such things," she said, feeling the tears again. "You do not know anything about me. I have endured things that you cannot imagine and I am beyond your reach. Please, Andreas… you are sweet and honorable and beautiful. But do not ask me again."

He reached out, cupping her soft cheeks, before leaning forward to kiss her gently on the lips. It was enough to bring a gasp of pain from her, pain and elation and utter joy, and he kissed her again to silence her. He wanted to kiss her fears way because he could see that she was full of them.

"Please," he murmured. "Just tell me who you are and where you live. Let me at least speak to your father."

Her eyes opened, bright with tears. "You do not know what you are asking."

His thumbs caressed her cheeks. "I am a grown man," he said. "And you have warned me, but it has not frightened me away. Tell me, Gavriella. Please."

He kissed her again and she broke down, her hands coming up to touch his face. He kissed her fingers, her palms, her cheeks, as she quietly wept. She was so overwhelmed she could hardly speak, unable to deny him, unable to agree with him. She didn't know what she wanted.

Her head was telling her one thing, but her heart was telling her another.

"I… must think on it," she murmured. "Please let me think."

"I will," he said, kissing her tender wrists. "We shall meet here again, tomorrow morning, and you will tell me what I want to know. Will you promise?"

He was kissing her arm, peeling back the shift and the red sleeve, tenderly kissing her flesh. Gavriella's heart was racing so that she could hardly breathe, but she managed to nod her head.

It was all she could do.

"I promise you that I will consider everything," she said breathlessly. "Let me go home and sleep on it."

"But you will meet me here in the morning."

"I will, I promise."

He smiled, leaning forward to kiss her on the cheek. "That's my good lass," he said. "I'll take you home now, but I will be here first thing in the morning and if you do not come to me right away, I will go and find you."

She swallowed hard, trying to recover her composure. "You must not," she said. "I do not know how my aunt will react to a man coming to call upon me, so please do not come to The Asher. It might get us both into trouble. Wait for me here. I will come as soon as I can."

"Swear this to me."

"I swear."

That seemed good enough for him. He pulled her out of her chair, but she was so wobbly kneed from his attention that it took her a while to regain her balance. They were out on the street, heading for The Asher, before she could walk a straight line again.

Andreas held her tightly the entire time.

By the time The Asher was in sight, Gavriella was feeling stronger. She tried to disengage herself from him, but he wouldn't let go of her hand. He kept kissing it until she finally had to gently but firmly pull away, smiling apologetically at him.

But he understood.

Andreas came to a halt across the street from The Asher, watching Gavriella cross the avenue and head to the entry door. When she turned to look at him, a final glimpse, he blew a kiss at her and she gave him a small wave. Her gaze lingered on him as the armed guards at the heavily fortified door opened for her, admitting her inside.

Once she was out of view, Andreas headed off to Lothbury.

But he was already wishing that it was tomorrow morning.

"GAVRIELLA? COME HERE."

Gavriella had just put a foot on the bottom of the stairs leading to the floor above when she heard her aunt's stern voice. She looked over to see the woman standing in the archway that led from the entry hall into the great hall, a severe-looking woman with a tight, white wimple and dark, perfect robes. There wasn't a thread out of place. Cold and emotionless, much like Gavriella's father was, Drucilla de Kennet, Countess of Blackburn, was a formidable woman.

Already, Gavriella was on her guard.

Her heart began to pound.

"Greetings, Auntie," she said, coming off the stairs and heading in her direction. "How may I be of service?"

Drucilla turned her back on her niece and walked into the great hall. Gavriella followed, noting that the hall was vacant except for a guard standing over near the hearth.

As Gavriella drew closer, she recognized the man.

He had opened the door for her at noon when she'd gone to

meet Andreas.

She braced herself.

"Gavriella," Drucilla said sternly. "I am told that you left here around the nooning meal and have only now returned. Tell me where you have been all afternoon."

Since the guard was there, Gavriella knew it would be of no use to lie. The man had seen her leave and had evidently told her aunt. At that moment, she decided then and there that she was going to be completely truthful. In truth, she'd done nothing wrong except go off with a man, unescorted. There were technicalities to that, such as not asking her aunt's permission or borrowing Camilla's dress, but Gavriella wasn't going to lie about it.

She wasn't the lying type.

"I went across the bridge, Auntie," she said. "There is an area over there with food and entertainment. I went to see the plays."

"Did you go alone?"

"Nay, Auntie."

"Who did you go with?"

"A knight named Andreas."

"Andreas *what*?"

Gavriella shook her head. "I do not know his family name, Auntie," she said. "But he is very kind and polite. We saw two biblical plays and then two more with fools. In one play, they even threw candy. It was very entertaining."

"I *saw* her, Mama!" Aurelia was suddenly entering the great hall, having just come from her bedchamber on the upper floor. Her gaze on Gavriella was loathsome. "I saw her leave with him earlier today and, just now, I saw them return together. Just now! He blew her a kiss!"

Gavriella was starting to put the pieces of the puzzle together. With Aurelia there, it was all coming to light. Now she knew why her aunt was so quick to condemn her – Aurelia, whom she thought was asleep when she had left earlier that day, evidently hadn't been asleep at all. Her greatest fear was realized when it occurred to her that Aurelia had seen her leave with Andreas and had then run straight to her mother with the information.

After the argument they'd had earlier, Gavriella knew that Aurelia was trying to get her into trouble, or worse. Gavriella didn't know her aunt well and all sorts of terrible things went through her mind – punishment, restriction – perhaps even a beating. There was no telling what her aunt would do to her with Aurelia poisoning her ear.

But if she went down, she was going to take Aurelia with her.

"Before Aurelia fills your head with lies against me, please let me explain," Gavriella said calmly. "Sir Andreas was perfectly polite and proper. He knew I had not been in London very long and offered to escort me to the place across the river where they have plays. I very much wanted to see the entertainment. We saw them, he bought me a meal, and he returned me home safely. That is really all there is to it."

Drucilla eyed her a moment before crossing her arms stiffly. "You should have asked permission, Gavriella," she said. "If everything was proper, as you say, then why did you not tell me where you were going? Why did you run off and not tell anyone where you had gone?"

She had a point and, in this case, Gavriella wasn't sure she wanted to tell her the truth of it. She didn't ask permission for obvious reasons – she didn't want to be denied.

She said the first thing that came to mind.

"I suppose I did not want to trouble you, Auntie," she said, trying to sound contrite. "I thought I could go and not be missed and you would not be troubled at all. I never meant to be any trouble to you, I promise."

"She's lying," Aurelia spat. She jabbed a finger at her. "Look at her! She has stolen Camilla's dress. Camilla didn't know anything about it at all. She's a thief *and* a liar, Mama. There is no telling what she did with that… that *man*."

Drucilla just stood there and shook her head at the behavior of her niece, wagging it back and forth. "Is this true, Gavriella?" she asked. "I did not want to believe what was in your father's missive, but how can I not believe it when I see the evidence right before my eyes?"

Gavriella was still eyeing Aurelia dangerously. "What evidence, Auntie?" she asked. "What do you mean?"

Drucilla uncrossed her arms and went to sit at the feasting table. She sat at the end, so heavily that the chair creaked, and immediately poured herself some wine.

"Sneaking out to meet a man," she said. "Your father told me what happened to you. He told me that you fornicated with a man and bore a child as a result. He told me that you needed my guidance to mend your ways but, already, you are doing here what you did at your father's home. You are off meeting strange men and doing God only knows what with them. Well, Child? What do you have to say to all of this? I cannot have your terrible influence around my daughters, Gavriella."

Gavriella was pale with shock that her aunt should speak so freely of that horrible event that had ruined her life. She said it in front of Aurelia, no less, who was staring at Gavriella in shock before assuming a gloating expression.

That threw Gavriella over the edge.

"Did my father tell you that I was abducted and beaten and raped?" she asked, her voice beginning to tremble. "I had no control over the men who abducted me from the village and assaulted me. I did not willingly fornicate with anyone, I assure you, Auntie. My father is embarrassed and frightened by what happened, so he sent me here so that he would not have to look at me. I was not a willing partner in anything, Aunt Drucilla, certainly nothing like your daughters are when they sneak out of your home in the middle of the night to attend a guild called Gomorrah where they kiss and dance with men they do not know, and I am sure they have done much more than that."

Drucilla's expression went from one of severity to one of shock. "They *what*?"

Gavriella was going for the proverbial throat. "Did you even know Aurelia leaves your house nightly to go to this place?" she said "You should ask the guards on night watch. Or mayhap you should watch for yourself. If anything, I do not need the horrible and scandalous influence of *your* daughters, who are shaming the House of de Kennet every single night."

She was nearly shouting by the time she was finished, pointing fingers at Aurelia, who let out a scream of shock and fear and anger. Drucilla was on her feet, looking between Gavriella and her daughter in horror.

"Silence!" Drucilla bellowed, holding out a hand to stop Gavriella's rant. "This is not about my daughters! How dare you say such… such terrible things about them!"

Gavriella wasn't going to back down. "Ask them," she said through clenched teeth. "Ask Camilla. Ask the guards who watch the postern gate at night because they let us pass most easily, which tells me that Aurelia is either paying them to look the other way or she is fucking them to keep them quiet. I am *not* the sinner here, Aunt Drucilla. Tend to the whores in your own house before you accuse my house of being dirty!"

Aurelia screamed and ran at her, hands like claws. Gavriella saw her coming and, after having beaten an armed knight in the head only hours earlier, she was ready for her petty, weak cousin. As Aurelia drew close, she lashed out an open palm, catching the woman in the face and sending her tumbling.

Aurelia crashed into the chairs and ended up on the floor as Gavriella pounced, grabbing her by the hair.

"Tell her what you do every night!" Gavriella cried. "Tell her how you sneak out and let men kiss your mouth and fondle your breasts! Tell her what a whore you are!"

Aurelia was screaming. "Let me go!" she said. "You have ruined everything, you stupid chit!"

Drucilla was on top of them, trying to separate them, but she didn't have the strength and Gavriella was surprisingly strong. She called out to the guard near the hearth and he stepped in, grabbing Gavriella around the waist and yanking her off her cousin. But not before Gavriella came away with a handful of red hair.

Aurelia was hysterical and, by now, the entire house had been alerted. Camilla had come down the stairs, now standing in the doorway and weeping fearfully at the sight of Gavriella and Aurelia fighting.

Gavriella caught sight of Camilla as the guard dragged her away.

"Tell your mother what you do every night, Camilla!" she screamed. "Tell her that you sneak out to that terrible place where men and women fornicate for all to see! Tell her how you let strangers kiss you!"

Camilla let out a cry, her hands to her mouth as she looked at her mother and sister. "She knows?" she wept in a question mostly directed at her sister. "She told Mother everything?"

Aurelia was being helped into a chair by her mother, her hand on her head where Gavriella had yanked the hair out by the roots.

"Tell Mama it is a lie," Aurelia insisted frantically. "Tell her that Gavriella is lying!"

Camilla had no idea what was going on. She was sweet, and weak-willed, and not particularly bright. "About what?" she said. "About Gomorrah? How does Mama know about it?"

Aurelia could see that her denials were crumbling. Her sister was too stupid to reinforce her claims. Therefore, she did the only thing she could do – she burst into tears.

"It was Gavriella who took us there!" she wept. "I did not want to go, Mama, I swear it, but Gavriella forced us to go. She threatened us if we did not!"

Gavriella was still in the grip of the guard. "*I* took you there?" she cried in outrage. "How could I take you to a place I did not know about until last night when you took *me* there?"

"Enough!" Drucilla shouted. The woman was shaken as she looked at her niece. "Gavriella, I have no choice but to send you back to your father. You are a disruptive influence to this house and you must leave immediately. Barnes, take her back to her chamber and lock her in. Then you will summon the men who brought her here. They are to remove her immediately. I am sending her home this very night."

The guard nodded and began dragging Gavriella away, who realized she was not to be believed at all. The countess was taking her daughters' side even though it was clear that what Gavriella had said was true.

But that didn't matter.

Drucilla didn't want the aggravation or the burden of her niece from the north.

Gavriella de Leia was going home.

When the guard locked Gavriella in the chamber she shared with Camilla, the impact of her aunt's decision began to weigh heavily on her. It was not the fact that the woman didn't believe her; nay, that wasn't the issue. It wasn't even the fact that Aurelia had it out for her and probably had since the day she had arrived. Clearly, remaining at The Asher would be a battle, every single day, with no peace from Aurelia. Gavriella didn't even really care about that.

What she did care about was Andreas.

She was supposed to meet him on the morrow, but she

wouldn't be there. Her aunt wanted her removed that very night from The Asher and Gavriella didn't even know where the man was staying. He'd said it once, but she couldn't remember. The more she thought about not showing up to The Fox and The Wolf the next morning, the more distraught she became.

It was all her fault that she didn't even know Andreas' last name. She'd kept up that guessing game even though he'd asked, more than once, to end it. But she wouldn't do it. She'd kept up the façade. Perhaps this sudden change in plans was a sign from God, cleaving her relationship with Andreas before it could go any further.

Perhaps this was the end, as it should have been all along.

There would be no more meeting the man in taverns or on the street because she knew, if things had continued between them, she would have eventually told him who she was and where she was from. Perhaps he would have continued to ask to speak to her father and, knowing that she turned to melted butter in the man's hands, she would have given him permission.

And Andreas would have found out her deepest, darkest secret.

Damaged goods.

The tears began to come.

Perhaps this was for the best, then. Not showing up to the tavern tomorrow morning was the best thing for both of them. As much as it broke her heart, she had to believe that this was, indeed, for the best.

When her guard came to collect her an hour later, she was packed and ready.

The door closed firmly on the best day she'd ever had in her life.

Or ever would have.

Farewell, my sweet Andreas.

CHAPTER TWELVE

"**...a**ND THEN SHE came flying through the doorway with an iron rod in her hand," Andreas was saying. "The next thing I realized, she had smacked de Alisal on the head with it. Even after I told her to stop, she hit him twice more before I was able to disarm her. The woman is a savage and I adore everything about that particular trait."

Will, Tor, and Theodis were greatly entertained by the tale of Andreas' visit across the London Bridge. They started laughing at Andreas as he spoke of the "savage" woman he took to see the entertainment across the river, but they'd been laughing steadily since the man returned to Lothbury and tales of his afternoon unfolded.

"And this is the same woman who ran screaming into that alcove at Gomorrah?" Tor asked. "God's Bones, Dray. How she has changed."

Andreas was into his third cup of wine since returning home. The sun had set, food was being set out for Edward and his family and their visitors, but all Andreas wanted to do was drink and speak of the woman he'd spent the afternoon with.

It was clear to all that he was quite smitten.

"Changed, indeed," he said. "She is not the same woman

you saw. She's smart, lively, humorous… a genuine delight. Even so, there's something about her that is quite mysterious."

"Like the fact that she will not tell you her name or where she lives?" Will asked, cocking an eyebrow that suggested the woman must have a great deal to hide. "That is not normal, Dray. If you like her and she likes you, then why won't she tell you where she is from?"

Andreas lifted his shoulders. "It was curious the way she phrased it," he said. "She said that, much like the rules of Gomorrah, there is an air of mystery about someone when you only know their first name. They could be a prince of Persia or the lowliest peasant, in truth, but as long as you do not know their background, you can imagine they are anyone to suit your particular fantasy."

As Will shrugged, Tor nodded in agreement. "That makes some sense," he said. "It does make it a little more exciting, I suppose."

Andreas took another drink of wine. "That is true," he said. "But tomorrow she promised to tell me everything I want to know. She has told me that she is meant for the veil, but I am going to speak to her father and ask the man if I can court her. Mayhap I shall bring my father with me. Troy de Wolfe is not a man to be refused, in any case. Besides… a woman like that would be wasted as a nun. God has enough women to serve him. Mayhap he will let me have this one."

Theodis drained his cup and slammed it to the table, grabbing for the wine pitcher. "Stop telling us all of the unexciting details," he said, pouring himself more wine. "Tell us the most important things, lad – did you kiss her and was it good?"

Andreas chuckled at his tactless friend. "I did and it was," he said. "But nothing scandalous or shocking, I assure you. A simple kiss to the hand. And her cheek. I think I kissed her neck, too. Probably her lips."

Theodis rolled his eyes. "It sounds as if you kept missing the target," he said. "Dray, you are a fool. Do I need to instruct you on how to kiss a woman?"

"Not now." Edward joined the table, putting his hand on Theodis' shoulder and squeezing hard enough to make the man wince. "We are about to be joined by womenfolk, including my wife, and she'll belt you in the mouth if you say anything offensive in front of her daughters, so please keep the conversation civilized."

Andreas, Will, and Tor snorted at Theodis, who had to rub his shoulder where Edward squeezed it as the man sat down between him and Andreas.

"Of course, my lord," Theodis said, eyeing Edward unhappily. "Civilized conversation only, I swear it."

A smile played on Edward's lips as he reached for the wine pitcher and poured himself a measure. His wife appeared with their two eldest daughters, Helene and Phoebe, who were now old enough to be allowed to sit at the feasting table with the adults while their younger siblings were fed in their chambers by their nurse.

At twelve and ten years of age, respectively, they were a dark-haired reflection of their father, except for Helene, who had hazel eyes through her mother. Helene sat down next to Andreas, her cousin, and he tended to her quite sweetly, as he always did with his younger female cousins.

All of them loved "Dray" very much.

"Dray?" Edward said softly. "What is it? What are you thinking of?"

Andreas hadn't realized he was staring at Helene, who had been named for his mother by her only surviving sister, Edward's wife. He smiled faintly, watching Helene's delicate profile as she tore up a piece of bread.

"I don't really know," he said. "I suppose I was wondering

how much Helene looks like my mother. Eddie… I can't even remember what she looked like. Sometimes I see her in my dreams and she is petite and blonde and I can hear that silly giggle she had. Do you remember that?"

Edward nodded faintly, looking at his nephew who never spoke of his mother. "I do," he said. "I remember Troy slapping his hand over her mouth to quiet her."

Andreas' gaze lingered on Helene for a moment before turning back to his wine. "I wish he hadn't done that," he said. "He should have let her laugh. He should have let her laugh all she wanted considering that laughter was silenced all too soon. I wonder… I wonder if you can tell me what she looked like. Do you remember?"

Edward's gaze turned serious. Sad, even. The conversation had taken a swift and unexpected turn, and he could tell that Andreas had imbibed a good deal of wine because the usually quiet man was not only speaking up, he was being emotional about it. Helene was a very touchy subject in the de Wolfe and de Norville households.

But he answered him.

"I remember," he said. "She was short and had blonde hair and big blue eyes. You inherited your eyes from her, in fact. You favor your mother a great deal."

Andreas didn't say anything for a moment as he tried to picture his mother in his mind. "Did you see her after she died?" he asked. "When she had been brought back to Castle Questing after she drowned, I mean. Did you see her then? And my sisters?"

The conversation had taken an even darker turn. It had gone from light and happy to serious and gloomy very quickly. Edward knew that Andreas was drunk, perhaps not terribly, but drunk enough to ask questions he wouldn't normally ask.

Edward cleared his throat softly.

"We shall speak of it at another time, Dray," he said quietly. "I want to hear more about this young lady you spent the afternoon with. Was it pleasant?"

"Did you *see* my mother, Eddie?" he asked, ignoring Edward's question. "I have never asked you that. I do not know why. I suppose I did not want to know, but that was years ago. You can tell me now."

Edward pondered the question. On the other side of the table sat Will and Tor, who had lost their mother in the same accident. They, too, were listening to the answer of a question neither one of them had ever asked, either. They had all been young men, off fostering when the accident happened, and their mothers had been buried by the time they made it home to grieve. Perhaps Andreas' question mattered, perhaps it didn't, but they were listening nonetheless. Andreas' focus on young Helene had him thinking about the mother he had lost.

"Dray," he said quietly. "There are three other people at this table who consider this a sensitive topic, not the least of which is my wife. We'll discuss this at another time."

Andreas understood. He sighed faintly, looking at young Helene, who was buttering her bread and oblivious to the conversation the adults were having. As Andreas simply nodded and took another drink of wine, Edward spoke softly.

"Aye, I saw her," he muttered for Andreas' ears only. "I helped bring her into the house when the soldiers brought her back from the accident. I helped lay her on the floor of Poppy's solar. She looked as if she were sleeping, Dray. You needn't worry."

Andreas turned to look at him, appreciating that he murmured words that only he could hear. Or so he thought. "I did not mean to ask uncomfortable questions," he said. "But it just occurred to me that I have met a woman I am interested in and I have no mother to ask questions of. Women know about women, don't they?"

"You can ask me."

Both Andreas and Edward looked across the table to Cassiopeia. She was the baby of the de Norville family – she had two older brothers, then her sisters were born, then another brother, and then her. When her eyes met Andreas, she smiled faintly.

"Please, Dray," she said. "I would consider it an honor. You can ask me what I think about this lady you spent the afternoon with. I think my sister would like it if you did."

Cassiopeia was actually two years younger than Andreas. He had spent a lot of time with her in his youth because she had been a late baby for her parents, born well after their older brood were young men and women. She really was the closest thing he would ever have to his own mother so he shrugged, suddenly uncertain of what he would even ask.

He had to think a moment.

"I suppose I would ask why a woman would be so secretive about her life," he said. "It is clear that she is attracted to me, and I am attracted to her, so why would she not tell me everything I want to know?"

Cassiopeia grinned. "Because you cannot learn everything about a woman in just a few hours," she said. "Getting to know someone takes time. She cannot tell you everything about herself all at once. Part of the joy of coming to know someone is the time it takes to do it. It is like unwrapping a gift that keeps going and going… and you keep unwrapping and unwrapping, finding new and delightful things."

Andreas sighed, thinking she made a great deal of sense. "But she is very secretive," he said. "As if… as if she is hiding something from me, though she assured me that she is not married nor betrothed. In fact, she says that she is meant for the veil."

"Then that is why she has been secretive, I am sure," Edward said. "You have asked uncomfortable questions, ones that are not your right to know. She is meant for the church."

"But I want to speak with her father."

Edward scratched his head, looking at his wife to see if she had anything to say about this impetuous man who would not be denied his wants. Cassiopeia took the hint.

"Tread carefully, Dray," she said. "If the woman is guarded and has already told you that she is meant for the veil, then you do not want to push her too much. It might scare her away. You must be gentle when dealing with a woman you do not know – or even one you do."

That was probably very true, though Andreas didn't want to admit it. His aunt and uncle were giving him excellent advice. It was up to him to take it.

"She agreed to meet me tomorrow and tell me what I wish to know," he said. "All I really want to know is her family name and where she lives so that I may speak with her father. Everything else… I can learn in time, I suppose."

"A wise attitude," Edward said as the food began to arrive. "And whatever you do, do not listen to de Velt. Women do not like to be spanked, forced, or otherwise, no matter what he says."

Theodis had his spoon in his hand, licking his lips at the trencher of roast bird set before him. But he heard Edward and frowned. "That is not true," he said. "I do not spank or force women. Well, not much. Not unless they want me to. Say, when did I become such a dolt when it comes to women in your eyes? I am not, you know."

Edward started laughing, pouring his nephews more wine. "Tay, you are a gorgeous creature and you know it," he said. "But do not advise Dray to push this lady into giving him what he wants. If she has already been hesitant, that kind of advice will only work against him."

Theodis shrugged and plowed into his food with gusto. In fact, everyone at the table did except for Andreas.

For once, he couldn't eat. Thoughts of Gavriella had his stomach tied up in knots, but they were knots of excitement.

He couldn't wait until the morrow.

Andreas sat with his uncle and cousins long into the night, long after the table was cleared and everyone else went to bed. The conversation flowed, as did the wine, and they ended up speaking more about his mother and dead aunt. Edward spoke mostly of what he remembered about them. Even though he wasn't much older than Andreas or William, he still remembered Athena and Helene, women that he had essentially grown up with.

When Andreas finally did go to bed, it was with thoughts of his mother on his mind.

He very much wished she was there to advise him.

Sleep did not come easily, however, and when it did, it was heavy. The wine had seen to that and Andreas awoke the next morning with a throbbing head, well after dawn. In a panic, and knowing that Gavriella would be waiting for him, he ignored his aching head and dressed quickly. He flew out of his uncle's home and rushed through the dusty streets of London until he came to the narrow alleyway where The Fox and The Wolf was located.

Only barely composed, he entered the tavern and fully expected to see Gavriella waiting patiently for him. He knew that she would be annoyed that he was late, but he knew that he could soothe her. He was just excited to see her again, that beautiful woman with the stunning blue eyes. He was excited to sit with her and talk to her almost more than he was excited to finally know her name and where she was from.

In his excitement, he ended up going twice around the common room looking for the table where Gavriella would be waiting for him and by the third turn around the room, it began to occur to him that she wasn't there. The tavern was full of people eating the very fine food that the tavern produced, but not one of those people was Gavriella, so he found his own table to sit and wait.

And wait.

Andreas waited all day for Gavriella to appear. He kept telling himself that she had only been delayed and that any second she would come in through the door, but she never did. He ordered food simply to keep the table, but he never ate the food. It sat there and grew stone cold as he continued to wait for a woman who had been so delayed that she still hadn't shown up by sunset.

But he refused to believe she wasn't coming.

Andreas ended up sitting there all night, even after the tavernkeeper locked the door for the night. He continued to sit and wait, wondering if Gavriella had misunderstood him about when to meet him at the tavern. He thought that perhaps she had thought he meant the *next* day and he was willing to put faith in that belief, but when dawn came on the following day, Gavriella still did not come.

But Andreas continued to wait.

After sitting there for two days and nights, William and Tor finally came looking for him and found him sitting at the table, now cluttered with old food and empty pitchers of wine, still waiting for the woman who hadn't shown up. Andreas was exhausted and heartbroken, and it took both William and Tor to convince him that it was time to leave. But even after they left, Andreas walked to The Asher and stood across the street with his cousins, watching the front door, watching for some sign of Gavriella.

But he saw nothing.

Gavriella had told him that she was afraid for him to come

to The Asher because she was unsure how her aunt would react to a man coming to call for her. He had mentioned that to William and Tor, and when the wait became too excessive, it took both of his cousins to convince him not to go to the door and inquire about Gavriella. But that didn't stop William from going to one of the guards at the entry door and asking them about the lady. One of the guards knew nothing, but the second guard told him that the niece of Lady Blackburn had been sent home. That was all he could tell William, who returned to Andreas to relay the news.

Now, he knew.

But Andreas sent William back to talk to the guard who could tell him nothing more than what he had already told him. He didn't know where she'd come from and he didn't know where she had returned, and not even the offer of a few coins from William could get him to change his story. He positively refused to ask the countess about her.

The guard finally chased William away by refusing to answer any further questions and William had to return to Andreas to tell him that there was no further information about his mysterious lady. All they knew was that she had been sent back where she had come from, and Andreas knew that was somewhere in Northumberland.

Andreas hadn't felt real disappointment in his life until that very moment. When he realized that he might never see Gavriella again, he felt disillusionment that was bone crushing. He only had one lead, that she lived somewhere in Northumberland, and he thought that if he started from one end of the province and worked his way to the other end, he might be able to find her or at least find someone who knew her.

He was willing to try.

Northumberland was quite large, but it wasn't heavily populated, so it was very possible he would find at least her trail. Perhaps the easiest way of doing that would be to inquire at all the churches, for if she was meant for the veil, certainly he would find her priest at some point.

That meant he had to go home as soon as possible.

The sooner he could get to Northumberland, the sooner he could find his Gavriella. In fact, if she had been sent home the very last night that he saw her, that meant she only had a few days head start on him and there weren't many roads into Northumberland, so he had hopes of possibly finding her on the road if they moved swiftly.

Four days after Andreas was supposed to meet Gavriella in that stuffy little tavern, he departed London along with William, Tor, and Theodis, heading for the wilds of Northumberland.

Andreas had never wanted to go home so badly in his life.

He was going to find Gavriella if it took him the rest of his life.

PART TWO
THE SCOTTISH MARCHES

CHAPTER THIRTEEN

Year of Our Lord 1293
January
Wolfe's Lair

THE BAILEY WAS filling up with dirty, war-scarred men and knights, funneling into the great bailey of Wolfe's Lair nearly as far as the eye could see.

It was an army returning from war.

The de Wolfe knights were filthy, sweaty, and in most cases, bloodied as well. They had just seen six days of a nasty battle in a long line of battles over the past five months, but this one had started when Clan Maxwell, reinforced with their allies from the north, had broken out in an ugly skirmish with Clan Elliot. There were pockets of fighting, and clans chasing clans, and all of those Scots had overrun the border north of The Lair.

Oddly enough, this wasn't a typical land grab, the type of thing that had been going on for centuries. There were wars between Clan Maxwell and its enemies, Clan Elliot and Clan Johnstone, but that feud was spilling over into de Wolfe lands and tearing up everything in its path.

The English found themselves caught up in a clan war.

It was a nasty, political conflict. The House of de Wolfe had tens of thousands of men at their disposal, but there was such a buildup of angry clans on the border that William de Wolfe, the Earl of Warenton and the head of the House of de Wolfe, had called upon the king to send more troops north to help contain the rage. Considering King Edward was mostly focused in Wales at this time, he hadn't been happy about moving men and material from the Welsh Marches to deal with the conflict happening along the Scottish border.

De Wolfe was holding the line, but he was calling in reinforcements.

Other great de Wolfe allies had come to their aid – de Lohr, de Winter, de Shera, du Reims, de Royans, de Reyne, and more. Wellesbourne and de Russe had also headed north with their massive armies, which the Scots saw as a buildup to an English invasion. Or, perhaps they saw it as an insult that the English should involve themselves in a bloody conflict between clans that was just growing worse. Whatever the case, that brought more Scots to the border.

The entire north of England was straining against a Scots surge.

Wolfe's Lair was right in the middle of it because, technically, it was in Clan Elliot territory. Wolfe's Lair belonged to Scott de Wolfe, the heir to the House of de Wolfe, but what made the situation complicated was the fact that Scott's twin, Troy, had married a chieftain's daughter from Clan Kerr. That particular clan was allied with Clan Maxwell but in the midst of these border wars, they were doing their best to remain neutral.

As Troy had put it, the whole thing was a goddamned mess.

On this icy winter's day as the sun set against an orange sky to the west and the embattled army filtered into the bailey for the night, Wolfe's Lair sat like an immovable sentinel against the dramatic Scottish landscape, protecting the armies that trusted her.

The Lair...

In truth, Rule Water Castle hadn't been called by its proper name in decades, ever since the de Wolfe family from nearby Castle Questing had annexed the former Scottish garrison for the de Wolfe barony of Kilham, now the Earldom of Warenton. Everyone in England and Scotland knew the place as Wolfe's Lair, or simply The Lair, an extremely fortified fortress that had an imposing look to it.

Much like infamous Hell's Guardhouse Castle about a day's ride to the southwest, seat of the terrible de Soulis family, Rule Water Castle was built in much the same design and it was almost twice the size. It was square, box-shaped, and four stories tall. The walls of the keep were also the exterior walls of the fortress, with massive flying buttresses by design. It also had an enormous moat that was fed by a nearby stream, a wide and muck-filled ditch that was at least twenty feet wide in places and had a massive retractable wooden bridge that crossed it.

The impression of Wolfe's Lair was one of intimidation. It sat on a flat plain, with rolling hills in the distance, and could been seen for miles. With its sheer, dark walls, it had the look of dread and danger about it. The entrance to the fortress was also much like Hermitage Castle in that it was a Norman arch, several stories tall, and had two enormous gates that had been forged from the strongest iron. These gates were thick, vastly heavy, and impossible to breach once closed.

The great gates protected the interior of the fortress, which included an enormous bailey in the center. The stables, trades, small chapel, and kitchens were all located in the vast bailey while the second level contained sleeping quarters for the soldiers. The third level contained living and sleeping accom-modations for the family and the fourth floor was mostly the wall walk, a flat roof over the third floor that spanned the perimeter of the fortress. The hall, a great thing that took up one entire side of the second floor, was designed to hold a thousand men at any given time.

It was into this hall that the de Wolfe knights moved.

Andreas was at the head of the exhausted de Wolfe pack, along with Will and Tor, Markus de Wolfe and his brother, Cassius, sons of their uncle, Patrick. They were joined by Brodie de Reyne, Troy's garrison commander from Scotland, along with Scott de Wolfe, Troy de Wolfe, and another de Wolfe brother, Blayth.

Blayth had been born James de Wolfe, but the horrible battle at Llandeilo that Andreas wouldn't speak of was where the man received a near-fatal head injury. The entire de Wolfe family believed he was dead for five years until he resurfaced with no memory of who he had once been. It had taken time, and the loving arms of his family, to return much of Blayth's memory, but given that he'd spent those years in Wales as part of the Welsh rebellion, no one knew rebellion and clan battles better than Blayth did.

His advice and experience during these recent battles had been invaluable.

These were knights in their prime, fighting men who kept the Scots from invading the north of England, but they were joined by their counterparts to the east, men who were preventing the Scots from infiltrating the entire eastern seaboard of England. Northwood Castle, Castle Questing, Wark Castle, Berwick Castle, and Kyloe Castle were just a few of the fortresses who had mounted massive armies to hold the border.

Northwood was commanded by the Earl of Warenton's best friend, Paris de Norville, and his sons Hector and Adonis, while mighty Berwick Castle was commanded by the Constable of the North, Patrick de Wolfe, and his knights Alec Hage and Apollo de Norville. Patrick had sent his powerful sons, Markus and Cassius, to The Lair to help their Uncle Scott. Strangely enough,

Troy de Wolfe's properties in Kerr lands hadn't been particularly threatened, but that didn't mean they weren't on high alert. Roxburgh Castle, usually heavily beleaguered by the Scots, was also on high alert, another de Wolfe outpost that was reinforced.

And waiting...

Holding the center of this unbreakable line from Berwick all the way to Wolfe's Lair, the furthest outpost to the west, was Castle Questing commanded by none other than the Earl of Warenton himself. Since half of his sons, and knights, were concentrated at Wolfe's Lair and also at Kale Water Castle and Monteviot Tower, Troy's holdings, several knights from Northwood Castle came to help hold perhaps the mightiest and most unbreachable castle on the entire border in Castle Questing. Legendary Northwood knight Michael de Bocage and his sons, Case and Corbin, came to Castle Questing as well as the entire army from Beverly Castle, a close de Wolfe ally.

Castle Questing was so vast that she had a three-thousand-man standing army and along with Beverly's troops, added a thousand more. When de Russe and de Lohr began to arrive, Castle Questing filled out quickly and armies set up their encampments on the hilltop around it. When everyone finally arrived, including the royal troops from Wales, they had a count of twenty-five thousand men, all of them waiting for orders from William de Wolfe.

The order, starting five months earlier, had been given. But in this most recent Scots brawl, more men than ever before had moved up from Castle Questing to help quell the fighting.

This particular battle had been different.

The Scots, in a deviation from their usual plans, had decided to breach the border between The Lair and Kale Water Castle near Kelso, otherwise known as Wolfe's Den, and plowed down through the rolling hills of Northumberland and swarmed the smaller allied castles of Makendon and The Lyceum. That brought de Wolfe from the east and the west, converging on the surge of Scots that were eventually driven back over the border.

Six long and exhausting days of battle. It had taken more than a shove to get the Scots back over the border and, now, the men from the west had returned to The Lair while those from Castle Questing had retreated to their base. As the doors to the great hall of The Lair flew open, men covered in old blood and congealed gore, sweat and filth, swarmed into the hall, heading for the tables where the servants had been frantically putting out pitchers of watered wine and ale, bread and beef.

Andreas went for the wine right away. He was covered from head to toe in grime and blood, though not his own. Somehow, in the past five months of heavy fighting, he'd managed to come away unscathed. The same thing could be said for most of his cousins and uncles, though a few had light to moderate battle wounds. Will had taken an ax strike to his left arm that pained him when he moved, while Markus had taken a strike to the thigh that had taken twenty-two stitches in fine cat gut to close.

Nothing that wouldn't heal, eventually.

Everyone was beyond exhausted, however. It had been six days of limited to no sleep and Andreas was ready to collapse, as were most of them. Sleep would come easily tonight, but they all needed to eat something and decompress a little. As much as they were able, at least, given that they'd been in fight or flight mode for the past six days. More like the past five months.

It had been a rough autumn and winter.

Bringing up the rear of the cavalcade of knights entering the hall were Scott, Troy, and Blayth. As the senior commanders of the western army, they were the tacticians. Their sons like Andreas and Will and Tor were simply the followers at this point. Andreas could see his father gathering the de Wolfe knights, herding them towards the table where Andreas and the others were. Tor, in fact, had already stretched out on the floor under the table until Scott bent over to call him out. Wearily, Tor climbed out as far as the edge of the table before laying down on the floor again.

Scott didn't try to get him up.

He knew how tired they all were.

Scott de Wolfe, Lord Kilham, was the heir to the entire de Wolfe empire. A brilliant man, usually gregarious and emotional, was oddly serious these days with the threat against his family's lands. He was a stellar battle commander, much used by the king when his father wasn't in need of him, so he was the natural leader for something like this.

Next to him was Andreas' father, Troy. Although he was Scott's twin, the two brothers looked quite different. Scott was blond, favoring their mother, while Troy had the dark of their father's Saracen blood. Troy was quick to temper, a ferocious fighter, and loved his family deeply. He was proud of all his sons, so much so that he'd brought Andreas' younger half-brothers along for the experience.

Gareth de Wolfe was nineteen years of age and more Scots than English by blood. His mother, Rhoswyn, was the chieftain's daughter of Clan Kerr and his father, Troy, was half-Scots through his mother, Jordan Scott de Wolfe. Gareth looked like Troy to a fault with his dark hair and hazel eyes, and he hated anyone bringing up the fact that he was mostly Scots. He would live and die English, he swore, and as he spied Andreas, he headed over to his oldest half-brothers for camaraderie and comfort.

Andreas had a soft spot for Gareth.

Bringing up the rear behind Troy were two more sons, Corey and Reed. They were younger than Gareth at seventeen years and fifteen years of age, and they were not yet knighted but had talent beyond their years. Reed in particular; at fifteen years of age, he had inherited the extreme height trait that ran through the de Wolfe bloodlines, seen most prominently in Patrick. He had glorious auburn hair and hazel eyes, and was at least a head taller than his father, who wasn't a short man by any means. He was a calm lad who obeyed orders, trained hard, and had fists of iron. He could also be excitable. Brother Corey was much more like his father – dark, quick to temper, but also quick to laugh.

And Andreas loved them all deeply.

But they also chattered like magpies and were noisy and aggressive, grabbing bread and food, shoving others aside to get at it. Scott finally had to smack Corey on the back of the head so the lad would get the hint and shut his mouth as Scott held up a hand to silence the table full of knights. Once he had their attention, he scratched his head wearily.

"Good men," he said. "It has been an exhausting six days, but a magnificent six days. You have all performed admirably and I am very proud of you, every single one of you."

The older knights were used to such praise and didn't react overly, but the younger knights puffed up. Corey and Reed puffed up. They were usually the pair to get worked up, feeding off each other. They grabbed their cups of watered wine and cheered for themselves, a chorus picked up by the other men in the hall until it was reverberating with their shouts.

Scott had to wait until it had all died down.

"Now," he said. "Just a few moments of your time and you can eat and sleep afterwards, but I have a few things that I must discuss with you. After we chased the Scots back over the border, my spies tell me that they have retreated to the Maxwell seat of Old Midlem, at least for now, but not before they destroyed some of Kelso."

"What of Northumberland's charity at Edenside?" Andreas

asked. "Aunt Mae has her foundling home right outside of Kelso and Uncle Tommy keeps men there to protect it. Did that escape unscathed?"

He was speaking of the Earl of Northumbria, Thomas de Wolfe, and his wife, Maitland. Maitland was well known for her benevolence and she had a foundling home just to the east of Kelso where unfortunately parentless children were raised, nurtured, and educated. It was a lovely place. But Scott shook his head to his nephew's question.

"I have not heard anything about Edenside," he said. "It is a foundling home and I cannot imagine the Scots would touch it, but I am sure Uncle Tommy has it amply fortified. In any event, Kelso has been damaged and Jedburgh also took a beating."

"So did the Scots!" Corey boomed, getting the younger knights at the table riled up. "We beat their arses like an old fishwife beats her stupid children!"

Some of the other men nearby heard Corey's shout and, soon, the room of weary men was going at it again, congratulating themselves for their victory. Scott rolled his eyes at the arrogance of youth, looking to Troy for the man to control his sons, but Troy simply grinned. He loved that they were so exuberant so he was more than willing to let them have their victory yell. As Scott and Troy shook their heads at each other in amusement, in resignation, Corey jumped onto the table where everyone was drinking and trying to eat, grabbing a knuckle of beef and holding it aloft.

"This is what I think of the Scots!" he shouted, taking a big bite of the meat and letting it hang out of his mouth. "I'll chew them up and spit them out!"

The room went mad. Food began to fly. Troy finally looked to Andreas and Gareth, who took the hint and pulled Corey off the table, settling him down between them. But the damage was done. The hall was worked up by exhausted fighting men who were pleased with their victory. Scott finally gave up trying to quiet them down and quit the hall through a door that led into the living and working quarters of the castle, followed by nearly everyone at the table with the exception of Corey and Reed, who were told to remain in the hall.

Even as they left the hall, they could hear Corey shouting of their triumph and the hall going wild for it.

The more sedate knights had followed Scott into his solar, a large and comfortable chamber, without the rabble-rousing that the hall was embroiled in at the moment. Scott sent servants running for more food and drink as the senior knights settled in to listen to what Scott had to say.

Tor ended up on the floor again in front of the hearth, with Andreas and Will and Gareth standing by him. Markus, nursing the painful thigh wound, stretched out next to him, feeling the heat from the flame with great satisfaction. As the knights settled down throughout the chamber, Scott spoke up again.

"As I was saying before Troy's wild animals chimed in," he said, eyeing his brother, "the Scots retreated back to Old Midlem, taking a piece of Jedburgh and Kelso as they did. I am also hearing reports that they are moving east, which means Kelso, Wark, Questing, and Northwood will be in their path. So will Pelinom Castle."

Andreas perked up at the mention of Pelinom. "They would be mad to attack the de Velt stronghold, Uncle Scott," he said seriously. "Theodis and his father, Atlas, are holding the fortress along with his brothers Rhett and Hugo. They have Pelinom and their outpost at Foulburn reinforced. Unless the Scots want Atlas de Velt to go on a rampage like his grandfather, Jax, did those years ago, they'll stay clear of Pelinom."

That wasn't an unreasonable statement. Jax de Velt's brutality one hundred years ago was legendary. The man would conquer entire armies and put every man on a stake, shoved up through his body, and leave him to die for all to see. That kind of barbaric behavior hadn't been seen since then, but every de Velt had that edge. Atlas de Velt was very much like his grandfather, a man of little mercy and even less patience, so the threat of the man seeking vengeance for an attack on his property wasn't unreasonable.

In fact, Scott grunted in agreement.

"That is why it is better to be allied with the son of the devil's spawn than in his path," he said frankly. "I like Atlas de Velt a great deal and the man is a loyal ally, but God help the Scots if they provoke Pelinom. I am not worried about de Velt, nor any other castle to the east because they are so heavily fortified. But after what happened to Makendon Castle and The Lyceum, I am concerned for the fortresses to the west. My spies already tell me that they have seen movement from the Scots heading westerly, passing through Johnstone lands as well as Murray. If those clans catch Maxwell moving through their territory, the situation is going to go from bad to worse."

Troy, standing next to his brother, scratched his head. "Then what do you want to do?"

Scott fumbled around on the enormous oak table, rifling through a clutter of vellum, until he came to what he was looking for.

A map.

He spread it out over the table as men crowded around.

"We are located here," he said, thumping the area of the map that was just to the north of the Scottish border, about midway from one end of the border to the other. "Here are Makendon and The Lyceum. They are about a day and a half south of us and we sent them three thousand men from Castle Questing. They're reinforced for now. But this is the area I am worried about."

He was gesturing to the west of The Lair, a fairly remote and wild area between The Lair and Gretna Green. Carlisle was just to the south. He took a quill and marked two spots, closer to Gretna Green.

"Here are two castles that could be in the path of the Scots should they decide to move towards Carlisle," he said. "The one deeper in Scots' territory is Hell's Guardhouse."

Andreas, who had been studying the map intently, glanced at him. "That's de Soulis."

Scott cocked an eyebrow. "Frankly, I hope the Scots overrun it and burn out de Soulis, so I'll not lift a finger to help them, but this fortress – south of Hell's Guardhouse – is one I am concerned with."

Everyone shifted around for a better look. "What's that one?" Cassius, who was from Berwick, asked.

Scott thumped on the map again. "That is Falstone Castle," he said. "They are de Wolfe allies, but they are a smaller castle with a good deal of land on both sides of the border. Lord Merek de Leia is in command, a decent fellow who has always been cooperative, so it is my intention to move troops to Falstone in case the Scots decide to make a mess of it like they did Makendon and The Lyceum. It's a preventative measure, really."

Next to him, Troy grunted. "Hell's Guardhouse should be their allies, but they are allies to no one," he said, rubbing his eyes. "That entire family is wicked to the bone."

Scott nodded. "Which is why I am only sending troops to Falstone," he said. "Christ, the atrocities of John and Nicholas de Soulis are legendary. I hope the Scots burn those bastards out."

"Worse than Ajax de Velt?" Cassius asked. "What that man did one hundred years ago is the worst thing I've ever heard of."

"But the family has redeemed itself," Andreas said, protective of Theodis. "Ajax settled down with a good woman and amended his ways. But the de Soulis'… their actions aren't borne of conquest or money. Their actions are based on the love of bloodshed and hatred. They've looted and burned, raped and pillaged."

"So did Ajax."

"But he had an end result in mind." Andreas was becoming more heated. "I'm not saying that what he did wasn't horrible. It was. But he did it with a goal in mind. There are rumors of de Soulis boiling men alive who do not pay his rents, simply for the pleasure it gives him to inflict pain. I've heard more than one person tell me that the man and his son are involved in the dark arts. They worship the fallen angel. De Velt, as far as I know, never did that kind of thing. He was simply bent on conquest."

Cassius didn't argue with him. He supposed there was a fine line between the two, atrocities that were more acceptable than others. As Andreas wandered over to a chair to plant his weary body, Cassius was more interested in the map. Behind him, Blayth moved forward and fixed on his brothers.

"De Soulis worships the devil and boils men alive," he said in his slow and deliberate speech. "But the man mostly keeps to himself."

Scott and Troy looked at their brother. "That is true," Scott said. "He does not cause any trouble with his neighbors. Not much, anyway. But he rains hellfire on his own vassals."

Blayth looked over the map. A big man with cropped blond hair, the entire left side of his head was scarred from the wound he'd received years ago and he was missing the vast majority of his left ear. His brain had been damaged to a certain extent, hence his slow speech, but he'd never lost his brilliance.

There was something sharp still there.

"If you do not support him and the Scots manage to raze

Hell's Guardhouse, then you will have a massive fortress, full of Scots, right at your backdoor," he said. "That's less than a day's ride from The Lair, Scott, not to mention all of the smaller fortresses and allies in the area that will be under threat. Is that what you really want?"

Scott pondered that a moment. Nothing Blayth said was untrue. The de Soulis' might have been a horrible family, but they kept to themselves and left de Wolfe properties alone. They'd never had any trouble with them. If he had to choose between de Soulis and the Scots, he knew which choice he had to make.

He finally shook his head.

"Nay," he said. "I suppose not. But they would not take our help even if I offered it. You've seen Hell's Guardhouse. It's as impenetrable as The Lair. As long as de Soulis keeps himself sealed up inside, the Scots cannot take it."

"Then mayhap you should send him a missive to do just that," Blayth said. "He may not know about the movements of the Scots towards the west."

Scott's focus lingered on his map for a moment before finally shrugging. "Very well," he said. "I'm not beyond at least warning the man. But let us return our attention to Falstone. Andreas?"

Andreas' head came up from where he'd been sitting near the hearth, looking at his hands. "Aye, Uncle Scott?"

Scott met his gaze. "You will take a thousand men with you and head for Falstone," he said. "I'll send word to Castle Questing to have two thousand more sent along. You will hold that fortress and if anything happens to Hell's Guardhouse… well, I'm afraid you may have to protect it, too. Blayth is right – as much as I don't care what happens to John and Nicholas de Soulis, we cannot let the Scots overrun it."

Andreas nodded smartly. "Aye, my lord."

"Take Gareth, Will, and Brodie with you," he said, looking to Troy. "Is it agreeable to send de Reyne along?"

Brodie de Reyne was one of the older knights in the de Wolfe arsenal. A tall and muscular man, he was from the prestigious de Reyne family, a very large family that had roots in Northumbria and York. He had a vivacious personality, something that ladies took to quite easily, and he had no shortage of female admirers.

With his blond good looks and bright smile, Brodie had quite a reputation as a lady's man, something that had ended when he'd met Scott's eldest daughter, Sophia du Rennic. Twice her age, it brought a good deal of consternation from Scott, who was particularly overprotective of Sophia since her biological father had perished years before. It had taken some doing on Brodie's part to woo her, and it had been quite an adventure, but he was part of the family now.

But the de Wolfe brothers still liked to pick on him from time to time.

Therefore, Troy nodded.

"Get that dolt as far away from me as you can," he said, but fought off a grin when Brodie smiled broadly at him. "Besides, I have Cassius de Shera in command of Kale Water Castle and I have a de Bocage son at Monteviot Tower, so for now, I can spare that fool. But beat him if he misbehaves."

As Brodie chuckled, Andreas stood up wearily. "Is there anything else I need to know before going to Falstone?"

Scott ran a weary hand over his face. "Possibly," he said. "We had a group of minstrels who passed through here right when the wars with the Scots was heating up," he said. "I was told that Lord de Leia may be suffering from some kind of madness. Some days, he seems well and other days, he does not. Be cautious going in, Dray. And once you're there, send a contingent of men down to Blackgate Castle to the south. As I recall, it's a small but important outpost. Warn them of the Scots' activity and ask them if they require reinforcements."

Andreas nodded. "I will," he said. "What about Carlisle?"

Scott sighed heavily. "They could possibly be a target," he said. "Carlisle Castle is a royal garrison right now and could have quite possibly already heard about the Scots, but it would be wise to send them word. We may need them if things grow worse."

Andreas was silent a moment, thinking on the assignment he'd been given. Something seemed to be troubling him.

"Uncle Scott," he finally said. "Falstone will be the last fortified castle in a line that stretches all the way from Berwick. There is still Gretna Green and then Carlisle. We're not covering the entire border and if the Scots move past Falstone, what then? It's quite possible that will happen because they've not been able to breach the border where we hold the line. But if they keep moving further west, eventually, they'll be able to break through."

Scott looked at his nephew. The brilliant knight who hadn't been the same since returning from London those months ago. Scott's sons, Will and Tor, spoke of a mysterious woman that Andreas had fallen for, one that had simply disappeared without a word.

They all knew what had happened.

Even if they hadn't, it was obvious that something had been amiss with Andreas. He was usually such a kind, gentle man with members of the family. But the past six months had seen a man who was particularly withdrawn. He didn't want to socialize or engage in the gatherings, and he didn't spend an inordinate time with his brothers or friends anymore.

He'd become a bit of a loner.

Troy was concerned, of course, but he knew his son. He knew Andreas would work through it somehow, although he didn't like the blow that he'd taken from the woman no one knew. But that blow had other side effects.

Whatever angst, sorrow, or disappointment Andreas was feeling had come out on the battlefield. Andreas had always been a formidable fighter, but the last five months against the Scots had seen him turn into a beast of a knight. He had more kills than any of them, brutal kills that took off heads or cut torsos nearly in two. Troy had seen him take off half of a man's head – just the top half – in a spectacularly gory death. He'd become so powerful and courageous that the armies had given him a nickname –

Loup tueur.

Killer wolf.

Still, others were calling him *WolfeBlade* because of the way he swung his sword. Left-handed and as fast as lightning, he could sneak up on a man that way and they never knew what hit them until it was too late. It was something that the right-handed fighters had trouble defending against.

In battle, Andreas had indeed become the killer wolf with a deadly blade.

Troy was proud of him for becoming such a legendary knight, of course, but he was also troubled by what drove Andreas to kill like that. He and the others could only assume, make best guesses at a puzzling situation because Andreas wouldn't speak on the woman from London, just as he never really spoke on his mother's death. Andreas wasn't a man to let others know his inner thoughts and feelings. That was simply his way.

Therefore, they were all trying to be sympathetic to that.

Especially Scott. There was a special place in his heart for the man who had lost his mother the same way his older sons had lost theirs, only Will and Tor had each other for comfort.

Andreas didn't even have that.

"I share your concerns, Dray," Scott said after a moment. "Rowanburn Castle is near Gretna Green but the last I'd heard, that place had fallen to the Scots. We cannot worry about it right now. My spies will keep an eye on the Scots' movements and if it looks like they're heading towards Gretna Green and Carlisle, then we'll do what we must at that time. Me, your father, and Uncle Blayth are on the west side of the border and Uncles Atty, Eddie, and Tommy are on the east side along with Poppy and Uncle Paris. The bulk of the border is well covered and because this is a clan war, I don't believe we really have to worry about them passing down into Carlisle."

Andreas lifted a hand, gesturing in the direction they had come from. "Why not?" he asked. "We just spent six days chasing them back over the border. Why do you think they'd not try to get through to Carlisle?"

"Simple," Troy said, answering for his brother. "Rhoswyn's clan says that Clan Maxwell is interested in regaining Scottish lands they believe belong to them. All of these other clans that have come down to fight on the borders don't seem to have a stake in the lands. Their stake seems to be in each other with political dealings. This isn't an invasion of England, though they make it look otherwise."

Andreas wasn't quite sure he agreed. "What does Poppy say?"

Poppy was what all of the grandchildren called William, their grandfather. Troy looked at his brothers, Scott and Blayth, who both nodded faintly.

"He has seen more action on the border than any of us," Troy said after a moment. "Poppy does not believe this is an invasion, but simply clan unrest that is spilling into England. But objectives change sometimes. We'll simply have to be vigilant."

There wasn't anything more Andreas could say, so he simply nodded his head. He was tired, they all were, and the conversation seemed to lag quite a bit after that. Tor and Markus were snoring on the floor in front of the hearth and Andreas had to step over them. As he approached his father, Troy reached out and put a hand on his shoulder.

"Come," he said. "Walk with me and let us discuss your approach to Falstone."

Andreas paused, looking at his father. "Why?" he said. "I think the situation is clear enough."

Scott was standing next to Troy, turning to his nephew. "I hope it is clear," he said. "But you understand I am sending you there for a reason."

"What reason?"

"Because since the beginning of this campaign, there has been no knight as courageous and ferocious as you," he said. "Falstone may need that should the Scots make it to their walls and I would rather have you in command of a siege more than anyone else."

He meant it as flattery, but Andreas suspected there was more to it. He could see it in their eyes. He knew he'd been a madman in battle. Perhaps they meant to take him off the line for a time simply to help him regain his control.

As if such a thing was even possible right now.

"Markus, Cassius, Tor, or Will would be just as courageous," he said. "I am no better than they are, but I do appreciate your faith in me, Uncle Scott. I will not fail."

Scott smiled faintly. "I know you will not," he said. "Eat and rest, now. You will be departing at dawn."

Andreas simply nodded. He forced a smile at his father and his uncle before turning away and heading back out to the hall where there was plentiful food and drink, and perhaps the opportunity not to have his father and half-brothers and family hovering over him, wondering if he was mentally composed.

Wondering if the killer wolf would take a rest.

Troy and Scott, joined by Blayth, watched him depart through the stone-arch doorway.

"He knows," Blayth muttered.

Scott turned to him. "Knows what?"

"That you gave him that command to get him out of battle before he gets himself killed."

Troy sighed heavily. "It is for his own good," he said quietly. "He's become a monster in battle and, sooner or later, that is going to catch up with him. It would be better if he spent a few weeks at a nice, quiet castle. Mayhap it will calm the fire in his blood."

Blayth thought on his powerful, brooding nephew. "Would it calm the fire in yours?" he asked. "All Dray has done since he returned from London is look for that woman he'd met there, the one who told him that she lived in Northumberland. He was just starting his search in earnest when these wars cropped up. He has unfinished business of the heart and sending him off to cool his blood will not stop that. It will only delay it for a time."

Both Blayth and Scott were looking at Troy, who was chewing his lip, pondering his son's situation. After a moment, he simply shook his head.

"It cannot be helped," he said. "He has unfinished business – I understand that – but the angst and fury he is displaying in battle is going to get him killed."

"He's not been reckless that I've seen," Blayth said.

Troy shook his head. "Not reckless," he said. "But not exactly cautious, either. I cannot lose him, Blayth. If I did, everything of Helene would be gone and I am not sure I could bear that. I know that sounds strange, given that I love Rhoswyn and we have many children together. We are quite happy. But I was happy with Helene, too, and Andreas is the last vestige of that happiness. It is a part of me that I cannot lose."

Scott understood. He put his hand on Troy's shoulder. "I see the same thing in Will and Tor," he said. "The last remnants of my life with Athena. I see them now and see the men they have become, and I know she would have been so proud. I have a wife I adore and nine children, and I would not trade my life for anything, but I understand when you say that you look at your eldest and see the remnants from a past life. It becomes part of your very aura, part of the air you breathe, and that is why I think sending Dray to Falstone is for the best. It will take him out of the action."

Troy nodded, but his heart was heavy. "And he knows it, as Blayth said," he mumbled. "But he's obeying his orders, like a good knight."

Before Scott or Blayth could reply, Corey and Reed came flying into the solar, heading for their father.

"Papa!" Corey said breathlessly. "Dray is going to defend a castle and he said we could come! May we, Papa? *May we?*"

Troy looked at his excitable boys and he started to chuckle. He looked at Scott. "Well?" he said. "Should we send the wild animals with him?"

As Blayth stood back and smirked, Scott was on the spot. Corey and Reed turned their attention to their uncle and nearly bowled the man over in their excitement.

"Uncle Scott," Corey said, his hands on Scott's shoulders, grabbing at him. "May we please go and help defend the castle? It would be very good experience for us!"

"Very good!" Reed echoed.

"*Please*, Uncle Scott!"

Scott was being buffeted between the two of them and he finally put up his hands, pushing them away.

"Very well," he said, simply to shut them up. "But you listen to Dray. Do everything he tells you. If I hear you have diso-beyed the slightest command, I will send you back to

Kenilworth and you'll stay there until you can learn to obey. Is that clear?"

The threat of the master knights of Kenilworth Castle, the premier training castle in England for knights, was a serious threat, indeed. Both Corey and Reed nodded eagerly and Troy grabbed Corey by the arm.

"Tell Dray you may go," he said. "Ask him what help he needs to prepare and do everything he tells you. If he has nothing for you, then you will take his armor, my armor, and your uncles' armor and clean it until it shines. You will do this before dawn or you do not go. Is that clear?"

The boys continued to nod, grabbing him and kissing him as he fought them off. Like their uncles, Scott and Blayth, they were kissers. They kissed everyone, something their mother loved but something their father thought was annoying. After sufficiently smooching on their father's head, they fled the solar, hooting and yelling like barbarians in their excitement. Blayth burst into quiet laughter and even Scott grinned as Troy covered his face.

"My God, what have I done to Dray?" he moaned. "And Rhos – my wife is not going to like that I have sent them away."

"Rhos is a warrior," Scott said. "She understands."

Troy's hands came away from his face. "Aye, she does, but that doesn't mean she'll like it," he said. Then, he sighed heavily. "But their presence may very well distract Dray from his angst. If he must be responsible for that pair, it may be the help he needs in cooling whatever burns in his blood."

Scott turned back to his table as some of the other knights began to filter out of the room. "Everybody's blood is burning these days," he said, looking back to his map. "The Scots are burning, Dray is burning. Unfortunately, we have to be concerned with both."

That was quite true. As the room cleared except for Tor and

Markus, snoring in front of the fire, Scott and Troy and Blayth took a seat at the table, drinking the watered wine and eating food that had been brought to them, speaking of something other than battle.

Family… friends… they were much more pleasant subjects than the rampaging Scots.

But something told them that this respite would be quite brief.

Tomorrow might bring them more hell than they could handle.

CHAPTER FOURTEEN

Falstone Castle

"THERE'S TROUBLE."

Gavriella paused, looking up from the tally of stores in the vault. A fungus had moved through the turnips they'd had stored for winter and, by the time they caught it, they'd lost half of their supply. She and a pair of servants were in the vaults underneath the keep of Falstone, separating the unsalvageable from the salvageable, when her father's only knight, the commander of his eight hundred man army, found her.

She found herself looking into Sir Lukas de Dere's serious face.

"What trouble?" she asked, pushing a stray lock of hair from her face. "More trouble than what we already have here? I am afraid this rot has gotten into other vegetables I simply do not yet see."

Lukas shook his head. He was a young knight, handsome with intense blue eyes and cropped brown hair, and he was deeply dedicated to his duty. So dedicated, in fact, that when his wife became sickly last year, he'd sent her home to live with her parents so they could tend her and he would not be distracted with it. He thought he'd been doing the right thing, but he longed for her every single day, distracted with the memory of her more than he probably would have been with her physical presence.

It was something he had to live with. Just like he had to live with the guilt of not being able to protect his liege's daughter when she'd been abducted by Nicholas de Soulis last year. He'd been forbidden to retaliate by Merek himself, who had given him a litany of reasons why it was a bad idea.

Lukas didn't agree with any one of them.

He was a man with many regrets.

"I just received a missive from the commander of the de Wolfe army, Scott de Wolfe," he said. "Evidently, the Scots are going on a rampage and there is trouble heading our way. A contingent of de Wolfe troops will be arriving today to help us in the event the Scots move against us."

Gavriella brushed off her hands and stood up. "War is heading in our direction?"

He shrugged his big shoulders. "It is possible," he said. "We have heard about the trouble to the north."

Gavriella nodded, but she was clearly anxious. "We have," she said. "But trouble rarely comes in our direction. We have a good relationship with Clan Johnstone."

Lukas could see that she was worried. "It sounds as if this goes beyond just Clan Johnstone," he said. "According to the missive, the entire House of de Wolfe, all the way to Berwick, has been dealing with this clan war. 'Tis clan against clan, and that is never a good thing."

Gavriella pondered that. "So de Wolfe is sending men to help protect us in case the situation grows worse?"

"Exactly."

Gavriella took a deep breath, trying to still her anxiety, as she turned to look at the enormous vault and its contents.

"We must be able to feed them," she said. "I was not expecting to feed an army, Lukas."

"I know," he said. "Do what you can. I'll discuss the situation with the commander when the army arrives. It is the dead of winter, so we cannot harvest anything further."

Winter hunger was always a serious threat, one always taken seriously and especially now with the arrival of an unexpected army. "I will see what we can spare," she said. "Did the missive say what time they would be arriving?"

Lukas shook his head. "Nay, but I would plan on feeding them the evening meal."

Gavriella nodded in resignation. As Lukas headed off to prepare for the incoming army, she returned to the turnips, piled up in two large heaps – the bad ones and the good ones.

She pointed to the pile of rotting ones.

"You heard the man," she said to the servants. "Lukas said we have an incoming army to feed. We shall have to go through every single turnip and cut away the rotted parts and try to salvage the remaining good. We shall need more help for this. Iva, go into the kitchens and find anyone who can help us. We'll need baskets to haul up the vegetables to the kitchen yard. Tell the cook we must make a stew to feed two thousand men, so we'll need the massive iron pot she uses for boiling hide. It needs to be cleaned and put over the fire in the yard. Hurry, now – there is no time to waste."

Iva, a tiny old woman who moved swiftly, took off running. That left Gavriella with the remaining servant, a woman she had known all her life. She sighed heavily.

"That leaves you and me, Meli," she said. "Get a knife and let's start going through these turnips. Cut the mold off completely and save what is left, even if it is just a tiny piece. Every little bit will help."

Meli, round-cheeked and dedicated, went to work alongside Gavriella, who picked up the knife that Iva had left behind and began cutting out the rot on one turnip at a time. She threw herself into it, as she threw herself into everything these days because it took her mind off the situation at Falstone.

The realities of what her life had become.

The truth was that it had all started last year with that horrible abduction she tried so hard not to think about. But the situation had only gotten worse since her return from London. Her flight from London had been a confusing, disorienting thing because it had happened so quickly. One moment, she was there and in the next, she was heading home. She did not regret her fight with Aurelia, however. In fact, she really didn't regret anything, not even the visit to Gomorrah, because she wouldn't have met Andreas otherwise.

The man who was on her mind every moment of every day.

She was still overcome by memories of the evening she left. Though she'd initially believed that the separation between them had been for the best, increasingly, she was overcome with remorse and longing. Being unable to get word to him had haunted her. All she could think about was Andreas sitting in that tavern, waiting for a woman who would never come. She wondered how long he had waited before he realized that.

She wondered just how much he hated her now.

Being made out to be a liar had been bad enough but, in the end, the inability to tell Andreas exactly why she hadn't been able to meet him was even worse. Had she known what would have happened on the afternoon she returned to The Asher, then perhaps she would have conducted herself differently.

Perhaps she would have been more obedient and more apologetic to her Aunt Drucilla. She had relived it over and over in her mind a thousand times, but every time she came to the part where Aurelia accused her of wrongdoing, she knew she would have fought back. She couldn't have stopped herself. Something about Aurelia brought out the fighter in her.

But that fight had cost her everything.

She had to explain the fight when she had returned home, showing up on her father's doorstep and telling the man that she had been sent home in shame. She knew, at some point, that her father and aunt would speak and that her father would eventually find out just why she had been sent home, so it wouldn't do any good to lie to the man.

Therefore, she tried not to.

She'd told him, quite frankly, that Aurelia was a vile girl who had forced her to go to a guild called Gomorrah. She told her father of all the horrible things she saw there and how Aurelia and Camilla let strange men kiss them and fondle them. She proceeded to tell her father that she had been trying to get out of the place and became lost when a nice man helped her to find the exit. The man, she explained, had been very proper and polite with her, so much so that she accompanied the man the next day to see entertainment.

Her aunt had taken exception to that.

It was the truth and Gavriella stood behind it. Of course, there was much more to it than her simple explanation, but her father wasn't going to ask for details and she wasn't going to tell. At this point, she controlled the narrative of the situation and she was going to leave it at that. If her aunt, at any point in the future, decided to make an issue out of it, Gavriella would deal with it at the appropriate time.

But the truth was that her father had been extremely displeased to see her returned to Falstone Castle. He hadn't expected to see her anytime soon and he hadn't really cared why she had come home, only that she had. It was clear that he didn't want her there and it had made for an awkward few weeks after her arrival.

Merek de Leia had never been an overly affectionate man and his standoffish behavior towards her hadn't been anything unusual. Gavriella quickly resumed her routine at the castle, resuming her duties as chatelaine and taking over other duties such as becoming more involved in meal preparation and any number of smaller tasks that she had always passed off on the cook.

At that point, she was looking for something to occupy her time.

Anything to make her feel useful.

Now that she had returned, she didn't want to think about what she'd left behind in London.

It was so strange, really. She had hated London at first, grieved because of why her father had sent her there, but Andreas had quickly changed her mind. The time spent with him had been something that had changed her outlook on life. It *had* changed her life. Then she'd come home again, home to the terrible memories of the child that she had given birth to on that stormy morning in April.

It was as if she had never left.

Her child, a son, had been born after just a few hours of labor. Truth be told, it hadn't been all that difficult to push the baby out, into the waiting hands of two servants and the cook. Her father wouldn't even call for the physic, nor would he call for a midwife because he didn't want anyone to know his daughter was pregnant. Even though the village of Deadwater knew about the attack, that was all they knew.

No one knew about the resulting baby.

In fact, the only people who really knew of the pregnancy were Gavriella's maids and the cook, women she had known her entire life and women who are very protective over her. The little boy was born healthy, screaming at the top of his lungs, and Gavriella was able to hold him and nurse him for a couple of weeks until her father insisted that the child be sent to the foundling home at Edenside.

The permanent reminder of her shame had to be removed.

Her beautiful, perfect son was taken away from her when he was barely two weeks of age, handed over to the nuns who had come from Edenside. They had been quite gentle with the infant, but Gavriella felt as if her heart had been ripped from her body. It was true that child had been conceived in a violent, terrible act, but in Gavriella's mind, that hadn't been the baby's fault. He was innocent, just as she was, and the day she returned home from London was the day she knew she would never be able to forgive her father for what he had done.

He had taken her son away.

A lad named Storm.

Those were the things he had sent her to London to forget, and she had for a short while. At least, she had forgotten the gut-wrenching pain she had felt from being separated from her baby and the horrific shame and anguish from the attack. She knew who had attacked her. She had known that from the beginning when she had identified the brand on one of the horses.

Assaulted by the most hated family on the borders.

And justice would never be served.

For those few brief days that she had been in London, the situation had seemed more distant and she had been better able to deal with it although the anguish hadn't completely gone away. She wondered if it ever would. It had been Andreas who had shown her something other than that dark and horrific anguish that seemed to follow her around like a fog.

Andreas, her knight in shining armor, a man who had shown her a glimpse of the world she never thought she would know.

And now, here she was, back home in a place she hated, with a father she hated, with no future and no way to reclaim her child. The past six months had been her greatest effort to try and forget about what had happened, but much as her son had been a reminder of the shame brought upon her family, her father was a reminder of that child she had lost. Every time she looked at him, she felt hatred anew.

It was just one of the things she hated about returning home.

More strange things were happening at Falstone these days.

When Gavriella had returned from London, there had been a new female servant who shadowed her father everywhere he went. The woman had been sent by an ally, she was told, but not even Lukas could tell her just who the ally was. He was very suspicious of the woman, but Merek didn't seem to mind having her around. Lukas had discovered why when he had walked in on them in Merek's solar and the woman's head was down between Merek's legs.

That told Lukas everything he needed to know.

The woman's name was Giddy and she was quite clever. Over the past six months, she had gone out of her way to separate Merek from everyone else. She ate with him in his chamber, she was with him while he conducted business in his solar, and wherever Merek went, she trailed along behind him. She was obedient and quiet, and always tried to be as inobtrusive as possible, but it was obvious that she had a stranglehold on Merek.

These days, he wouldn't go anywhere without her.

Then came the madness.

Somewhere in the past six months, Merek seem to have developed a madness that ebbed and flowed. It seemed to be better in the morning and worse in the evening. He conducted business with Lukas in the mornings, because by mid-afternoon, he was almost completely incoherent.

Giddy was always with him, madness or no, following him around and tending to him, and Lukas was convinced that the woman had something to do with whatever was happening to Merek de Leia.

But he couldn't prove it.

Merek would rage at anyone who suggested that he separate from Giddy. When Gavriella had returned from London and saw what was happening, she'd even suggested it to her father and he lashed out at her, nearly hitting her in the face. After that, Gavriella stayed away from him and away from Giddy, who had tried to befriend her at first, but Gavriella made it very clear she wanted nothing to do with her.

These days, Falstone was something of a horrible mess.

And now, the Scots were on the rampage.

As Gavriella sat on the floor of the vault and cut away pieces of rotten turnips, she tried not to think of what her life had become. What Falstone had become. If things hadn't been bad enough when she left, they were worse when she had returned. But she was jolted from those moody thoughts when Iva returned with the cook and two more servants, taken from the keep. They were maids, but they could use a knife as well as anyone, so Gavriella handed her knife over to the cook, a woman named Jocosa, as she stood up and brushed off her hands.

"Lukas tells me that we're expecting an army here by this evening," she said. "We'll need to make great batches of stew in the iron pots used to boil the hides. We have turnips, carrots, onions, and the sausages we made when we slaughtered the pigs in the autumn. We can boil the sausages with everything and make a nice stew."

Jocosa was already on the ground, tossing the cut turnips into a big basket she'd brought.

"I'll add barley to it," she said. "I can make it last a few days, depending on how many men we're feeding. Do you know?"

Gavriella shrugged. "Lukas says at least two thousand," she

said. "We do not know how long they are staying, so you'll have to plan to feed them for at least a month. Can you do that?"

Jocosa looked around the vault. She was a big woman, round and strong, and she knew her business. "Aye, my lady," she said after a moment. "I'll determine what to feed them without using everything we have. Leave it to me."

That was Jocosa – a woman who never had a harsh would or a negative comment. Truthfully, she was one of the people who kept Gavriella sane around this place and Gavriella smiled, patting the woman on the shoulder.

"You have my thanks, Jo," she said. "I must see what Lukas is doing about their accommodations. I suppose we should house the knights in the keep, so I should make room for them."

Leaving Jocosa to handle the turnips, Gavriella headed out. The vault had two exits – a narrow staircase to the floor above and then a second exit built right into the wall, with exterior stairs that led up into the bailey. She had seen Lukas go in that direction, so she followed.

It was an icy day. They'd had snow two days before that had melted, but the freezing temperatures had turned everything to ice. The bailey was caked solid and there were frozen ponds throughout. Given that Falstone had limited space inside that crusty, frozen bailey, Gavriella knew that they were about to be crammed full of men with the incoming army and the horses.

It was about to get quite cozy.

Rounding the keep, she came into the main body of the bailey. The enormous gatehouse was directly ahead and she could see men scurrying about, including Lukas, who was speaking to one of his men. When he looked up and saw her approach, he excused himself and made his way in her direction.

"The army has been sighted a few miles out," he told her.

"Our scouts have seen them moving towards us and it looks like more than a thousand men. There are at least five knights that our scouts saw, mayhap more he did not."

Gavriella lifted her eyebrows. "I wanted to ask you where you wish to house the knights," she said. "We have those two chambers on the ground floor of the keep that the servants use, but they can sleep elsewhere if we need to house the knights."

Lukas nodded. "It would be the polite thing to give the knights their own chambers," he said. "If you could see to that, I would be grateful."

Gavriella smiled. "I will," she said, noticing that he seemed rather harried. "Do not worry so, Lukas. We shall feed them and house them. There is nothing to be concerned over."

Lukas cast her a long look. "Nothing except your father," he said. "I have not even told him yet."

"I will do it."

"It should come from me."

"Then let me tell him that you will come to him when time allows. He is probably already watching the bailey and wondering what the activity is about."

Lukas resisted the urge to look up to the top floor of the keep where Merek's chamber was located. "He'll send that bitch down here to demand answers," he muttered. "Mayhap you'd better tell him what has happened so he will not send her down here to get in my way."

Gavriella patted his arm. "I will," she said. "I will keep her away."

"You seem to have better luck at it than I do."

She could hear the frustration in his voice. He turned away, heading back to the commotion at the gatehouse as Gavriella turned for the keep.

No one wanted to deal with Merek these days with that woman by his side.

Taking a deep breath, she headed inside.

The keep of Falstone was cylinder shaped, and quite large, with several chambers on each level except for the top level, which had one great room belonging to Merek. The first level, accessed by stone steps in a fortified forebuilding, contained an entry hall, her father's solar, a small hall, and three smaller chambers. This was where she planned to house the knights. The level above that was a level with two large bedchambers, one belonging to Gavriella, and then her father's level on top of that.

Heading up the stairs to the keep entry, she found one of the male servants in her father's solar, sweeping out the ashes in the hearth, and she instructed him to start preparing two of the chambers for at least five knights and perhaps more. Beds needed to be brought in and mattresses needed to be prepared.

There were logistics to preparing guest accommodations and she sent the man off to do her bidding before taking the mural stairs that led to the upper floors. She has just come off the stairs onto the level where her bedchamber was when Giddy suddenly emerged from the stairs that led up to her father's chambers.

Their eyes locked.

"You, there," Giddy said imperiously. "Gavriella. Your father wishes to know why his men are running around like mad. What is happening?"

Giddy never addressed her formally. Her manner always conveyed little respect. That had started when Gavriella had made it clear she wanted no friendship with the woman and it continued even now. Giddy was an older woman with big breasts and big hips, wearing garments that were always tightly cinched at the waist to make her breasts look larger. She had red hair, piled on top of her head, and Gavriella thought she wore rouge because her cheeks were always unnaturally red. Giddy, which probably wasn't even her real name, was clearly a low-born woman who tried to throw her weight around.

Even with the lord's daughter.

Gavriella eyed the woman a moment before pushing past her without answering.

She could hear Giddy calling after her, demanding she stop, but Gavriella ignored her. She continued up to her father's chamber to find the man sitting in front of the hearth, enjoying a big pitcher of wine. Gavriella had noticed that her father seemed to drink quite a lot these days, always spurred on by Giddy.

The woman was constantly supplying him with drink.

"Greetings, Father," she said without a hint of warmth. "Lukas has asked me to tell you that he will join you shortly to provide more information, but he has received a missive from the House of de Wolfe."

Merek had the cup in his hands, half-filled with wine, as he turned to his only child. There was no hint of warmth in his gaze, either.

"De Wolfe?" he repeated. "What do they want?"

Giddy came around behind Merek's chair, standing over him as she eyed Gavriella angrily.

Gavriella wouldn't even look at her.

"There has been some trouble with the Scots," Gavriella told her father. "De Wolfe seems to have had a good deal of trouble with them and he fears they are heading in our direction to cause trouble, so he is sending men to reinforce Falstone against a potential Scots attack. Lukas will give you more detail when he can, but that is the commotion you have been seeing. We are preparing for the army's arrival."

Giddy's hand went on Merek's shoulder, Gavriella was certain, in a possessive gesture just to irritate her, but Gavriella still wouldn't look at her. She was focused on her father, who seemed concerned that de Wolfe was sending an army to them.

"We've not had trouble from the Scots in years," he said. "He must have more reason to send men to protect us. I would speak with the commander of the army when he arrives."

Gavriella nodded. "I will tell Lukas that," she said. "Anything else, Father? I thought to house the knights in the keep because there is really nowhere else to put them. We shall be quite crowded, but we shall manage."

Merek nodded and started to stand up, but Giddy pushed him down. "Rest, my lord," she said. "Your knight will come to you. You need not strain yourself."

Merek did as she asked, like a man with no will. Gavriella peered at him. "Father?" she said. "Do you require something?"

"If he does, I shall do for him," Giddy interrupted.

There was something controlling in the woman's tone and Gavriella did look at her, then. "I was not speaking to you," she said. "I was asking my father."

Giddy stiffened. "I am capable of bringing him whatever he needs, Gavriella."

Gavriella's eyes narrowed. "You will address me as 'my lady'," she said. "You are only a servant, after all. Know your place, Woman. You will show me the respect I deserve, as the lord's daughter."

Giddy's pink cheeks grew pinker. "I have Lord Merek's confidence," she said, sounding like a snarl. "If anyone should know her place, it should be you."

Gavriella had had enough. She'd gone around a few times with Giddy before, but the woman didn't seem to get the message. She walked up to her father's chair, putting her face in Giddy's.

"You are a servant and nothing more," she hissed. "We do not even know where you came from. You showed up here one day telling us you were a gift from an ally, but *which* ally? I am going to start sending out missives to every ally and neighbor we have and ask them if they sent you. Should I do that, Giddy? If you cannot tell me more, then that is what I need to do."

"You'll do no such thing. I am no business of yours."

"Any business of Falstone's is my business also. I am going to find out where you really came from if you will not tell me."

"I do not answer to you."

"And *you* do not belong here."

Outraged, Giddy lifted a hand as if to strike her, but Gavriella was faster. She slapped the woman, open-palmed, as hard as she could. Giddy's coiffed hair went flying everywhere and she staggered, nearing falling over into the hearth.

Gavriella was on top of her.

"Did you truly think to strike me?" she demanded, pushing Giddy back to her knees when the woman tried to stand up. "Strike me and I shall have you thrown in the vault for striking the lord's daughter. I'll leave you there to rot. Do you understand me?"

Giddy was furious. "And the men would do your bidding only because they know you shall reward them," she seethed. "I know what you've done, lady. I know that you are not as pure as you want everyone to believe."

Gavriella's eyes widened. She was about to wrap her hands around Giddy's neck but her father was on his feet, grasping her by the arms and pulling her away.

"Nay, Gavy," he said. "Go, now. Prepare for our guests."

Gavriella yanked herself from her father's grasp. "How can you keep her here, knowing how she treats me?" she demanded. "*Why* do you keep her here, Father?"

Merek waved her off, giving her a feeble push towards the chamber door. He didn't want to talk about the situation, or deal with it, and he headed back to his chair as Giddy stood up and brushed herself off. This was the Merek they'd been dealing with since Giddy had arrived – apathetic, befuddled, weak.

Very weak.

Infuriated, Gavriella focused on Giddy.

"Your days here are numbered, wench," she said. "Do not become too comfortable. As soon as I find out where you really came from, I'll throw you out myself."

All Giddy had to do was put her hands on Merek, possessively, and the message was clear. Unless Merek dismissed her, she wasn't going anywhere. And she probably wouldn't leave even if he did. She had a good thing going and she wasn't going to let it go so easily.

Enraged, Gavriella quit the chamber and slammed the door.

She met Lukas when she was halfway down the stairs.

"Is he –?" Lukas began.

Gavriella cut him off. "He's with that… that *whore*," she said, close to tears because she was so angry. "I told him about the army. He's expecting you."

She pushed past him but he grabbed her before she could get away completely. "What happened?" he asked, genuinely concerned. "Why are you so upset?"

Gavriella was trying to stave off the tears. "Lukas, how can we get rid of that woman?" she asked. "It is bad enough here with my father the way he is, but she makes the situation so much worse. What can we do?"

Lukas sighed heavily. "I have tried, my lady," he said. "Your father wants her here."

Gavriella shook her head in frustration. "I have been hearing the same thing since I returned from London," she said. "Mayhap I could give her some money to go away. Mayhap that's what she is after, anyway. I have a very bad feeling about her, Lukas. She is after something."

"I know," Lukas said quietly. "I feel the same way. If I wasn't such an honorable man, possibly she could meet with an accident and we could be done with her. But so far, she's really done nothing but keep your father company. She's not stolen anything that I can see, and she hasn't done anything treacherous."

Gavriella wasn't satisfied. "She's rude and insufferable," she said. "I am going to offer her money to see if she will go away."

"If your father finds out, he may become angry."

Gavriella looked at him. "My father and I have been at odds for some time now, Lukas," she said. "One more thing will not make any difference. But I do apologize for being short with you. That woman has me up in arms. My father is waiting for you and I am off to ensure the knights have a soft bed and a clean chamber."

Lukas smiled faintly at her. "Your efforts are appreciated," he said. "And do not let Giddy get the better of you. That is what she wants. You are far better than she is and she knows it. Do not let her use that against you."

Gavriella took a deep breath, forcing herself to calm. Lukas was like the big brother she never had, always kind to her, always protective. There had never been anything romantic between them, not even before he married his wife. Gavriella had simply never felt that way about him. He was more like family and that was the only way she would ever look at him. In any case, she was glad to have him around.

He was the one stable thing around this place.

"Thank you, Lukas," she said. "I do not know what I would do without your kindness. I will not let her get to me."

"Good," he said. "I'd better see to your father before that cow comes looking for me. And you must see to those chambers. Make haste, my lady. The de Wolfe army approaches."

Gavriella nodded and continued down the stairs, pushing Giddy out of her mind. She had other things to focus on. Men to bed, food to provide. All in a day's work as the chatelaine of

Falstone.

Little did she know what, however, she would soon be facing.

Her stars were about to change.

CHAPTER FIFTEEN

"**L**OOK TO THE east," Gareth said. "A storm is coming in. See it?"

Andreas was astride his muscular war horse, the one that had replaced the horse he'd had for eighteen years who had fallen in battle three months ago. The horse's name had been Otho, a gray beast missing one eye, but he'd been hell in a fight. Oddly enough, it hadn't been a weapon that killed him – he'd simply seized up in the middle of a fight and dropped dead, leaving Andreas pinned beneath him. It had taken his father, his brother, and several men to lift the horse enough so he could be pulled out from underneath.

Andreas missed that horse.

He was still getting used to the Belgian charger he now rode, the one as dark as a moonless night. The horse was gorgeous, young, and powerful, but Andreas felt like all he did was wrestle the beast to keep him controlled. The horse seemed to have the same disposition in battle or out of it – vicious and edgy. He swung that big head around and knocked men down with ease, a particularly valuable trait in a fight, but not so much when they were simply riding along and not trying to kill anyone.

It was Cassius who had named the horse The Hammer, but it was Andreas who felt like *he* was the one being hammered every time he rode the damned thing.

"I see it," he said after a moment, cuffing The Hammer on the side of the neck when the horse threw his head once again and bashed into Gareth's horse. "That means snow. We must get to Falstone before the weather lets loose. I do not want to be caught on the open road with a snowfall."

Gareth agreed with him. "Should I send a man ahead to tell them of our imminent arrival?"

Andreas was looking ahead at Falstone in the distance. "I want you to look at the location of the castle," he said. "Is it fair to say that from their position, they would be able to see our approach?"

Gareth was young and eager, but he wasn't stupid. He knew what his brother was getting at. "Aye," he said sheepishly. "So they already know we're coming."

Andreas fought off a grin. "They do," he said. "But that does not mean you cannot send someone ahead to give them exact numbers so they know where to position everyone. From the looks of it, the castle isn't terribly sizable. There might be some logistical issues."

Gareth nodded. "Agreed," he said. "May I ride ahead?"

"You may."

Flashing a smile that looked very much like their father, Gareth spurred his horse onward, thundering down the road that was a mixture of mud and ice. As he charged off, another knight rode up to take his place.

Andreas glanced over at Brodie.

"He reminds me of you at that age, Dray," Brodie said, grinning. "So eager. So ridiculous."

Andreas had known Brodie most of his life. The man was about eight or nine years older than Andreas was, so they'd done much growing up together, as Brodie had served Troy since he had been newly knighted. If Andreas had ever had an older brother, Brodie would be it.

"Ridiculous or not, I'm still better looking than you are," he said. "I still cannot believe my cousin married you. I thought we'd warned Uncle Scott sufficiently about you."

Brodie laughed, low in his throat. "Your poison did not take root, thank God," he said. "Sophia and I are quite happy. I should be an inspiration to you, in fact."

Andreas looked at him as if he'd said something utterly ridiculous. "Inspiration?" he repeated. "For what?"

"Because I married late in life and I married for love," he said. "You can, too."

That stripped Andreas of any hint of humor he might have had. He shut his mouth, facing forward as they drew closer to Falstone. Brodie may have been sociable and outgoing, but he wasn't insensitive. Like everyone else in the de Wolfe ranks, he knew what had happened to Andreas in London those months back.

He hadn't meant to hurt the man.

"Dray," he said softly. "You know I love you. I did not mean that as a flippant comment."

Andreas nodded. "I know."

"I meant it as encouragement."

"That is not necessary," he said. "Send word back along the lines. I want the wagons moved forward. I want to get those into Falstone's bailey sooner rather than later. If they're last in the line, then we may not be able to fit them in at all."

He was changing the subject and Brodie went along with it, though he felt badly about it. He whirled his horse around and headed back along the column towards the six provisions wagons they'd brought with them. That left Andreas riding point with Will mid-pack and Corey and Reed covering the rear. They weren't full-fledged knights, but they were properly armed and quite skilled even at their young age. They were so damned excited to be riding with the army that they had obeyed every order Andreas had issued down to the last letter.

They didn't want to chance being sent home.

Riding alone, Andreas tried not to let Brodie's comment bother him. He knew the man had meant well. Therefore, he shook it off, as it was becoming easier to shake off those things these days. Thoughts of that woman from London leaving him sitting alone at The Fox and The Wolf were easier to push aside.

He just tried not to think of her at all.

He couldn't even bring himself to remember her name.

It was better that way.

The storm from the east was moving fast and Andreas had the army pick up the pace as Falstone drew closer. With darkness on the approach, he could see that the gatehouse was open wide because there was a good deal of light from within. The entire fortress glowed against the night sky, the silhouettes of soldiers standing at the gates.

Andreas pushed his men until they were essentially running and they began pouring in through the gatehouse. The wagons, with the horses running, charged up through the column and into the open bailey, with Corey and Reed on their excitable horses escorting the charge.

Very quickly, the bailey of Falstone began to fill up, but the Falstone men were ready. They had the wagons continue to the stables while the men were organized into groups, each group with several Falstone soldiers to assist them. By the time Andreas came to the gatehouse, the last of his army was pouring in, with Will yelling encouraging insults to keep them moving. The man had quite a talent for bellowing insults, getting the men moving but in a way that was both threatening and encouraging. That was his gift. When the last man entered the bailey, Andreas and Will followed.

The massive gates shut behind them.

Andreas was met by Gareth and another knight he didn't recognize.

"Dray," Gareth said. "This is Sir Lukas de Dere, commander of Falstone. De Dere, this is my half-brother, Andreas de Wolfe. Our father is Troy de Wolfe, Lord Braemoor."

Andreas dismounted his steed, greeting the blue-eyed, handsome young knight. "My lord," he said. "You received my missive?"

Lukas nodded. "We did, earlier today," he said. "We are grateful for your presence, of course, but will you provide me with the details of what is occurring that we should need such reinforcements? We've seen nothing at all in our lands that could be interpreted as threatening."

Andreas handed the reins of his horse over to Gareth. "I would be happy to tell you everything," he said. "May I make sure my men are well-tended first? It looks as if a storm is approaching from the east."

Gareth answered, "We have the men pitching tents already, Dray," he said. "De Dere showed us where we could set up our encampments."

"We are going to be crowded, but manageable," Lukas said. "Food is being prepared for your men and they will have a hot meal within the hour. We're moving the horses and wagons into the stable yard as we speak."

It sounded like everything was being taken care of and Andreas nodded. "You have my thanks," he said, returning his focus to Gareth. "I will go with Sir Lukas. Tell Brodie I want him to oversee the settling of the men and send him and Will to me when they are finished."

Gareth nodded. "Where will you be?"

Andreas looked at Lukas for that answer. "In the great hall," he said. "It is on the other side of the keep. Some of your men may sleep there if they wish. It will probably be warmer than the tents."

Andreas nodded. "That is appreciated," he said, glancing at Gareth. "Go about your business. I will see you later."

With that, he followed Lukas towards the great hall as the wind began to pick up. Already, little white flakes of snow were blowing around, indicative of the incoming storm.

"This weather has not stopped the Scots?" Lukas asked.

Andreas pulled off his helm before they reached the enormous doors to the hall, running a gloved hand through his damp hair.

"Nothing stops them," he said ironically. He took a second look at Lukas. "I do not believe you and I have met before."

Lukas nodded. "I do not believe so, either, though we may have attended a few battles together," he said. "Falstone never seems to be involved in much. We're not as large as the de Wolfe properties and the Scots do not seem to be much interested in us."

They entered the hall at that point, met by the warm, stale air from two large hearths blasting out flames and sparks. When they reached a table next to one of the hearths, Andreas set his helm on the tabletop and began to remove his cloak.

"That is a fair assessment," he said. "I've never heard of much action at Falstone. You're in your own little valley here, which is a good thing unless the Scots decide to use it in their trek south."

"And that is what you are afraid of?"

Andreas hung his cloak on a peg next to the hearth. "Possibly," he said. "You asked for the details of what has happened and I can tell you this – we have a clan war on our hands with Clan Maxwell against Clan Elliot and Clan Johnstone, and anyone else they feel who has wronged them. It's a situation that seems to be growing until no one will remember how it even started. Eight days ago, they burst over the border and we spent almost a week chasing them back over. My grandfather has twenty-five thousand men in and around Castle Questing, enough to send a serious message to the Scots. We will not tolerate their foolery. I am here in case they decide to head into England via this route. We do not want Falstone to fall victim to their rampage."

Lukas digested the situation. "Nor do I," he said. "I have informed Lord de Leia of your missive. He shall be here shortly to speak with you as well."

Andreas stood there, warming his hands by the fire, as he looked over his shoulder at Lukas.

"We were told there was an… issue with Lord de Leia," he said. "Do you care to elaborate?"

Lukas cocked his head. "What issue?"

"Madness."

"Who told you that?"

Andreas looked back to the fire. "It is a simple question, de Dere," he said. "We are here to help. We are not here to pass judgment on your lord. But I must know what we are facing. Either your lord is showing signs of madness or he is not. I need to know."

Lukas was silent for a moment. Andreas could see him moving around the table from the corners of his eyes until he came to stand next to him.

"I do not know who told you this and I suppose it does not matter," he said, lowering his voice. "Lord de Leia has never been a particularly strong and active lord when it comes to his army, but he was always accommodating to his allies. I am sure you know this."

"I do. My father considers him a valuable ally or I would not be here."

Lukas was looking at him closely, perhaps for any sign of a man who might go back on his word and refuse to help if he knew the truth. But Lukas had to assume that Andreas, being a de Wolfe, was a man of honor. Not that he had much choice at the moment.

He took a deep breath.

"The burdens of Falstone are not burdens to be assumed by anyone else, my lord," he said quietly. "We are capable of handling our own issues. But we also value the House of de Wolfe, as our great ally, so because of that admiration, I will explain the situation as best I can. Let me say from the outset that it is not dangerous. At least, not yet. But it is… puzzling."

Andreas was looking at him again. "How so?"

Lukas folded his big arms across his chest, thoughtfully. "Because I am not entirely sure how it happened," he said. "As I said, Lord de Leia is not a man who was ever actively involved in leading his men. He is not a warrior, although he went through the usual training as a lad. He simply prefers to give orders and let others carry them out."

"Like you."

"Like me," Luka confirmed. "I am his only knight and have been for more than ten years. I have always had a free hand to make important decisions regarding the army and Falstone in general because Lord de Leia trusts me. But several months ago, a woman appeared. She said that she was a gift from an ally for Lord de Leia, a servant to tend to his every need. I would have sent her away except Lord de Leia happened to be present when she arrived and what he heard intrigued him. He allowed her to remain and she will not leave his side. That is when the trouble started."

Andreas was listening intently. "Why?" he asked. "What does she do?"

Lukas smiled without humor. "Everything you think a

woman would do to a man," he said grimly. "I caught them in a compromising situation, once, and that tells me the woman makes herself useful to Lord de Leia by using her body any way she can. But it is more than that – she keeps him supplied with drink. A great deal of drink. She keeps him sequestered, from me and from his daughter, and she is rude and demanding. As for the madness, I believe that is related to the drink, but there is more to it somehow. It seems to me that Lord de Leia is sane some moments, insane in others, and all I can tell you is that it started when that whore arrived. I apologize for my language, but that is exactly what she is. And Lord de Leia will not send her away."

It seemed like a strange situation, indeed, and Andreas considered it.

"It is possible she was sent by an enemy and not an ally," he said. "Is she English?"

"Aye."

"Who is Lord de Leia at odds with?"

Lukas stared at him for a moment before averting his gaze. He seemed quite hesitant, whereas only moments earlier, he had had been forthcoming to Andreas' questions. Sensing this, Andreas peered at the man.

"He *does* have enemies, then?" he asked. "Is it possible this woman was sent by them?"

Lukas wouldn't look at him. "I have considered that," he muttered. "But it makes no sense why they would send this woman to Lord de Leia."

"*Who* are his enemies?"

Lukas turned his head in Andreas' direction, but he still wouldn't meet his eyes. "De Soulis."

Andreas rolled his eyes. "That bunch, is it?" he said. "I am not surprised. But you are not going to like what my father has dictated."

That forced Lukas to look him in the eyes. "What?"

Andreas grunted unhappily. "Even though my father would much rather see the House of de Soulis purged from Hell's Guardhouse, he doesn't want the Scots holding that massive place, so if they are attacked, my orders are to defend them."

Something in Lukas' expression changed, then. It was as if a curtain were drawn over his features, because his face turned dark. Everything about him turned dark. Andreas saw the transformation right before his very eyes. A calm, congenial knight turned to stone.

"Let them die," he growled. "Let the Scots overrun them and cut their bodies into a thousand pieces and feed them to the dogs. I would rather see Hell's Guardhouse filled with a thousand Scots than see de Soulis within those walls. They deserve to die in the most hideous way possible."

It occurred to Andreas that there was some very bad blood between Falstone and Hell's Guardhouse that his father either hadn't known about or simply failed to tell him. Andreas refused to believe it was the latter, so he would go on the assumption that Troy hadn't known anything.

That meant the de Wolfe army was now pulled into something they knew nothing about, Scots be damned.

He fixed on Lukas.

"You are going to explain that comment," he said, though not unkindly. "I brought a thousand men here, including my own blood, to defend Falstone from a Scots incursion, and now I am told there is bad blood between Falstone and Hell's Guardhouse? I do not have orders that cover any confrontation between you and de Soulis, so you will be very clear as to what is going on here so I can make the best decision I can for my men and for the House of de Wolfe. Have you been battling de Soulis and we were unaware?"

Lukas stared at him a moment before turning away and

returning to the table, where he sat heavily.

Andreas followed.

"Answer me, de Dere," he said, sitting next to him. "Are my men in jeopardy now?"

Lukas shook his head. "Nay," he said. "De Soulis has not brought their army against us."

"Then what in the hell is going on?" Andreas demanded, displeased with Lukas' evasive answers. "Tell me immediately or I shall take my men, return to my father, and tell him of the situation here. Then you can explain it to Troy de Wolfe when he comes down around your ears for withholding information that may have jeopardized his men."

It was a threat and Lukas knew it. He scratched his head in a nervous gesture.

"Every fortress has its little secrets, its personal hell," he said quietly. "We have ours, as well. Nay, your men are not in jeopardy from de Soulis, but what they have done to us is beyond reprehensible. Do I think that whore has been sent by them to further weaken the House of de Leia? Possibly. Anything is possible. My lord, I will explain everything to you, but you must swear to me that you will only tell your father and no one else. If this information got out… it would shame Lord de Leia and his daughter greatly. That personal hell I speak of."

"You have my word," Andreas said. "What has happened?"

Lukas took a deep breath. "Falstone has three villages within her domain," he said, barely audible. "Deadwater, Liddel, and Larriston. Deadwater is the largest, named for the lake to the north that tends to stagnate in the summer. The village is a busy one and a peaceful one. We have never truly had any issues with Scots, although about six years ago, a raiding party passed through. Reivers. But until last year, that was the only real trouble we'd ever had. 'Tis as if we live in a land with secret borders, repelling all evil."

"Until last year."

"Aye."

"What happened last year?"

Lukas pondered the question before continuing. "De Leia's daughter was in Deadwater with two of her maids," he said. "She'd been traveling to the village for years without an escort, so this was not unusual. But there was a group of knights in town and they abducted her. She was beaten and violated. When we found her, she could not tell us who had done this heinous thing, but she could identify the brand on one of the horses. She drew it for us and it was a brand we recognized."

Andreas got the message. "De Soulis."

Lukas nodded sadly. "Aye," he muttered. "De Soulis."

Andreas frowned, distressed by the tale. "And your lord did not seek to punish them?"

Lukas shook his head. "He was so ashamed by what had happened that he did not want to summon his allies, de Wolfe included," he said. "It was strange... he turned into a man who simply wanted it all to go away. We do not have a large enough army to go after Hell's Guardhouse on our own and he would not let me summon help, afraid this terrible secret would become public knowledge. And when he realized that attack resulted in a pregnancy for his daughter... God, it was a nightmare. He kept her hidden away as if she had somehow been a willing party to all of it. He was so ashamed of her that when the child was born, he sent the infant away to Edenside and sent his daughter to London. He was trying to erase all evidence of what had happened. He refused to acknowledge anything."

It was quite a tale. Andreas shook his head slowly. "My father knew nothing of this," he said in a low voice. "If he did, I am sure he would have told me. I am sure he would have encouraged your father to seek vengeance. What happened is not right."

Lukas shook his head. "Nay, it is not right," he said. "And Lord de Leia's daughter… she is the victim in all of this. Gavriella did not deserve any of what happened to her and her father made her feel as if it were all her fault. But none of it was. That's the sad part. She's such a sweet, beautiful woman and now… now, there is no chance she'll ever find a decent marriage after this, although I suspect that is why de Leia has been keeping it all a secret. He does not want a prospective husband to know."

It took Andreas a moment to process the name of de Leia's daughter. *Gavriella.* It was such a unique name that, surely, there couldn't be two women with the same name in Northumberland.

Could there?

Andreas didn't hear much after that. He felt the room rock. In fact, he found himself gripping the table until his equilibrium returned. He was in such disbelief that although he heard Lukas as the man continued to speak, he didn't really comprehend the words. He just sat there, feeling as if a wall of stone had just fallen on him.

My God…

Gavriella!

When he had returned from London, he'd started his search for the woman he knew as Gavriella, but he'd been starting towards the east. His plan was to ask every priest from Castle Questing to the sea, hunting down anyone who might know of a woman named Gavriella.

But he'd been searching in the wrong direction.

She had been at Falstone all along.

He suddenly felt sick.

Sick enough that he hung his head, struggling with his composure as Lukas rattled on about Lord de Leia and the way he treated his daughter like a disease. *What happened to her wasn't her fault,* he'd said.

An assault...

A child...

Andreas remembered thinking in London how Gavriella gave every indication of someone with dark secrets. With something to hide.

Now, he knew why.

He put a trembling hand to his mouth, his face, as if trying to wipe away his shock.

His utter despair.

"My lord?"

Lukas' voice broke through his haze of disbelief and he suddenly looked at the man, realizing he'd been lost in his thoughts.

"Aye?" he said simply as a reflex action, then realized he looked foolish. "My apologies. I was thinking of... of de Soulis. They have a reputation for being brutal and unsavory, but usually only to their vassals. They do not venture out of their properties too often."

Oblivious to the fact that Andreas looked somewhat pale, Lukas nodded. "That is true," he said. "Unfortunately, they ventured into Deadwater and the results were catastrophic. For Lady Gavriella, anyway. I was saying that it is very possible that they sent this woman who calls herself Giddy, but I do not know their purpose behind it. I suppose it's possible they are trying to get their hands on Falstone somehow. In that sense, I am grateful you have come, my lord. Lord de Leia would not let me summon you."

Andreas was still reeling, trying to pretend that he wasn't. It took him a moment to focus and collect his thoughts, made extremely difficult by the fact that he knew Gavriella was here, somewhere.

He had to find her.

"It seems as if there is far more going on here than meets the eye," he said as steadily as he could. "Thank you for taking me into your confidence and telling me. I will tell my father, but without Lord de Leia's cooperation with de Soulis, you know that there is very little we can do."

Lukas nodded. "I know," he said with regret. "But you cannot imagine how good it feels for me to actually tell someone what has been happening here. I am the only knight here and there are very few people I can speak in confidence to."

Andreas took a second look at the man. All shock of Gavriella's revelation aside, he took a brief moment to focus on Lukas de Dere. He realized that he felt sorry for him. Andreas had any number of cousins, friends, and uncles he could speak with. Even a father and grandfather that he adored. But Lukas evidently had no one at all.

A difficult situation, indeed.

"I hope this establishes trust between us, de Dere," he said. "I do not want you to feel as if you are alone in the world. I am the garrison commander of Monteviot Tower, which isn't terribly far from here, and I embarrassed to say that I've not taken the time to become acquainted with my neighbors such as Falstone. Most of my family's properties are concentrated to the east and that is where our focus lies, but I fear we have forgotten our western neighbors in the process. You have my apologies for that. I will make sure we make amends."

Lukas smiled weakly. "Thank you, my lord."

"You will call me Andreas, please."

Lukas' smile grew. "I am appreciative, truly," he said. "I will answer to Lukas."

Andreas returned his smile, but it was hollow. His mind had all it could take of focusing on de Dere and was now whirling back to Gavriella.

He had to find her.

"Now we can move forward, Lukas," he said. "I understand the situation here and the issues with de Soulis, for which I am most grievously sorry, but my focus for now is on the movements of the Scots."

"Understood."

"That does not mean we will not deal with de Soulis at a later time."

The way he said it came out as a growl, causing Lukas to peer at him rather closely. "Deal with them?"

Andreas couldn't put it into words. He had too much else going on in his mind. "Do not ask me to elaborate at the moment," he said. It was the truth. "Not until I speak with my father. Meanwhile, I would like to settle my knights. Where are we to bed down?"

Lukas stood up. "I will summon Lady Gavriella," he said. "She is chatelaine and she will show you the hospitality of Falstone. And, please… do not ever mention to her what I told you. She would be greatly shamed that I confided something like that to a stranger."

Andreas shook his head. "I would not dream of betraying your confidence."

Satisfied, Lukas headed out of the hall, but not before he ordered a servant to bring food and drink to the commander of the de Wolfe army.

I will summon Lady Gavriella.

All Andreas had to do was wait and she would come right to him. After all these months, he could hardly believe it. What would he say to her? What would *she* say to *him*? His heart was thumping against his ribs and his palms were sweating as he thought of her, feeling the same way he did the moment he went to meet her at The Fox and The Wolf.

Excited.

Hopeful.

Happy…

Even though he knew something terrible had happened to her, something that most men would look upon as a disgusting event that would easily change their minds about a woman, Andreas didn't look at it that way. Gavriella had been forced to endure something no woman should have to endure. When he thought about that sweet, beautiful woman being abused, he could feel the bile rising in his throat.

The anger rising in his heart.

Pure, black rage.

Aye, she'd been hiding something. Now, he knew what it was.

And he didn't care.

But it was quite possible she didn't feel the same way about the situation, or about him. She was the one who left him sitting there, after all. She was the one who had run out.

He was going to find out why and hope it didn't emotionally destroy him forever.

He braced himself.

CHAPTER SIXTEEN

"GAVY?"

Lukas was standing in the kitchen doorway as Gavriella stood with the cook, both of them sampling the stew the old woman had made from a wooden bowl. Spoon in hand, Gavriella looked up when she heard her name.

"I am here, Lukas," she said, peering around one of the pillars that held up the low, barrel-vaulted ceiling. "Do you require something?"

The doorway leading into the kitchen was low and he was hunched over as he stood in it. "The de Wolfe army has arrived," he said. "I promised them a hot meal within the hour. Are we close?"

Gavriella nodded, licking the spoon. "Almost," she said. "We have a nice stew and plenty of bread."

"Are you cooking the stew in the yard?"

"Aye."

"Then you're going to have to cover it because it is going to snow soon," he said. "Be ready to start serving the meal in about an hour."

"We will."

Lukas threw a thumb over his shoulder. "The commander

of the de Wolfe army is in the hall," he said. "Will you please show him where his knights will sleep?"

Gavriella nodded quickly, removing the apron she was wearing. As Lukas headed off, she hung her apron up on the peg as she left the kitchen, heading into the ground level of the keep. She wanted to check on the chambers before she attended the commander, so a quick perusal of the rooms showed that they were indeed prepared, if not a little crowded. There were three beds in each chamber, all six with comfortable mattresses and blankets. A fire burned in the hearths, so the chambers were nice and warm.

Satisfied, she headed towards the hall.

Gavriella was clad in a heavy woolen dress against the cold temperatures, a garment made out of undyed wool. It was a pretty garment, with long sleeves that she could wrap her hands up in to keep them warm. As she came out of the keep and noticed the snowflakes starting to fall, she smoothed at her hair, which was braided and gathered at the nape of her neck. Since she'd been working in the kitchens, and around fire, it was best to keep her hair out of the way. She continued to smooth at it, tucking strands behind her ear, as she reached the door to the hall.

There were a few servants moving about the great hall and the hearths were blazing, making it almost cloyingly warm. She could see a figure sitting near the southernmost hearth, his back to her. As she drew closer, she could see that he had a cup of something steaming. Warmed wine, she assumed. He was a very large man, she could see from the breadth of his shoulders, and his head was lowered so she couldn't get a good look at him.

She came up behind the man, clearing her throat softly.

"My lord?" she said politely. "I am Lady Gavriella. My father is Lord de Leia. Welcome to Falstone."

The man stood up and looked at her, tall and imposing, like a god from Olympus. Everything about him radiated power. Though the hall was dimly lit, even with the blazing hearths, there was no mistaking the features.

For a moment, Gavriella thought she was dreaming.

Then, reality hit.

"Andreas!" she gasped.

He smiled faintly and her knees collapsed. She ended up on the bench next to her, but had Andreas not grabbed her to help her find it, she would have ended up on the floor. As it was, they sat down together, staring at each other, gripping each other.

The shock in the air was palpable.

"Greetings, my lady," he said softly. "You look… beautiful."

Gavriella's mouth was hanging open as she looked at him. Then, she looked at his arms, his chest, squeezing and poking as if to convince herself that he was real.

"It really *is* you," she whispered, trembling. "Andreas… *how* is this possible? How did you find me?"

He didn't say anything for a moment. He didn't even answer her question. He simply sat there and looked at her.

"Will you answer a question for me?" he asked quietly.

"Anything!"

"Why did you not show up in the tavern those months ago?"

As he watched, tears filled her eyes. Little did he know that, at the time, she had resigned herself to never seeing him again, thinking it was for the best. Had the situation kept going the way it had, the lady with secrets would have had to reveal them.

Damaged goods.

But here he was, as big as life, and she didn't think that way anymore. She was so glad to see him that she was nearly faint with it. Perhaps it was foolish of her, but she couldn't help it.

"Because my aunt sent me home the very night we returned from Southwark," she said, trying not to weep. "My cousin saw you and I return together and she told my aunt… terrible things. I was sent home against my will, I assure you."

"Your *cousin* saw us?" he said. "What did she say?"

She let go of him with one hand, using it to wipe the tears that were starting to trickle. "Awful things, Andreas," she said. "They knew that I had been missing all day and they were waiting for me when I returned from our most remarkable day. When I told them where I had been, I was accused of terrible things. Such horrible things. My cousin and I fought, and my aunt banished me from The Asher as a result. She sent me home that night."

He stared at her a moment before sighing heavily. "Is *that* what happened?" he said. "But why did you not send word to the tavern? You knew I would be there."

The tears were spilling over. "I knew you would be there, but it was impossible to send you a missive," she said. "I was locked in my chamber until my escort took me away. I had no way of sending you word. Not even the servants would come near me, so there was no one to ask. Andreas, I am so sorry. I know it seemed as if I did not come to you deliberately, but I swear to you that is not true."

He began to nod his head as if the events were becoming clear now. He mulled it over, finally snorting with realization. "So that's what happened," he said. "It was not because you did not wish to see me again."

Her hand found his and she squeezed it tightly. "Nay," she said softly, her eyes alight with warmth and joy. "That is not true, I swear it. You are all I've thought of for the past several months, but I did not know if I would ever see you again because I was so foolish."

"What about?"

"For playing that foolish game and not telling you everything about me. I should have told you everything the first night I met you."

He grinned. Then, he chuckled softly, taking her hand and bring it to his lips. He very much wanted to do more, to take her in his arms, but he didn't dare. Not when there was a chance someone would see them.

"It does not matter now," he breathed, kissing her hand tenderly and feeling her warmth against his flesh. "You are here. You have been here the entire time."

"I have," she said. "And you… you are from the House of de Wolfe."

He nodded slowly, her hand still at his mouth. "My father is Troy de Wolfe, Lord Braemoor," he said. "My grandfather is William de Wolfe, the Earl of Warenton, and my garrison is Monteviot Tower, which is a day's ride from here. I was so close to you the entire time. I still cannot believe it."

She was in full agreement. "Nor can I," she said. "I swear to you that I was going to tell you everything you wanted to know on that morning. I… I was going to tell you who my father was. In case you wanted to speak with him, still."

There was a question in that statement. She was asking him if he was still interested in her after everything that had happened, after all these months. As he looked at her, he felt as if the separation had never happened. He was here, she was here, and that was all that mattered. All of the confusion and disappointment he'd felt faded away.

His eyes glimmered with mirth.

"You're not meant for the veil," he said.

It wasn't a question. The smile faded from her lips. "Nay," she said. "But… but there is something…"

"There you are!"

A booming voice interrupted them. Startled, Gavriella

yanked her hand out of his grasp and as she quickly stood up, several big knights entered the hall, all of them bearing de Wolfe tunics. Gavriella had seen Andreas wear the same tunic in London and he wore it now. He'd told her that it had been of a wolf, but she had never made the connection to the House of de Wolfe and she should have. Living in the north her entire life, she knew the name well. Now, she was surrounded by de Wolfe knights, Andreas included, and she dipped into a polite curtsy as the knights came near the hearth.

"My lords," she said. "I am Gavriella de Leia. My father is Lord de Leia. I have been asked to show you to your accommodations."

She darted off, towards the entry, and the men swung around to follow.

Andreas brought up the rear.

He was simply watching her.

Like a balm or a salve, she soothed his soul, so deeply encased in a shell of self-protection, but he felt as if simply reveling in her aura filled him with a peace he had never experienced. To hear her reasons for not meeting him in the tavern on that day in question brought about more relief than he'd ever known. She hadn't simply left him there to make a fool of him.

She didn't show up because of circumstances beyond her control.

God, it was good to hear that.

"The men are getting settled," Brodie was saying. "I've got some of them packing into the stables because… Dray? Are you listening?"

Andreas hadn't been. He had been watching Gavriella, several paces ahead. "I am," he lied, though he'd heard the word "stable" and assumed what he was talking about. "You can put a few hundred in the hall, but tell them they are to keep it clean.

The moment it starts smelling like wild animals live there, I will throw them out into the snow. Is that clear?"

Brodie nodded. "It is," he said. As they headed out into the bailey, he lowered his voice. "Did you find out what is going on around here?"

Andreas nodded. "Not now," he muttered. "When Lady Gavriella leaves us, I will tell you what the de Leia knight told me."

Brodie was still looking at him strangely. "Are you well?" he asked. "What is wrong?"

Andreas looked at him. "What do you mean?"

"I mean you look odd."

Andreas didn't want to say anything, not here. He waved him off. "Later," he muttered. "I'll tell you everything later."

Brodie shut his mouth.

The group entered the keep of Falstone, a massive, circular-shaped structure. Gavriella took them to two chambers on the entry level, in a corridor just off the entry so there was swift access to the exit.

The chambers were smaller and crowded, but cozy and clean. Andreas immediately ordered Gareth, Corey, and Reed into the smaller of the two chambers while he, Brodie, and Will took the larger one. Although Andreas loved his half-brothers, he didn't want to sleep in close quarters with them. If Corey and Reed kept him awake with their fighting and chatter, he wasn't sure how he could explain to his father that he'd been forced to smother them.

He was only able to briefly thank Gavriella for her hospitality before she left them to settle in, but not before they passed lingering looks at one another. He very much wanted to follow her and continue their conversation, but he knew she had duties with so many new visitors.

He had duties, as well.

There would be time enough for their continued reunion later.

The chamber he and Will and Brodie had settled in was crowded, but not so crowded that a table and a chair had been worked into the corner. There was a pewter pitcher there, a thick and heavy thing, and three cups. Will put his hands on the pitcher and quickly took them away.

"Damnation," he hissed. "Hot. Who wants mulled wine?"

Brodie held up a hand. "Me."

Will poured two cups, looking over to Andreas, who was removing his tunic in preparation for removing his mail coat.

"Dray?" he said. "Wine?"

Andreas shook his head. "Nay," he said. "But you two indulge. There is much to tell and you should be well-fortified."

"I suspected as much," Brodie said, taking his cup from Will. "So you met with de Leia's knight? What did he say?"

Once the tunic was off, Andreas extended his arms to Will, who took the hint and pulled off his mail coat. Andreas took it from him and tossed it onto the end of his bed.

"Strange things are afoot here," he said. "All is not peaceful at Falstone."

That brought interest from Will and Brodie. "Like what?" Will asked.

Andreas went to work on the damp padded tunic he wore underneath his mail coat. "Lukas de Dere is de Leia's only knight, and my impression is that he is a decent man, but he has sworn me to secrecy on what he told me, so you must never repeat it to anyone." As Will and Brodie nodded seriously, he continued. "It all started when I mentioned Hell's Guardhouse. I told him that if it was threatened by the Scots, I was ordered to go to its defense. That brought a strong reaction from de Dere. Let them die, he told me. Let the Scots overrun them and cut their bodies into a thousand pieces and feed them to the dogs.

He further said that he would rather see Hell's Guardhouse filled with a thousand Scots than see de Soulis within those walls. He said that they deserved to die in the most hideous way possible."

Will lifted his eyebrows. "Clearly the man hates his neighbor," he said. Then, he rolled his eyes as if a thought had just occurred to him. "Dray, don't tell me we've come here only to involve ourselves in some manner of dispute between Falstone and Hell's Guardhouse."

"That was my first thought, too," Andreas said. "But it's not so much a dispute between Falstone and Hell's Guardhouse as it is a truly heinous injustice that Nicholas and John de Soulis have committed against Falstone."

"What did they do?" Will asked.

Up until this moment, Andreas had been quite neutral about the situation. He'd been able to relay it without any emotion whatsoever. But Will's question was pushing him deeper into a subject he found himself increasingly distressed over. Not just any distress; a deep-seated, painful distress, burrowed down in the pit of his belly because it had to do with Gavriella.

God, how he wanted to run to her at that moment and take her in his arms.

God, how he wanted to run to Hell's Guardhouse and burn it to the ground.

He took a deep, steadying breath.

"De Dere told me that last year, Lord de Leia's daughter, the woman you just met, was in the nearby village of Deadwater," he said, trying to maintain his neutrality. "To make a long and sordid story short, Nicholas de Soulis abducted and violated her, an attack that left the woman with child. Rather than seek justice, Lord de Leia has instead chosen to ignore the situation in the hopes that it will simply fade away. De Dere believes he is hoping it will be forgotten as to not jeopardize her chances of marrying well. In any case, de Leia is turning a blind eye to it all."

By this time, Will had closed his eyes and hung his head, fighting off the very idea of Nicholas de Soulis violating an innocent woman. Brodie grunted unhappily.

"Bastard," he muttered. "You mean that very woman who was just here?"

"The same."

"Christ," Brodie said, shaking his head. "The poor lass. She's quite lovely. What a terrible, terrible thing. And her father did nothing?"

"Not a thing."

"No wonder there is bad blood," Will said, lifting his head to look at Andreas. "Hell, I agree with de Dere. Let the Scots overrun Hell's Guardhouse and give them what they deserve."

"I do not disagree with you," Andreas said. "But there's something more going on, something very odd that may be linked to de Soulis. About six months ago, a female servant showed up here, saying she was a gift from an ally for Lord de Leia. She made herself indispensable to him, if you understand my meaning. The woman has worked her way into de Leia's bed. De Dere isn't sure why de Soulis would send her to Falstone, and he's not even sure that's who sent her, but the woman is here and her arrival coincided with the bouts of madness Lord de Leia seems to be having."

Will frowned. "De Soulis sent her to drive de Leia mad?"

Andreas lifted his big shoulders. "Possibly."

"And that is related to the attack on the daughter?"

"Your guess is as good as mine," Andreas said. "No one seems to know, and no one can get close to her or to de Leia. According to de Dere, the woman has separated the man from everyone."

"Then she is in control," Brodie said softly.

Andreas and Will looked over at him. "It seems that way," Andreas said. "That is why we must be wary of any orders coming directly from de Leia. I'm not entirely sure what is going on here, but I intend to find out. With the Scots on the rampage, a mad lord, and a neighboring castle that could possibly have an eye for this place, that is what I meant by Falstone not being peaceful. There is a good deal happening here."

That was an understatement. After a few moments to ponder the situation, it was Brodie who finally spoke.

"De Soulis is known to be greedy, Dray," he said. "You know the man taxes his vassals into the grave. He's a cruel lord and master. And Falstone is not far from them. Mayhap he sees something here that he wants. What if the attack on de Leia's daughter was only the beginning? What if this servant was sent by him to also bewitch the lord himself? And if that doesn't work, will they go back to the daughter again? I think this is a more dangerous situation than it appears."

Andreas thought he was doing quite well at behaving objectively on the subject, but Brodie brought out the fears he couldn't quite bring himself to voice. He suddenly sank back onto the bed and sat there, fighting off visions of de Soulis putting his hands on Gavriella's soft body. Again.

As if one attack hadn't been good enough.

He couldn't be objective any longer.

"Will," he finally muttered, unable to look at them. "Do you remember when we were in London those months back?"

He was off the subject, causing Will to look curiously at his lowered head. "Of course."

"And when we went to Gomorrah?"

"I remember that very well. Why?"

Andreas sighed faintly. "The woman who ran into the

chamber where we were, the one who was hysterical. The one I escorted out. Do you remember her?"

Will's brow furrowed. "I remember the event, but I do not remember the woman specifically. Why do you ask?"

Andreas lifted his head to look at him. "That was Lady Gavriella."

Will's eyes widened. "That was *her*?"

"Aye."

Now, Will's mouth popped open. "The one you took to Southwark?"

"The one who left me sitting in the tavern, alone, for days until you came for me."

Will was astonished. "God's Beard," he hissed. "Dray... did you know this? Did you know she was de Leia's daughter?"

Andreas was shaking his head before William even finished asking the question. "She never told me her family name, remember?" he said. "That was why I went to the tavern that morning. She was going to tell me everything. But she did not come and I returned to Northumberland to find her. I was well on my way when this madness with the Scots started and I had to focus on that. But now... now, I find her here. She's been here the entire time."

Brodie really had no idea what was going on, but Will did. He went to Andreas, dropping to his knees in front of the man as he sat upon his bed.

"Dray, speak to me," he pleaded seriously. "Meeting that woman changed you. I know you were heartbroken when she failed to show herself. Did she even tell you why?"

Andreas nodded. "She told me," he said. "She was staying at her aunt's home in London and her aunt disapproved of her going to Southwark with me. There was some sort of fight between Gavriella and her cousins because of it, so her aunt sent her home immediately. That is why she never came to the tavern."

It made sense to Will, but he still wasn't satisfied. "And now that you've found her," he said. "I know you felt something for her and when she left, it was as if there were a dark cloud hanging over you. We could all see it. She left you in a dark and unhappy place. I am delighted that you have found her, for your sake, but given what you've been told about de Soulis… are we going to find ourselves laying siege to Hell's Guardhouse?"

Andreas looked at his cousin. He was only a few months older than he was, so they were the same age. They'd grown up together. They'd experienced life and death together. Their fathers were brothers and their mothers had been sisters so, in a sense, Will was a brother to him a well.

He wasn't going to lie to the man.

"Not at the moment," he said, smiling weakly. "I have a task to complete here and I am trying very hard to keep my priorities straight. But truthfully? I wish I was with her right now instead of you two. Now that I've found her… I made the decision in London those months ago that I was going to speak to her father about courting her. That has not changed. But I will not speak to him until the crisis with the Scots passes. I am not impulsive, nor am I foolish. I am a commander of a de Wolfe army at the moment and that is where my focus is. But that woman is never leaving my sight again."

Will looked at him, seeing the sincerity and feeling some relief to hear that. He put a big hand to Andreas' cheek. "Good lad," he murmured. "But what about de Soulis?"

Andreas' expression hardened. "Even if her father will do nothing, I do not subscribe to that inaction," he said. "When I marry Gavriella, and I do say *when*, it is clear that Nicholas de Soulis took that which belongs to me – her innocence. The woman bore his child, for Christ's sake. The torment he put her through is beyond belief. What about de Soulis, you ask? The man is going to pay with every last bone in his body. When I get finished with him, being overrun by Scots will have been preferable."

Will believed him implicitly. Given what he'd seen in battle with the man over the past several months, Andreas was more than capable of tearing both John and Nicholas apart given the chance.

He had a feeling this task to protect Falstone was going to turn into something much bigger for the House of de Wolfe.

At least, bigger for Andreas.

He put his hand on the man's knee. "If you marry the lass, then it is your right to seek vengeance," he said. "But not today."

Andreas shook his head. "Nay, not today," he said. "Now, I am going to retrieve my saddlebags from Gareth, wash some of this stink off my body, and find Gavriella before the evening's meal begins. And that is all I have to say about the situation. For now."

Will remained crouched down as Andreas stood up and used him for leverage to maneuver through the small chamber and to the door. Once he quit the chamber, Will stood up and looked at Brodie.

"We are in for a good deal of trouble," he muttered. "He's going to drag us all into a battle against Hell's Guardhouse."

Brodie, who had pieced enough of the conversation together to realize what the situation with Andreas was, glanced at the man.

"And you blame him?" he asked quietly.

Will shook his head. "Nay," he said. "That's the problem – I don't. Neither will Uncle Troy, or Poppy, or my father. No one will blame him. And they'll go to war because of it. Hell's Guardhouse is going to fall."

Brodie, who had been around longer than Will and Andreas, nodded slowly in approval. When he spoke, his words were full of venom.

"I hope so."

CHAPTER SEVENTEEN

THE SNOWS CAME.

Gavriella stood at the kitchen door, the one that opened up into a small yard, watching the men struggle with the canvas they'd strung over the enormous iron pot filled with stew, bubbling away on the fire. They'd set it up like a tent. The snow was falling steadily, but the men had to make sure it didn't build up too much on top of the canvas and collapse it right into the food.

It was an ongoing task.

The meal in the great hall was in full swing. Because of the snowfall, men were crammed into every corner of the room. The hearths were working overtime, belching out heat and smoke and flames against the frigid night. There were four long tables in the hall and it could seat hundreds of men at any given time, and those tables were completely filled. They were so full that men were even sitting on top of them in some places. Dogs wandered underneath.

Gavriella was overseeing the meal, making sure that the army that had come to protect Falstone was satisfied. Jocosa had prepared that lovely stew and the men were gobbling it up. Because the hall was so full, there were still men out in the bailey, in the tent city that had been erected to house them. There were several fires going out there to stave off the icy temperatures, but the men outside were provided with the same meal as the men inside – plus extra ale to help with the cold. There were a few servants moving out in the bailey, making sure that the men were taken care of, as Gavriella remained in the kitchens to ensure that the food stayed hot and plentiful.

It was a busy night.

It was also a difficult night.

Andreas...

She was still reeling with shock at seeing the man. Part of her still thought she was dreaming. Women like her weren't blessed with good things. It was a strange God who allowed something horrible to happen to her, and then brought the only man she'd ever cared for back to her doorstep. Was it God's apology for the de Soulis attack? Gavriella could only wonder. She'd only had a few brief moments with Andreas alone before her duties had taken her away. She so desperately wanted to see him again.

She desperately wanted to talk to him again.

It seemed to her that he was still the same Andreas she had left in London. All of her fears that he might hate her for leaving him sitting in that tavern seemed to be for naught. She had lived for the past six months with the fear that he would have grown to hate her for it, but that didn't seem to be the case. When he'd looked at her today, she could see the same warmth that had been there six months ago, and when he kissed her hand, it felt the same as it did back then.

Delight...

Joy.

Everything felt the same.

But that didn't mean the situation was ideal.

There was still something about her that he didn't know.

Now, he knew her name and he knew where she lived, and nothing seemed to have changed with regard to him wanting to speak with her father about courting her. Nothing would make her happier, of course, but she couldn't let him do it without telling him what had happened last year. Her father seemed so willing to hide what had happened, but she simply wasn't.

Not when it came to Andreas.

The truth was that she never really thought she would get to the point where she would have to tell him. After she'd fled London those months ago, she wasn't sure she would see him again, so facing this situation was something she had pushed from her mind. Of course, she had always hoped he would find her, and it was a situation she would deal with at the proper time. But the reality was that he was here now and she was going to have to face it head on.

She thought far too much of Andreas not to be completely honest with him.

Even if it destroyed her.

God, this was such a bittersweet moment for her. She was so glad he'd come, yet terrified her joy would be short-lived when he found out the truth of what had happened on that sultry July day last year.

The nightmare that would be part of her for the rest of her life.

"My lady?" Jocosa came up behind her, the woman's face red and sweaty from the bread ovens. "The servants say your father has come to the hall."

Shaken from her thoughts of Andreas, Gavriella looked at her in surprise. "He has?" she asked. "He's not attended a meal in the hall for months."

"He's here now."

"Is that woman with him?"

"She is."

Gavriella's expression darkened. "I suppose it was too much to hope that she would make herself scarce," she said. "I should join my father. We have guests, after all."

Jocosa nodded, taking the apron from Gavriella and shooing her towards the hall.

But Gavriella was already on the move, swiftly in fact, because her father was unpredictable these days and she wanted to be in the hall if he started to get out of hand. The evenings seemed to be worst for him and, knowing that Andreas and his men were in the hall, she didn't want her father embarrassing all of Falstone in front of the House of de Wolfe. He might even give Andreas second thoughts about seeking permission to court her purely based on Merek's erratic behavior.

Aye, she needed to get into the hall.

Quickly.

She wasn't exactly dressed in something she would have preferred to wear with guests in attendance, but that couldn't be helped. She was still in the heavy woolen dress she'd been wearing all day. Gavriella crossed the snowy yard and entered the great hall through the servant's alcove, immediately confronted by a vastly crowded chamber. There was barely room to walk with all of the men seeking shelter from the snow, but she pressed on, finally spying Andreas first as he sat at the table that was close to the southern hearth.

Her heart began to pound at the sight of him.

In fact, she had eyes only for him as she approached, trying desperately not to appear as if she were staring at the man, but it was difficult. He was very much worth staring at. As she drew closer, he happened to catch a glimpse of her and she couldn't help but smile. He smiled in return, though faintly. Not enough to really be noticeable, but it was to her. The warmth in his expression was unmistakable.

But so was the back of her father's bald head.

He was sitting across the table from Andreas and Gavriella only really noticed because the man shifted in his seat and ended up in her line of sight. It was like having cold water thrown on her. The warm feelings she experienced while looking at Andreas had taken a dousing.

Now, she was looking at her father.

There was no warmth there.

"Greetings, Father," she said. "I did not know that you were coming to the hall tonight. I would have greeted you when you arrived."

Merek glanced at her, looking her up and down. "You need not attend," he said. "Go back to the kitchens where you are useful."

It was a nasty insult right away, in front of guests no less, and Gavriella was humiliated. She could feel her cheeks grow hot and it was a struggle not to insult the man in return. As she tried to think of something to say that wouldn't start a fight, Andreas spoke up.

"I think not, my lord," he said. "She brings light and beauty into a hall filled with men. She is needed far more here than in the kitchens. My lady, you are welcome to sit with us. You have been a gracious hostess since our arrival and we appreciate your company."

He said it so sweetly. Gavriella looked at him, deeply touched and grateful, as he smiled at her. The bench he sat on was full, and he was at the very end, but he thumped one of the young men with him on the back of the head and instructed him to stand up. The lad did, frowning as he rubbed the spot where Andreas had thumped him, and Andreas scooted down the bench so there was a place for Gavriella to sit down. As she moved to take the spot next to him, Merek spoke.

"I can see you have met my daughter," he said. "I am glad she made herself useful to you and your men, but I do not want to see her when I am eating. It is my wish that she return to the kitchen."

Gavriella was just about to take a seat but she came to an uncertain pause. Uncertain because she didn't want to disobey her father in front of their guests. Even if he had shown her great disrespect, she didn't want to show him the same.

But even if she was willing to back away, Andreas wasn't.

"And it is my wish that she remain," he said steadily. "As a gracious host, it is expected that you accommodate my wishes, and as a knight who brought a thousand-man army to protect you from rampaging Scots, you owe me that gratitude. I would like for the lady to stay."

It was not a request, but a command. He was clearly challenging Merek. Gavriella looked at him in shock, but he was looking at her father. Glaring at him was more like it. Conversation that had been buzzing around the table with the other knights now suddenly came to a halt as there was evidently some kind of disagreement between Merek de Leia and Andreas de Wolfe. As Andreas waited for the next volley, the red-haired woman who had accompanied Merek into the hall, standing behind him, spoke up.

"This is Lord de Leia's property, my lord," she said. "If he does not wish for his daughter to remain, then she will not remain. It would be rude of you to demand otherwise."

Andreas' eyes flicked over to the woman. "I do not normally lower myself to address a servant who has overstepped herself, but I will in this instance," he said, his voice low and threatening. "Keep your mouth shut unless you are spoken to. This does not concern you."

Her head snapped back as if he'd physically struck her and Merek frowned. "By what right do you come to Falstone and make such demands?" he said angrily. "I did not summon your army, de Wolfe. You are here because your father sent you here, not because you were invited. I came to the hall to greet you in a gesture of goodwill, but I'll not have you insult my companion or countermand my orders. My daughter is better suited to the kitchens and that is where she will go."

Something in Andreas' eyes flickered dangerously. "Why?" he asked simply.

"Because I wish it."

"I will again ask – why?"

"Because that is where she belongs."

As Andreas and the others watched, the redhead poured wine into Merek's cup from a flask she'd brought herself. Not from the pitchers on the table or from the drink the servants were providing, but from her own personal flask.

It was most curious.

But Andreas wasn't backing down.

"As I understand it, she is your chatelaine," he said. "She was most hospitable this afternoon, kind and intelligent. She would be an asset to any house, so I am curious why you will not let her remain and entertain your guests, yet you allow that one to remain."

He was pointing a finger at the redhead from the hand that gripped his cup of hot wine. It was a gesture not meant to be polite. Frustrated, Merek glanced at the knights at this end of the table, Lukas included.

He focused on him.

"If my daughter will not leave by her own will, then you will remove her."

Lukas, who had remained silent through the odd and strained exchange, looked over at Gavriella. He could see by the look on her face that she knew this situation wasn't going to end well if she didn't do as her father told her.

"It is no trouble," she said, backing away from the table. "I have plenty to keep me busy in the kitchens, my lord. In fact, there is some fresh bread that was coming out of the ovens when I left. I will bring that to you personally."

With that, she scurried away before Andreas could stop her. He watched her rush back through the hall and disappear before turning his attention back to Merek, who was draining his cup.

Already, he didn't like the man.

Truth be told, he didn't even know him. He'd been sitting across the table from the man for two minutes before Gavriella appeared, so they'd only been introduced when everything happened. Even in that short time, he could see how Merek treated his daughter. The man who sent her to London because he was ashamed to look at her. Maybe he hadn't really believed Lukas' assessment until that moment, but he could see very plainly that it was true.

And that didn't sit well with Andreas.

But something else occurred to him. *Careful, man, if you want to ask his permission to court her...*

"I was telling Sir Andreas that our lands have been peaceful for quite some time," Lukas said, breaking the tense silence. "We've not seen any signs of the Scots, fortunately, but it sounds as if they are giving the House of de Wolfe a terrible time. Personally, I'm grateful they've come."

Merek had drained his cup by then and the woman was filling it back up. After a moment, he snorted.

"They never come here," he said. "I have lived here my entire life and we've had more trouble from local English lords than the Scots. What makes you think they're going to come this way?"

He was looking at Andreas, who was trying very hard to be polite at this point.

"As I told de Dere, they've been all over the borders as of late," he said. "We just spent six days in close combat with the

Scots before finally chasing them back over the border. Our spies told us that they were moving in this direction. Of course, they could pass you by, but my father thought it was prudent to send you reinforcements in case they did not. He does not want to see Falstone fall to the marauding Scots and I suspect you do not, either. It is safer for Falstone if we remain for a time."

Merek sucked down whatever the redheaded woman had put in his cup, licking his lips with gusto. "De Wolfe," he muttered, rolling the name over his tongue. "When my grandfather was a lad, there was no House of de Wolfe in the north. They rose to power rather quickly."

Andreas wasn't sure if there was an insult in that. "My grandfather, William de Wolfe, was the younger brother of the Earl of Wolverhampton," he said. "He had to earn his way and he did. He was much rewarded by Henry III."

Merek was looking at his cup. "My grandfather fought for Henry, too," he said. "Only he did not receive any rewards for it."

Maybe he wasn't as worthy.

Oh, how Andreas wanted to say that. It was a struggle to bite his tongue. He wanted something from de Leia and they'd already started off on the wrong foot, so he labored to keep the conversation pleasant.

More pleasant than it had been, anyway.

"How did the House of de Leia come by the Falstone property?" he asked.

Merek wouldn't look up from his cup, finally holding it up to the woman so she could pour more drink into it.

"It was built by an ancestor who came to these shores shortly after the Duke of Normandy," he said. "De Leia is a fine Norman family. There was a time when we held a good portion of the north. Before the de Wolfes and the Grays and the Percys. Before de Vesci claimed everything along the east coast and all we had to worry about were the Scots from the north. Never each other."

He downed half the cup in his hand. It was clear that he was quickly becoming inebriated and Andreas caught Lukas' expression, suggesting the worst was yet to come. Andreas could see that the knight was on-edge.

"My father says you have been a loyal ally," Andreas said evenly. "I would not be here if he did not think so. He means to help protect you against the enemy."

Merek looked at him, then. "He does not even know who our enemy is," he said, starting to slur his words. "Our enemy is not the Scots. It's even worse than that. English in wolf's clothing and I do not mean the de Wolfes. I mean another, more sinister wolf even than that."

Given what Andreas already knew, he suspected who the man meant. "I would wager to say there are few worse than the Scots this far north," he said, but sought to shift the subject. "How far do de Leia lands go, anyway?"

Merek pointed in a general northly direction. "Over the border," he said. "We run all the way to Hell's Guardhouse. *That* is the enemy I speak of. With a name like that, of course the devil lives there. That whole family is full of devils. Where has de Wolfe been to protect us from those bastards? You speak of protecting an ally, but where were you when they attacked my daughter?"

Andreas froze. That wasn't the subject he wanted to be on, not in the least, especially with Gavriella approaching the table with a big basket of fresh bread. He could see her out of the corners of his eyes. She was trying so hard to be a good chatelaine and an obedient daughter, but she had a fool for a father.

Andreas could see that quite clearly.

He could see her moving closer and he wanted to change

the subject as swiftly as possible.

"How far are your lands to the south?" he asked, trying desperately to shift the conversation. "My father told me that you hold a good deal of land up here. What do you do with it? Sheep?"

"Mostly sheep," Lukas answered. He could see what Andreas was trying to do. "We do have an entire meadow towards the east that contains cattle but, mostly, it's sheep. We have massive herds that the Scots and others have pilfered from time to time, but that has been rare. It is a blessing that we've been left alone as much as we have."

Gavriella had reached the table at that point, setting the basket of bread down. In her other hand, she had a bowl of butter, which she sat down next to it. Andreas dared to look up at her, concern in his expression, and the smile on her face turned into a questioning grimace. She had no idea why he looked so concerned.

But she would soon find out.

Merek's hand shot out and grabbed her by the wrist.

"Here is a victim of the enemy de Wolfe did not protect us from," he said, quite obviously drunk now. "My only child, my daughter. She is a beautiful woman and should marry into a fine family, but not now. She cannot. De Soulis spoiled her by taking what did not belong to him and no one will want her. He violated her in unspeakable ways. You wonder why she is only good for the kitchen? Because she's *dirty*. Dirty, I say!"

Andreas was prepared to punch the man in the mouth simply to shut him up. "She is nothing of the kind," he snarled. "Shut your lips, you fool. You are embarrassing yourself in front of everyone."

Merek blinked as if he hadn't realized that. He looked at his daughter, who was already in tears with what he had said, struggling to pull away from him, and he yanked on her hard enough to snap her head back. She gasped and would have fallen onto the table had Andreas not grabbed her.

But Merek was on a streak. Whatever the redhead had given him had loosened his tongue and he wouldn't, or couldn't, stop it. It was Andreas who finally broke his grip on Gavriella, pulling her away as Merek stood up, pointing a finger at her.

"Every time I look at her, I feel sick," he said. "She has ruined this family. De Soulis touched her and they bore a child together, so I should simply give her over to him and be done with it. That is what he wants, you know. He wants her and he wants the child, but like a fool, I sent my daughter to London and the child to Edenside simply to get them away from me. I cannot bear to look at either of them. I… I should have killed her when I was told de Soulis' seed had taken root. At least I would have saved my family's honor. But she is damaged goods now. Mayhap I should simply kill her now and be done with it!"

Andreas lashed out a massive fist and caught Merek in the jaw, knocking him unconscious in an instant. As he went flying backwards, onto the floor, Gavriella yanked herself away from Andreas and went on the run, barreling thorough the hall and heading for the exit. Will, Brodie, Gareth, Corey, and Reed were on their feet, preparing to defend Andreas against an undoubtedly furious Lukas and the rest of the de Leia army, but no one seemed to be moving towards them. In fact, Lukas was still in his seat, looking at Merek on the ground quite unemotionally.

Andreas had remained at the table only because he was certain he was about to be part of an enormous brawl for striking the lord of Falstone, but no one was moving against him. It took him a moment to realize that.

He caught Lukas' eye.

"He threatened to kill her," he said, sounding as if he were stumbling over his words. "The man is spewing violence and curses… I cannot allow that to go on. I will apologize for striking him if you think I should, but know that I would not mean it. I am not sorry in the least."

Lukas sighed heavily. "You have done what I have wanted to do for quite some time," he said, clearly distressed. "Have no fear. He will remember nothing in the morning."

Andreas was still coiled, still braced for a fight. "What did he mean when he said de Soulis wants his daughter and her child?" he asked. "Has he made an offer of marriage for her?"

Lukas shrugged. "If he did, I was not made aware of it," he said. "Lord de Leia used to consult with me on everything, but ever since that… that incident he spoke of, he's not confided anything in me. I do not know what he means, but I intend to find out."

Throwing his leg over the bench, he stood up, looking at his unconscious liege. The disgust on his face was evident. As he bent over to gather de Leia under the arms and drag him out, Will suddenly spoke up.

"That redhead," he said. "The one feeding him all of the drink. Where in the hell did she go?"

They all started to look around, realizing that de Leia's companion had simply vanished. For a woman who had been hovering over him all evening, her sudden absence was odd. And concerning. Andreas had a very uneasy feeling.

He had to find Gavriella.

CHAPTER EIGHTEEN

NOW, HE KNEW.

That wasn't exactly the way Gavriella had planned to tell Andreas, but her father had gone on a rampage and spoiled everything. Something he'd kept secret since it happened, he had willingly and recklessly poured out to a table of mostly strangers, Andreas included.

Now, they all knew.

Gavriella found herself praying for a hole in the ground to open up and swallow her.

If her luck held steady, however, no hole would be forthcoming. She would be forced to face her torment, her shame. She'd come running out into the kitchen yard, blindly, tramping through the snow until she came to the shelter that provided cover for the additional bread ovens, which were warm from having been used this night.

Standing next to the bread ovens, she stood in the shadows and wept.

Everything was ruined.

All of the hopes and dreams she'd had for a future with Andreas had just been summarily dashed by her drunkard buffoon of a father. Everyone knew what had happened now. It wasn't as if Merek could take the words back and force them to forget.

She desperately wished such a thing was possible.

But it wasn't.

Around her, the snow was falling gently now, having let up since the burst earlier in the evening. There was about a foot of snow on the ground, but the bailey of Falstone, and the yards, were lit by heavily fatted torches and lanterns, the warm glow of light pushing through the darkness.

But it was darkness that would never leave Gavriella.

She could feel it right down to her bones.

Hopelessness.

The tears wouldn't stop falling. She'd never be able to face any of those men now and, most importantly, she'd never be able to face Andreas. How could she when he knew her deepest, darkest secrets? That kind, chivalrous knight who had helped her find her way from Gomorrah, the same kind and chivalrous knight who had spent the day with her watching entertainment in the most glorious day of her life.

The same man who had found her, against all odds, here at her home in Northumberland.

All of it… gone.

She'd told him once that she was meant for the veil in an attempt to tell him that she was unmarriageable property. *Damaged goods.* Now she was thinking that the church might be the only alternative for her. She refused to remain with her father any longer and she certainly couldn't find a decent husband. She would go to Edenside where her son was and ask if she could remain, taking care of the children in exchange for a roof over her head.

In exchange for being with her son.

Perhaps it was the best option she had.

More tears fell.

"Gavriella?"

Andreas' voice filled the air, soft yet strong, like velvet against steel. He'd startled her so that she gasped aloud, turning to see that he'd essentially boxed her in against the oven she was standing next to. When their eyes met, he smiled gently.

"I did not mean to startle you," he said.

Gavriella opened her mouth to deny it, but she couldn't quite manage it. She'd already lied to the man enough, or at the very least, withheld truths. There was no reason to protect herself any longer. She had no idea why he'd come to speak to her; perhaps to kindly tell her that he was no longer interested or to show her some kind of pity.

The mere thought made the bile rise in her throat.

"It is of little matter," she said, brushing away tears that were falling faster than she could wipe them. "Now you know everything, Andreas. You know everything I did not tell you. I told you in London that people hide things, and now you know why – there was much for me to hide."

He had a pained expression. "Gavriella, I…"

She held up a hand. "Please," she said, her voice trembling. "Let me speak of this while I still have courage. Last year, on a lovely day in July, I was in the village of Deadwater. I had gone to seek the merchant who imports fine threads from London. As I was walking to the merchant, four armed men came charging down the avenue. They asked one of the merchants if he knew who I was and the man confirmed that I was Merek de Leia's daughter. The knights proceeded to abduct me and take me to a livery on the edge of town where I was held down by three of them while the fourth man hit me so hard that I was knocked unconscious. When I awoke, he was on top of me, doing things that a man would do to his wife. I tried to fight him, to scream, but it was me against four big men. I never had a chance. When the man was finished, he rode off and left me there. It was Lukas who found me and brought me home. We determined that it was de Soulis because I saw a brand on one of the horses that Lukas and my father recognized. A child resulted from this attack and he was sent away after he was born and I was sent to London. That is when you met me. And now… now, you know. My life laid open. I am damaged goods, as my father said."

Andreas was watching her with a heavy heart. She was pale and shaking, refusing to look at him, and he felt as bad as he possibly could.

"I already knew," he said quietly.

Her head jerked up, her eyes wide. "You… you *knew*?"

"I did."

She was looking at him in confusion and disbelief. "But… *how*? How did you know?"

"De Dere," he said hoarsely. "He did not tell me to gossip, only to explain the relationship between Falstone and her neighbor to the north, Hell's Guardhouse. One thing led to another and the situation came out. So, I knew before your father shouted it out for the world to hear."

She stared at him a moment before breaking down into tears again. "When we met in London, I tried to discourage you," she wept. "Do you not recall? I told you that I was not meant for marriage. I led you believe that I was meant for the veil because it was better than telling you the truth. The truth that something horrible happened to me that I shall have to live with for the rest of my life."

Andreas pondered that a moment. "And you should not have to assume that burden alone," he said gently. "Gavriella, I am not sure how to say this gracefully so I shall come out with it. Nothing has changed with me. Not my determination to court you nor my desire to marry you. I knew that you were hiding something from the first – it was something we even discussed. But I also knew that you would belong to me, no matter what. Once you were finished being rude to me, there was something about you I could not get away from. I told you before that I see a sunrise in you, a new day, and I do not want to see that sun set. Sometimes, you meet the person who speaks the language of your heart and you just… *know*."

She hadn't stopped weeping. Her hand was over her mouth as she looked at him and when she spoke, it was through splayed fingers. "You still feel the same way even after… after knowing everything?"

"After knowing everything."

Her hand came away from her mouth. "But after what my father did… everyone will know what happened now," she said. "This shame we tried to keep secret will be something everyone knows and when they look at me with disgust, they will look upon you with disgust, too. You know that is what is going to happen and it should not. You do not deserve that."

He was moving closer to her now. "I am a de Wolfe," he said, his voice a gentle growl. "I come from the most powerful family in the north, one whose reputation is beyond contestation. I am a knight of the highest order, an elite warrior, and when a de Wolfe chooses a mate, it is for life. There are no regrets. We marry for love and we marry a woman who is worthy of that devotion. I think that you are more than worthy, so if there is any condemnation for something that was beyond your control, I will dare whoever speaks of it to cast the first stone. And then I will kill them. Is this in any way unclear?"

By the time he was done, she wasn't weeping any longer, but looking at him as if mesmerized. His words were powerful and honest and poignant. It was finally starting to sink in that he hadn't come to condemn her.

Quite the contrary.

"It is clear," she whispered, hardly daring to hope. "But,

Dray… you must know that someday, I intend to reclaim my son. He was an innocent in all of this and I cannot stomach the thought of him being in a foundling home. My father insisted on it, but I did not want to send him there. He is *my* child, my flesh and blood. I realize it is a lot to ask, but do you think… *could* you… accept him?"

He didn't hesitate. "He is part of you. Of course I could."

Her jaw dropped in shock. Although Andreas was already showing an inordinate amount of compassion in her situation, she wasn't entirely sure that would hold true to the living, breathing result of the horrible attack that had robbed her of everything.

She could hardly believe it.

"Oh… Dray," she breathed, feeling overwhelmed. "Is it true?"

"All of it."

"It seems like a dream."

"It is no dream," he said. "May I prove it?"

She was nodding, but her eyes were filling with tears again as he took a couple of steps and ended up standing right next to her. Their proximity to one another was intoxicating – painful and frightening and exhilarating.

"The last time a man was this close to me," she murmured tightly, "terrible things happened. I am afraid, but I do not want to be afraid of you. When I asked you to prove your words, mayhap I was also asking the same thing of myself. I must prove to myself that a man's touch – that your touch – is nothing to fear."

He could feel her fear, fear she was trying so hard to push aside. It hurt his heart to see her so afraid, but it also filled him with the rage of the devil.

"You did not shy away from me in the tavern," he said softly. "I was able to get quite close."

She nodded, trembling because he was so close to her. "It is true," she said. "But that happened so quickly. I did not have time to be afraid."

"But now you do."

"A little."

"Then let me show you how to be fearless," he muttered. "Try to put aside what you've experienced in the past. Let me show you what it is meant to be like. What it will always be like with me. I swear that I will only, and always, be gentle with you. Do you trust me?"

"I do."

Their breaths hung in foggy puffs in the air between them as he gazed into her eyes before reaching out and pulling her against him. She didn't resist; she was fluid, boneless, a warm mass of fabric and hair, heart and flesh, and his mouth slanted over hers hungrily.

Prove it, she'd said.

He did.

He had to prove it to them both.

Andreas had never kissed a woman like that in his entire life. A man who kept his emotions at bay, it was as if they were all barreling out now and he couldn't stop them. He had Gavriella aloft, in his arms, kissing her so deeply that he drove his teeth into her lower lip.

Tasting the blood, he licked it hungrily.

It was sheer bliss.

"Now," he whispered huskily. "I want you to remember this moment. When I showed you how a kiss can be between a man and a woman. Are you still afraid?"

Dazed, Gavriella swallowed hard. "Nay."

With a smile on his lips, he swooped in for another kiss, this one more deeply than the first one. He rather liked the taste of her, the feel of her in his arms. Certainly he'd kissed women before, but there had been something lacking in each kiss he couldn't put his finger on.

There was nothing lacking in this one.

He was looking forward to many more just like it.

Over near the kitchen door, servants suddenly appeared, talking about providing stew to men who hadn't received any yet. They were bickering, back and forth, and Andreas stopped kissing Gavriella and set her to her feet, remaining in the shadows as the servants dished more stew out of the pot in the center of the kitchen yard before disappearing back inside. When they were gone, he turned to her.

"Let tonight be a foretaste, my lady," he said, a glimmer in his eyes. "I will speak to your father first thing in the morning, providing he does not remember what happened tonight."

Gavriella still had a grip on him, holding tightly to his warm, powerful form. "He usually does not," she said. "In fact, he usually…"

She suddenly trailed off and he looked at her, noting that she was looking at something over in the stable yard. Andreas turned to see what had her attention. He could see a small figure moving through the snow towards the stables before disappearing inside.

"What is it?" he asked her. "Who was that?"

Gavriella cocked her head curiously. "I've seen that cloak," she said. "I think that is Giddy."

"Who is that?"

"The woman who will not leave my father's side."

The light of recognition went on in Andreas' mind. "The woman with the red hair."

"Aye," Gavriella said. "It is strange that she would be out here on this night."

Andreas cocked a disapproving eyebrow. "It seems to me that everything about her is strange," he said. "After you fled the hall, she disappeared. Your father was on the ground and she was nowhere to be found."

Gavriella looked at him. "Why was he on the ground?"

Andreas looked at her, trying not to appear contrite. "Because I struck him," he said. "He was speaking of… madness and would not shut his mouth. I struck him to shut him up."

She regarded him for a moment. "He was speaking about me, wasn't he?"

"Aye."

He averted his gaze and Gavriella smiled faintly. "You have made yourself my champion, have you?" she said. "Even against my father?"

"Especially against your father."

She started to chuckle, touched by his actions and words, but was cut short when a horse and rider suddenly thundered from the stable, heading for the gatehouse. It was dark, and a light snow was falling, but still, the rider was heading out of Falstone on a night when travel would have been inadvisable.

Andreas released Gavriella and tried to peer through the dimly lit bailey as the rider reached the gatehouse.

"*That's* Giddy?" he asked.

Gavriella could see the distant figure as the gate sentries opened up a small section of gate, a man gate, to allow the figure to pass through.

"Aye," she said. "But where in the world is she going? She has not left Falstone since I returned home those months ago and now, abruptly, she must leave? Most peculiar."

Andreas didn't have an answer for her but he knew, instinctively, that it couldn't be good. As he watched, the horse and rider slipped through the gate and disappeared out into the night.

He grasped Gavriella by the hand.

"Come on," he said.

She held on to him with one hand, lifting her skirts away from the snow with the other. "Why?" she asked. "Where are we going?"

Andreas didn't look at her. He had much on his mind. "To find answers."

Gavriella didn't say anything. She simply went along with him. Whatever he needed to accomplish was fine with her.

Her champion.

Something was rotten at Falstone and Andreas was going to find out what it was.

CHAPTER NINETEEN

Hell's Guardhouse

"Edenside," Giddy said breathlessly. "The child is at Edenside!"

She had just burst into John's bedchamber and the man had been dead asleep, but Giddy's shrill voice had him sitting up in his bed before he even realized he'd moved. In fact, he nearly pitched himself over the side of his bed as Giddy ran to him, grasping at him.

"Did you hear me?" she said urgently. "The child is at Edenside!"

John was struggling out of a deep sleep. He rubbed his eyes furiously. "Edenside?" he repeated. "The child of de Leia's daughter?"

"Of course," Giddy said as if he'd just said something foolish. "Who else? God's Beard… six long months with that… that *animal* and he finally revealed the whereabouts tonight. I had to come and tell you as soon as I heard!"

John was more lucid now as he processed what she was telling him, but her shouting had brought Nicholas. He was suddenly in the doorway of his father's chamber, dressed in smelly, crumpled clothing and rubbing his eyes.

"What has happened?" he yawned, then realized he was looking at Giddy. "You? What are *you* doing here?"

Giddy sauntered up to him. "I found your bastard, my handsome lad," she said seductively. "All of those months plying the man with wine mixed with that weed called vervain finally came to fruition. The old fool finally revealed that he'd sent the infant to Edenside."

Nicholas peered at her in disbelief. "The truth serum actually *worked*?"

Giddy nodded. "It must have," she said. "Whatever the apothecary in Gretna Green sold you as effective in prying the truth out of a man finally worked, but it took six long months for it to have an effect. The child is at a place called Edenside. Have you heard of it?"

Nicholas hadn't. He looked at his father, who was sitting on the bed, scratching his head. "Edenside," John muttered thoughtfully. He looked at Giddy. "And he said no more?"

Giddy shook her head. "Why should he say more?" she said. "He has revealed where the child is. Now you must go and get it!"

Nicholas frowned as he stumbled to his father's bed, eyeing the man. "What is Edenside?"

John was thinking seriously on that very thing. "The name sounds familiar," he said, pausing for a moment before continuing. "I seem to remember attending a gathering at Roxburgh Castle a few years ago and they were speaking of... something. A great scandal had happened involving Kelso Abbey. Something about their foundling home selling children. I swear to you that they mentioned Edenside."

Nicholas' eyebrows lifted. "Edenside is a foundling home that *sells* children?" he said, aghast. "If de Leia sent the child there, then mayhap they've sold *my* child."

John held up a hand to his angry son. "They did it illegally and were punished, as I recall," he said. "This was a few years ago, as I said. Damnation… I wish I had paid more attention to that conversation. But I am fairly certain that Edenside is part of Kelso Abbey."

Nicholas was electrified by the news. "Then we have a location," he hissed, smacking his hand on the post of his father's bed in triumph. "God's Bones, we have a location! We must leave immediately!"

"The snow is falling," Giddy said. "It may be difficult to start such a journey tonight."

"But you made it here from Falstone," John said. "How did you find your way?"

She shrugged. "I was born here," she said. "I know the land and the roads. The road that passes Falstone Castle intersects with a road that leads to Hell's Guardhouse. I simply had to make sure to stay on the road. The clouds must not be thick because there was a glow to them, as if the moon was right behind them. You know what I mean, when they seem silver and the land is the color of steel. It is still dark, but one can see."

"Even through the snow?"

"The snow was light enough when I left Falstone," she said. "Now that you know where the child is, you may as well wait until morning. I am sure the child will still be there tomorrow."

She had a point. No one was doing any traveling on this night, except for Giddy, and she had a reason. It probably hadn't been wise of her but, to John, it was indicative of the fact that she finally had the information he wanted and she was anxious for her payoff.

But he wasn't finished with her yet.

"You did well, Giddy," he said. "I am pleased."

Giddy flushed. "It was an honor, my lord."

"What do you know of children?"

She shrugged. "I've had two myself," she said. "They live

with my mother in Carlisle."

"Then you know how to tend them."

"My mother knows better."

John looked at his son. "Then we retrieve the child and send it with Giddy to Carlisle," he said. "That would be the perfect solution so that we are not responsible for the child, but it is still within our control. She can bring it back to us when… when the time comes."

Nicholas shrugged. "We do not need the child until the summer solstice," he said. "Pay her well and send the child with her."

Giddy was listening to the conversation, a volley going back and forth between father and son. "I do not wish to tend this child," she told John. "I do not even tend my own."

John shook his head. "You can take it to your mother's house," he said. "We will send coin along so your mother will be compensated. Surely she would take care of the child until we retrieve it in the summer."

Giddy's eyebrows lifted. "My mother would tend the devil himself for the right price," she said. "I'll take the child there. But I want what you promised me for spending those months in de Leia's bed."

John nodded. "Do not fret," he said. "You shall have your due, I swear it. Nicholas, send word to the servants. They are to have our mounts prepared at dawn."

Nicholas left the chamber without another word, leaving Giddy with John. She was watching the old man run his hands over his face wearily. Something he said had her curious.

"Why do you want the infant returned by the summer solstice, my lord?" she asked.

John's hands came away from his face and he looked at her. "Do you want to be paid?"

"Of course, my lord."

"Then do not ask questions. If I wanted you to know, I would have told you."

That shut her up swiftly. She liked living at Hell's Guardhouse and doing what she did best, and she was quite happy to be away from Falstone and that lord who smelled of compost, so she didn't want to stir up any trouble.

She backed away, towards the door.

"Is there anything else you require from me, my lord?"

John lay back down, pulling the covers up over him. "Not tonight," he said. "But be prepared to ride with us on the morrow."

"Me?" She stopped at the door. "Why should I ride with you to Edenside?"

John turned his head in her direction, glaring. "You do not think Nicholas or I will tend an infant, do you? You are coming along to do just that."

She almost reminded him that she didn't even tend her own children, again, but thought better of it. She didn't think he would take it well.

She had seen what the man was capable of when he didn't take things well.

At dawn the next morning, Giddy was ready for travel.

CHAPTER TWENTY

Falstone Castle

"MY LORD, WE must have a word with you."

Lukas and Andreas were standing in the open door of Merek's bedchamber as the man stood over a basin against the wall, dry heaving because he was so hungover. It was dawn on a surprisingly clear winter's morning, the storm from the previous evening having cleared out sometime during the night. After a couple of particularly nasty heaves, Merek turned his head to look at the pair.

"God, what?" he grumbled. "Now? Can it not wait?"

"Nay, my lord, it cannot," Lukas said. "We have something of a mystery on our hands that is… concerning."

Merek gave one final heave before wiping his mouth and turning for his clothes, thrown in a heap on a chair.

"What is concerning, Lukas?" he asked. "And why is de Wolfe here?"

"Because he was the one who brought it to my attention, my lord," he said. He passed a glance at Andreas before continuing. "What do you remember of last night, my lord?"

Merek paused, tunic in hand. "Last night?" he repeated. "When?"

"In the feasting hall?"

Merek paused. "I was in the feasting hall?"

That answered Lukas' question. It was as he'd told Andreas – the man hardly remembered anything after a drinking binge.

The knights entered the chamber and shut the door.

"My lord, your companion, Giddy, left late last night," Lukas said quietly. "Andreas saw her ride from the stables. She has not returned."

That brought some awareness from Merek. He looked around the chamber as if he hadn't noticed she'd been gone. Puzzled, he looked at the knights.

"She left?" he asked.

"She did," Lukas said. "Did you send her away?"

Merek frowned. "Of course not," he said. "Why would I do that?"

"I do not know," Lukas said. "When evaluating a situation, one must eliminate the possibilities one at a time. So, you did not order her away?"

"I did not."

"Then she left of her own accord," Lukas said, looking around the chamber. "Is anything missing? Did she steal something and run off?"

Merek didn't say anything for a moment. He pulled the tunic over his head, clumsily, moving slowly and aimlessly around the chamber. He went to a table that contained a clutter of things, pulling forth a metal box and peering inside. Then, he closed the lid and wandered back over to the bed, sitting heavily.

All the while, Lukas and Andreas were watching him, waiting for an answer, but Merek didn't seem too eager to provide them with one. In fact, after his initial flash of emotion at the disappearance of the woman who had been his constant companion for months, he didn't seem to be showing any reaction at all. He was simply sitting on his bed, staring off into the dim chamber.

Lukas and Andreas exchanged curious glances.

"My lord?" Lukas finally said.

Merek turned in his direction but he didn't look at him. "She did not steal anything," he said. "And she did not run off. She simply returned to where she came from."

Lukas and Andreas looked at each other again, this time in puzzlement. "Did you know she was leaving?" Lukas asked.

Merek shook his head. "Nay," he said. "But I knew she would at some point. She was not meant to stay."

Lukas was becoming frustrated with the man's answers. He moved around the bed so that he was standing in front of him.

"My lord, please tell us what you know," he said. "There was a time when you used to confide everything in me, but that all stopped when that woman came around. You stopped speaking to me as if I had done something to displease you. I am yours to command, my lord, and we have had an excellent relationship for ten years. I am only trying to help you and you know that, so if there is something you know that you are not telling me, I wish you would simply come out with it."

Merek looked up at him. After a moment, he smiled weakly. "Dear Lukas," he said. "Always trying to do the right thing. Always willing to help me even if I cannot help myself."

Lukas nodded. "Of course, my lord," he said sincerely. "That is why I am here. I am your devoted knight. Will you not tell me what you know about everything?"

Merek grunted and looked away. "Everything," he muttered as if disgusted with the very word. "There was nothing you could have done. I was as curious about her as she was about me. I knew her presence here was not a good one, but I let her stay. It is difficult to be so lonely."

Lukas was quickly growing exasperated. "*Who* is she?"

Merek was still looking at the floor. "She's really gone, is she?"

"She is."

Merek scratched his nose. "I had been expecting it," he said. "You want to know everything? I suppose I shall tell you. There is nothing you can do about it now, anyway. Giddy was not a gift from an ally, Lukas. She was sent by John de Soulis to spy on me."

Lukas' eyes widened and he looked at Andreas, who also appeared surprised. "*What*?" Lukas finally hissed. "How do you know this?"

Merek sighed heavily. "It is my belief that it goes back to something that happened several months ago," he said. "You know Harman the Wise, of course. The physic from Deadwater. He came here months ago to tell me that he overheard John and Nicholas de Soulis speaking of getting their hands on the infant my daughter delivered in order to fulfill some sort of prophesy. They wanted the child and they wanted my daughter. They even wanted Harman to smuggle the child out of Falstone and give it over to them, but he refused. He came to me instead to tell me so that I could protect both my daughter and the child."

By this time, Andreas was standing next to Lukas, his features dark with rage. "And what did you do?" he growled.

Merek looked up at the very big, very tense knight. "I did nothing," he said. "My daughter was in London and the child was not here, so I did nothing. I sent Harman away and I've not seen him since. There was no reason to do anything, de Wolfe, and I fail to see why this concerns you so."

Andreas hadn't pictured this as the moment he would ask for Gavriella's hand, but he was backed into a corner now and had little choice. He suspected Lukas already knew of his inclination towards Gavriella so he might as well get it all out in the open.

He wanted them to know he had a massive stake in this situation.

"Because I met your daughter when she was in London," he said, trying not to sound threatening. "I met her, spent time with her, and I want to marry her. I know what happened with Nicholas de Soulis and because of my feelings for your daughter, your problem with the House of de Soulis has become my problem, as well. You have refused to punish them for what they did, but I promise that I am not as weak. I bring the de Wolfe power with me and when I am finished with them, they will be dust in the wind. My lord, this is not exactly how I envisioned asking you for your permission to wed your daughter, but I am asking you now. I swear that I will love her and protect her all my life."

When he was finished, Merek was looking at him as if he'd just spoken in tongues, but Lukas was smiling. Reaching out, the knight put his hand on Andreas' shoulder.

"I thought there might be something you had in mind simply from the way you were acting, but I could not be sure," he said. "I cannot tell you how happy I am to hear this. I have known Gavy for half of her life and she is a sweet, compassionate lass. I could not hope for a finer husband for her."

Andreas was trying to focus on Merek, but Lukas' words had him fighting off a grin. "To be honest, I was not sure if you had designs on her," he said. "You are quite protective of her."

Lukas shook his head. "I am already married," he said. "My dear wife, Amy, is sickly and lives in Carlisle with her parents so that they are able to tend her. They can do it much better than I can, considering the duties I have here at Falstone. Gavy is like a sister to me and nothing more, I swear it."

Andreas let his grin break through, but only briefly. There was still the matter of Merek, who had yet to say a word. Both knights finally turned to him, expectantly.

But Merek only had eyes for Andreas.

"You… you want to *marry* Gavriella?" he finally said.

Andreas nodded. "If you will allow it, my lord."

Merek blinked. In fact, he started blinking rapidly as if staving off tears. "My God," he finally said. "Truly?"

"Truly."

"I never thought this moment would come. I thought she would be my burden for the rest of my life."

Andreas didn't like the way the man spoke of his daughter. He'd never liked it. "She will be *my* burden," he said. "And a joyous one at that. Do I have your permission, my lord?"

Merek was still having difficulty with the whole concept. "She is my only child, you know. My heiress to Falstone. 'Tis not much, but the House of de Leia is an honorable family."

"I know. May I?"

When Merek realized this was no joke, and no whim, he nodded. "Aye," he said. "By God… you may. Take her and welcome."

That pleased Andreas immensely. He looked at Lukas to see that the man was still smiling at him. But now that he had permission, he had a few things to say to Merek that he didn't want to say before he had the man's agreement.

He wasn't going to hold back.

"I will," he said. "And if I ever hear you insult her again, in any fashion, you will not like my reaction. You have a strong, intelligent, and beautiful daughter who will be treated with the utmost respect. You refused to do anything to de Soulis when he touched what by all rights now belongs to me, but I am going to do something about it and you will give me the answers I need in order to accomplish this. Do you understand?"

Merek understood his words, but he wasn't clear on why. "What can I tell you?"

"I am not sure," Andreas said. "But I will ask questions until I am satisfied. Now, you said this physic, Harman, came to warn you that de Soulis wanted Gavriella and the infant?"

"Aye."

"And you think that Giddy was sent by de Soulis?"

"I am certain of it."

"*How* do you know?"

Merek cocked his head. "Because she would ply me with wine nightly and ask me about the infant," he said. "Knowing what Harman told me, who else would want to know that?"

"But you said that you were warned they wanted Gavriella, too," Andreas said. "She has been returned from London for several months and they've not come for her. Did Giddy ever try to lure her away?"

"Not that I am aware of."

Things just weren't adding up for Andreas. He looked at Lukas a moment before turning away, his mind churning through everything he'd been told.

"The old physic warned you that there was some kind of prophesy to fulfill," he muttered. "I have no idea what that may be, but let us push that aside for the moment. De Soulis wanted the infant *and* Gavriella, but Gavriella has been at Falstone for months and they've not come for her. Instead, Giddy has been focused on asking about the infant."

Lukas and Merek were watching him as he reasoned out the situation. "That is true," Merek said. "That seemed to be of the most interest to her."

Andreas paused by the window before turning to look at Merek. "What did you tell her?"

"Edenside."

It was Lukas who answered, not Merek. Suddenly, Lukas' eyes widened as he looked at Andreas. "He blurted it out last night at sup," he said. "Don't you remember? Lord de Leia said that he'd sent Gavriella to London and the infant to *Edenside*."

That fact hit Andreas like a revelation. "And she disappeared after that," he said. "My God… she fled from the hall and then I saw her leave the stables last night, in the midst of a snowstorm."

"Because she is running back to Hell's Guardhouse to tell John de Soulis," Merek finished. "If she left last night, she is already there."

Andreas had his answers and he didn't like them. "Damnation," he growled. "They've been looking for that infant all along and now they know where it is. If they want the infant that badly, my guess is that they will go and fetch it. And we have already given them an advanced start."

He was moving for the door, as was Lukas. "How does it tie into that damned prophesy?" Lukas demanded. "*What* do they want it for?"

Andreas was already through the door. "I do not know, but knowing that bunch, it cannot be good," he said. "You will have my horse saddled. I'll find Gavriella and tell her what is going on."

"Wait, please."

They were almost through the door, but Merek's soft plea forced them to pause.

"My lord?" Lukas said impatiently.

Merek just sat there for a moment before slowly pushing himself off the bed to face the two knights heading out to help him and his family. Even if he had lost the will to aid his family in any way, there were those willing to do it in spite of his apathy. He didn't even know when the apathy began, only that it had. Perhaps it had started when he lost his wife, and then when his daughter was attacked… well, that seemed to suck everything out of him. Every dream, desire, goal, or sense of pride.

Gone.

But perhaps he had even more reason than that, as Lukas and Andreas were about to find out.

"There is something you should know," he said quietly. "I have spent my entire life upholding the good de Leia name. Or, trying to. My father, Henri de Leia, was a good man, as was his father before him. But we have suffered with the House of de Soulis as our neighbors for generations and the sins committed against us by those bastards are beyond measure. It has been our cross to bear. There is a history there that you should be aware of, lads. Nicholas de Soulis' attack against Gavriella was not the first time a de Soulis has violated a woman in my family. It is only the latest."

Andreas and Lukas looked at the man with some sorrow. Given the reputation of de Soulis, they weren't surprised to hear it. But Merek's confession was unexpected.

"Then this has happened before," Andreas said quietly.

Merek nodded. "Aye," he said. "I was the result when John de Soulis' father raped my mother as a young girl. She was only fifteen and newly married to my father, and as she told me upon her deathbed, she allowed Henri to think that he was my father. She never told him the truth, mayhap for the same reason I had when I sent the infant to Edenside and my daughter to London. Pride, honor… peace of mind. Because no one can win in a battle against de Soulis. They have Lucifer on their side, and no one can win against the Fallen One."

Andreas eyed the man with pity, with frustration. "I am truly sorry for you, my lord," he said sincerely. "But surely you do not believe that they fight with Lucifer at their side."

Merek sighed heavily. "It has long been rumored that they believe in such things," he said. "I would not be surprised if their obsession with this infant has something to do with it. I suppose that is why I never told Giddy. Even if I wanted the child, and my daughter, out of my sight, that doesn't mean I was willing to throw them both to the wolves. Maybe, in my own way, I was protecting them. I should have been more honorable about it."

"But you let Giddy continue? Why did you not just send her away when you realized who had sent her?"

Merek shrugged. "Loneliness, and fear, does strange things to a man sometimes," he murmured. "Some attention is better than no attention at all. But I make no excuses. I thought you should know… everything. And I am sorry."

Perhaps they did understand everything, but it didn't change the situation. Andreas simply dipped his head as if to acknowledge what he'd been told before quitting the chamber. He was almost to the stairs when he heard a voice behind him.

"I am going with you."

Andreas stopped, turning to Lukas as the man walked up behind him. "Nay," he said. "You must stay here to protect Gavriella. I do not know why de Soulis has not tried to take her before now, but they may try now that they know where the infant is. I am asking you to remain here with her. Will you, please?"

Lukas frowned, but he didn't fight Andreas. "Aye," he said begrudgingly. "But do not go alone. Take your knights with you, at least. If you have to fight de Soulis for the infant, do not go into a fight with them undermanned."

"True enough," Andreas said. "Please find my cousin, Will, and tell him what has happened. He is trustworthy. You may tell him everything. Tell him to gather one hundred men and be prepared to depart within the hour."

They split up, going about their duties. Andreas went on the hunt for Gavriella, finding her in the kitchen yard taking an inventory of the stores they'd used the previous night. She was very glad to see him and when he told her that he had permission to marry her, she threw herself at him gleefully and he spun her around as the kitchen servants grinned. For a brief and shining moment, they gave in to their delight.

A moment of joy among hours of darkness.

But their joy was short-lived when he told her what he and Lukas suspected and where he was going. Andreas really wasn't surprised when she insisted on going with him. In truth, he didn't have the heart to stop her.

There was no way he could have.

A mother determined to get to her child.

Within the hour, they were mounted along with Will, Brodie, Gareth, and Corey, leaving Reed riding hard for Kale Water Castle to summon help from Troy. The Lair was closer, but Andreas wanted his father's help because his Uncle Scott had enough to deal with at the moment, Scots and all. Lukas was left at Falstone to command the army. It was his post, after all, and he would man it till the death.

As he watched the group of knights and one hundred soldiers pour out of Falstone's gatehouse, he seriously wondered how this situation was going to end. He had several scenarios in his mind and only one of them good.

When one was dealing with the House of de Soulis, the devil was in the details.

Or, so the rumors said…

CHAPTER TWENTY-ONE

THE JOURNEY TO Edenside Foundling Home was a little more than a day's ride from Falstone under normal conditions, but having suffered through a recent snowstorm, these weren't normal conditions.

Far from it.

Even though the day following the storm had dawned bright and remained so, the appearance of the sun and the rise in temperature had turned the roads into soup and the rivers into torrents. The snow was melting and the water runoff was great. More than once, the horses had been up to their knees in muck.

But that didn't stop them.

Andreas was trying to be thoughtful of Gavriella and not push too hard but, as it ended up, she was the one pushing them and setting the pace. She was heavily clad in warm clothing, so she was protected against the temperatures as she pushed her sturdy horse through swollen streams and muddy roads like a madwoman. There was a frenzy to her movements, a desperation.

She had a son to retrieve.

It came to the point where the men were simply trying to

keep up with her.

Andreas let her lead the way, mostly because there was no way to stop her, and it occurred to him how much the separation from the baby must have hurt her. He thought back to the moment he'd first met her, how hysterical and sad she had seemed. *Guarded.* She's been rude and planted behind a shield of her own making. Given what he knew now, he understood completely, but the fact that she was rushing almost recklessly to collect her son told him much, much more.

How much she had been hurting.

It also began to occur to him what a rational nature she had because she didn't view the child as something horrific, a reminder of the worst moment of her life. She didn't equate him to the violent and vile act of his conception and Andreas thought that was quite remarkable. As a knight, he'd been trained to keep emotions out of the violence perpetrated in battle. An emotional fighter was often a man with a death wish. But a woman with that kind of capacity for reason and understanding of a violent moment in her life was remarkable, indeed. With every moment that passed, Andreas was more and more impressed by her.

And the group pushed on.

In truth, no one said a word about Gavriella wanting to push that hard. They simply followed her. When they reached spots in the road that seemed impassable, someone always found a way around it. Because the days were shorter, the sun set much earlier than normal and evening came beneath what was, strangely enough, called a *wolf moon*. It happened in January every year and was thought, by some, to have been called a wolf moon because the wolves seemed to bay at it more than any other moon.

Andreas thought it was rather appropriate.

That big, bright moon illuminated the countryside so they

could see their way into Kelso. It had been dark for a few hours by the time they reached the border village with its great abbey, a soaring icon of stability and religion against the night sky. Andreas had been here, several times, and it occurred to him that he should probably send word to his Uncle Thomas about the situation since Edenside was his wife's charity.

Mae de Wolfe, Thomas' wife, had taken charge of the charity right after a scandal that had seen those in charge of the children selling them off for most unsavory purposes in most instances. She had taken a charity rocked by pain and scandal and mistrust and had made it into something fine and good.

When he first heard that Gavriella's infant had been taken there, he knew the child would be well-tended. He'd tried to tell Gavriella that before they left that morning, but she had been too preoccupied with the idea of seeing her son soon. Until the advent of Andreas, it was something she could have never even dreamed of. A distant father, a dark situation, and no hope.

Andreas had once called her a new day. What he hadn't realized was that he was her new day, too.

The village of Kelso was quiet at this time of night and Andreas forced Gavriella to slow down so she wouldn't awaken the entire village by thundering through. Reluctantly, she did, and Andreas took the lead, directing the party through the village and to the eastern side, which had been heavily burned by the Scots. The road continued all the way to Berwick, but the Edenside Foundling Home was just a few minutes out of town along this very path.

Andreas could see it up ahead.

Gavriella, of course, had never been to the home, so she didn't know they were there until Andreas reined his horse to a halt in front of it.

In fact, it didn't look like a foundling home at all.

Edenside had been a fortified tower house many years ago

before the church took it over. There was a big, round tower with tiny windows towards the top and the entire complex was surrounded by a masonry wall that was quite tall, having been built and reinforced by the Earl of Northumbria. There was a massive gate in the wall, heavy oak and fortified by thick iron strips. As Brodie ordered the escort to spread out and dispatched a few scouts to comb the area, Andreas helped Gavriella off her horse and, along with Will and Gareth, approached the gate.

There was a big iron bell attached to the wall next to the gate. It was meant to be used if a child was dropped off, but Andreas rang the bell loudly. As the echoes sounded off the walls, off the top of the tower, he looked at Gavriella, standing next to him.

He was holding her hand, but she was squeezing his hard enough to cut off circulation. Even through his gloves, he could feel it.

Her nerves had the better of her.

"Do not fret," he said softly. "We shall have the child back in no time."

She looked at him, her expression strained even though she was trying to smile. "I know," she said. "I simply… God, Dray, you have no concept of how much it tore me apart when my father ordered my son away. He was so young… only a few weeks old. I know I should have hated the babe and I should have wanted him to disappear because of the violence he reminded me of but, as I told you, he was innocent. He was a victim as much as I was. But I will admit that when I first realized I had conceived, I prayed that I would lose the pregnancy."

He squeezed her hand. "That is understandable," he said softly. "What changed your mind?"

Her smile turned real. A soft, gentle gesture. "When I first felt him move," she said. "Something changed at that moment. I am not sure why, but it did. When he was born, it wasn't as difficult as I had been told. He came right out and when I looked in his face, I understood the meaning of true love. I… I've never really had that. Someone to love me, I mean. Not even my father does. But Storm… he was all mine and he loved me, and I loved him."

"Storm?"

She nodded. "That is his name," she said. "He was born on a stormy April morning, so I named him Storm. Mayhap someday, he will harness the wind as a great knight."

Andreas smiled. "He will be raised as a de Wolfe," he said quietly. "Storm de Wolfe. Does this displease you?"

She shook her head, gazing up at him. "Nay," she said. "It is the greatest blessing I could ask for. That you are willing to treat him as your own. Truly, Dray… your compassion is astounding. I am humbled in the face of it."

He lifted her hand, kissing it. "It is I who am humbled," he murmured. "And you have someone to love you in me. Don't you realize that?"

She nodded, her free hand coming up to touch his face, so sweetly and so tenderly. "I do," she said. "But I still think I am dreaming."

"If you are, then we are dreaming together."

She grinned just as a small door within the gate lurched open and a small, wimpled face appeared.

"What does thee wish?" came a quiet voice.

Andreas shifted from the besotted lover to the imposing knight in a heartbeat. He peered at the face on the other side.

"My name is Andreas de Wolfe," he said. "My aunt and uncle are the Earl and Countess of Northumbria. Please admit us."

The woman didn't move right away. She was trying to see

the men in the darkness and what they were wearing. When Andreas realized that, he stood back and opened his cloak so she could see his de Wolfe tunic. It was one of the most recognizable in northern England.

That was enough to open the gate.

Andreas entered, leading Gavriella by the hand, followed by Will and finally Gareth. Brodie and Corey remained outside with the men. The tiny nun closed the gate, motioning for her guests to follow.

"Come with me," she said, heading for the tower.

They pursued the woman into the stout, round tower. The entry level was surprisingly roomy, with a big entry chamber that had an enormous hearth and then a secondary chamber off that, containing a long table and sturdy benches. It was the dining hall. As the old woman bolted the door behind them, a woman in robes came down the stairs. She was swathed in unbleached wool from head to toe, her face round and rosy as she focused on the visitors.

"I am Sister Fiona," she said. "May I ask what brings thee at this late hour?"

Andreas didn't even have a chance to respond because Gavriella recognized her. She rushed the woman.

"Do you remember me?" she said, nearly plowing the woman over in her eagerness. "My name is Gavriella de Leia and you came to Falstone Castle last year to collect my son. He was newly born and my father forced me to give him over to you. Do you remember? His name was Storm. I told you that before you took him away."

There was a plea in her tone. *Begging.* She wanted the woman to remember her so badly and the woman, in fact, studied her closely for a moment.

"Falstone," Sister Fiona said slowly. "A newly born infant, male."

"Aye!"

Sister Fiona nodded. "I remember," she said. "Thou were quite distraught, as I recall. Thou asked me to take good care of thy little boy."

Gavriella nodded quickly. "I did," she said, tears stinging her eyes. "I have come to retrieve him. I am to marry Sir Andreas. He is a de Wolfe. His aunt and uncle are patrons of this charity. Please… may I have my son?"

The sister's focus lingered on her a moment, her features conveying surprise. Her gaze moved to Andreas, standing behind Gavriella with two other big knights.

"I see," she said after a moment. "Sir Andreas, thou art related to Lady Northumbria?"

Andreas nodded. "I am," he said. "Her husband is my father's brother."

"Who is thy father?"

"Troy de Wolfe, Lord Braemoor," he said. "He is the lord of Kale Water Castle. It is not far from here."

Sister Fiona nodded. "I know of it," she said. "And you are to marry this lady?"

"I am. I will be a good father to the lad, I swear it."

Sister Fiona looked between Andreas and Gavriella for a moment before her focus finally settled on Andreas.

May… may I speak with thee a moment, my lord?" she asked. "Alone, please."

It seemed like a strange request, but if it would get her child any faster, Gavriella was willing to do anything. Perhaps the old woman wanted to interrogate Andreas to make sure he would be a good father. Andreas walked past her, putting a gentle hand on her shoulder as if to beg for her patience, as he followed the old nun into the next chamber.

As Gavriella twitched and paced in the entry hall, Andreas had a sneaking suspicion that something was wrong. It was the way the woman had looked at Gavriella when she recognized her. The woman came to a halt and turned to him.

"My lord," she said quietly. "I did not wish to tell the young lady in front of everyone, so as her betrothed, I will let thee tell her."

Andreas' stomach lurched. "Tell her what?"

The old woman wasn't without sympathy. "Last month, several of the children contracted a fever," she said softly. "The lady's son was one of them. He was a sweet child, a healthy child, but the fever weakened him greatly. We lost four children to the illness, the lady's son included."

Andreas closed his eyes and lowered his head. "God," he groaned. "He's dead?"

"Aye." Sister Fiona watched him struggle. "I am so very sorry. I remember thy lady when I came to take the child. She was utterly heartbroken over it, but I also remember her father. He was quite… firm, I am sorry to say. I do not know what the circumstances of the child's birth were and I did not ask, but it seemed to me as if it was an… unfortunate birth."

She meant illegitimate, but she was too tactful to say so. Andreas dragged a hand over his face.

"Unfortunate, indeed," he said. "But I assure you, it was through no wrongdoing of her own. She was so happy to collect her son and now… it does not seem fair that tragedy seems to follow her wherever she goes."

Sister Fiona nodded faintly. "Am I to understand you are not the father?"

"Nay."

"But you would raise the child as your own."

Andreas shrugged. "The child is part of her. That is all I see."

A smile creased the old woman's lips. It was a touching thing to say. "Sir Andreas," she said softly. "Sometimes God moves in ways that we do not understand but always with a purpose. I do not profess to know what his purpose was for allowing a child's death, but it must not be in vain. We must have faith."

Andreas snorted. "Faith," he muttered. "Is that what I am to tell her? That we must have faith in God because he has allowed another tragedy to befall her? What should I tell her that purpose is, Sister?"

Sister Fiona didn't have an answer. "She is young to know such hardship."

Andreas turned his head as if to see her through the wall that separated them. "She is young and compassionate and sweet, and she has never committed a sin in her life, yet bad things seem to find her," he said. "I told her I would protect her, but I cannot protect her from this. I do not even know how. Already, I feel as if I have failed her."

"She loves her son very much?"

"Very much. You said yourself how heartbroken she was when they were separated."

Sister Fiona watched him struggle with his emotions, his faith, his everything, and an idea occurred to her. A mother without a child… and so many children in her care without mothers.

Perhaps she could fix what Andreas could not.

"Go to her," she said. "But do not tell her what I have told you. Not yet."

He looked at her, torn between grief and curiosity. "Why?"

Sister Fiona was already heading out of the chamber. "Please," she said. "Have faith, Sir Andreas. I will only be a moment."

By that time, she was into the entry, heading for the stairs. Andreas came out after her, watching the woman with confusion as she disappeared up the steps. But Gavriella rushed to him, distracting him.

"Where is she going?" she asked.

Andreas had no idea what to tell her. "I do not know," he said honestly. "She told me to wait a moment before…"

Gavriella's features lit up. "She is going to retrieve him!"

Andreas looked at her and he could see the unrestrained joy. Utter, complete joy. She dashed away from him, running to the base of the stairs and looking up the stairwell eagerly. As he stood there, Will came up beside him.

"What's wrong?" he hissed.

Andreas' gaze was fixed on Gavriella as she literally trembled with joy. "The worst thing you can possibly imagine," he whispered. "The baby is dead."

He heard Will grunt, as if in pain. "God," he muttered. "Then where did the nun go? Not to get the body, I hope."

That thought hadn't occurred to Andreas. "Christ," he hissed. "If she does, I'll kill her where she stands and answer for it later."

There was rage in that statement. Will backed off, feeling a great deal of pity for his cousin and Gavriella. In silent support, he remained by Andreas' side, both of them watching the stairwell until Gavriella finally shrieked because she saw something moving up in the stairwell. As they watched, Gavriella burst into quiet tears as Sister Fiona came down the stairs with an infant in her arms.

A dark-haired, blue-eyed boy.

Weeping with joy, Gavriella took the child out of Sister Fiona's arms and held him up to get a good look at him before hugging him tightly. The babe was clearly still very young, a stout little lad who was wrapped tightly against the cold weather. As Gavriella hugged the baby and rocked him gently, Andreas came to stand next to her.

"Look at him," Gavriella wept happily. "He's so big! When

he was born, he had light hair, but it has turned darker over the months. My mother had dark hair, you know. I think he looks a little like her now. He's more beautiful than I remembered!"

Andreas was trying not to look too stunned and too confused. He forced a smile as she held the lad up so he could get another look at him. He really was a gorgeous little thing with dark hair against his pale skin, chewing his hands and wide-eyed at all of the activity.

"He's quite handsome," he concurred, putting a big hand on the baby's head, dwarfing it. "Why not sit down with him and become acquainted? I must speak to the sister about... a donation."

Gavriella didn't notice the tone of his voice, as if he were both confused and annoyed. She was too focused on the baby. As she went to sit in the chair next to the hearth, setting the baby on her lap and speaking sweetly to him, Andreas made his way over to Sister Fiona, who was watching the exchange carefully. When she saw the knight approach, she simply lifted her thin eyebrows.

"He was in need of a mother," she murmured. "She was in need of a son. See how happy she is? Now, she does not have to know the truth unless thou feels the need to tell her. Does thou?"

Andreas sighed faintly, looking at the pair. Now, Will was standing next to them, admiring the baby, who was starting to squeal happily. "Nay," he said, resigned. "Sister, I am not entirely sure this is the right thing to do, but she is overjoyed and, for that, I am grateful. If you feel this is the right thing, it is not something I will spoil."

"As I said, one must have faith."

"I'll try."

Sister Fiona smiled encouragingly, giving him a bold wink before heading over to Gavriella to tell her a little about the child she believed to be her son. The little lad was nearly the same age as the child she lost, perhaps slightly younger, and he'd come to the foundling home after both of his parents, Scots from Clan Maxwell, had died in the clan wars that had been going on for the past several months.

But Sister Fiona wasn't going to tell her that.

Truth be told, the little nun knew the child to be the grandson of a chieftain, one of the very men who was wreaking havoc on de Wolfe lands. Oh, she knew *all* about it. She was far from being a naïve woman who tended children, because being a dependent of the Earl of Northumbria, she knew a great deal of what went on this far north. And she knew the little lad's name to be Peyton Maxwell. But now… now, he was to be Storm, raised by a de Wolfe.

But Andreas and Gavriella never need know any of it, and if little Peyton's relatives came looking for him, she'd simply tell them he'd met the same fate as Storm.

He'd have a better home with the House of de Wolfe, anyway.

A little lie she was certain God would forgive her for.

As Sister Fiona sat down next to Gavriella to tell her about her son, there was a knock at the heavy entry door. The tiny sister who had admitted them went to the door and unbolted it to reveal another nun, the one who worked in the stable yard and kitchens, with Brodie behind her.

Andreas spied him immediately.

"What's wrong?" he asked.

Brodie was wise enough to motion them outside rather than shout out the message for all to hear. Andreas, Will, and Gareth emerged into the bailey, facing him.

"Our scouts have just returned from Kelso," Brodie said in a low voice. "They have spotted de Soulis entering the other end of town. He'll be here in a matter of minutes, Dray."

It wasn't unexpected news. It simply confirmed what they'd all suspected. In fact, Andreas felt a little as if he'd been hit with a fist to the gut. Nay, the news wasn't unexpected at all, but it was the realization that Merek had been right, after all.

Giddy *had* been looking for the child.

"How many men?" Andreas asked.

"The scouts think at least one hundred," Brodie said. "As many as we have."

Andreas said a quick prayer that it wasn't more.

It was time to move.

"Get our men into the bailey," he said. "Quickly, get them out of sight. We'll all wait here for de Soulis to ring that bell."

Gareth and Will were already moving for the gate, already shouting at the men to get inside. But Brodie remained focused on Andreas.

"And then what?" he asked. "What are you going to do when they ring that bell?"

Andreas began to rub his hands together, like a man ready for a fight. He was greatly anticipating it.

"When they ring that bell, both gates open and our men pour out to attack," he said. "They will not be expecting it, so we'll use the element of surprise. They think that they have been clever all this time, trying to find out where Gavriella's infant was. Now that they're here, they're going to get a big surprise. And, Brodie – no mercy."

Brodie liked that order. A smile flickered on his lip. "I'll spread the word."

"We have men with crossbows," Andreas said. He pointed to the wall that surrounded the foundling home. "That wall isn't much, but we're going to use it. Get them on it. When the fighting starts, I want them to take out everything that moves."

"It shall be done. Anything else?"

Andreas looked him straight in the eyes. "Nicholas de Soulis is mine."

Brodie's smile bloomed. "Make it hurt, Dray."

"I'm going to do a far sight more than that."

Brodie believed him.

"HALF OF THE damn village is burned," Nicholas said. "Do you suppose it was the army that passed on the road before us?"

The de Soulis contingent was at the edge of Kelso, all one hundred and thirty of them. They'd ridden hard since before dawn, all the way from Hell's Gatehouse, and by now they were showing their fatigue. It had been a long, cold day. But the sight of a village that had been recently burned in an act of warfare had their attention. Now, they were on edge.

John shook his head to his son's question.

"Nay," he said. "The priests at the abbey said it was the Scots. Did you not hear them?"

Nicholas shrugged. He hadn't heard much after the fearful priests, pulled away from their evening prayers, had told the heavily armed de Soulis group where the Edenside Foundling Home was located. The priests had given the knights directions and promptly slammed the door in their face.

But it didn't matter.

The de Soulis men had what they wanted.

"Nay," Nicholas admitted after a moment. "I wasn't really listening. They had already told me what I wanted to know."

John eyed his distracted son. "They said that there is trouble with the Scots these days," he said. "That being said, I do not want to get caught up in anything. Let us retrieve this child quickly and be done with it."

Nicholas spurred his horse forward and the others followed, including Giddy, who was cold and sore from having been in the saddle so long. But she didn't complain, even when the entire contingent followed Nicholas with breakneck speed. They were all anxious to finish their task so they could retreat to Kelso and find a tavern or two to warm themselves in.

But all Giddy could think about was the infant she was about to be saddled with.

They galloped down the road, spying the tower house and wall that the priests had described as belonging to Edenside. The walls were made from pale granite and, under the bright moon, they gleamed white, like a beacon. The entire de Soulis contingent raced up to the walls, with Nicholas and John dismounting their horses quickly. They didn't even give commands to the men, who simply grouped around, waiting.

No one was watching anything. Their minds were thinking of the warmth they would seek out when their task here was finished. They were thinking of the whores who would warm their beds, of the tankards of ale they would drink. No one was thinking about anything other than that until one man happened to see something on the walls.

It looked like a helmed head.

He peered at the shape in the distance curiously.

"Does a place like this have guards?" he wondered aloud.

He was a lesser soldier, towards the rear of the pack, and only those closest to him heard the question. One man, an old cuss with a missing eye, turned to him.

"I don't know," he said. "I don't even know why we're here. Someone said something about a baby, but I don't even know whose baby or why. What is this place, anyway?"

"A foundling home," another man said impatiently. "De Wolfe is the patron, so it probably has guards. It probably has…"

Those were the last words he uttered before a rain of bolts came flying at them from over the walls, heavy crossbow bolts that were meant to disable horses. They were enormous. Several men went down, as well as the woman who had accompanied them. She took a bolt to the chest and fell into the snow, dead.

It was a shocking sight.

Immediately, the de Soulis contingent was under attack. What had looked like a sleepy little orphanage was evidently anything but and the de Soulis men were caught off guard.

The battle was underway.

ANDREAS WAITED UNTIL someone rang the bell before the soldiers with crossbows let loose. Then, someone yanked the gates open.

Andreas was the first one out.

They had caught the de Soulis men by surprise and although Andreas didn't know the father and son on sight, he assumed they were the men who had rung the bell. They were extremely well dressed and heavily armed, and as he headed for the younger one, Will went for the older man, who wasn't able to unsheathe his broadsword before Will was able to slice him from his collarbone to his groin.

It was a deep cut. Blood and guts came squeezing through the breach and the man pitched to his knees as the younger man screamed. *"Father!"* That told Andreas all he needed to know and as the younger man moved to aid his father, Andreas lifted his sword against him. The younger man could see his life flash before his eyes and he managed to get his sword up in time to block a blow that would have surely taken off his head.

The fight was on.

The de Wolfe soldiers showed no mercy, as they'd been instructed. It wasn't just a fight they were after; it was a massacre. They were cutting soldiers down swiftly because the men hadn't been given a chance to even draw their weapons. That was only true of the men close to the gate, however. The men further back could see what was happening and they had every chance to unsheathe broadswords and crossbows. Some fled, but most stayed to fight.

The de Soulis men began to launch bolts of their own.

Beneath the wolf moon, the men from the House of de Wolfe cut down enemy after enemy. It was a night of much slaying, with Andreas in the middle of it. He was doing battle against the younger of the pair who had been at the bell, a man who was surprisingly good with his sword and surprisingly strong. If Andreas had been looking for an easy kill, he didn't find one.

The knight was giving him a good fight.

But it was close quarters fighting. There were men all around them battling and dying. On the north side of the road was dense forest growth and to the south, on the other side of the foundling home, was the River Tweed. Men were already being pushed into the trees, however, and Andreas could hear them fighting in the growth.

But he was focused on his opponent.

He was fairly certain who he was.

No words were spoken between them. None were necessary, mostly because they were trying to kill each other. Big broadswords were flying through the dark and when they met, sparks flew. But Andreas had the advantage. He always had the advantage because he was left-handed when most men were right-handed, and he'd learned to use that against his opponents.

This opponent was no exception.

In short order, Andreas had driven the man back towards the heavily forested area. His plan was to box him against the trees and then let nature take its course. But not before he told the man who he was and made him understand that any plans he had for Gavriella and the infant had failed.

He wanted Nicholas de Soulis to know who it was who had beaten him.

But that was his last coherent thought before someone came up behind him and clobbered him on the back of his helm.

Andreas went down to his knees, seeing stars dance before his eyes. He could hear grunting and fighting all around him, but he kept his eyes on his opponent, as much as he was able, seeing the man come at him with a sword raised. As he lifted his own sword, someone dashed in front of him and he could hear sword upon sword and then finally a groan. A body hit the ground next to him, lying face-up in the snow.

It took him a moment to realize it was Corey.

Andreas went mad.

Shaking off the stars, he charged his opponent, taking the man out by the knees. As he went down, somehow, Andreas lost his grip on his sword and began using his fists, pounding the man in the face until the blood began to fly. Teeth went flying. He knew he'd broken his nose because he'd heard it crack.

Then, he picked his opponent up and lifted him over his head, throwing him again a tree trunk.

As his opponent fell to the ground, Andreas pounced. He punched, kicked, and threw his opponent back onto the road and then rolled him down the other side towards the river. More punches, more kicks, more broken bones. It was the bloodiest, brutal beating in the history of brutal beatings, with every blow having Gavriella or Corey's name on it.

And it went on for some time.

Andreas didn't even realize when the fighting around him had stopped for the most part. He didn't see his father's army roll up from the west, subduing any remnants of the de Soulis resistance. He was focused on his opponent, who had now become his victim. When they ended up almost at the river, Andreas finally stopped throwing punches with his torn gloves and bloodied knuckles.

His opponent lay on the ground in front of him, eyes open but unable to move his body. In fact, the man's face didn't even look like a face anymore. It was smashed and contorted.

It looked like death.

"Your name," Andreas growled, exhausted. "What is your name?"

The bloodied lips formed words. "De… de Soulis, you bastard," he rasped. "Nicholas de Soulis. You killed my father, you son of a whore. I will kill you for that."

Andreas heard the man's name with a great deal of satisfaction. "Not before I kill you first," he rumbled. "But you and I are going to have a conversation before that event. I am from the House of de Wolfe. What in the hell do you want with the de Leia infant?"

The eyes blinked, looking at him with increasing horror. "De… de Wolfe?" he repeated thickly because his mouth was smashed. "Nay… nay, you shall not emerge the victor. *I* will! I shall avenge my father!"

He was spraying droplets of blood on the snow as he tried to shout. But Andreas ignored his distress.

"*Why* do you want the de Leia infant?" he asked again. "That is why you have come here, so you may as well tell me. What's this about a prophesy?"

Nicholas stared at him a moment. "Prophesy?" he said. Then he tried to smile, but it was all garbled and twisted. "True

Thomas said so."

"Said what? Be plain."

Nicholas tried to move, to sit up, but he was so badly beaten that his body would not permit it. He managed to lift his head and that was nearly all he could do.

"I will tell you, de Wolfe scum, so you will know that your days in the north are numbered," he said. "I do not need the de Leia infant. I can have another. I can have many. But all I need is one."

"For what?"

Nicholas started to laugh, or something that sounded like a laugh. "A child must be sacrificed," he said hoarsely. "The blood must be spilled at the ring of the nine stones upon the summer solstice. I will bury the body to feed the stones, to nourish the demons of the stones, and they will give their power to the House of de Soulis. We shall rise against the wolf. We will kill you all!"

Andreas was looking at him as if he'd gone mad. "Sacrifice a child?" he said, trying not to let his horror show. "Is *that* what you wanted this baby for?"

Nicholas' strength gave out and he fell back into the snow. "A baby of noble blood," he said. "De Leia's daughter fought me, but it was of no use. My seed took root, as I had hoped, and the child was born. But I can have more. I can have many more and one of them will fulfill the prophesy. De Wolfe *will* fall. The de Soulis family was the most powerful in the north until the rise of de Wolfe. You took that from us. You took our dignity, our lands. But we shall gain them back, mark my words."

Andreas was having a difficult time comprehending what he was being told. "You *intentionally* impregnated de Leia's daughter?"

Nicholas started laughing again, a weird sound because his mouth was so swollen. "It was a pleasure," he muttered. "She is my cousin, after all."

Andreas had heard enough. A wild story of fulfilling a prophesy by impregnating Gavriella and harvesting the child for evil purposes. It was the wildest thing he'd ever heard. But clearly, Nicholas believed it. He believed it enough to ruin a young woman's life and attempt to regain the child of that ruinous act.

It was a horrific and vile tale.

One that Gavriella would never know. The woman had already suffered enough.

Although Andreas had lost his broadsword, he had an array of daggers on his body, including a large one on his left hip, next to his empty broadsword sheath. He unsheathed the dagger, its enormous and razor-sharp blade gleaming in the moonlight, and went over to Nicholas as the man lay in the snow looking up at him.

"And she is my love," he said, his voice raspy. "This is for anguish you have caused her family."

With that, he tossed the dagger into Nicholas' left shoulder, where it plunged deep. As Nicholas let out a cry, Andreas unsheathed another dagger from its place along his right forearm.

"And this is for taking that which did not belong to you," he said. "Her innocence."

The second dagger flew into Nicholas' groin. The man screamed as Andreas unsheathed a third dagger located in his left boot.

"This is for Corey," he said.

Another dagger flew, this one into Nicholas' left thigh. Nicholas moaned and wept as Andreas removed a fourth dagger from his right boot. This one was long and slender, the blade serrated on one side. It was meant to slit throats silently and efficiently, or any other body part worth slitting. Andreas moved up to stand over Nicholas, looking down at the man as he wept in pain.

The fourth dagger went flying, right into Nicholas' neck, severing the windpipe.

He wasn't dead yet, but Andreas knew it would only be a matter of seconds and he wanted to make sure Nicholas de Soulis knew why he'd been killed.

And *who* had killed him.

"And that is for Gavriella," he muttered. "For the pain and agony you dealt her, I'm privileged to watch you suffer for it. My name is Andreas de Wolfe. I want you to know the name of the man who bested you, you vile bastard. The day you touched Gavriella de Leia is the day you signed your death warrant. I hope you rot in hell."

Nicholas' eyes were wide and panicked as he slowly suffocated to death. Andreas crouched down beside him, watching the life go out of the man and feeling a hollow sense of satisfaction. Certainly, he felt avenged. He felt as if Gavriella were avenged. But he found himself wishing Nicholas' death had lasted longer.

Loup tueur.

The killer wolf had struck again.

"Dray?"

He knew that voice. In his determination to make Nicholas pay, he hadn't even been aware of his surroundings. Standing up, he turned to face his father.

Troy was in full battle regalia, sword in-hand, looking at his son most urgently. But one look at his father and Andreas dissolved into tears.

"Papa," he said tightly. "Corey fell. He tried to save my life and he was struck down."

Surprisingly, Troy waved him off. "He took a gash to his chest and fainted," he said, coming to stand next to his son as his attention moved to the body at his feet. "He's perfectly fine, although I'm not sure he'll live down fainting in battle. Your brothers are already teasing him mercilessly about it. But you... what in the hell happened?"

Learning Corey wasn't mortally wounded did Andreas in. He sobbed as his father put his arm around him to comfort him.

"God," Andreas wept, wiping his eyes. "I thought he was dead."

"He's not dead," Troy assured him softly. He'd never seen Andreas weep, not ever, which was indicative of the emotional situation at hand. "Dray, what happened? Please tell me. Gareth could not tell us much, only that you were in trouble, so I took half my army and rode here like a madman. Thank God it was not too terribly far. We came as quickly as we could."

Andreas took a deep breath, struggling to regain his composure. Corey was well, Gavriella was well, and that was all that mattered. He kept telling himself that.

Everything was going to be all right.

He gestured to the body on the ground.

"That," he said wearily, "is Nicholas de Soulis. To understand this situation, I must start from the beginning. It is a complicated tale, but I will try and simplify it. When I was in London, I met a woman. She was special, Papa, and I knew... I knew she was the woman for me. I do not think you ever thought you would hear me say such a thing."

Troy grinned. "Never," he said. "Will told me that you had met a woman, but he did not know more than that. He said that she disappeared, however, and that was why you were so moody when you returned to the north. I saw that moodiness in every battle we fought."

Andreas nodded. "I know," he said. "I was... hurt. Disappointed. Angry. That emotion found an outlet against the Scots.

But I have discovered that she left London to return home – to Falstone Castle."

Troy's eyebrows lifted when he realized what his son was saying. "You *found* her?"

Andreas smiled weakly. "I found her," he said. Then, he looked to Nicholas' form in the snow. "But this bastard violated her. She became pregnant as a result. As it turns out, he did it intentionally so he could harvest the child and use it to fulfill some strange prophesy given to him by True Thomas. Have you heard of him?"

Troy was listening seriously. "A Scotsman," he said. "A soothsayer, I think. I've heard the name, but I have never met him."

"He was enough of a soothsayer that Nicholas de Soulis listened to him," Andreas said with disgust. "He was supposed to sacrifice a child of de Soulis blood at the nine stones near Hell's Guardhouse and it would give him the power to defeat the House of de Wolfe."

Troy looked at him in shock. "This was about *us*?"

Andreas nodded wearily. "Aye," he said. "Ultimately, it was all about us. De Soulis hated the House of de Wolfe and wanted to see us fall. I will tell you more about it later, but right now, I must see to…"

He happened to look up, towards the walls of the foundling home, and caught sight of a bundled-up figure standing several feet away.

He recognized the clothing.

A lump came to his throat.

"'Tis all right, sweetling," he said, holding out a hand to her. "Everything is as it should be. There is no longer any threat from de Soulis."

Gavriella hadn't been standing there very long. She'd been watching the battle from the top of the tower house and she had seen, clearly, when it had ended. There was no longer any fighting, so she left her son in the care of Sister Fiona and ventured out to find Andreas.

To make sure he had survived.

It was the strongest pull she'd ever known.

But her concerns were for naught. He was standing and whole. She could see a bloodied body in the snow and an older man with Andreas. She came towards him, trying not to slip in the snow, but the closer she came, the more she realized that Andreas was beaten and bloodied himself.

"Andreas!" she gasped. "You're bloody!"

He grinned. "Not much," he said, taking her by the hand and pulling her to him. "Gavy, I want you to meet someone. This is my father, Troy de Wolfe. Papa… this is Gavriella de Leia and I have her father's permission to marry her."

Troy found himself looking at a delicate blonde beauty. She was exquisite. Reaching out, he took her hand and kissed it warmly.

"My lady," he said. "It is the greatest honor to meet you."

Gavriella found herself looking into the face of a man who looked a good deal like Andreas through the eyes and nose.

"It is a privilege, my lord," she said. "But I am very sorry to cause so much trouble. I am so sorry that this was surely an inconvenience for you."

She had a silky voice, sweet like honey. "It was no inconvenience," he said. "I am simply relieved that everyone is sound and whole."

"As am I," Gavriella said, looking to Andreas, who seemed awfully beat up to her in spite of his assurance that he wasn't. "Is… is it finally over?"

Andreas nodded, turning slightly so she could see the body in the snow. "The remains of Nicholas de Soulis," he said quietly. "He paid for his deeds every way I could make him."

Gavriella glanced at the body before quickly looking away. "God's Bones," she breathed. "He's dead. He's truly dead."

There was relief and astonishment in her voice, as if she could hardly believe it. Andreas put his arm around her and turned her in the direction of the foundling home.

"He is," Andreas said. "I want you go to inside while I clean up this mess. You do not need to be part of it."

She wouldn't let him push her away. "Nay," she said, turning to face him. "You did this for me. I would be a terrible woman, indeed, if I let you face this all alone. You must at least let me help clean up the mess I caused you to make."

Andreas loved that about her. She was a selfless woman in too many regards to count. He smiled, pulling her into his powerful embrace. For a moment, he just looked down at her, those lovely eyes, that little nose that twitched whenever she found something funny, and those lips that were so incredibly delicious. He forgot about his father standing there who, in fact, had turned away to remove the daggers from de Soulis when he saw his son in an amorous embrace.

All Andreas could see was Gavriella.

"You did not cause me to make any mess," he said softly. "But know that I would make a million more, and gladly so, if only to keep you safe and happy. From this day forward, you are a de Wolfe, Gavy. You belong to me and I belong to you. As I told you, de Wolfes mate for love and we mate for life. There will never be anyone but you, from now until the end of all things."

Gavriella wrapped her arms around his neck, gently kissing his cheeks, finally his mouth. "I was thinking something," she murmured.

"What were you thinking?"

"That I always thought attending Gomorrah was the worst day of my life. As it turns out, it was the best."

He grinned. "Mine, too," he said. "Thank God you were hysterical that night or we might have never met."

She kissed him again. "You were my champion that night," she said softly. "You will always be my champion, on that night or any other. I do not remember when I started loving you, Andreas. It seems as if I have always loved you. I cannot remember when I have not. You once said that you saw a sunrise in me, a new day, and you did not want to see the sun set. I think that sunrise dawned the moment I went crashing into that chamber and you found me there. That will always be the beginning of my world with you in it."

Andreas kissed her, then, deeply and emotionally. Around them were the remnants of a battle, but neither one of them noticed. In their minds, it was just the two of them in the entire world.

"I have been waiting all of my life to hear that," he murmured against her lips as he hugged her tightly. "Thank you."

"For what?"

"For loving me as I love you."

Gavriella put both of her hands on his face, gazing into his eyes.

"Always," she whispered.

Later that month, when Andreas had the goldsmith in Berwick make a wedding ring for Gavriella, that was the word he had inscribed on the inside.

Always.

And he meant it.

EPILOGUE

Kale Water Castle
Two months later

"There once was a lady fair,

With silver bells in her hair.

I knew her to have,

A luscious kiss… it drove me mad!

But she denied me… and I was so terribly sad.

Lily, my girl,

Your flower, I will unfurl

With my cock and a bit of good luck!

Your kiss divine,

I'll make you mine,

And keep you a-bed for a fuck!"

THE GREAT HALL of Kale Water Castle erupted with cheers and shouts of approval as Blayth, standing on a feasting table with a lute in his hand, took a deep and exaggerated bow.

It was a tradition, after all.

The naughty wedding song.

He sang it at every wedding to the cheers of his brothers

and the scolding of his mother, only she wasn't here at the moment, which took some of the fun out of it.

Oh, well. He'd just have to sing it for her later.

"Excellent, Uncle Blayth," Andreas said, meeting him as he climbed off the table. "A de Wolfe wedding wouldn't be a wedding at all without that song. But don't look now – Aunt Evelyn and Aunt Katheryn aren't happy. They might take a switch after you in Matha's stead."

Blayth spied his sisters, Katheryn and Evelyn, seated with other women on the dais, including the bride, Gavriella. Lukas, Brodie, and Brodie's wife, Sophia, were also at the table because Sophia and Gavriella had become fast friends, being close in age. In fact, Sophia and Gavriella were in animated conversation, as were Brodie and Lukas, but there was one member of that group who wasn't part of the conversations going on. She was sitting alone. Blayth's gaze settled on his Aunt Jemma.

And she did not look happy.

The mere sight made Blayth recoil.

"I would not worry about my sisters," he said. "But Aunt Jemma is glaring at me and that cannot end well. I must find my wife so that she may defend me from Aunt Jemma."

Andreas was feeling his alcohol. The finest alcohol in all of England and France, provided by Troy and Merek. There was more drink at this wedding than he'd ever seen in his life, at any one event.

He laughed at his uncle's statement.

"Asmara will probably help her beat you, so I would not look for reinforcements there," he said. Then, he pointed to a group of men several feet away. "There is an entire line of de Wolfe men. Mayhap they can help you stave off the women bent on murder."

He pulled Blayth over to a group of men in conversation. It was rare when the entire de Wolfe family got together, but the wedding of Andreas to Gavriella de Leia was a grand event, indeed.

Scott and Troy and Blayth were joined by brothers Patrick, Edward, and Thomas. They were also joined by Merek, who was so drunk that he could barely stand, along with Hector de Norville, and Andreas' grandfather, Paris. Theodis was also there, having come all the way from Pelinom Castle for the wedding. He had been in conversation with Will and Tor until he saw Andreas approach.

"My beautiful lad," he said happily, hanging on Andreas. "So this is where your lady from Gomorrah ended up? As your wife? I must say that I am astonished."

Andreas had to snort at his inebriated, happy friend. The wedding wouldn't have been the same without him.

"Aye, it is astonishing."

"But it is wonderful!"

"Aye, quite wonderful."

"Dray, my friend," Theodis said, forcing Andreas to look at him. "I've got even more excellent news."

"What is that?

Theodis thumped him on the chest. "I've not had the opportunity to tell you that my father has finally agreed to allow me to serve with you," he said "Can you imagine? We will be invincible at your new post. We will dominate the borders. De Wolfe and de Velt, side by side!"

That was good news, indeed, the result of seeds planted with Atlas de Velt almost two months ago when Andreas assumed a new post. Andreas had been waiting for such news and he hugged his friend.

"We will, indeed," he said, noticing that Paris was heading in his direction. "But let us speak of it on the morrow, Tay. Do not leave here without seeing me, please. Swear this to me?"

Theodis kissed him loudly on the cheek. "Of course I will,"

he said. "I love you, my friend."

"I love you, too."

As Theodis staggered off because his cup was empty, Paris took his place at Andreas' side. He put his arms around his grandson, hugging him tightly.

"Dray," he said, another obviously drunk man. "Come with me. I must speak with you alone."

Andreas was practically holding him up. "I do not have too much time, Bonny," he said, addressing Paris by the name all of his grandchildren called him. "I have a new wife waiting for me and I am anxious to spend time alone with *her*."

Paris waved him off. "In a moment," he said, dragging him away from his uncles. "Come with me."

Andreas looked at his uncles, shrugging, as Paris pulled him from the great hall and into the night.

Outside, it was a bright spring evening, with a smattering of stars spread across the sky. The snows of the winter had been short-lived, thankfully, and a beautiful spring was upon them.

A perfect time for a wedding.

Paris came to a halt and faced his grandson.

"I want to speak to you before you go to your wife," he said. "Since your mother is no longer here, I had hoped you would marry before your grandmother passed away so that she could speak to you, but that unfortunately did not happen. Now, it is left up to me to say to you what I believe Helene would have said to you on this day of days."

Andreas' humored expression faded. "You do not have to, Bonny," he said, putting his hands on the old man who had once been one of the most powerful knights in the north. "I know my mother is here, in spirit."

Paris looked at him closely. "You are my only living link to her, Dray," he said, suddenly seeming quite sober. "You are the closest thing I have to her. When I look at you, I see the shape of her face. You have her smile. You are all that is left of her."

Andreas was quickly becoming emotional, something he didn't particularly want to do. "Bonny, I've gone all day without thinking of her overly," he said. "I will be honest when I say it is painful for me not to have her here. I appreciate what you are saying and I miss her greatly as well, but I do not want to go to my marital bed crying for my mother, if you know what I mean. I would look foolish."

Paris chuckled. "I am sorry," he said. "I did not mean to make you sad. I simply meant to remember her. This would have been a very important moment for her."

Andreas nodded. "I know," he said, sighing. "And for me. When I look at all of the grandchildren here tonight, it makes me think of Arista and Acacia, wondering what kind of women they would have grown up to be. Arista was lively and annoying, and Acacia was gentle and creative. I did not get to see them often because they were born when I was fostering, but when I returned home from time to time, I remember sitting on the floor with them while they played their games. Sometimes they would run circles around me while I tried to grab them, or they would put dried posies in my hair. Silly things, really, but sweet things. They were sweet."

He was smiling in remembrance which made Paris smile, too. "They were very much like me," he said. "A little wild, I suppose. Do you know who reminds me of them? Hector and Evelyn's boys, Atreus and Hermes. They are such idiots sometimes. But Acacia and Arista reminded me of them greatly when they were young."

Andreas put his hand behind his grandfather's neck, pulling the man close. "I promise I will not forget my mother," he assured him softly. "I would never forget her. She was my best friend when I was young and I have missed her every day since we lost her. She is always in my heart, Bonny, and I shall remember her to my own children. They will know her."

Paris smiled at his grandson, one he had a soft spot for. He patted him on the cheek before digging into the pocket of his fine tunic and pulling forth an item. He took Andreas' hand and pressed it into his palm. Andreas held it up, looking at it. It was small and gold, a little brooch with a flower in the center of it. The petals were red stones, garnets, while the center was black onyx.

He looked at Paris curiously.

"A flower?"

"A poppy," Paris said. "I used to always call your mother my 'fragile flower' because she was a sweet, delicate lass. Athena was always tall and strong and sure of herself, but Helene was gentler. Quieter. A fragile lass, like an angel. The day she married your father, I gave her that brooch. It was to remind her that she would always be my fragile flower. When your father cleared away her things long after her death, he gave that brooch back to your grandmother, but she gave it to me, knowing I had been the one to give it to Helene. I realize that it is meant for a woman, Dray, but that is all I have to give you of your mother. I gave it to her on her wedding day and, tonight, I give it to you on yours. To remember her by."

Tears came to Andreas' eyes as he looked at it. He was so touched, something given to his mother, now given to him. It meant the world to him.

"Thank you, Bonny," he said huskily, leaning over to kiss the man on the head. "I did not know about this. I shall treasure it always."

"Good," Paris said. "It belongs with you. I do not know if you were ever told this, Dray, but your parents' marriage – and your birth – did not go as planned."

Andreas was blinking away tears, grinning as he looked at his grandfather. "What you mean to say is that my mother was pregnant with me before she married my father."

"Oh, you know about that, do you?"

"Aye, I know that."

Paris watched Andreas pin the brooch onto his fine silk tunic and the sight of it choked him up. "You were the grandchild who nearly bought about the breakup of the House of de Wolfe and the House of de Norville," he said. "I remember holding you right after you were born, wondering if you would be worth the trouble."

Andreas glanced up from admiring his mother's brooch. "Am I?"

Paris' eyes glimmered at him. "Very much so," he said. "You are a fine tribute to both houses. You may bear the de Wolfe name, but you look like a de Norville."

Andreas chuckled. "So I have heard."

Paris' gaze lingered on him for a moment longer before he patted him on the cheek. "Go, now," he said, turning Andreas back towards the great hall. "Do not keep your wife waiting."

Andreas hugged his grandfather tightly. "I will not," he said softly. "Thank you, Bonny. For everything."

The two of them headed back into the hall, Paris retreating to the table where his youngest daughter, Cassiopeia, sat as Andreas continued to the dais where his wife was sitting with the women. He leaned on the table, catching his wife's eye.

"Gavy," he said. "Unless we want a parade of drunken men escorting us to our chamber, for I have seen it far too many times, I will meet you there. Aunt Jemma, will you escort my wife up to our chamber without attracting the attention of the wild throng?"

Jemma's amber gaze drifted over to the group of de Wolfe, de Norville, and Hage men standing in a bunch over near the hall entry.

"Aye," she said in her heavy Scots burr. "They willna dare

try tae follow me."

"I know," Andreas snorted. "That is why I asked. If you will take her through the servant's entrance, I will find my way out another way. I thank you for your assistance."

Like a covert operation, they split up. The last Gavriella saw of her husband, he was moving for the entrance where the gang of knights were gathered. Jemma took her by the hand, pulling her away from the dais.

"Come along, lass," she said. "Hurry!"

Gavriella did.

It had been a day made of dreams and, as she had told Andreas, she still felt as if she were living one. Perhaps she would always feel that way but, at the moment, she was feeling a little anxiety, too. Over the past two months, she'd been told horror stories of how the de Wolfe and de Norville men liked to storm wedding chambers or not allow the newly wedded couple any privacy at all.

But she was coming to think that with Jemma at her side, the men would obey.

It seemed to her that the women in the family had all the power.

Kale Water Castle, or the Wolfe's Den, was Troy's enormous fortress on the Scots side of the border just as Wolfe's Lair was. While Wolfe's Lair was massive and tall, but rather compact in the amount of space it covered, Kale Water Castle was gigantic simply in the acreage it did cover. It was a rare concentric castle this far north, meaning it had two sets of walls, one within the other, and an inner bailey that could hold thousands.

It was across this bailey that Jemma and Gavriella moved quickly, heading for the keep that was the jewel in the crown of the fortress. It was big, tall, and rectangular, with a wooden staircase leading to the entry on the second floor.

Quickly, they dashed up the stairs.

Once inside, they took the mural stairs up to the floor above where there were four chambers. They went to the chamber on the southwest corner, which was a small sitting room with an adjoining bedchamber, and Jemma opened the door to reveal the warm, comfortable chamber beyond. As soon as they stepped in, Jordan looked up from her sewing.

"Shhh," Jordan said, pointing to her husband on a chair next to the hearth. "Poppy and the bairn have been sleeping there for about an hour."

Jordan had referred to her husband as Poppy, the name all of his grandchildren and great-grandchildren called him. Gavriella laughed softly, moving over to William, who was slouched in the chair, his head tilted back and his eyelids closed. He held Storm against his broad chest and the baby was sleeping peacefully against his Poppy. When she bent over to catch a glimpse of her son, William peeped open his eye.

"Do not wake him," he whispered. "It took him a long time to fall asleep. Matha says he is sprouting new teeth."

Gavriella smiled at William, a man she had truly come to adore over the past couple of months. "You are very sweet to tend him," she said. "But wouldn't you rather be down in the hall with your sons now? You did not have to watch the baby all evening."

William had a trencher-sized hand on the baby's back, patting him gently when he started to stir. "I will see them soon enough," he said. "It is not often that I have a chance to become acquainted with my newest great-grandchild."

"He loves you, too."

William smiled at her. They'd become quite fond of one another. The baby was settling back down and everyone was moving about quietly until the chamber door burst open and Andreas appeared.

"They're right behind me," he said breathlessly. "Aunt Jemma, I need your help. Can you stand at the door and chase them away? If you do not, I fear they might batter the door down. Uncle Tommy was even talking about climbing in through the windows."

The baby's head shot up at the sound of Andreas' voice and he started wailing. With a heavy sigh, William stood up with the sobbing baby, trying to comfort the little lad.

"I can do better than that," he said, heading for the door with the sobbing baby. "I'll get rid of them."

Gavriella was following him, her arms out because she wanted to take the baby, while Jemma swatted Andreas on the buttocks because he'd woken the baby up so rudely. Andreas truly had no idea why he was being beaten until his grandfather kicked open the door only to find at least four inebriated men standing there, Troy included.

"Do you see what you did?" William hissed at them. "You woke up the baby. Now, *who* is going to put him back to sleep?"

That moved the group away from the door faster than anything else possibly could have, except for Troy, who took his grandchild from his father and began rocking the baby gently. Properly contrite, he succumbed to his father's guilt. As William stood there, satisfied with his tactics, Jordan and Jemma headed for the chamber door.

"The babe can sleep with Poppy and me tonight," she told Andreas. "You two enjoy at least one night without a weepy baby. We will tend to him."

Andreas looked at his wife, who looked like she was about to weep herself. He could tell she wanted her son, but it was their wedding night, after all. He put an arm around his grandmother's shoulders.

"I'll come and get him in a little while," he said. "I do not think Gavy wishes to be parted from him for very long."

The expression of gratitude on Gavriella's face spoke volumes.

Jordan understood.

When the cries of the baby faded as Troy carried him off, Andreas shut the door and bolted it, facing his wife. For a moment, they simply looked at one another before breaking down into soft laughter.

"I thought we'd never be rid of everyone," Andreas said, stepping away from the door and holding out his hand to her. "Finally, some peace."

Gavriella took his hand and he pulled her close, hugging her tightly.

"More dreams, Dray," she whispered. "These are the best dreams of my life."

He couldn't disagree. "Of mine, too," he murmured against the side of her head. "So much has happened over the past couple of months, I feel as if my head is still whirling with it."

Gavriella pulled back to look at him. "So much, indeed, but you are well-deserving of all of it," she said. "Not only are you a new husband, but you have a new post. With those hideous men finally gone from Hell's Guardhouse, I am so proud to think that the king has appointed you the garrison commander of the fortress. It is a very important position."

Andreas shrugged modestly. "I was already there," he said. "We could not leave it unmanned after the deaths of those vile men, especially not with the Scots on the rampage, so someone had to assume command. It just happened to be me."

"It just happened to be you because you are the best man for the job," Gavriella said firmly. "I am very proud of you, my love."

He smiled faintly. "That is all that matters to me," he said. "Theodis told me tonight that his father has agreed to permit him to serve with me, so we will have a powerful force, indeed.

I'm very happy about that. I've missed Tay."

"I know you have. I am excited for him to join you, too."

He pointed a finger at her. "I've spent the past two months cleaning that place up and making it livable for you and Storm, but it needs a woman's touch."

"And I cannot wait to assume my role, by your side," she said sincerely. "I will be bringing some of my servants from Falstone. Iva and Jocosa. I must have their help."

"As you wish," he said. But his gaze lingered on her for a moment. "Gavy… are you sure you feel comfortable living there? It did belong to that man whose name we no longer speak of. If you do not feel comfortable, sweetling, you must tell me. I do not want to force you to live somewhere that upsets you."

Gavriella shushed him, taking his hand and pulling him towards the bedchamber that was attached to the smaller chamber they were in. "I feel perfectly comfortable," she said. "I've never been there in my entire life, so it is of little matter to me. You say you have cleaned out all reminders of those men we no longer speak of, so why would I not be happy there? You are there and it is my right to live with you. Not at Falstone, a half a day's ride away."

He smiled ironically, since she had been living with her father during their betrothal period because of all of the activity surrounding the deaths of John and Nicholas de Soulis and also because of the clan wars, which had thankfully started to die down. Immediately after the de Soulis deaths, William de Wolfe petitioned King Edward for control of Hell's Guardhouse, or The Hermitage as he called it, and it was quickly granted by Edward with the agreement that the king could station royal troops there if he needed to.

William thought that Edward might view the property as a foothold into Scotland for the submission of the Scots, but he agreed because he didn't want to see the fortress go to anyone else. With the addition of The Hermitage, and Andreas de Wolfe as its commander, the power of the House of de Wolfe was growing.

And so was the family.

Andreas couldn't have been more thrilled.

She had pulled him into the bedchamber by this time, which was warm and fragrant with rosemary and lavender Rhoswyn and Andreas' sisters had spread around the chamber. He went over to the hearth to stoke it while Gavriella went to the bed and began pulling back the coverlet. Andreas glanced over his shoulder, watching her.

"Can I tell you something?" he said.

She smiled at him as she fluffed up a pillow. "Anything. You know that."

His attention returned to the fire. "When we have been alone over the past couple of months, *really* alone, it has been very difficult not to give in to my natural instincts with you."

She cocked her head curiously. "What do you mean?"

He tipped his head in the direction of the bed. "That."

After a moment of confusion, it occurred to her what he meant. "Ah," she said, returning to the pillows. "You have been perfectly chivalrous, my love."

"I know. But I did not want to be."

She started laughing. "It is not as if we haven't… touched one another. We had moments of weakness."

That was true. They had done a fair amount of fondling, kissing, and caressing, but Andreas had held off bedding her.

"I know," he said, poking the fire one last time. "But I did not bed you for one very good reason."

"What was that?"

He stood up from the fire and turned to her. "Because I did not want to rush it or be an opportunist," he said. "The one and only time you have partaken of such a thing was not a good experience. I wanted our first time together to be very special and very tender. It is very important to me that I show you this is something wonderful. It is nothing to fear."

The man was unbelievably sweet and considerate. It was that gentle soul that had touched her from the first, a man of great compassion. Gavriella stopped fussing with the pillows and went to him.

"I have had much time to think on this moment," she said. "At first, I thought I would be afraid, but I no longer think that. You are my husband and you are the man I love. I am more than willing to learn what you want to teach me. I want this to be something wonderful, too."

His expression was warm on her. "Are you certain?"

"I am."

"Then it is usual for the couple to remove their clothing and get into bed."

Gavriella laughed softly and began to undress in front of him. Over the past couple of months, in those heated moments alone, she'd practically undressed, anyway, as the man buried himself in her breasts or slipped his hands under her skirts, so she wasn't ashamed or reluctant. She unfastened the ties of her blue silk garment, the one that made her look like an angel. She was just peeling it off her shoulders when she noticed him fumbling with something on his shoulder.

"What is that?" she asked.

He held it up for her to see. "Bonny gave me this," he said, showing her the flower brooch. "He told me that he had given it to my mother when she married my father. It was the only thing of hers that he had to give to me."

Gavriella carefully took the brooch from him, looking it over closely. "It is so beautiful," she said. "What kind of flower?"

"A poppy, he said," Andreas replied. "He used to call my mother his 'fragile flower'. The poppy had some significance to them because of it."

Gavriella's gaze lingered on the brooch before carefully handing it back to him. "Your Uncle Edward and Aunt Cassie have a daughter named Helene, don't they?"

"Aye."

"Then mayhap we shall name a daughter Poppy, after your mother's brooch," she said. "And also after your grandfather. That is his name, too."

He set the brooch to the table next to the bed before kissing her on the forehead. "That is very sweet," he said softly. "I think I would like that, very much."

Smiling at him, Gavriella finished undressing down to her shift. Over on the other side of the bed, Andreas had finished pulling his clothing off and leapt into the bed, pulling the coverlet up. He leaned back on his arm, watching her most expectantly. She didn't disappoint. She let her shift fall away from her shoulders, revealing her perfect breasts and shapely torso.

The warm smile on Andreas' face turned into something seductive.

"Come to me, sweetling," he purred.

She did. As she climbed in and he reached for her, she happened to see the *stigmata* on the inside of his right forearm. She'd seen it before, but she'd never really asked him about it. Tonight, it caught her eye again.

"What's that?" she asked.

Andreas tore his eyes from her full breasts to look at what she was pointing at. "The mark of de Wolfe," he said. "All of the grandsons of William de Wolfe bear the mark of the de Wolfe standard somewhere on their body. It is a mark of honor."

"It looks like strength to me," she said softly, lifting her eyes to his. "Just like you."

Andreas couldn't wait any longer. His mouth came down on Gavriella's, so hard that he drove her teeth into her lip. He kissed her deeply; there was passion and lust and adoration there, feelings that made him pull her more tightly against him. He could taste her blood as he sucked her lips, aware that her arms were going around his neck. Her breasts, soft and warm, were pressed against his chest.

Laying down, he pulled her down with him.

Andreas could feel her squirming on top of him, rubbing herself against him, and it drove him mad. His mouth moved down her neck to the exposed cleavage and he quickly rolled over so that she was beneath him, lifting her arms and trapping them above her head. With his mouth on her breasts, he managed to wedge himself in between her legs. With one hand holding her wrists above her head, the other hand moved to the moist heat between her legs and he stroked her gently before inserting a big finger into her.

Gavriella shuddered.

"Are you comfortable?" he asked, his lips against her right breast. "Shall I continue?"

Gavriella's answer was a short nod. "Aye," she breathed. "Continue."

Andreas did, suckling on her nipple. "Do you feel me inside of you?" he whispered in between tugs. "This is where I will take my pleasure with you, as you've never known pleasure before."

He thrust two fingers into her, moving them in and out, mimicking what he would soon be doing with his engorged member. Gavriella groaned with pleasure every time he thrust his fingers into her tight, wet heat, preparing her for his entry. It wasn't long before he could feel her body start to quiver, the beginnings of her release, so he quickly removed his fingers and thrust his manhood firmly into her as her body was overcome with a climax.

Andreas could feel her body convulsing around him as he carefully but firmly thrust into her. She was very hot and wet, her gasps of pleasure filling the air until he slanted his mouth over hers to silence her, kissing her with deep and abiding passion. He was so highly aroused that he released himself sooner than he had anticipated, spilling deep and feeling his seed mingle with her wet heat.

It was sheer heaven.

The sounds of heavy breathing filled the air as Andreas slowed his thrusts, finally coming to a stop as he struggled to catch his breath. Beneath him, Gavriella lay still, eyes closed as she clung to him. Andreas watched her in the firelight, thinking he'd never seen anything more beautiful. She was finally his, in every sense of the word, and when she lowered one of her arms, her breasts quivered and the sight was enough to arouse him again. There was nothing about her that didn't set fire to his loins. In little time, he was very slowly and sensually thrusting in and out of her again as his manhood began to pulse back to life. It was a far less frenzied pace and a far more emotional one. His face was buried in her neck, inhaling her essence, as his hips moved in the primal rhythm.

"Dray," Gavriella gasped. "Oh… *Dray…*"

Her hands found his taut buttocks and Andreas responded by covering her mouth with his, his kisses hot and tender. The pace was slower now, his thrusts as gentle as they could be. When Gavriella shifted and opened her legs wider to him, welcoming him deep for a second time, he held her pelvis fast against his. He rubbed himself against her, grinding against her, and when Gavriella's tremors began again, he thrust into her, hard, before releasing himself in another, shorter, burst of glory.

The fire in the hearth snapped softly as heavy breathing filled the room. Andreas lay atop his wife, his body still joined to hers, thinking a great many things at that moment. Mostly, he was astounded. He hadn't known it was possible for him to climax twice in a row like that but, then again, everything with Gavriella had been something new for him. A love he never expected, a wife he was deeply in love with, and a new son that he loved as if the child were his own flesh and blood.

So many wonderful, unexpected things for the young man who had felt so alone in life, for the knight who had been going through life alone. But he was alone no longer.

And loving every minute of it.

It was the life he'd always wanted and never even knew it.

When Andreas rose a couple of hours later, after bedding his wife one more time, he pulled his clothes on, without his boots, and headed to his grandparents' chamber to retrieve his son.

His son.

He found his grandfather asleep with the baby on his chest again and it took both Jordan and Andreas to separate the pair with the promise that William would get to hold his great-grandson again on the morrow. Andreas carried the sleepy baby all the way back to his chamber, putting the infant to bed between himself and his wife.

As Gavriella and Storm fell back asleep, Andreas lay awake long into the night, watching the pair sleep, wondering how on earth he'd become such a fortunate man. For someone who had known such grief and loneliness, deeply affected by his mother's death as a lad, to a man whose cup of abundance was running over, he kept going back to what Gavriella had said, time and time again.

I feel as if I am dreaming.

Andreas, too, felt very much as if he were dreaming. And he was quite willing to go on dreaming because the life he'd ended up with was something only spoken of in dreams and fairytales, where a dashing knight rescues a damsel in distress and lives happily ever after.

For Andreas and Gavriella, those dreams and fairytales became reality for them both and Andreas knew, wherever his mother was, that she would have been proud. Proud of that unexpected son who had grown into a fine and honorable man, and a noble tribute to his father and grandfathers.

Aye, his mother would have been proud, indeed.

The de Wolfe and de Norville legacies lived on… through him.

Always.

⌘ THE END ⌘

De Wolfe Pack Generations:
WolfeHeart
WolfeStrike
WolfeSword
WolfeBlade

Children of Andreas and Gavriella:
Storm
Sage
Taran
River
Poppy
Arista
Acacia
Fox
Lily

The Parents, Children, and Grandchildren of de Wolfe

(Note: Don't be intimidated by these family trees – refer to them if you need clarification on a relationship)

<u>William (deceased 1296 A.D.) and Jordan Scott de Wolfe</u>
Total children: 10
Total grandchildren: 75 (including 4 deceased, 7 adopted, 3 step-grandchildren)

Scott (Troy's twin) – (Wife #1 Lady Athena de Norville, has issue. Wife #2, Lady Avrielle Huntley du Rennic, has issue)

With Athena
- William (married Lily de Lohr, has issue.)
- Thomas "Tor"
- Andrew (deceased)
- Beatrice (deceased)

With Avrielle
- Sophia (with Nathaniel du Rennic)
- Stephen (with Nathaniel du Rennic)
- Sorcha (with Nathaniel du Rennic)
- Jeremy
- Nathaniel
- Alexander
- Seraphina
- Jordan

Troy (Scott's twin) – (Wife #1 Lady Helene de Norville, has issue. Wife #2 Lady Rhoswyn Kerr, has issue)

With Helene

- Andreas
- Acacia (deceased)
- Arista (deceased)

With Rhoswyn

- Gareth
- Corey
- Reed
- Tavin
- Tristan
- Elsbeth
- Madeleine

Patrick – (Married to Lady Brighton de Favereux, has issue)

- Markus
- Cassius
- Magnus
- Titus
- Thora
- Kristiana

James – (Wife #1 Lady Rose Hage, has issue. Wife #2, Asmara ap Cader, has issue)

With Rose

- Ronan
- Isabella

With Asmara (as Blayth)

- Maddoc
- Bowen
- Caius
- Garreth (known as Garr)

Katheryn (James' twin) – (Married to Sir Alec Hage, has issue)

- Edward
- Axel
- Christoph
- Kieran
- Christian

Evelyn – (Married to Sir Hector de Norville, has issue)

- Atreus
- Hermes
- Lisbet
- Adele
- Aline
- Lesander (goes by Zander)

Baby de Wolfe – (Died same day. Christened Madeleine)

Edward – (Married to Lady Cassiopeia de Norville, has issue)

- Helene
- Phoebe
- Hestia
- Asteria
- Leonidas
- Dorian

- Dayne
- Stephan
- Pallas

Thomas – (Married Lady Maitland "Mae" de Ryes Bowlin, has issue)

- Artus (adopted)
- Nora (adopted)
- Phin (adopted)
- Marybelle (adopted)
- Renard & Roland (adopted)
- Dyana (adopted)
- Alexander
- Cabot
- Matthew
- Wade
- Tacey
- Morgan

Penelope – (Married to Bhrodi de Shera, Earl of Coventry, hereditary King of Anglesey)

- William
- Perri
- Bowen
- Dai
- Catrin
- Morgana
- Maddock
- Anthea
- Talan

Holdings and Titles of the House of de Wolfe and close allies as of 1292 A.D.

Scott de Wolfe – Lord Kilham, heir to the Earldom of Warenton (Heir: William "Will" de Wolfe)

Troy de Wolfe – Lord Braemoor (Heir: Andreas de Wolfe)

Patrick de Wolfe – Earl of Berwick (Heir: Markus de Wolfe, Lord Ravensdowne.)

Blayth (James) de Wolfe – Baron Sydenham (Heir: Ronan de Wolfe)

Edward de Wolfe – Baron Kentmere (Heir: Leonidas de Wolfe)

Thomas de Wolfe – Earl of Northumbria (Heir: Alexander de Wolfe, Lord Easington)

Wark Castle (Wolfe's Eye):

Larger outpost for the Earl of Warenton. Literally sits on the border between England and Scotland.

- Titus de Wolfe (son of Patrick de Wolfe) commander
- Ronan de Wolfe (son of Blayth/James de Wolfe)

Berwick Castle (Wolfe's Teeth):

Massive border castle, strategically important, de Wolfe holding and seat of the Earl of Berwick, Patrick de Wolfe

- Alec Hage, commander
- Edward "Eddie" Hage, commander
- Hermes de Norville, second

Castle Questing (Wolfe's Heart):

Massive fortress, seat of the Earl of Warenton, Scott de Wolfe.

- Apollo de Norville, second
- Nathaniel Hage
- Owen le Mon

Rule Water Castle (Wolfe's Lair):

The largest outpost in the de Wolfe empire, known as The Lair. Seat of William "Will" de Wolfe, Viscount Kilham, heir apparent to the Earldom of Warenton.

- Magnus de Wolfe, second
- Adonis de Norville, second
- Perri de Shera, son of the Earl of Coventry and Penelope de Wolfe de Shera (squire)

Monteviot Tower (Wolfe's Shield):

Smaller outpost in Scotland, strategic. Holding of Troy de Wolfe.

- Brodie de Reyne, commander

Kale Water Castle (Wolfe's Den):

Larger outpost on the England side of the border, strategic.

- Troy de Wolfe, Lord Braemoor, commander
- Troy also commands Sibbald's Hold, former home of Red Keith Kerr (his wife's father). A minor property commanded by son Gareth de Wolfe.

Kyloe Castle (Wolfe's Howl):

Seat of the Earl of Northumbria, Thomas de Wolfe

- Christoph Hage, second

Roxburgh Castle (Wolfe's Claw – unofficially)*

Large royal-held castle near Kelso, formerly manned by knights from Northwood, but awarded to the House of de Wolfe by royal decree for meritorious service to the crown. Volatile location, often attacked by Scots, and is manned by both royal and de Wolfe troops.

- Blayth (James) de Wolfe, Lord Sydenham, commander
- Axel Hage, second

*Note: Because of the extreme volatile location and nature of this garrison, Blayth (James) de Wolfe was given the title Lord Sydenham and the Sydenham Barony, a small but strategic barony between Wark Castle and the town of Kelso.

Northwood Castle:

Massive border castle, very important and strategic. Belonging to the Earls of Teviot. Not part of the de Wolfe empire, but strongly allied to de Wolfe by marriage and blood. The Earl of Teviot is John Adrian de Longley, Adam de Longley's eldest son. Adrian's mother is Cayetana Fernanda Teresita Silva y Fausto de Longley, Princess of Aragon.

- Hector de Norville, captain of the guard (also Lord Bowmont)
- Atreus de Norville, second
- Tobias de Bocage, second

Castle Canaan (Kendal) Wolfe's Bite:

The Earl of Warenton's southernmost holding, not directly related to the Scottish border but a source of additional troops if needed. Inherited the property when he married the widow of Castle Canaan.

- Stephan du Rennic, commander

Seven Gates Castle (Kendal):

- Seat of Edward de Wolfe's Barony – Kentmere in Kendal that adjoins brother Scott's lands at Castle Canaan
- Isleworth House, Surrey

Hell's Guardhouse (The Hermitage)

- Andreas de Wolfe, commander
- Theodis de Velt, second

Kathryn Le Veque Novels

Medieval Romance:

De Wolfe Pack Series:
Warwolfe
The Wolfe
Nighthawk
ShadowWolfe
DarkWolfe
A Joyous de Wolfe Christmas
BlackWolfe
Serpent
A Wolfe Among Dragons
Scorpion
StormWolfe
Dark Destroyer
The Lion of the North
Walls of Babylon
The Best Is Yet To Be

De Wolfe Pack Generations:
WolfeHeart
WolfeStrike
WolfeSword
WolfeBlade

The de Russe Legacy:
The Falls of Erith
Lord of War: Black Angel
The Iron Knight
Beast
The Dark One: Dark Knight
The White Lord of Wellesbourne
Dark Moon
Dark Steel
A de Russe Christmas Miracle
Dark Warrior

The de Lohr Dynasty:
While Angels Slept
Rise of the Defender
Steelheart
Shadowmoor
Silversword
Spectre of the Sword
Unending Love
Archangel
A Blessed de Lohr Christmas

The Brothers de Lohr:
The Earl in Winter

Lords of East Anglia:
While Angels Slept
Godspeed

Great Lords of le Bec:
Great Protector

House of de Royans:
Lord of Winter
To the Lady Born
The Centurion

Lords of Eire:
Echoes of Ancient Dreams
Blacksword
The Darkland

Ancient Kings of Anglecynn:
The Whispering Night
Netherworld

Battle Lords of de Velt:
The Dark Lord

Devil's Dominion
Bay of Fear
The Dark Lord's First Christmas

Reign of the House of de Winter:
Lespada
Swords and Shields

De Reyne Domination:
Guardian of Darkness
With Dreams
The Fallen One

House of d'Vant:
Tender is the Knight (House of
d'Vant)
The Red Fury (House of d'Vant)

The Dragonblade Series:
Fragments of Grace
Dragonblade
Island of Glass
The Savage Curtain
The Fallen One

Great Marcher Lords of de Lara
Dragonblade

House of St. Hever
Fragments of Grace
Island of Glass
Queen of Lost Stars

Lords of Pembury:
The Savage Curtain

**Lords of Thunder: The de Shera
Brotherhood Trilogy**
The Thunder Lord
The Thunder Warrior
The Thunder Knight

The Great Knights of de Moray:
Shield of Kronos

The Gorgon

The House of De Nerra:
The Promise
The Falls of Erith
Vestiges of Valor
Realm of Angels

Highland Warriors of Munro:
The Red Lion
Deep Into Darkness

The House of de Garr:
Lord of Light
Realm of Angels

Saxon Lords of Hage:
The Crusader
Kingdom Come

High Warriors of Rohan:
High Warrior

The House of Ashbourne:
Upon a Midnight Dream

The House of D'Aurilliac:
Valiant Chaos

The House of De Dere:
Of Love and Legend

St. John and de Gare Clans:
The Warrior Poet

The House of de Bretagne:
The Questing

The House of Summerlin:
The Legend

The Kingdom of Hendocia:
Kingdom by the Sea

The Executioner Knights:

By the Unholy Hand
The Mountain Dark
Starless
The Promise (also Noble Knights of
de Nerra)
A Time of End
Winter of Solace
Lord of the Shadows
Lord of the Sky

Gothic Regency Romance:
Emma

Contemporary Romance:

**Kathlyn Trent/Marcus Burton
Series:**
Valley of the Shadow
The Eden Factor
Canyon of the Sphinx

**The American Heroes Anthology
Series:**
The Lucius Robe

Fires of Autumn
Evenshade
Sea of Dreams
Purgatory

**Other non-connected
Contemporary Romance:**
Lady of Heaven
Darkling, I Listen
In the Dreaming Hour
River's End
The Fountain

Sons of Poseidon:
The Immortal Sea

**Pirates of Britannia Series (with
Eliza Knight):**
Savage of the Sea by Eliza Knight
Leader of Titans by Kathryn Le
Veque
The Sea Devil by Eliza Knight
Sea Wolfe by Kathryn Le Veque

Note: All Kathryn's novels are designed to be read as stand-alones, although many have cross-over characters or cross-over family groups. Novels that are grouped together have related characters or family groups. You will notice that some series have the same books; that is because they are cross-overs. A hero in one book may be the secondary character in another.

There is NO reading order except by chronology, but even in that case, you can still read the books as stand-alones. No novel is connected to another by a cliff hanger, and every book has an HEA.

Series are clearly marked. All series contain the same characters or family groups except the American Heroes Series, which is an anthology with unrelated characters.

For more information, find it in **A Reader's Guide to the Medieval World of Le Veque**.

ABOUT KATHRYN LE VEQUE

Medieval Just Got Real.

KATHRYN LE VEQUE is a USA TODAY Bestselling author, an Amazon All-Star author, and a #1 bestselling, award-winning, multi-published author in Medieval Historical Romance and Historical Fiction. She has been featured in the NEW YORK TIMES and on USA TODAY's HEA blog. In March 2015, Kathryn was the featured cover story for the March issue of InD'Tale Magazine, the premier Indie author magazine. She was also a quadruple nominee (a record!) for the prestigious RONE awards for 2015.

Kathryn's Medieval Romance novels have been called 'detailed', 'highly romantic', and 'character-rich'. She crafts great adventures of love, battles, passion, and romance in the High Middle Ages. More than that, she writes for both women AND men – an unusual crossover for a romance author – and Kathryn has many male readers who enjoy her stories because of the male perspective, the action, and the adventure.

Kathryn loves to hear from her readers. Please find Kathryn on Facebook at Kathryn Le Veque, Author, or join her on Twitter @kathrynleveque, and don't forget to visit her website and sign up for her blog at www.kathrynleveque.com.

Please follow Kathryn on Bookbub for the latest releases and sales: bookbub.com/authors/kathryn-le-veque.